Also by Lucy Score

BOOTLEG SPRINGS SERIES
Whiskey Chaser
Sidecar Crush
Moonshine Kiss
Bourbon Bliss
Gin Fling
Highball Rush

KNOCKEMOUT SERIES
Things We Never Got Over
Things We Hide from the Light
Things We Left Behind

BENEVOLENCE SERIES
Pretend You're Mine
Finally Mine
Protecting What's Mine

RILEY THORN SERIES
The Dead Guy Next Door
The Corpse in the Closet
The Blast from the Past
The Body in the Backyard

SINNER AND SAINT SERIES
Crossing the Line
Breaking the Rules

Whiskey Chaser

LUCY SCORE *WITH* CLAIRE KINGSLEY

Bloom *books*

Published by Bloom Books, an imprint of Sourcebooks
P.O. Box 4410, Naperville, Illinois 60567-4410
(630) 961-3900
sourcebooks.com

Cataloging-in-Publication data is on file with the Library of Congress.

Originally published in 2018 by That's What She Said Publishing, Inc.

Printed and bound in the United States of America.
POD

To the country girls and moonshine drinkers.

And my BRAs.

Chapter One

Scarlett

I hated funerals. They smelled like lilies and sadness. There were too many hugs and soggy tissues. And the black dress I found on the Target clearance rack made my neck itch where the tag curled against my skin.

"I'm so sorry for y'all's loss, Scarlett." Bernie O'Dell's stoop-shouldered six-foot frame engulfed me in an awkward hug. He'd closed up the barber shop today for the funeral. He'd been one of Jonah Bodine's only friends who'd stuck with him until the bitter end, even when he no longer deserved friends.

I gave Bernie a weak smile and a pat on the arm. "Daddy was always grateful for your friendship."

Bernie's eyes misted, and I handed him off to Bowie, my good brother. Not that Jameson and Gibson were bad, but Bowie was a high school vice principal. He was used to dealing with emotions that terrified the rest of us.

"God has a plan," Sallie Mae Brickman announced with a reassuring squeeze on my hand. Her hands were always ice cold no matter what time of year. It could have been a hundred degrees on the Fourth of July, and Sallie Mae's hands could keep her lemonade half frozen.

"I'm sure he does," I said, anything but sure there was a plan or a god. But if it made Sallie Mae feel better to believe, then, by all means, she was welcome to the faith.

The receiving line was getting backed up like a bad septic system with Bernie sharing a fishing story with Jameson. My brother was something of a reclusive artist, and this was probably his personal nightmare. Our father dead in a box behind him and a line out the door of well-meaning Bootleggers.

Bootleg Springs, West Virginia, was, in my humble opinion, just about the best place in the world to live. We had a storied history of bootlegging during Prohibition—my own great-grandfather Jedediah Bodine was legend here for bringing prosperity to our tiny town with his moonshine and hooch—and we were in the midst of a tourism boom thanks to our hot springs and half-dozen spas. We were small but mighty. Everyone knew everyone. And when one of us died—no matter their standing in the community while living—we all spiffed up, baked our casseroles, and shared our condolences.

"Hey, babe." Cassidy Tucker, the prettiest, snarkiest deputy in all of West Virginia, was dressed in her uniform and dragging her sister June along behind her. My best friend since preschool, Cassidy knew exactly the hot mess that was stewing beneath my sad countenance. I hugged her hard and dragged June Bug into our embrace.

June thumped me on the back twice. "I'm sure you're relieved you don't have to worry about your father's public intoxication anymore," she said gruffly.

I blinked. June was... different. Human relationships bewildered her. She was much happier spouting off sports stats than making small talk, but that didn't stop me and Cassidy from forcing her into social situations. Besides, she was a Bootlegger. Everyone here was used to her quirks.

"That's a good point, June," I said. Everyone else was too polite to mention the fact that my father drank himself to death. But just because he made really shitty life choices didn't mean he wasn't part of the fabric of Bootleg. We all tended to forget shortcomings when the person was laid out in a satin-lined box in the Bootleg Community Church.

"What?" June asked Cassidy, raising her eyebrows as they stepped on down the line. Cassidy patted June on the shoulder.

Old Judge Carwell grasped my hand in both of his, and I sneaked a peek to my right at Bowie. He was hugging Cassidy… with his eyes closed. I made a mental note to rib him about it later. *Smelling a deputy's hair at your father's funeral, Bowie? Just ask the girl out for fuck's sake.*

"Sorry about your daddy, Scarlett," Judge Carwell wheezed. The man had been looking to retire from his judgeship for fifteen years now. But Olamette County wouldn't hear of it. Change didn't come easy in Bootleg.

"Thank you, sir," I said. "And please thank Mrs. Carwell for the cornbread she sent over."

Carolina Rae Carwell's cornbread was famous in four counties. I'd wrestled Gibson, my oldest brother, for the last piece this morning. I fought dirty enough that I won.

I was glad for the sustenance now. It looked like everyone was turning out to say their sorrys and to gossip about how sad Jonah Bodine's life had been and what a blessing it was that it was all over.

The real blessing would have been my daddy waking up after yet another drunk blackout and deciding to change his ways ten years ago. Instead, my father committed wholly to the idea of being a drunkard, and now the four surviving Bodines were front and center in the church we hadn't stepped foot in since Mama died.

Yep. I was a twenty-six-year-old orphan. Thankfully, I had my brothers. Those three brooding boys were all I needed in life. Well, them, a cold beer, a good country song, and my little lake cottage. I could get by without much else.

———

"Well that was a shit show," Gibson muttered, flopping down in the first pew. He stretched out and toed off his shoes. A temperamental carpenter and cabinetmaker by trade, he was allergic to suits. He was the quintessential tall, dark, and handsome bad boy. With anger issues. To the rest of Bootleg, he was an asshole. To me, he was the big brother that ran out and bought me tampons in the middle of the night when I was out.

Much to his consternation, he had our daddy's good looks. Dark hair, icy blue eyes, and that beard that went from nice and neat to mountain man in two days. Gibson was the spitting image of Jonah Bodine, and he hated it.

Jameson lowered his tall frame to the green carpeted steps in front of the altar. He put his hands over his face, but I knew better than to think that he was crying. Sure, he was overcome, but it was from being too social for too long.

Bowie slipped an arm around my shoulder. "Hangin' in there?" he asked.

I gave him a wry smile. "Yeah. You?"

"Yeah."

Reverend Duane had given us some privacy before Daddy was packed up for burial. None of us were real keen on the idea. We'd survived the visitation and the funeral. The burial was private. And it was the last thing standing between us and a whole lot of liquor.

I spared a glance in my father's direction. I didn't get when people said it looked like the dead were just sleeping. To me, the second Jonah Bodine's spirit left his body, there was nothing lifelike about it. I'd had that exact thought four days ago when I found him dead in the bed that he and my mama had shared for twenty-two miserable years.

Of all us Bodines, I was the closest to Daddy. We worked together. Or, rather, I had taken over the family business from him when he couldn't keep himself sober enough to finish a job. I'd learned to drive at twelve. That summer, Mama had started sending me to work with Daddy to make sure he wasn't

4

drinking on the job. He was. And I learned to drive stick sitting on a stack of folded-up quilts.

And now he was gone. And I didn't know how in the hell I felt about that.

"Bonfire still on tonight, Scar?" Gibson was looking at me like he knew I wasn't entirely in the "ding dong the drunk is dead" camp.

"Yeah, it's still on."

My little cottage with its swatch of lakefront beach was the perfect place to ring in the weekends, and we did so with bonfires, floats, and impromptu concerts—Bootleg had its share of musical talent.

While tonight would be just another party to my brothers, it would be my own private send-off to the father I'd loved despite everything.

"So, Bowie," I said, eyeing him up. He had our mama's gray eyes like me and daddy's dark, dark hair. "Was it just my imagination, or were you trying to inhale Cassidy Tucker? How many other neighbors did y'all sniff in the receiving line?"

He clenched his jaw, which only served to highlight the sharp Bodine cheekbones. "Shut up, Scarlett."

I grinned, my first real smile of the day. "Only pickin'," I promised.

Bowie had never admitted it, but the man was carrying a torch. As far as I knew, he'd never done a damn thing about it. Me, on the other hand, if there was a guy I liked? I let him know. Life was short, and orgasms were great.

Chapter Two
Devlin

The house smelled like sugar cookies and dust. My grandmother had been in Europe for a few weeks, enjoying a spring holiday with her partner, Estelle. When they heard about the trouble I was in, the shambles my life was in, they offered up their comfortable lakefront home in some tiny no-one's-ever-heard-of-it-town in West Virginia.

I'd never been here. Not with a life in Annapolis. Gran came to us for holidays and events. We were the busy ones, she'd insist, though we all knew the real reason. My mother—her daughter—would throw a passive-aggressive fit about venturing into the backwoods for any amount of time.

However, this backwoods was currently my only option. I'd fucked up *and* been fucked over. I was banished, temporarily. And now, I wanted to do nothing but sit here with my eyes closed and will away the past few months.

Including the moment when I broke Hayden Ralston's nose.

Violence was never the answer as my father had so helpfully

pointed out. But the dark pleasure I'd felt from the crunch of that asshole's cartilage suggested otherwise. It was out of character for me, a man who'd been groomed for public approval from preschool.

I stared out into the night through the deck doors. I'd opened them in hopes of freshening the stale air inside, but all I'd done was invite the pounding music from next door into my solitude. Some upbeat country singer was infringing on my angst, and I didn't appreciate it. I didn't come here to be subjected to what sounded like a spring break hoedown. I came here to wallow.

With a sigh, I shoved my way out of Gran's plaid wingback and stalked to the door. The sliding screen door protested when I shoved it open. Another item to add to my fix-it list. If Gran and Estelle were nice enough to harbor a broken man, then I was nice enough to help patch up a few things that could be fixed. Myself included.

The smell of campfire bled onto the lot through the woods when I stepped out onto the deck. If one hard-partying redneck stepped the toe of a cowboy boot over the property line, I'd scare the shit out of him and his friends with a trespassing charge.

I followed sounds now foreign to my ears through the woods. Laughter, hoots of delight. Fun. Inclusion. Belonging. I didn't know what any of those things felt like anymore. I was an outsider looking in, both from my old life and here at this rustic juncture. This limbo of before and after.

The path between the properties was well-worn, but by human or animal feet I wasn't sure. When I broke through the woods, it was like crossing the border into another universe. Revelry. Couples slow-danced and laughed under the stars in the front yard. A dozen others crowded around the bonfire that snapped and crackled, sending up plumes of blue smoke into the night sky. The roll of the land was gradual down to the shimmering lake waters. The house—a cabin really—reminded me of a dollhouse. Tiny and pretty.

The music changed to a country anthem that even I'd heard

before, and the crowd reacted as if they all just won the lottery. Someone cranked the volume even higher, and I remembered why I was there.

"Whose house is this?" I asked a gyrating couple on the impromptu dance floor.

"Scarlett's," the woman answered with a twang so thick I almost didn't make out the word.

Of course her name was Scarlett.

"She's over yonder on the pickup." Twangy's man-friend jerked his bearded chin in the direction of a red pickup truck backed up to the fire. A cheering crowd surrounded its tailgate.

The couple went back to swaying back and forth, forehead to forehead. I stalked across the grass in the direction of the ruckus. *Ruckus?* It appeared that the backcountry was already rubbing off on me.

I weaved my way "yonder" through the crowd to the rear fender of the truck and stopped cold. She had her back to me, facing the crowd. She wore a short denim skirt, a plaid shirt that was knotted at the waist, and cowboy boots. The legs connecting the boots and skirt were leanly muscled. She had long brown hair that hung down her back in waves. She was tiny, but the curve of her hips was anything but subtle. She looked like every man's girl-next-door fantasy, and I hadn't even seen her face yet.

She tilted her head back, the ends of her hair brushing the small of her back. The crowd cheered even louder.

"Drank, drank, drank!" I supposed it was the cheer to "drink" just with an accent.

With a flourish, the slip of a woman righted herself, opening her arms to her adoring audience, revealing the empty 32-oz. plastic mug in her hand. She spiked the mug off the tailgate and curtsied, offering me a shadowy look at just how high that skirt was riding.

The crowd loved her. And I had to admit, if I weren't a shell of a man, I would have fallen just a little bit into that camp. She danced a little boogie in those boots and leaned over to offer high fives all around the bed of the truck. Until she got to me.

She had a wide mouth and a sprinkle of freckles across the bridge of her upturned nose. Her eyes were big and thickly lashed.

"Well, well, y'all. Look who finally came out to play." Her voice was as sweet and potent as the moonshine my grandmother had brought to Thanksgiving dinner.

Before I could react, before I could demand that she turn the damn music down and have some respect for her neighbors, she had her hands on me. My shoulders to be precise. She planted and sprang, and I only had time to act on instinct.

I grabbed her by the waist as she hopped out of the bed of the truck. My arms reacted a little slower. I held her aloft and our eyes met. Sterling gray, wide, and sparkling. Was she laughing at me? Slowly, slowly, I lowered her to the ground, her body brushing mine every inch of the way down.

She was tiny, a West Virginian forest fairy that came to my chest.

"It's about damn time you showed up."

"Excuse me?" I managed to string two words together and congratulated myself.

She put her fingers in her mouth and let out a shrill whistle. "We can turn the music down now," she yelled, or hollered, or whatever it was they did in this godforsaken town.

The volume immediately cut almost in half.

"Do I know you?" I asked, finally finding my words. I was quite certain there was no way this beer-swilling creature and I knew each other.

She ignored my question, grabbing my hand instead and pulling me to a trio of coolers halfway between the house and the bonfire. She bent and fished through the ice before producing two beers.

"Here," she shoved one at me. "Everybody, this here's Devlin McCallister. He's Granny Louisa's grandson."

"Hey, Devlin," the people circling the beer coolers chorused in an Appalachian twang.

Confused, off kilter, I glanced down at the beer in my hand and, with nothing better to do, twisted off the top. The music was down. Mission accomplished. I should go.

"C'mon," she said jerking her head toward the crowd near the fire. "I'll introduce you around."

At this moment, I couldn't think of anything I'd like less than being subjected to introductions. I just wanted to crawl back to Gran's house and hide there until...

It was one thing when I was a state representative. A married man with a nice house and a five-year-to-D.C. plan. But now that I was a nearly divorced, newly disgraced lawmaker on leave? I wasn't exactly in a hurry to start making small talk with anyone.

"Devlin, this is my brother Jameson," she said, pointing her fresh beer bottle at a man in a gray t-shirt. His hands were shoved into his pockets, shoulders hunched, as if he too didn't care to be here.

I nodded. He nodded back. I liked him immediately.

"And this here is my brother Gibson," she said, laying a hand on the flannelled shoulder of a man quietly strumming a guitar.

He eyed me as if I were in a police lineup and grunted.

People sure were friendly 'round these parts.

"And this is my brother Bowie," she said, knocking shoulders with a guy in a waffle knit shirt holding a beer. The family genes were abundantly evident when all three of them were in close proximity. Scarlett, on the other hand, had finer features, and in the firelight, I could see more red than brown in her long hair.

"Hey, Devlin. What's up?" Bowie offered his hand and a quick smile.

"Hey," I parroted, apparently having lost the ability to perform during even the most casual of introductions. My Queen of All Social Etiquette mother would die of embarrassment if she could see me now.

"Granny Louisa's asked that we all make Devlin feel right at home," Scarlett said, giving Gibson a pointed look.

He snorted. "Whatever."

Scarlett slapped him on the back of the head. "Be-have." She said it like it was two words.

"Yeah, yeah," Gibson grumbled and went back to his guitar.

"He's the strong angry type," Scarlett said by way of apology. "Jameson's the artistic, leave-me-alone type. And Bowie just loves everybody. Don't you Bowie?" She fluttered her lashes at him, and he gave her a glare.

"Don't you start that bullshit again," Bowie said, pointing a warning finger at her, but there was no heat behind his words.

Scarlett laughed, and it sounded like the twitter of birds on a sunny Sunday morning. The light in her laughter turned something on inside me.

"And you are?" I heard myself saying the words.

She gave me the side-eye.

"Why, I'm Scarlett Bodine, of course."

Someone turned the music up to head-throbbing levels again, and Scarlett let out a bred-in-bone whoop when she recognized the twangy song. It made me remember why I'd come in the first place.

"I'd appreciate it if you'd turn the music down," I snapped.

"What?" she yelled.

I leaned down into her space, avoiding the arms she tossed in the air in time to the music. "Turn down the music!"

She laughed. "Devlin, it's a Friday night. What do y'all expect?"

I'd expected the tomb-like quiet of a backwoods town whose residents were in bed by eight while I licked my wounds. I'd expected my wife to remain faithful. Hell, I'd expected my entire life to turn out differently.

"Not everyone likes a party," I said, sounding like an old man who'd kick kids off his lawn. "Turn it down, or I'll call the cops."

"Well, excuuuuuuuse me. I didn't realize that *fun* was *illegal* where you're from," Scarlett snipped.

"Causing a disturbance is illegal where *everyone* is from, and you're *disturbing* me."

"Well, bless your heart. Maybe y'all need to lighten up?" Scarlett suggested, batting her eye lashes with false sympathy.

I wasn't sure of anything right now except for the fact that it had been a mistake to come here. Bootleg Springs was not a place to hide and heal.

"Just turn it down," I muttered. I turned around and headed for the sanctity of the woods.

"Real nice meetin' you," she called after me. One more thing to be sure of. Scarlett Bodine was lying.

Chapter Three

Scarlett

I broke the egg and let it dribble into the bowl with the others. "Dang it," I muttered and fished a piece of shell out of the yolky mess. Finding a fork in the drawer next to the sink, I sloshed it around until the eggs were the appropriate soupy mess.

I nabbed the bacon from the pan one second before it turned to charcoal and tossed the slices onto a plate where they splintered into breakfast meat shrapnel.

"Just what the hell are you doing?"

Devlin was standing in the kitchen staring at me like I was some kind of common criminal. Granted, I had kinda broken into his house. But, in my defense, Granny Louisa asked me to.

I would have explained all that to him, but he'd appeared wearing only a pair of low-riding cotton pajama pants. I would have bet my best boots that he wasn't wearing any kind of underwear either. With great reluctance, I dragged my gaze away from what promised to be a spectacular package and let it roam his naked torso.

He snapped his fingers. "Hello!"

"Hi," I answered chipperly.

Devlin rolled his eyes and put his hands on his narrow hips. "What are you doing in my kitchen, Scarlett?"

"I'm making you breakfast." Maybe the man just wasn't very quick in the mornings. What the hell else would I be doing in his kitchen holding a plate of bacon?

"I mean, *why* are you making me breakfast? How did you get in here?"

I cocked my head to the side. "Granny Louisa asked me to look after you, and she always leaves the downstairs door open. I let myself in."

"You broke into my house—"

"Granny Louisa's house," I corrected him.

"You broke in here to cook me breakfast?"

I was starting to wish I'd just ordered him a sticky bun for delivery and called it a day. He obviously didn't know what an honor it was to have Scarlett Bodine cooking up a mess of scrambled eggs for him. Men fantasized about this exact moment, and here he was bitching about it. It was literally the only meal I knew how to make. I'd learn to cook. Eventually. But for now, I lived off of sandwiches, scrambled eggs, and diner food.

To be real honest, I doubted I was missing much. And none of the men I'd dated ever complained about me being better in the bedroom than the kitchen.

"You can't just come into someone's house," Devlin began again. He acted like he was explaining 2+2 to a kindergartner.

"Sure, I can. We all do it. Just bein' neighborly. Better get used to it," I said, dumping the eggs into the pan.

"I don't want to be neighborly." He was gritting his teeth, and there was a sexy tic in his jaw. He was even better looking than Granny Louisa had told me. I was surprised because she wasn't a woman to undersell anything.

"Well, you don't much have a choice now," I told him, swiping a spatula from the pitcher on the counter and flipping

14

the eggs. "Coffee's on," I said, nodding in the direction of the coffeemaker. "Maybe you'll feel better after you have some caffeine."

He stared at me for almost a full minute before he finally moved toward the coffee. *That* I could make blindfolded with one arm tied behind my back.

"Scarlett, I don't want you coming into this house uninvited," he said after his first sip.

I plated up the eggs, threw a couple of slices of extra, extra crispy bacon on the side and handed it over to him. "Oh, you're just sayin' that."

"I am saying that. But I'm also meaning that. I'm not here to make friends or be neighborly."

"Then why are you here?" I asked. Who in their right mind would come to Bootleg Springs for solitude? Hell, we practically went door-to-door at the rentals just to introduce ourselves to our new tourist friends. Devlin was in for quite the rude awakening.

The doorbell rang, and I smirked. I'd installed it special for Granny Louisa. Instead of a bell ringing, it was Beethoven's 5th. It never failed to put a smile on Granny Louisa and Estelle's faces.

"Doorbell," I announced in case he was too dimwitted to know what it was.

"I gathered that," he said dryly and stalked to the front door. I helped myself to a cup of coffee and checked my schedule. I had another half hour before I had to leave for my first job of the day. I'd finally convinced Jimmy Bob to let me fix the gutters on the Rusty Tool. The hardware store's façade was about twenty years past due for an update, and I was sick and tired of getting doused with overflow every time I walked by the store on my way to the diner.

After that, I had a maintenance call at one of my properties. This week's renter somehow managed to deprogram the garage door. Then, I was popping in to change furnace filters for Sheriff and Nadine Tucker and giving their air conditioner the once over to make sure it was ready for summer. I planned to squeeze in a drive-by to get a look at the boat lift on EmmaLeigh and Ennis's dock. EmmaLeigh texted this morning to tell me it was stuck in the up position.

I heard voices from the foyer, and then the door closed.

Devlin walked back into the kitchen staring down at the plate in his hand.

I peered through the plastic wrap. "Those Millie Waggle's brownies?"

"I guess. I didn't catch her name. She didn't say much."

Millie dressed like a Sunday school teacher and baked like a chocolate-loving sinner. She tended to get a bit tongue-tied around men higher on the scale than a five out of ten. I wished I would have seen her expression when disheveled Devlin opened the door shirtless. The poor girl probably wouldn't speak for the rest of the day.

I helped myself to a brownie and took a bite. "Mmm, oh yeah. That's a Waggle brownie. My lord, that woman is a sinful genius."

Devlin was eyeing me with something unreadable in those brown eyes. Interest? Disgust? Both? He made it too much fun to push his buttons.

"Well, better eat before your eggs get any colder. What do you want for supper?" I asked, batting my lashes.

The tic was back in his jaw. My work here was done.

"I eat alone," he insisted.

I grinned up at his grumpy, sexy-as-hell face. "We'll see about that."

He turned away from me and yanked open a drawer, the handle coming off in his hand. "This place is falling apart," he muttered.

"I can fix that," I promised Devlin. It was just a little knob for Pete's sake. He acted like the entire house was crumbling around him.

He grabbed a slip of paper off the counter and scrawled something on it.

Curious, I snatched it off the counter the second he walked away. *Sliders don't slide, deck needs refinished, creaky stairs, ugly ass carpet, leaky upstairs sink, drawer hardware.* I flipped it over and felt my eyebrows wing up.

"Well, I can definitely take care of the first list for you, but you might need professional help for the second." The back of the paper was a list of apparently everything that was wrong with Devlin McCallister's life. Starting at the top: *married the wrong woman.*

He grabbed it out of my hand.

"Thanks, but no thanks. I don't need your help with anything. And I definitely don't need you snooping around here pretending to fix things. I've got a list long enough for a handyman."

"And just where will you find one of them?" I asked, tongue in cheek.

He stomped across the kitchen and glared at his granny's bulletin board. He snatched a card off of it triumphantly. "I've got it covered," he insisted.

"They're pretty busy this time of year what with the tourist season startin' up."

Stubbornly, Devlin dialed.

My phone rang in my pocket, and I fished it out. "Bodine Home Services. Scarlett speaking. How can I help y'all?"

Devlin hung up on a growl.

Chapter Four
Devlin

About two minutes after I threw Scarlett out of the house, my phone rang.

"Now why in heaven's name would you go and kick Scarlett Bodine out of my house?" Gran demanded without preamble.

Great. My next-door neighbor was a tattle tale. "Hello to you, too. And how's Rome?"

"Don't you 'how's Rome' me," Gran said. "You're my favorite grandson in the world, Devlin, and I know you're going through a rough patch. But you can't be rude to our neighbors."

"Gran, she broke into your house and made me cold, runny eggs." I scraped them into the trash and settled for more coffee. My appetite had deserted me months ago.

"That's just Scarlett being friendly."

"You live in a town where breaking and entering is considered friendly."

"Do I need to remind you that you live in a world where your friends and family backstab you to get to the top of the food chain?"

"I think you're being a little dramatic," I said, smiling despite myself. Gran was vocal about her disinterest in the political world my parents and I moved within.

"Look, I want you to be nice to that Bodine girl. I understand that maybe you're not looking for company, but her daddy just died last week, so I'd appreciate it if you'd at least make an effort to be polite."

And just like that, I felt like the biggest asshole in Appalachia. I sank down on one of the dining room chairs. "I wasn't aware of that."

"Well, now you are. Do better."

I looked down at the list on the counter. "Yes, ma'am."

"Now, here's Estelle. She wants to say hi."

Gran handed me off to her girlfriend. "Hey, handsome," Estelle said in her singsong voice.

"Hey, Stell. How's your European tour?" I asked glumly.

"Magnificent. We stayed up 'til dawn yesterday drinking champagne with a bunch of old ladies from Denmark. But I'm worried about you." Estelle and my grandmother had been together for the last ten years. It had been a complicated transition, even for my liberal parents, but now I couldn't imagine my grandmother without her skinny, sassy counterpart.

"I'll be just fine," I lied.

"Bootleg is a good place for healing," Estelle said. "Make sure you do some of that and don't hole yourself up like Henrietta VanSickle."

"I hate to ask."

"Henrietta VanSickle lives in a cabin in the mountains and comes down to town once a month for groceries. Rumor has it she took a vow of silence twenty years ago. Never broke it yet."

Or maybe Henrietta Van Sickle was burned out on real life and just wanted to be left alone, I projected.

A vow of silence and a remote cabin? I liked that idea enough to store it away as my official Plan B. I had no Plan A for getting my life back. But at least I knew I now had a backup.

"Listen, the tour bus is leaving for the naked cabaret. Do

your gran and I a favor and get out once in a while. Maybe take Scarlett with you. No one has more life in her than that girl."

I made a non-committal noise. "Have fun at the naked cabaret."

We said our good-byes and disconnected. I stared at the phone in my hand and at the business card on the counter.

"Call me when y'all change your mind," Scarlett had said chipperly as I hustled her out the front door.

"Fuck." I muttered to myself.

———

"These steps need redone," Scarlett said, writing more notes on her clipboard and studying the deck stairs. "And that window on the end is rotted out. I can replace it so the place is sealed tighter for winter."

Twenty-four hours after I'd thrown her out, she was back at the house going over my list of shit that needed to be fixed and adding her own ideas to it.

I followed her wordlessly around the house wondering if she was this good at her job or if she saw an opportunity to make some money off of an out-of-town asshole.

"And, please for the love of all that's holy, tell me you're gonna let me rip out that cabbage rose carpeting upstairs."

It really was an eyesore.

"You do carpet too?"

"I got a guy. But I can rip the old stuff out and save you some money. Me and that carpet have hated each other since your granny moved in."

"Add it to the list." It was one of the benefits of being partner in a family law firm. My paychecks kept coming, even after I'd potentially destroyed my reputation.

She nodded briskly.

The list was getting longer and longer, and at this point, I wanted to say yes to everything just to see what this girl could do.

She didn't look like any handyman I knew. Granted, it was

a sexist observation and entirely unlike me. Despite wearing a tool belt and a headlamp, Scarlett looked more like an elementary school art teacher than a heavy-lifting blue-collar business owner. She was still unsettlingly gorgeous.

I was used to beautiful women. My father had been a U.S. Senator, and we'd spent most of our lives between Annapolis and Washington, D.C., before he retired into consulting. Everyone there was flawless, at least on the outside. Scarlett, by contrast, rolled up in a pickup truck with dirt on her chin and sawdust and mud on the knees of her jeans. Her very nicely fitting jeans.

She looked like she belonged on a poster on a teenage boy's wall in those sexy jeans and fitted Henley. I'd never considered tool belts to be sexy, but on Scarlett's swaying hips, I was willing to reconsider my stance.

"All right," Scarlett said, tucking the contractor pencil back in her belt. "I'm gonna run the numbers for you so you have an accurate quote, but I can give you an estimate right now."

She named a figure that didn't make me light-headed. "That's with the friends and family discount for Granny Louisa," she said, making another note in her notebook.

I peered over her shoulder at it. She had the handwriting of a three-year-old trying to figure out whether they were right- or left-handed.

"You can think about it and let me know," she said, ripping off a corner of the paper and handing it over.

"Let's do it," I decided. I wanted to see if she could do it all just as much as I wanted to give my grandmother and Estelle a "thank you" for letting me stay.

"All right," Scarlett said. "I can start on the deck tomorrow and fit in some of the smaller projects here and there. I've got a roof job and some dry-walling this week, but after I'll have a bit more time."

"Sounds good," I said.

If she was surprised by my agreement, she didn't let on. "Awesome. Listen, while I'm here. I'm gonna check your roof. I did some patches last year, and I wanna make sure there aren't any new loose shingles."

I looked up. The roof was three stories above ground. The first floor was a garage and walk-out basement.

"Okaaaay." I wasn't exactly enthusiastic about the idea of anyone crawling around that high up off the ground.

"You don't have to go up," she said, patting my arm like I was a scared kid. "I got this."

She hustled over to her pickup and pulled the extension ladder off of the rack. Whistling, she held it over her head and hauled it up around to the front of the house. I jogged after her.

"Want me to carry that?" I offered.

She shot me an amused look. "I think I can handle an aluminum ladder."

She propped it against the front of the house and extended it all the way up. At least from this elevation it was only two stories up, but still. She placed a booted foot on the first rung and rocked the ladder until it dug into the flowerbed.

Scarlett scrambled halfway up the ladder before I reached out to hold it. "Are you sure you should be doing this?" I called after her.

She hung one-handed at the top and laughed. "Don't worry, Dev. I don't expect you to get up here with me."

It wasn't that I was afraid of heights. They'd never bothered me before. It was that, right now, everything terrified me. The unknown, hell, the *known*. Being away from work, my home, away from Annapolis. The only thing that was worse than being away from it was the idea of going back. I'd become risk adverse to the point where leaving the house felt like a monumental task. I'd been in Bootleg for three days and still hadn't ventured any farther than across the property line to Scarlett's party.

I squinted up in time to see Scarlett swing her leg onto the roof and disappear. The skies seemed bluer today, the sun sharper. And that hollow feeling in my gut, the one that had taken up residence when I'd discovered my wife of three years reviewing our prenup at the breakfast table, didn't feel quite as empty. The last of the daffodils fluttered against my shins in the breeze.

"Fuck it," I muttered under my breath. I could climb a damn ladder and sit on a fucking roof. I still had my balls. Johanna hadn't gotten those in the divorce.

I climbed. Sure, maybe my fingers ached from the tight grip on the rungs. And maybe my knees shook a little bit. But when I crested the lip of the roof, when I very carefully stepped onto the shingled expanse, I took a deep breath, and it was the first one in months that didn't feel like it was choking me.

"You made it." Scarlett grinned at me from her position on the peak where she was examining the chimney.

"I did." I looked to the lake, an even better view here than in the house. It stretched on, a shimmering expanse that beckoned the gaze and held it. The trees, green with new leaves, shivered in the breeze. The wind felt stronger up here. I wondered if it was strong enough to move the clouds that had anchored themselves above me.

"Patches held up, and I'm not seeing anything new that you need to worry about," Scarlett announced standing up and bopping toward me as if she were on flat ground.

"Good."

"Not bad, right?" she said, staring out over the waters.

"Not bad," I repeated.

She took a bracing breath, filling her lungs with spring sunshine. "I love this time of year. Everything comes back to life."

God, I hoped it was true.

We both heard it. The rattle of metal, and I turned to watch in horror as the ladder listed to the side and disappeared.

"Ah, fuck," Scarlett swore and jogged to the edge of the roof.

I scrambled after her and grabbed the back of her belt when she peered over the edge. "Jesus, Scarlett, can you maybe not plunge off my grandmother's roof?"

"I've been climbing on rooftops since I was twelve years old," she said, rolling her eyes at my concern.

"And how many have you fallen off of?" I asked.

"Six or seven." She shrugged, unconcerned.

I towed her away from the edge for my own peace of mind. "We're trapped. We're stuck up here." I could feel the panic rising in me, and I hated it. I hated myself. The anxiety that had reared its ugly and inconvenient head when I found out my whole life was a sham rushed back, socking me in the chest with the force of a fist.

"Sit your ass down," Scarlett said, her voice stern. She pushed me down, and I dug my heels into the shingles and tried not to think about how high up we were. She sank down in front of me and stared hard until I met her gaze. "We're gonna be just fine. I've got my phone in my pocket. Okay?"

She was talking me down. I hated the fact that it was necessary.

I nodded. She squeezed my knees through my jeans. The contact helped.

"Heights bother you?" she asked, her accent softening her words.

I shook my head and closed my eyes. "Life bothers me."

She cupped my face, and I opened my eyes. Her clear gray eyes—so close to sterling—were inches from me. Her lips, soft and pink, hovered just out of reach. "You, Devlin McCallister, are gonna be just fine."

It sounded like a promise. Or maybe it was a threat. I didn't care. I clung to the words like a lifeline in a storm.

"I'm going to hold you to that."

"Well, let's see how this relationship progresses, and we'll see if there's anything else you can hold me to." She gave me an exaggerated wink, and I felt my lips quirk.

Scarlett ruffled my hair like I was a kid. "I'm gonna call my brother. He'll get us back on the ground quicker than gravity."

She didn't leave my side but sat down hip-to-hip with me.

"Gibs, what are you doing?"

I couldn't hear his response, but I imagined it was something snarky.

"Good, then you have time to help your favorite sister out. I'm up on Granny Louisa's roof—"

She stopped and frowned. "I did not fall off this one… No. I don't need an ambulance… Jesus, Gibs, chill out. The ladder fell. Dev and I are stuck on the roof, and I'm getting hungry."

She listened, rolling her eyes heavenward.

"Thank yooooou," she sang before disconnecting. "He knows it's an emergency when hunger is involved. He'll be here in ten."

Chapter Five
Scarlett

Gibson gave me the growly once over when my boots hit the ground. "I didn't fall off of anything. I swear," I sighed, punching him in the arm. He smelled like sawdust and stain.

Devlin climbed down after me. He looked considerably less green around the gills once his feet were on solid ground.

"Thanks for the rescue," Devlin said to Gibson.

My brother, being a rude bastard, grunted. I kicked him in the ankle. "Ow! God damn it, Scarlett!" He gave me a shove and I laughed.

"I apologize for my brother being a crabby bastard, Dev. I interrupted him while he was workin'. He likes that about as much as when I interrupt him sleepin'."

Gibson sighed. "It's fine. I was done staining anyway."

"Gibson here makes the finest cabinets this side of the state," I told Devlin. "I've been after your granny to let him have a crack at her kitchen. I think I'm wearin' her down."

"You need anything else?" Gibson asked.

"You're free to go," I said grandly, dismissing him.

He started to walk away, grumbling about what an epic pain in his ass I was, but only made it a few paces. "Here." He pulled a candy bar out of his back pocket and tossed it to me.

Say what you want about Gibson Bodine, but my brother has a heart of gold. It's just under a whole bunch of thorns. And maybe some gargoyles and fire-breathing dragons. But it's there, and it's a whole lot bigger than anyone else knows.

"Thanks, Gibs," I said, unwrapping the chocolate. Without another word, he jumped in his truck and left. At least he didn't do a burnout in Granny Louisa's driveway. He wasn't a total Neanderthal.

"Let's go get some lunch," I said to Dev.

"Lunch?" he repeated.

"You know, the meal between breakfast and supper?"

"I know what lunch is."

"I'm thinking Moonshine if you want to go."

"You drink your lunch?"

"It's a *diner*, smarty pants. Best open-face turkey sandwich I've ever had." He still looked a little pale for my liking. I wasn't about to leave a man in the midst of a crisis alone. And there was nothing Whit's food couldn't fix.

He didn't look convinced.

"How many visitors you had today?" I asked, playing the ace up my sleeve.

"Counting you and your brother? Four."

I nodded. "They're curious about you. If you show your face in town, you won't be the broody stranger. They won't feel the need to come ringin' your doorbell and handin' you baked goods if you leave the house every once in a while."

He didn't look convinced. "You're saying if I go into town, they'll leave me alone?"

"Not entirely. But you won't be getting near as many strangers on your doorstep."

"I don't know, Scarlett. I've got a lot on my mind."

"Man's gotta eat. C'mon. I'll buy." I hooked my arm through his and gave him no choice.

The poor guy didn't put up a fuss when I shoved him into the passenger seat of my pickup. I'd seen that look before. That shell-shocked panic. Once, when we were younger and much, much dumber, the four of us were messing around on the ice. Jameson had fallen through. His eyes had the same stunned look as the ice gave way under his feet. We'd pulled him out as a sopping wet human chain. And then lay there on the ice shivering and laughing and half-crying. It's what we did when one of us was in trouble. From the looks of it, Devlin didn't have much of a human chain behind him.

I gave him the twenty-cent tour through town. "And those are the hot springs. They keep the lake nice and toasty and draw tourists like crazy. We've got a couple of spas on this end of town. And that's The Lookout." I pointed to the bar on the hill. "Did your gran tell you anything about the history of Bootleg?"

"She did not," Devlin said. He scrubbed his palms over his jeans. His nerves were still evident, but at least he was progressing to full sentences.

"Well, Bootleg Springs was the most prosperous town in West Virginia during Prohibition."

"Ah, hence the name," Devlin said, catching my drift.

"My great-granddad Jedidiah Bodine was the first to set up a still, and his moonshine became infamous. Soon, the rest of the town was brewing, and every Thursday night, they'd load up boats with liquor. A watch was always stationed up at The Lookout. They'd cross the lake into Maryland where they'd hand off the hooch, and it was distributed to D.C. and Baltimore."

Devlin made a non-committal noise, but I kept up my incessant chatter as I cruised down Main Street and pointed out more places of interest. The spot where Jedediah led the police on a merry car chase that resulted in the blowing up of his still. That event was still celebrated annually with an enthusiastic reenactment complete with pyrotechnics.

I eased to the curb half a block down from the diner. Moonshine took up the entire first floor of a three-story brick building. The whole block smelled like bacon and home fries. Leftover olfactory souvenirs from the breakfast crowd.

I led Devlin inside and slid into my favorite booth at the back of the diner. From this vantage point, I could see all the comings and goings of my neighbors.

Devlin eyed the greasy menu on the table with skepticism. I, on the other hand, didn't need to look at mine. I always get the same thing.

"Well, hi there, Scarlett," Clarabell the head waitress and proprietress of Moonshine said, plucking the pencil out of her brassy red beehive. She and her husband, Whitfield the short order cook, had been serving up plates of goodness for twenty-plus years now. "How y'all doing?"

"We're doin' just fine, Clarabell," I said, ignoring the fact that Devlin had just had a rooftop freak-out. "Thank you for the pepperoni rolls last week. That was real thoughtful of you."

"You're so welcome. I'm glad you enjoyed 'em. Now, what can I get for you today?"

"I'll have the open-faced turkey and a Pepsi," I said, sliding the menu to the edge of the table.

Devlin looked up from the menu, indecision written all over his handsome face. "I'll have what she's having," he said.

Clarabell gave him her trademark crooked smile and picked up the menus. "Sorry about your daddy, Scarlett," she said before bustling off behind the counter.

It was a strange reality check, knowing that a week ago I'd been sitting in this very booth across from my father, trying to sober him up with coffee and home fries.

"My grandmother told me about your father," Devlin began. "I'm sorry."

"Thanks," I said, my voice gruff. I hadn't had time to get used to the idea of life without him. Every morning, my first thought was how hard it would be to wake Dad up and get him ready for work if he was in any shape to accompany me. It was still my first thought, but now it was followed with the realization that it was no longer necessary. I remembered in exacting, painful detail walking into his bedroom and finding him cold.

It was a hell of a way to start every morning since. But if I kept busy enough, I could run from it until I could stand to face it alone. "It wasn't much of a surprise," I confessed. "Seemed like it was only a matter of time."

I didn't want to tarnish my daddy's memory any further by rehashing all the ways he failed my family. Not to a man who'd never meet him.

"I'm sorry." Devlin said it simply authentically sweetly.

"Thanks," I said and changed the subject. "How you feelin'?"

Clarabell returned with our drinks and a wink. Devlin toyed with the straw she left for him.

"I feel like I owe you an explanation," he said.

I watched his face. Even though his brow was marred by a frown, he wasn't hard on the eyes. He had that square jaw thing going for him. And stubble. I was a sucker for a manly five o'clock shadow. His eyes were coffee-brown and troubled. His hair was a cross between light brown and blond and currently only styled by the nervous fingers he shoved through it.

"You don't owe me anything until I've done the work," I said. If he wanted to keep this relationship strictly professional, that was an option. Though I admitted I'd be the teensiest bit disappointed.

"I've been going through something lately," he said. "Nothing like losing a parent, though."

"Let's not play my pain is worse than yours," I said, giving his hand a squeeze before picking up my soda. "Pain is pain."

He grimaced. "I was married. Technically still am for a few weeks at least."

"Divorce or plotting her murder?" I asked lightly.

The corner of his lips curved up. "I'll let you know."

"What happened?"

"I was under the misconception that we were partners. I

thought we were building something, following the same path. I didn't realize her path involved fucking someone else."

"Ouch."

"Sorry, that sounded harsh," he winced.

"Did you know him?" Growing up in Bootleg gave all residents a leg up on interrogations. We knew how to pump the unsuspecting for details regardless of whether or not it was our business.

Devlin gave a sigh, weighing his words carefully. "You know, I think I might have known him better than I knew her. I worked with him. We were both legislators in the Maryland House of Delegates."

"Were?" I pressed.

"We're out of session right now, and I am on a leave of absence to get my shit together."

It felt like there was a *lot* more to that story than he was willing to spill. I decided to be patient... for now.

"Did you confront her?" I asked, resting my chin on my hand.

"Not in any meaningful, satisfying way. I didn't even know she was cheating. I had my eyes on a Senate race in a few years. Political careers are built decades in advance. It meant less attention on the present. Maybe I should have paid more attention."

"Did she know about your career goals?" I asked.

"Of course."

"Then it's her own damn fault, Dev, not yours."

"I could have tried harder, been more available—"

"Yeah and she could have *not* put someone else's dick in her," I said bluntly. "Don't be looking for reasons why she's right and you're wrong. You didn't make her go fuck someone else. So stop wasting your time being all 'what if this?' and 'what if that?' It's a waste of time and energy. And it's not going to make you feel better."

Devlin blinked at my bluntness.

"You're going to regret not confronting her," I predicted.

"If I ask you something, will you give me a straight answer?"

31

"Sure."

"What's a pepperoni roll?"

"Are you fucking serious?" I gaped at him. "Jesus, Mary, and Joseph. Clarabell, get this man a pepperoni roll stat!"

Chapter Six

Devlin

The few bites of pepperoni roll I managed after the open-faced hot turkey sandwich that took up the entire plate were indeed delicious. My appetite had been MIA for a couple of months as had my motivation to go to the gym. Consequently, my strength and energy were waning. My physique, once a source of pride, had withered in the mirror.

Maybe a pepperoni roll or two would be my path back to the gym, back to life.

Scarlett slapped my hand when I reached for my wallet. She paid at the cashier stand and chatted with Clarabell about a softball game that sounded more like a competitive drinking match.

Clarabell gave me a wink and a finger wiggle before making her rounds down the line of booths.

I reached for the door to hold it for Scarlett, but she paused just inside the door at the community bulletin board. She tapped the pads of her fingers to the name on a MISSING PERSON poster. From the looks of it, the poster was old.

"Who's that?" I asked, staring at the black-and-white photo of a teenage girl.

Scarlett's pretty mouth opened in a perfect O. "Granny Louisa didn't tell you?"

"Tell me what?"

She ducked out the door and tugged me with her.

"There are two things Bootleg is famous for," she lectured, slipping back into tour guide mode. "Bootlegging and the disappearance of Callie Kendall."

I frowned. The name sounded familiar. Vaguely.

"Callie's family summered here. Her parents still do. Callie went missing right here in Bootleg twelve years ago this summer."

"As in kidnapped? Murdered?"

Scarlett slapped a hand over my mouth and glanced over her shoulder. "You hush now unless you want to get in an hour-long debate on all the conspiracy theories Bootleggers have."

We got back in her truck. And I noticed the marked difference between arriving at the diner and leaving it. I felt steadier. More connected. Interested. Just listening to Scarlett was like a lifeline to the living.

She had so much energy. It was hard to remain numb around her. Despite the fact that her father had died a week ago, she was the one comforting me.

"So, what happened to Callie?" I was curious about the story, but if I were to be honest, I just wanted Scarlett to keep talking.

"Well, no one knows for sure. It was just another summer day. We were at the lake until dark. Everyone scattered to go home for supper. She never made it. Somewhere between the lake and the springs, she vanished." Scarlett pulled onto the street and circled the block. Tidy brick buildings with colorful store fronts and funny names on their signs lined the street.

"You knew her?" I asked.

"Sure. She was two years older than me, and I wanted to be just like her. She was always so smart and fun. Always had cool clothes. And I was just… well, me."

34

I had a feeling no one else on the planet would think of Scarlett in those terms at any point in her life. "Just me" didn't do her justice.

"And no one ever found her? Were there any suspects?"

Scarlett shrugged. "The local cops talked to just about every adult in town about their whereabouts and whatnot. Callie's parents came forward and said that she suffered from some depression, some mental issues. I think they believed she'd up and run off or…"

Scarlett wrinkled her nose and stared through the windshield.

"Suicide," I filled in for her.

"Yeah."

"What do you think?"

Scarlett laughed. "Everyone's got their theories. There's the 'murdered by a drifter' theory. Then there's the 'ran off with a boy' theorists. Some think it was politically motivated. Her daddy's a judge, so some people think one of his rivals took her. Mostly everyone else agrees with her parents."

"But you don't?" I guessed.

Scarlett shook her head. "It may be a little hero worship coloring my memories, but Callie was a steady kind of person. Empathetic, thoughtful. She wasn't the type to just pick up and leave. I never saw any signs of mental shenanigans. Maybe some anxiety, a little fear. But nothing that was a red flag for me."

"Do you think she's dead?"

Scarlett chewed on her bottom lip. "I don't want to believe that. I'd like to think that she ran away to join the circus or make movies or something. But it's been so long with no word. I don't know what other answer there is."

"Twelve years, and you still have the posters hanging up," I observed.

Scarlett shot me a grin. "We have trouble lettin' go of the past around here. Besides, we want Callie's parents to know she was never forgotten. They may only summer here, but that doesn't mean they're not part of the Bootleg family."

"Loyalty or an inability to move on?" I asked.

"Little bit of both. The fact is she was just a good girl from a good family who disappeared. And if I think too long about the fact that I'll never know the answer, I go crazy and start coming up with harebrained explanations. I don't know if Callie is alive out there or not. But I like to imagine her alive and well and having a real good time."

"What do your brothers think happened to her?"

"Gibson thinks she was murdered and dumped in the lake, but he's a Suzy Sunshine like that. I don't know about Bowie and Jame. Bowie always wants to believe the best in people, and no one ever knows what Jameson's thinking."

"I bet people usually know what you're thinking," I teased.

"I don't see much point in sittin' around keepin' my mouth shut. Life's too short." She clammed up immediately as if the reminder was directed at herself. Her father's life had been too short.

I reached across the console and squeezed her arm. Her frame was so small that it was still a surprise to me. It seemed like such a personality would need a bigger container. "Thanks for everything today, Scarlett."

She brightened. "Just bein' neighborly."

I dropped my hand. But she leaned over and squeezed my knee. "You're gonna be all right, Dev. Bootleg will fix you up, and you won't even remember that dumbass ex-wife's name by the time we're done with you."

"I feel like you're threatening me with blackout drunkenness."

"Well, you *are* in the home of the best moonshine in the state. I've got my great-granddaddy's recipe, and I just might be willing to spare a mason jar for a neighbor who needs to forget."

"It's not the stuff that'll make me go blind, is it?"

She snorted. "That only happened on the first couple of batches. My great-granddaddy was real sorry about it, too."

"You're messing with me, aren't you?"

"Little bit."

36

Chapter Seven
Devlin

My neighborly neighbor showed up on my deck Saturday at two o'clock squishing her forehead against the glass of the door and knocking. I'd seen a lot of her this week. She'd tackled the work on her list with gusto, fitting me in around other work projects. I would have been flattered that she was prioritizing my tasks, but I knew that Scarlett Bodine was keeping an eye on me.

"I'm fine, Mom," I said into the phone for the sixth time as I pulled the door open for Scarlett.

"Your father and I just want to make sure that you're staying focused."

The McCallisters were nothing if not focused. By the time I was in third grade, I knew I'd follow my father's steps into politics. I'd never bothered to wonder if it was what I wanted.

"I'm fine. I'm focused."

Scarlett ducked inside and danced on the balls of her feet.

"Good because we're going to have to work to undo the

negative press before next year's session begins. And it's an election year. I hope this hasn't set us back too far."

I could hear the clink of china as she set her afternoon cappuccino down on its saucer. My mother was the perfect politician's wife. A lifelong volunteer, the perfect hostess, a natural social butterfly. She was the perfect supportive partner to my father's career. I thought I'd made the same choice in Johanna.

"I'm prepared to do the work," I promised.

"I'm glad to hear it. For now, we feel it's best if you continue to stay off everyone's radar for a few more weeks. Hopefully someone else will give them something to talk about this summer."

Scarlett hopped from foot to foot looking like a kid on Christmas morning in front of a mound of unopened presents.

"I'm sure some scandal will arise," I promised my mother.

"Just make sure it's not your own. If you and Johanna can't work this out, you're going to have to make sure everyone knows it's an amicable split."

There was zero chance of us working it out and also no chance for the divorce to be an amicable one. But I didn't feel now was the right time to explain that to my mother.

"I've got to go Mom. My neighbor is here."

"Ugh, I can only imagine. Are they wearing overalls?"

My mother hated the fact that her mother loved Bootleg. My grandmother invited Mom to Bootleg when she first moved here, and after one weekend in town, my mother vowed to never return. "Those people eat roadkill," she insisted at dinner parties when it was appropriate to paint her mother as a charming eccentric.

"I'll call you later, Mom," I said dryly.

I disconnected and tossed the phone on the coffee table. "Why are you dancing around my living room?" I asked, surprised that I was actually looking forward to the reason.

"Grab some flip-flops and let's go!"

I looked down. I was dressed for a workout in shorts and

a tank top. The weather had warmed considerably, taking it into the mid-seventies. With the aid of the sunshine and buzz of spring life, I'd actually made it a mile at a slow jog and had managed a few sets of push-ups and sit-ups today. A small step forward but certainly not the kind of attire I usually left the house in.

"I don't own flip-flops."

She goggled at me like I'd just confessed to hating babies. "Fine. Old sneakers then."

"Don't own those either."

"You're a deprived man, Dev. Bare feet are fine. Just don't whine about mud." She started dragging me toward the door.

I dug my heels into the living room rug. "Where are we going?" I asked.

Scarlett had an interesting habit of dragging me where I didn't want to go.

"Deck party. It's the perfect day for it. I've got a cooler of sandwiches, beers, water. And I'm not takin' no for an answer. So get your fine ass moving."

I wasn't exactly sure where to start. What was a deck party? And did she really think I had a fine ass? Or was that more a statement about the whole package? Because I was feeling as far from my normal self as I ever had.

"Stop overthinking and come with me," she ordered.

I grabbed my phone from the table. "Fine, but if this turns out to be some kind of Bootleg initiation where you take me cow tipping and leave me in the middle of a corn field, I'm going to hire a different contractor."

She rolled her eyes, and this time when she tugged my hand, I let her drag me out the door.

"A. There's no such thing as tipping cows. Urban myth. B. If I left you in a corn field right now, you'd be just fine seein' as how it doesn't hit knee high until the Fourth of July."

She kept a hold of my hand and pulled me through the woods in the direction of her house. I tried to remember the last woman who so freely held my hand. Dating Johanna had been more like a job interview. We both had specific goals. I was looking for the right partner for my career. She was looking for a husband who would provide financial security and the ability to pursue her volunteerism. Looking back it seemed a bit... archaic. Sterile?

Scarlett glanced over her shoulder at me and grinned, and I felt... something.

She beamed up at me, and I felt... tall, interesting, stirred. I was by no means in any position for a spring or summer fling. But this bubbly brunette with a sweet southern drawl was starting to paint pictures in my head.

We peeled away from her cottage and headed down the wooden dock over the dark lake waters.

"Who's ready to party?" Scarlett crowed.

The end of the dock erupted in hoots and hollers. It was a twelve-by-twelve floating deck with an outboard motor, railings with built-in cup holders, and folding camp chairs. Her brothers were there, all three of them, and two women close to Scarlett's age.

"Cass, this is my friend Devlin. Dev, this is my BFF Cassidy. She's deputy sheriff here in Bootleg."

Cassidy peered at me over her sunglasses and offered a wave. She had dirty blonde hair cut in short layers. Her green eyes considered me impishly.

"A pleasure," I said.

Cassidy raised an eyebrow. "Well, he's a hell of a lot more polite than your last 'friend,'" Cassidy said.

Scarlett flipped her the bird and cheerfully continued her introductions.

"This tall drink of water here is Cassidy's sister June. June, this is Devlin."

June was tall with stick-straight hair a shade or two darker than her sister's. They both had the same upturned nose.

"Are you two having sexual intercourse?" June asked. Her face remained impassive as if she didn't really care if we were or not but was merely making small talk.

I cleared my throat. "No. We're not." I noticed that the Bodine brothers relaxed visibly, and I realized I might have narrowly avoided a physical altercation.

"We're all here," Scarlett announced, not the slightest bit perturbed by the sex question or the fact that her brothers looked like they would have cheerfully beaten me to death and dumped my body in the lake. "Let's cast off."

Bowie fired up the motor while Cassidy untied the lines. Jameson gave the deck a shove away from Scarlett's dock, and we were underway. June queued up a playlist, and something country and upbeat poured out of the railing-mounted Bluetooth speaker.

"What do you think?" Scarlett asked, plopping a straw cowgirl hat over her dark hair. She looked like she belonged on the cover of a country album in her short, shredded denim cutoffs and her I Heart America white tank. Her blue flip-flops showed off pink toenails. And was that a peek of a red bikini I was seeing? God help me, it was. And I was trapped on a tiny barge with her three brothers.

I didn't feel like now was a good time to share exactly what I was thinking. Instead I stated the obvious. "Your deck is floating."

"There's a sandbar in the middle of the lake. On warm days, everyone heads there."

"To do what?"

She looked up at me from under the brim of her hat like she felt sorry for me. "To have fun, Dev. When's the last time you had any of that?" She laid a palm against my chest, and while I *really* liked how it felt there, I heard Gibson clear his throat.

Message received.

I took a step back, and Jameson helpfully shoved a cold beer into my chest. "Maybe this will help you cool off."

"Thanks," I said weakly.

We motored out around the boulders that jutted into the lake and into open water. Geographically, the lake was huge. I

41

could barely make out the opposite shore which, if Scarlett's tall tales were correct, was Maryland. We were heading away from town, and I noticed the lakefront homes grew sparser, replaced by rocky ledges and thick copses of pine trees. There wasn't much civilization on this end of the lake, and had I been alone, I might have enjoyed it.

I shouldn't have come. I wasn't prepared to socialize, especially not with an entirely different culture.

Someone behind me hooted. There in the center of the lake was a long strip of sand and a half-dozen other floating decks. I'd spent summer days on the Potomac on the deck of a sailboat, but I'd never seen anything quite like this.

With the expertise of a riverboat captain, Scarlett piloted us up to the sandbar, beaching the deck gently. Gibson flipped open a section of the railing and tied it to the neighboring deck, effectively lashing us to them and creating a doorway.

Greetings were exchanged, music stations synched, and inner tubes were launched into the dark lake waters.

"Isn't it a little cold for that?" I asked Scarlett.

"Hot springs, remember?" She leaned down and scooped up a handful of water, splashing me in the face. It wasn't the icy bath I'd anticipated.

She laughed, and I mopped my face with the hem of my t-shirt. Was it my imagination, or had her gaze locked on to my abs? It made me wish I hadn't given up on working out. A few months ago, she would have had something to stare at.

I dropped my shirt back in place, and she gave me a friendly grin. "Now, you just sit right down and enjoy yourself," she said and danced over to the neighboring deck.

In our flotilla, there were 20-somethings shotgunning beers, parents sunscreening little kids, and even a deck full of senior citizens in floppy hats playing Bunco.

I sat on the edge of the deck with my bare feet in the water and wondered how my life had come to a screeching halt and dumped me here. And why I wasn't more upset.

"Flippin' contest!" someone shouted.

The Bootleg population represented on the lake cheered, and the chant started. "Flip! Flip! Flip!"

The Bodine brothers shared a look and rose as one. Cheers erupted.

"You're going to need to move back for ballast," June said, appearing at my elbow. June, Cassidy, and I lined up on the edge of the deck closest to the sandbar while the brothers made a show of peeling off their shirts and stretching.

"Wait for me, y'all!" Scarlett barreled over from the next-door deck. She stripped off her tank top, and I swear I went deaf for a second or two. I've seen people move in slow motion in movies, but I'd never experienced it in real life. She shucked her cutoffs, and they hit me square in the chest. With a grin, she stood before me in a cherry red bikini that made it very clear exactly how sexy she was.

When she followed her brothers and climbed up on the top rail of the deck, I felt my heart stop.

The swimmers in their inner tubes cleared the water. "Get it, Bodines!"

"Shake your tail feathers!"

I didn't know what that meant, but I sure as hell wasn't prepared for what happened next.

Starting with Bowie on the right, they turned their backs on the lake one by one and executed perfect back flips into the water.

"Holy sh—"

I didn't even get the words out when Scarlett jumped, tucking her knees to her chest and spinning backward.

"Wooooooo!" Cassidy shrieked in my ear.

"Excellent form," June commented.

They surfaced, one at a time, the family resemblance evident in the matching ear-to-ear grins. Scarlett bobbed in the water and splashed Gibson. He dunked her and swam over to an empty tube.

"Water me, McCallister," he ordered.

Still stunned by Scarlett's ball-of-fire body and precision

43

gymnastics, I dug through the cooler and tossed him a bottle of water.

Scarlett hauled herself aboard and caught the towel Cassidy threw at her. "How's the water, dare devil?" Cassidy asked.

"Warmer than the air," Scarlett said, bending at the waist and flipping her head upside down to towel dry her hair. Was I the only one staring at her ass in that tiny scrap of fabric?

A quick scan of the nearby decks told me I was *not* the only one. Every male who wasn't related to Scarlett was avidly enjoying the view.

I crossed to her, blocking everyone else's view, and handed her a beer.

"Thanks, Dev. Stick around here long enough, and we'll have you back-flippin' in no time."

I couldn't imagine anything less likely.

Chapter Eight

Scarlett

The sun dipped low on the horizon casting a pinky orange glow across the surface of the lake. The shadows grew longer, the coolers slowly emptied, and the music played low in the background as we listened to crickets and tree frogs. I leaned against the railing enjoying the heat that pumped off of Devlin's body next to me. He'd relaxed today, smiled, laughed, made small talk.

Misty Lynn Prosser did her best to catch Gibson's eye while she bounced on the lap of her on-again, off-again fuck buddy Rhett. Misty Lynn had the misfortune to be the person I hated most in this world. She'd kicked Gibson when he was down, right after our mama's death. She cheated on him and laughed in his face when he called her out on it. Gibson didn't hit women. But I sure did.

Her nose still hooked to the right just the slightest bit from my fist. Bootleg Justice was swift and brutal when necessary.

I still hated her guts to infinity and back again. But this was Bootleg. So Misty Lynn showed up at every party, every bonfire, every softball game just like the rest of us. And while she blew Rhett in the Shop 'n Buy parking lot, I knew she still wished she was Gibson's girl.

Devlin shifted next to me, nudging my shoulder with his. He pointed with his water bottle toward the sun as it finally disappeared behind the trees. I smiled.

He'd argued baseball with June for almost a solid hour. And he'd given my bikini more than a passing glance. I liked seeing that heat in his whiskey brown eyes. That slow thawing of the ice inside him. There was life in him yet. He just needed to be reminded of it.

Dusk fell. It was my favorite time of day. Sure, there were merits to the sunrise, and the sunset was no slouch either. But dusk was when the world got quiet. Dusk was when Daddy swung Mama into an impromptu two-step in the kitchen on the good days when supper was getting done and the right song came on the radio. Dusk was when I sat on my screened-in porch and reminded myself how lucky I was. Every day, I used this time to count my blessings.

I had a house I loved, a truck that started every morning without fail, a business that made me indispensable, and I had my brothers. What more could I want?

Besides maybe someone like Devlin to fool around with. I side-eyed him as he chatted with Bowie and EmmaLeigh's husband, Ennis. There was something there that sent my blood singing. Sure, he was a pleasure to look at. But there was something else there. Several somethings. He was going through a rough patch, and I was a sucker for someone who needed a little extra loving. But the way he looked at me was a lot different from the way every other man in town did. It was downright impossible to be sexy and mysterious with a guy who'd dared you to eat paste in kindergarten.

But Devlin didn't know me as Jameson's little sister or Jonah's daughter. He looked at me like I was a *woman*. And I liked it.

It was right about that time that the right song came on

and someone cranked the volume. Those with enough energy jumped into the Cowboy Boogie in bare feet.

"What's happening?" Devlin asked in my ear as the decks rocked and swayed with the motion.

My skin pebbled in a thousand different places with him so close.

"It's a line dance, and we should probably move—"

It was too late. Rocky Tobias' enthusiastic arm caught me across the chest, and I felt myself falling. Strong arms reached around me, but dang if that gravity didn't have other plans. We hit the water in a splash, and I came up laughing. Devlin surfaced next to me spitting lake water.

"Are you okay?" he asked, his hands searching my arms for injuries.

My t-shirt floated up around my waist, leaving my bikini bottoms as my only barrier to him.

I slipped my arms around his neck. The water was deep here on this side of the sandbar. He froze for a moment at my touch and slipped under the water. He came back up sputtering.

I could barely see his face in front of me in the darkness.

"What are you doing, Scarlett?" he asked gruffly.

"Tryin' something," I told him. I wrapped my legs around his waist and let him keep us afloat. The water was warm. The dark made us both braver than usual.

I leaned in and pressed my wet mouth to his, anticipating that nice little zing I always felt when kissing a new man.

But a zing wasn't what hit me. Devlin hesitated for about a whole half-second, and then he was tasting me like I was a buffet of desserts and he was a man starving. His mouth was hard, bruising against mine, and when I opened to whisper "wow," he entered my mouth as if he owned it. His tongue was strong and sure and *hungry*.

I plastered myself against him and felt him go hard. *That* to me was power. Devlin kicked his legs to keep us from going under, and I wriggled against his hard-on, wondering what we could get away with under the water.

He fed on me with an unsuspected rawness that made my mind go blank. All I could do was feel. I'd only thought to tempt him, tease him into a response. But this was something I hadn't expected. I had awakened the dragon, and now he was going to consume me. And I dog paddled along happily to my doom.

Devlin's hand skimmed up my back and grabbed a fistful of hair, yanking my head back. He pressed kisses along my jawline, my neck. He bit at the strap of my bikini top, and I gasped in shock at the need that had fired up to red line.

I hadn't anticipated the power of his need and what a shockingly beautiful thing it was. To be taken by him, desperate and hungry? *Oh, hell yeah.*

I wanted his touch everywhere. I wanted him to brand me in this lake that I loved. To take me in the darkness like we were two night creatures. I wanted to belong to him right here in the water.

"Y'all about done maulin' each other?" Cassidy asked from the deck.

We were in the spotlight of someone's flashlight, and there was quite the audience gathered on the decks to watch us.

Devlin's hands flexed on my waist, just under my breasts.

"To be continued," I whispered in his ear.

"Get on the damn deck, Scarlett," Gibson snarled.

I swam back to the deck, and a strong hand grabbed my arm and hauled me aboard. "Careful there," Bowie cautioned me. "You don't know him."

"I know enough of him," I shot back, feeling rattled. It was hard to go from revved to full brake.

My brothers closed ranks around me—cockblockers—and left it up to Cassidy and June to haul Devlin aboard.

"I think it's time we call it a night," Bowie announced.

"You all suck," I drawled.

"You need to stop foolin' around and find a nice guy that you can settle down with," Gibson announced. "Someone we can beat the hell out of, if necessary."

"Shut up, Gibs. I'm not settlin' down until—"

"Thirty," he interjected. "Yeah, yeah. You made Mom a promise. I get it. She didn't want you to make the same mistakes she did." He said it like he'd heard it all a million times before.

"I don't see you all hurryin' down the aisle. Do I?"

"That's different," Jameson said, offering up a rare opinion.

"If one of you assholes says 'because I've got a dick and you've got a vag,' I swear to Christ almighty I will murder you, and they'll never find your body."

"Cut us some slack, Scar," Bowie butted in.

"No. You all need to cut me some slack. You raised me. It's your fault. So deal with it."

I shoved my way between them. But instead of heading over to Devlin's side, which would turn him into an instant target, I stood in the only unoccupied corner of the deck and plotted the murder of my brothers.

They were overprotective to be sure, but had I been a man, they'd have no issue with me wrestling in the water with someone. But no. Because I had a vagina, they thought they could dictate my sex life. It wasn't cute anymore. Not like when I went to junior prom and they lined up on the front porch and glared down Freddy Sleeth until he all but ran back to the car. Or when I had my heart broken by Wade Zirkel senior year. Gibson had shoved that boy in the trunk of his car and driven around for an hour before he let Jameson and Bowie take one shot each at him.

I had yet to tell them that I'd accidentally slept with Wade a few times at the tail end of this past winter and it hadn't ended well. He'd flirted up Zadie Rummerfield at The Lookout while I was playing pool. I'd dumped a pitcher of beer over his head and flattened one of the tires on his pickup on my way out.

He still had some of my stuff at his apartment, and come hell or high water, I was gonna get it back.

"You all right, babe?" Cassidy asked, handing me a towel.

"Just peachy with three asshole misogynists for brothers." I made sure the comment was loud enough for everyone to hear.

"They love you," Cassidy reminded me unnecessarily.

"That doesn't give them an excuse to shame me," I said, dropping my voice.

"They're not trying to shame. They're trying to protect you."

"I'm an adult."

"Does an adult really start wet humping a stranger in a lake in front of her brothers?"

I stuck my jaw out. "Careful, Cass. It's almost soundin' like you're on their side."

"I'm always on your side, Scarlett. But there comes a time when we all have to grow up."

Damn the pragmatic deputy in my best friend. Sometimes I had the distinct feeling that Cassidy had gone and grown up without me, leaving me—her best friend in the world—to fumble through life all by my lonesome.

I spotted Devlin on the other side of the deck as Gibson grumpily motored us home. He was watching me with an unreadable expression on his fine face. I'd taken him by surprise in the water. Hell, I'd taken myself by surprise with my reaction. But what surprised us both was Devlin's reaction.

It was times like these that I wished I still had a mama to talk to.

We reached my dock in subdued spirits. I hopped off and tied the lines, ignoring my brothers and Cassidy, who'd also landed on my shit list. I muscled a cooler off the deck and griped when someone took it from me.

But it was Devlin. And from the sparks that exploded from just a brush of his fingers, I knew the kiss hadn't been a random fluke. I wasn't sure if I was eager to explore it or if I should run in the opposite direction like my mama had made me promise.

"Never, ever get married before thirty, Scarlett Rose," she'd told me time and time again. It was common knowledge that she and Daddy had to get married right in the middle of their senior year of high school, pregnant with Gibson. Theirs had been a volatile relationship with more downs than ups. But the ups were still the highlight reel of my childhood.

Jameson took the cooler from Devlin, and Gibson bumped Devlin with his shoulder on purpose.

"There's no reason for you to be actin' like an asshole," I announced to my oldest brother.

Wearily he looked at me. "Can we just not for once, Scar?"

"Whatever." I shrugged. I was tired, too. I wanted to go home, alone. And sit in the dark. This melancholy was familiar. I'd lived with it daily for a year or so after Mama died. And since Daddy... well, it had found me again. And tonight, I was tired of running from it. I'd soak in it, feel it, suffer through it. And then tomorrow I'd start fresh.

"Who's that?" Bowie asked, tensing as a stranger walked toward us in the dark.

He stopped at where the dock met the land.

My brothers stood shoulder to shoulder in front of me, and it didn't escape my notice that Devlin wedged himself in between Gibson and Jameson.

"Is there a Scarlett Bodine here?" the stranger asked.

He didn't sound like West Virginia, and I couldn't see his face in the dark. Cassidy turned on the flashlight she went everywhere with, blinding the man.

"Can we help you?" she asked, all no-nonsense deputy now.

"Looking for Scarlett," he said.

"Jesus," I whispered. That voice. The face. It was like staring at a ghost.

"And who might you be?" Cassidy asked.

"Jonah Bodine."

Chapter Nine
Scarlett

The stranger had my father's face but someone else's eyes. Looking at him next to my brothers, anyone would have thought he was a fourth Bodine boy.

"Jonah Bodine?" I repeated, peering over Devlin's shoulder on my tip toes.

He nodded and held up a hand to block the beam of Cassidy's flashlight. "You mind?" he asked.

I wedged my way between my brother and Devlin. "I'm Scarlett," I said, walking down the dock to meet him. The bodyguard crew moved as one behind me, crowding in against my back. "You have my father's name… and face."

"Guess that makes him *our* father," Jonah said with a shrug.

There was a lot that went unsaid in that simple statement. The rounding of his shoulders against what sure sounded like the truth. His lined brow, the narrowing of his eyes, the bitterness behind his words.

"Look, I don't know who you are, man," Gibson began.

"He's our brother, jackwagon," I said, whirling around to

glare at him. I always was the one to recover fastest from a sucker punch. "Dang it! Another fucking brother." I was pretty tired of being the only girl in the cock-blocking, judgmental, overprotective family.

"Bullshit," Gibson argued.

"Christ. Look at him. Take one good look at him and tell me he's not Bodine blood," I snapped.

"Y'all got some ID?" Cassidy asked.

If Jonah thought it was weird to hand his driver's license over to a girl in cutoffs and a Madonna tank top, he didn't say so.

"Be right back," Cassidy announced, heading toward her car. "No one kill anyone while I'm gone."

Jameson stared at Jonah. "How old are you?" he asked finally.

"Thirty."

Bowie flinched next to me. He was thirty, and I imagined there'd be some kind of feelings there. "Hang on, Cass," he called and jogged after her.

"What are you doing here?" Gibson demanded. There wasn't anything friendly in his tone.

"Saw the obituary. Saw I had siblings," Jonah said simply. "Your dad and my mom. She was a waitress in a diner." He added the last defiantly as if he was daring us to say anything against his mama.

"Did you know? I mean, did you know our dad?" I asked.

"Met him once when I was a kid and once when I was nineteen in the summer."

I did the math.

"Fuck," I breathed. Jonah Bodine Sr. had gone looking for his other son—or his son's mother—right around the time my own mother died.

"This is ridiculous," Gibson began.

"What do you want?" Jameson asked shortly.

Jonah shrugged again.

"Dad had nothing," Gibson spat out. "So, if you think you're gettin' rich off of some drunk's estate, think again."

"I don't want anything from him," Jonah said.

I stepped between them just in case Gibson decided to take a swing. Devlin moved with me.

"Well, I'm Scarlett," I said, holding out my hand. "And I bet you have a lot of questions."

Jonah looked at my hand for a minute before shaking it. "Hi, Scarlett," he said softly, his voice so like my father's made it feel like I was having a conversation with a ghost.

"Devlin," Dev said, introducing himself. "I'm staying next door," he said.

Jonah nodded. "I'm Jonah."

"This is bullshit," Gibson muttered.

"Then why don't you walk away like you always do? Go mope in your fortress of solitude," I snapped.

"We don't know anything about this guy, and you want to be his friend?"

"Just 'cause you don't like what he has to say doesn't mean you have to be a dick about it," I retorted.

"He checks out," Cassidy called from my driveway. She ambled back down with Bowie at her side and handed Jonah his driver's license back. "Jonah Bodine, thirty, currently of Jetty Beach, Washington State. Few speeding tickets. No real bumps with the law."

Bowie offered his hand. "Not sure what the etiquette is here. But I'm Bowie. I guess I'm your half-brother."

"This is fucking ridiculous," Gibson railed.

"Go home, Gibs," I told him.

He ran a hand over his beard, and I saw anger in his ice blue eyes.

"Go on home until you can act like a human being," I ordered.

"Where are you staying?" Gibson asked Jonah. It didn't sound remotely friendly.

"Don't tell him," I ordered Jonah.

"Scarlett," Jameson said quietly, laying his hand on my shoulder.

"We're not goin' brother against brother tonight," I said stubbornly.

Gibson stormed off, and a moment later, we heard his muscle car rev up. He peeled out of my driveway sending gravel flying.

"If I have to arrest a Bodine tonight, I'm gonna be pissed," Cassidy sighed.

"Where *are* you staying?" I asked Jonah.

"Don't have a place yet," he said. "I wanted to see how the introductions went to see if I'd be sticking around."

I grinned. "I think they went all right, don't you?"

Devlin snorted next to me.

"Shut up, Dev. Nobody got decked."

"Why don't you stay with me, Jonah? I got a couch and a lot of whiskey."

"No!" The chorus was loud and insistent. Jameson, Bowie, and Devlin were glaring at me and shaking their heads.

"What?"

"You can stay with me," Devlin insisted. "I've got guest rooms. We can borrow the whiskey."

"Fine. Whatever," I muttered. "I'll see you for breakfast tomorrow, Jonah. We'll talk. Bowie, why don't you see June and Cass home? And Jame, do you mind checking in on Gibson on your way?" Gibson was an asshole, but he was my asshole.

"So, their father had an affair and impregnated someone else?" June asked Cassidy on their way to the driveway.

"Looks that way," Cassidy said, throwing a look over her shoulder. Bowie followed them a pace or two behind.

"Don't do anything stupid," Jameson said, pointing a callused finger in my face.

"Yeah, yeah. Don't let Gibson goad you into a fight," I replied.

With a wary look back at us, Jameson crossed the yard to my driveway.

"Well, that was fun," I said. "You don't by chance have any sisters do you, Jonah? I'm gettin' sick of the never-ending geyser of testosterone around here."

He shook his head. "Only child."

"'Til now," I reminded him. I couldn't quite tell in the dark, but I thought his face softened at my words. Whether Jonah realized it or not, he was one of us now.

I was suddenly exhausted. It settled on my shoulders like an unshakable weight. "Do y'all need anything for the night?" I asked.

Devlin rested his hand on my shoulder. "Go to bed, Scarlett. We'll see you in the morning." I wasn't sure what about his touch undid me, but I was one second away from blubbering all over him.

I reached up and gave his hand a squeeze and nodded at Jonah. "I'll see y'all tomorrow." With that, I left them in the dark and headed into my house. I didn't bother with the lights. I wanted the darkness. Wanted it to wrap me up and make me stop feeling things. I missed my dad. But was I really missing him or the man he should have been? The one we'd see glimpses of over the years. The two-steppin', bacon-frying, handyman who always had time for a conversation. Where had that man gone?

He'd disappeared into a bottle and never came out.

I looked at the shelf in my kitchen that held my booze collection. But nothing called to me. Nothing promised me happiness or numbness. Is that what he'd found in the bottom of that bottle, I wondered.

I thought about Gibson, his reaction to Jonah. My big brother had borne the brunt of my parents' unhappy marriage. And I had no idea what the existence of another Jonah Bodine would make him feel.

"Damn it," I muttered under my breath. I wanted to wallow in my own feelings of misery, not worry about my brother's.

I dug my phone out of my bag.

Scarlett: I'm not sorry. But I hope you're okay.

He made me wait almost a full five minutes before responding.

Gibson: I'm not sorry either. Go to bed. We can fight tomorrow.

And just like that all was right between us. Bodines didn't break promises, and we definitely didn't apologize. Well, Bowie did. And he was damn good at it. But me? The words always got stuck in my throat and came out in a jumble of excuses and finger pointing.

I stripped out of my wet clothes and pulled on a tank top and shorts. I got myself a glass of water and then sat down on the swing on my porch. The symphony of crickets was deafening on the cool night air.

Usually I thought about all the things I had to be grateful for. But tonight, I let myself stew in all the things I wished were different. And maybe I thought once or twice about that kiss.

Chapter Ten

Devlin

You can take your pick of the rooms upstairs," I told Jonah, jerking my head toward the hallway off the kitchen.

"Thanks."

He studied the house with a disconnected interest as if he was cataloging everything and storing away the details.

"Nice place," he ventured as he looked into the night through the deck doors in the living room.

"It's my grandmother's. She's traveling."

"And you're the house-sitter?" He dropped his duffle bag on the floor.

"I'm the grandson going through a rough patch who needed a place to stay."

Jonah nodded, no judgment in his gaze. "Looks like you picked a good place to ride out the rough."

"You ever been here before?" I asked.

Jonah shook his head and returned to the kitchen, shoving his hands in the pockets of his jeans. "No. Never had a reason to when Jonah was alive."

"Bad guy?" I asked. Scarlett had yet to talk much about her father, but I could tell her memories of him were softer, warmer, than Jonah's.

"He was no hero to me," Jonah admitted.

Since we were here, I opened the fridge and pulled two beers out of the six-pack Estelle had thoughtfully left for me. I slid one across the counter to him.

He twisted the top and crossed the kitchen to study a picture on Gran's bulletin board. "This your grandmother?" he asked.

It was Gran and Estelle wrapped in a cheerful embrace at the top of Pike's Peak in Colorado.

"My grandmother and her lesbian life partner." He'd seemed touchy on the subject of his mother, and I was the same when it came to Gran. I dared him to say something about West Virginia and a bi-racial lesbian couple.

"Cool," he said, returning to the island where he slid onto one of the flower padded barstools.

"So, what are you hoping to get out of this visit?" I asked him.

He shrugged one shoulder. "Honestly? I have no idea. The Jonah Bodine I knew had no interest in me and vice versa. His kids? My siblings?" He sounded like he was rolling the word around in his mouth, trying it out. "That's a different story."

"Family," I murmured.

"Drink to that," Jonah agreed, raising his bottle. We drank in silence for a few minutes.

"So, Scarlett?" Jonah finally said, letting the question hang in the air.

"What about her?" I could feel my hackles rising.

"I noticed you're pretty protective of her," he grinned, looking pointedly at my white knuckled grip on the neck of my beer.

I relaxed my hands and slouched against the counter. "She's something," I said. "Unlike any woman I've ever met before."

"Are you... together?" Jonah asked.

I thought about the kiss in the water. Her soul-stealing mouth moving against mine and how I'd been seconds away from doing something really stupid. She made me feel… alive. Intensely alive.

"She just lives next door," I said carefully.

"Hmm," Jonah said, not believing me.

"Does your mother know you're here?" I asked, the lawyer in me waking from his long hibernation. Redirect, go on the offensive, keep them off-balance.

"She does not," he said staring intently at the label on his bottle. "Yet."

———

We made the morning trek to Scarlett's little cottage and knocked on her front door. It was even more like a dollhouse up close, I realized. Her postage stamp screened-in porch housed one porch swing and a small round table with two chairs. Her front door was painted navy blue.

I knocked once and peered through the glass.

She was folded over, digging through her refrigerator, when I knocked.

She slammed the fridge and danced to the door. Scarlett smiled brightly when she welcomed us, but I saw the shadows under her eyes. It looked as though I wasn't the only one who hadn't slept last night. But my thoughts had been occupied by the kiss. I doubted that hers had.

"Morning, boys. I have some bad news. I've got one egg and two strips of bacon."

Jonah and I both looked around us in wonder. She'd taken the interior of the cabin and turned it into a sanctuary with green plants, soft quilts, and worn furniture. It was cozy, friendly. Her skinny coffee table was occupied by a laptop and a neat stack of work orders. The kitchen was the size of a shoebox. Tiny and L-shaped with about a foot and a half of usable counter space. The floors were pine. The walls were stucco. Above the stone fireplace's thick wood mantel hung a twisted iron heart.

60

Jonah said something about not needing much more than coffee for breakfast.

"Oh, no. I promised y'all breakfast," Scarlett said. "We'll just go to Moonshine."

"It's a diner," I told him before he could ask. "Great pepperoni rolls."

Scarlett beamed up at me, and I instantly felt ten feet tall. If I had that face smiling up at me every day, there wouldn't be much in life that I couldn't accomplish. I wanted to kiss her again or at least ask her about the kiss. What it meant? Would I be lucky enough to get another one from her? But not with an audience.

I should have backed out, let the two of them go together. But I knew I'd have to answer to Scarlett's brothers if I were to leave their baby sister with a stranger. Plus, if I was being honest, I wanted another pepperoni roll.

I volunteered to drive. Scarlett rode shotgun, and Jonah took the seat behind her so he'd have more room for his legs. Scarlett was unusually quiet on the short drive, focusing her attention on her phone.

When she caught me looking, she flashed the screen at me. It was a group text between her and her brothers. I wondered if we'd end up with more Bodines for breakfast.

Moonshine was busy, but Clarabell wrangled a table for us in the back.

"You sure keep comin' in here with some attractive men, Scarlett," Clarabell said with a wink of her blue-shadowed eye.

"I've got a reputation to uphold," Scarlett joked and opened her menu.

Clarabell hustled off to get our coffees, and Scarlett eyed Jonah. "Question that I'm gonna need an answer for real fast. Are you okay with folks here knowing you're my half-brother?"

Jonah looked up from his menu and scanned the restaurant. "I suppose so."

"Good, because secrets don't keep in Bootleg, and I figure I've got about forty seconds before someone comes up and wants to know who you are. And that family resemblance is gonna have tongues a waggin'."

Jonah shifted uncomfortably in his seat. I felt bad for him. No one really wanted to face that kind of scrutiny.

Scarlett reached out and patted his hand. "There's no sins of the father here in Bootleg. No one's gonna blame you for existing," she promised.

"Tell me they've got eggs benedict today." Bowie appeared over my shoulder and snatched Scarlett's menu from her hands.

"Hey!"

"Mornin' all," he said, sliding into the chair next to Jonah.

"Glad you could make it," Scarlett said, stealing my menu.

"You think I'd really miss our first family breakfast?" Bowie quipped.

"Well, here's yet another gorgeous hunk of man," Clarabell cooed, dropping off mugs. She looked back and forth between Bowie and Jonah, and I saw the recognition hit her like a ton of bricks. "Well, I'll be…"

"Clarabell, this here is our half-brother Jonah," Scarlett said as casually as if she were discussing the spring weather.

"Well, it's a pleasure to meet you, Jonah. I expect you'll be staying with us for a while."

Let the fishing begin, I thought with a cough to hide my laugh.

"I'm playing it by ear," Jonah said, flashing her a friendly smile.

"Clarabell, can I have the meat lover's omelet with white toast, extra grape jelly?" Scarlett asked, snapping the menu shut and passing it back to me. She began shoveling creamer and sugar in alarming quantities into her coffee.

"Why sure thing, sweetheart."

"Coffee when you get the chance," Bowie ordered. "And the eggs benedict."

"Same," Jonah said, handing over his menu.

"I'll do three egg whites, the turkey bacon, and wheat toast," I said closing the menu.

"Aren't you gonna get a pepperoni roll?" Scarlett asked, batting her lashes at me.

"And two pepperoni rolls to go," I added. If I still had a houseguest, I needed to feed him something for lunch.

"We'll just hang on to this one in case anyone else in the brood shows up," Scarlett said.

"Be right back with your coffee, Bowie," Clarabell said. She practically sprinted back to the counter, and I could almost feel the word spreading like wildfire. Heads swiveled in our direction. Jonah focused his attention on the top of the table, fiddling with the sugar packets.

"So," Bowie began.

"So," Scarlett said.

"Y'all order yet?" Jameson muscled his way over and snagged an empty chair from a neighboring table putting it at the foot of our table.

Scarlett lit up. "'Bout time," she said. But when she thought no one else was looking, I caught her mouth the words, "Thank you."

"So," Jameson began.

I was starting to feel like the odd man out. This was a family matter. Blood and DNA were ranged around the table, anxious to talk history. And the McCallister in me wanted to get up and leave. My family would never discuss private matters with outsiders.

"You know, I might just see if I can get my breakfast to go—" I started.

"Hush up, Dev. We've got no secrets," Scarlett insisted.

Jameson shrugged his broad shoulders. "No problems here."

Bowie nodded his assent in the stay or go vote. "Fine by me."

All eyes turned to Jonah. This was his first time to weigh-in on a Bodine family situation.

"It's cool with me," he said. The look of relief on his face told me he wasn't keen to be left alone with his new family just yet. "Besides, you drove us."

"Isn't this cozy?" Gibson appeared next to Scarlett, and everyone tensed around the table. The entire diner went silent as everyone strained to hear.

Scarlett nudged the empty chair at the foot of the table at him. "Pull up a chair, Gibs."

Gibson glanced in Jonah's direction and looked away again.

Chapter Eleven

Scarlett

I held my breath and waited for my brother to make his move. I really hoped it wouldn't be a fist to Jonah's face. Thankfully, my desperate prayers were answered, and Gibson grudgingly took the seat I kicked at him.

Clarabell, clairvoyant waitress that she was, arrived with a coffee for Gibson. "You boys want breakfast?" she asked Jameson and Gibson.

She took their orders—waffles for Jameson, who was as much a sugar whore as I was, and just the coffee for Gibs.

"I'm guessin' we all have some questions for one another," I began.

"I want to know why you're here," Gibson said to Jonah without looking at him. His tone was flat and lacked the heat of his anger last night.

"Curiosity mostly," Jonah answered.

Devlin shifted in his chair next to me. He was uncomfortable with the situation, but since Jonah was his temporary roommate and I was planning on sleeping with Devlin at some point, he might as well stick around and get his ears full.

"About us?" I asked Jonah.

He nodded. "I don't care about your father—our father," he corrected himself. "He had no interest in me and my life, and I'm happy to return that favor. But I didn't know about you."

"I'd be curious, too," Bowie admitted. "Why don't we do some preliminary introductions at least?"

Sallie Mae Brickman was leaning so far back in her chair to catch the scraps of our conversation I worried she'd end up on her ass in her Sunday best.

"You already know that I'm Scarlett. I'm the youngest and only girl. I run Bodine's Home Services, and I've got a few rental properties here in town."

"I'm Bowie, your age, which puts us as the second oldest in the crooked Bodine totem pole. I'm the vice principal at the high school."

Jameson hated shit like this, so I enjoyed watching him squirm.

I grinned at him. "Come on, Jame. It's not that hard."

"Jameson, second youngest. I work with metal."

"He's a pretty amazing artist," I supplied for Jonah. It was true. What Jameson couldn't seem to put into his human interactions, he twisted and welded in metal form. His popularity had skyrocketed since he'd been commissioned to do a large-scale installation in a park in Charleston.

"You know who I am," Gibson said, his tone surly.

"Yeah, we get that you're the resident asshole, brother dearest. Tell Jonah something he doesn't know," I suggested helpfully.

"I'm the oldest. I'm a woodworker."

I snorted. "Gibson likes working with wood."

"Nothing makes Gibs happier than havin' a handful of wood," Bowie agreed with a wink.

Even Gibson managed a smirk at that while the rest of us busted up laughing.

"It's a double entendre about erections," I whispered to Devlin who appeared not to have gotten the joke.

"I get it," he said dryly.

"Your turn, Dev. Tell Jonah who you are."

"I'm Devlin. I have nothing to do with your situation."

"What *do* you do, McAllister?" Gibson asked, shifting his pissed-offness to Devlin.

"I'm a disgraced lawmaker in the Maryland State Assembly."

I choked on my coffee and sent a fine spray across the table.

"Thanks, Scar," Bowie said, mopping up the mess.

"Disgraced in what way?" Jameson pressed. Jameson was interested enough to ask questions. That was a first.

"I was going to get around to telling you this part," Devlin said, looking at me sheepishly.

"Oh, boy." I could only imagine. This was the part where he told me he ran over his soon-to-be ex-wife or, *worse*, took a vow of chastity.

"My wife was cheating on me, and I was too busy to notice," Devlin said matter-of-factly. "When I did notice, it wasn't pretty. My divorce will be final in a few weeks."

He shot me the side-eye.

"Uh-huh." I knew all this already.

"I'm on leave and under orders to lay low because, on the last day we were in session, I assaulted the guy she was sleeping with."

Bowie slapped the table and hooted.

Gibson gave an almost imperceptible nod of approval. "Bet that felt good," he predicted.

The corner of Devlin's mouth quirked up.

I reached under the table and squeezed his knee. His truth seemed to embarrass him. But a man who'd punch out an asshole didn't scare me. Hell, in Bootleg, that was an admirable quality.

"Your turn, Jonah. Spill your guts," I said cheerfully.

"I'm Jonah Bodine. My mom gave me my father's name, but that's the only piece of him I ever had or wanted. I live in Washington State, and I'm a personal trainer. Until a week ago, I thought I was an only child. I don't want anything from you. Just maybe a chance to get to know you. If you're not all assholes." Jonah reached up and rubbed the back of his neck. My brothers and I shared a glance. It was a nervous trait we'd all seen in our father.

"Why didn't he want anything to do with you?" Gibson asked.

"Jeez, Gibs," I rolled my eyes. "Maybe tone it down a notch?"

"No, it's okay," Jonah shrugged. "My mom never talked about him much. We used to live in Virginia. I guess she met your dad at a diner when he was passing through. I didn't ask for details. She didn't know he was married. She said he tried to make it right, but she didn't want to ruin a family. So we made our own."

"You said last night you'd met him twice?" I prodded.

Jonah nodded. "First time when I was like six or seven. We were still in Virginia then, and he came to the house one day. I was playing in the yard. We threw ball. I didn't know. I was just a kid. When my mom came out, she freaked. Sent me inside. They talked for a long time in the yard, and then she cried the rest of the night."

Gibson was staring hard at the table. Bowie was frowning into space. Jameson was his usual unreadable self. I wasn't sure who I hurt for more.

"Before I put y'all's food down, is there gonna be anyone else joining you?" Clarabell asked, carting a tray of steaming breakfast food.

Devlin answered for us all, and she doled out the hot plates.

"Be back with refills," she promised and hustled away.

We dug in in silence and let Jonah's story settle over us.

"You said you saw him twice," Gibson said, finally breaking the silence.

Jonah poked at his eggs. "We moved cross-country when I started college. One weekend, I came home with a basket of

68

laundry, and there he was at my mother's house. He was drunk, upset about something, and she was treating him like a sick kid. I blew up. She had a boyfriend at the time, a nice guy. I thought he was back to mess things up for her again. I left, went back to school. We never spoke about it again."

"I don't know if y'all did the math, but that lines up with when Dad disappeared after Mom died," I said quietly.

"So, he waited all of five seconds after she died before running back to the woman he had an affair with?" Gibson asked bitterly. "No offense," he added at Jonah.

"Do you think Mom knew?" Bowie asked.

No one answered him.

I didn't know what the best answer would be. Mama and Daddy's relationship was volatile at best. In most ways, their relationship never progressed past the high school years. Petty jealousies, unrealistic expectations. They fought more than they got along, and we'd grown up thinking it was normal. There was a good reason none of us Bodines had settled down. We didn't know how.

Cassidy and June's parents, Sheriff Harlan and Nadine Tucker, were another story. Steady and strong. I know there'd been times over the years when they'd stepped up for each one of us when our own parents weren't capable. I was grateful. And jealous.

Devlin cleared his throat. "It sounds like the next best step would be for you all to spend some time together. Get to know each other and decide if this is a relationship you want to develop or let go."

We all looked at him.

"Look at you bein' all lawyerly," I crooned.

"Well, would you look at that, Bodines?" Bowie announced. "A mature suggestion that actually makes sense."

"I guess it's less taxing than beating the shit out of each other," Gibson mused. He waved Clarabell over. "Clarabell, I changed my mind. I think I'll have the eggs benedict."

Chapter Twelve
Devlin

It appeared that the Bodines had reached a tentative truce. It was good news for them, but I still had yet to get Scarlett alone to talk to her about that kiss. I had thought of little else, and the longer we went without talking about it, the stupider I felt bringing it up.

I watched her through the deck doors. It was another beautiful spring day. A Monday, and I had no place to be but staring out the door onto the deck where the afternoon sun was shining, the birds were singing, and a beautiful woman was swearing a blue streak at a particularly bad-tempered joist.

She wore those ass-hugging jeans and an old V-neck t-shirt. Her work boots were doll-sized and scarred from years of abuse. She wore her hair back in a high ponytail that made me want to wrap it around my fist. *A new temptation.*

"That's my new sister you're staring at there," Jonah said wryly.

"Got a problem with it?" I asked.

Jonah smirked. "Don't know yet. What are your intentions?"

I gave a dry laugh. That was the thing about Scarlett. She inspired instant and unshakable loyalty.

"I don't know what my intentions are. I can't get her alone to talk to her long enough to find out."

"I'm torn by newfound family loyalty and roommate gratitude," Jonah warned.

Scarlett hammered the wayward joist into submission with a triumphant shout and was working on positioning the new board on top of it when her phone rang. I watched her idly as Jonah prowled the kitchen. "You want eggs?" he asked.

We'd worked out a deal on splitting groceries and utilities. and like magic, food appeared in the fridge. An added bonus? Jonah could cook.

"Sure," I said.

"You son of a bitch!" We both heard Scarlett growl into her phone. It was different than the litany of curse words she'd laid down on the timber.

Jonah left the eggs on the counter, and I started to open the door.

"If you don't give me my shit back, I will burn down your life!"

Jonah and I exchanged a glance.

"Yeah, that's real funny Wade," Scarlett shouted. "You know what I'm gonna do? I'm gonna go find a nice tiny jar that I can store your little baby balls in. And when I find it, you better hide because I'm coming for you and your microscopic balls."

The unlucky bastard on the other end of the call must have hung up on her because Scarlett held the phone in front of her face and gave a scream of rage. She wound up and hurled the phone off the deck into the yard.

Jonah whistled. "Nice arm."

She reached for the nail gun and started to wind up again.

In a display of emergency teamwork, Jonah got the door open, and I nipped her around the waist before she was able to launch it into the yard. She fought like a wild animal in my arms. I outweighed her by a good hundred pounds and had a foot on her. It was almost comical... at least until the heel of her boot connected with my knee.

I pressed her against the siding of the house. "Scarlett," I said calmly. "Breathe."

She growled, and Jonah backed up a few paces.

"Breathe," I ordered again.

She sucked in a seething breath.

"If I let you go, are you going to break anything else?"

"Just Wade Zirkel's face."

Good enough for me. I released her. "Who's Wade Zirkel?"

She crossed her arms in front of her, temper snapping off of her like downed wires. "A big mistake I made a few weeks ago. He has some of my stuff and thinks he can hold it hostage until I 'come to my senses'."

I knew two things for sure. I hated Wade Zirkel, and I hoped I never, ever made Scarlett Bodine this mad.

"I'm takin' my lunch," Scarlett announced and stormed down the deck stairs.

It was two o'clock on a Monday, and she'd already eaten her sandwich with her toes in the water.

I looked at Jonah over my shoulder. "What would Bootleg do?"

Apparently, Bootleg would text Scarlett's brothers. At the diner, with a tentative family truce in place, everyone had traded numbers. Today, Jonah called his first family meeting. Bowie was at school but demanded that he be conferenced in.

"Now what did she do?" Gibson demanded, slamming the door of his Dodge Charger in my driveway. Jameson climbed out the passenger side.

"Wade Zirkel," I said, filling them in on the situation.

"I hate that fucking guy," Jameson muttered.

"Guess he didn't learn his lesson last time," Gibson said. "Get the trash bags."

72

"Awh, hell," Bowie said from the screen of Jonah's phone. "I'll meet you guys there. But I can't get blood on me. I've got a parent conference tonight."

Gibson eyed me up and pointed. "Bring a change of clothes for Bow," he said.

"What exactly are we doing?" I asked.

"Bootleg justice," Jameson and Gibson said together.

The ride to Wade Zirkel's apartment was relatively quiet. Jonah and I sat in the back, the roll of trash bags and a clean shirt and pants between us. I still wasn't sure if the bags were for Scarlett's possessions or Wade Zirkel's body.

It occurred to me that this was probably something I shouldn't be doing while laying low. But I didn't like that some asshole thought he could treat Scarlett like this. And I *really* didn't like the idea of him being anything to her.

Gibson pulled up to the curb in front of a duplex and revved the engine twice. A warning. I saw the blinds twitch on the first floor.

Bowie's SUV pulled up behind us, and he got out in khakis and a button-down. He took his tie off and threw it through his open window.

"I can't believe she gave this asshole the time of day again," Jameson muttered.

"This is the last time," Gibson promised. "Get the trash bags."

I grabbed them out of the backseat and was relieved when I noted none of them were carrying weapons. "So what's the plan?" I asked casually.

"We're going to scare the shit out of this douchebag and get our sister's stuff back," Gibson said.

I nodded thoughtfully. "Uh-huh. Sure. And how are we going to do that?"

"Just follow our lead," Bowie sighed, rolling up his sleeves.

Jonah and I exchanged a look, each of us wondering exactly what was going down and how much legal trouble we'd be in.

We climbed up onto the skinny concrete porch, and Gibson ignored the bell in favor of a heavy fist to the door.

The blinds twitched again.

"Might as well open the door, Wade," Bowie called out.

We all heard the sound of the deadbolt sliding open. Wade Zirkel peered through the inch of door that he cracked open. He had a ball cap on and a polo shirt that was plastered over "I go to the gym seven days a week" muscles. He was the kind of fake-tanned, bleach-toothed, former quarterback who was still riding high on his high school fame. I hated him even more.

"Well, hey there, Bodines. What do I owe the pleas—"

Jameson shouldered his way through the door, shoving Wade back a few paces.

"You can't just come in! That's breaking and entering," Wade squealed.

"Actually it's only trespassing," I pointed out.

"We're not here for pleasantries," Bowie announced. "We're here for Scarlett's stuff."

"I can call the cops," Wade announced, puffing out his impressive chest. The handsome bastard looked like a cross between Paul Walker and Vin Diesel from the car movies.

"Do you really want to do that?" I asked him. "The fines for trespassing are a lot lighter than harassment and larceny. Did you know you can face up to six months in prison for petty theft?" I asked him.

Wade blinked, his tan face going a shade of red.

"That's right, Wade. We brought ourselves a lawyer," Bowie said. "Now, are you gonna let us take Scarlett's stuff, or are we going to have to do this the hard way?"

Wade bobbed his head under his red Zirkel Auto Sales hat. "Help yourselves," he said meekly.

"Do we know what stuff she has here?" Bowie asked me in a whisper. I shrugged.

Gibson stalked up to Wade and stared the man down. He was a big guy, but the second Gibson Bodine invaded his personal space, he shrank into himself, shoulders stooping, gaze gluing to the floor.

"I want a sandwich," Gibson announced.

Wade gulped audibly. "Okay."

"Make me a sandwich, Zirkel."

"S-s-sure. Roast beef or t-t-t-una?"

If Wade made it through this encounter without pissing his pants, I'd consider it a miracle.

"Come on," Bowie said, leading the way down the hall and up the stairs. "Gibs will babysit him." He handed out trash bags.

"You all take the bedroom. I'll start in the bathroom."

I had no idea what we were looking for. I found a pink hoodie on the floor of the closet and threw it in the bag along with a pair of leggings that I doubted belonged to Zirkel. I really hated the idea of Scarlett being here with this guy. He was an overgrown asshole with a pretty face who obviously didn't know how to treat women.

Jonah tossed me a Bodine Home Services t-shirt and a pair of socks with hearts all over them.

Feeling irritable, I grabbed the stack of scratch-off lottery tickets off of the nightstand and added them to the bag.

"Find stuff?" Bowie asked, sticking his head out of the bathroom.

Jonah picked up a scrap of material off the shag carpeting. "What's this?" It was black-and-white-striped and stretchy.

"That's Misty Lynn's 'get lucky' tube top," Bowie said, glowering at the shirt. He snatched it out of Jonah's hand.

I briefly wondered what kind of alternate universe I'd landed in. Here, your neighbors knew what outfit you wore to get lucky. In Annapolis and D.C., you kept your secrets on lock down because, sooner or later, someone would use them against you.

"And we hate Misty Lynn?" Jonah guessed.

"She cheated on Gibson when Mom died," Bowie said shortly. "And apparently Mr. Zirkel had no problem mixin' it up with her and Scarlett."

There was a tic beneath Bowie's eye. "Take the shower curtain," he growled at us before marching downstairs.

Jonah and I looked at each other and shrugged. I headed into the shoebox of a bathroom and yanked the shower curtain off its hooks.

"Why do y'all have Misty Lynn Prosser's shirt on your bedroom floor on top of Scarlett's stuff?" Bowie's raised voice carried up the stairs.

"We should probably get down there," Jonah suggested.

I wasn't sure if he was worried about missing out on the action or being there to prevent any murders.

Wade was sputtering his excuses in the kitchen. And Gibson was glaring at the man like he'd like to beat him to death with his own arms.

"Did you cheat on our sister with Misty Lynn?" Bowie demanded.

"N-n-no. I swear! We were already broken up when—"

Gibson grabbed Wade by his shirtfront. "Just what kind of a dumbass are you? You trade in my sister on that Venus fly trap?"

The sandwich knife Wade had used to build Gibson a roast beef club with what looked like the last of his bread was safely lost in the pile of dirty dishes in the sink. I decided I didn't want to be a witness to whatever happened next, so I headed into the living room, the shower curtain rustling in the bag against my leg.

I watched Jameson pop the batteries out of the TV remote and drop them into his bag. The remote, he tossed over his shoulder behind the couch. He took all of the throw pillows on the couch and stuffed them in the trash bag.

I looked around at the shabby room. More shag carpeting. Some framed movie posters hung in cheap plastic frames. A collection of expensive sneakers had a home on a shoe rack just inside the door. There was a single couch and a seventy-five-inch big-screen TV mounted to the wall.

The whole place felt sad.

I tried to imagine Scarlett here curled up to watch one of the movies in the collection that Jameson was going through.

Every third Blu-ray he'd open and dump the disc into his bag. He picked up another one and grunted.

He held up *The Godfather* in my direction.

"Keeper," I agreed.

Jameson tucked it, case and all, into his bag.

I opened the coat closet and found a Bodine Home Services fleece and a purple parka. I stuffed them both into my bag.

"I swear that toaster oven ain't Scarlett's," Wade said, trailing in on Gibson's heels. Jonah and Bowie followed him.

Gibson spun on his heel, and Wade stopped in his tracks and Bowie and Jonah stepped in behind him. "But she's welcome to it," he gulped.

"You're damn right she's welcome to it," Gibson snarled. "And anything else she wants because you're a douchebag who never grew up. And if you ever go near Scarlett again, you'll be missing more than some appliances. You get me?"

Wade, eyes wide enough to pop out of his sockets, nodded frantically. "I get you. I sure do. And I'm right sorry. I'll tell her that if y'all—"

"I think it's best if you never speak to her again," Bowie said amicably. "Also, stay away from Misty Lynn for fuck's sake. She's bad news. And your dick'll fall off."

"I will," he said, Adam's apple bobbing.

We filed out, one by one. Jonah paused in Wade's face in front of me. "Don't fuck with Scarlett again," he said, his voice low.

"She's too good for you," I said, piling on. "Don't you forget that."

We convened around Gibson's Charger with our trash bags.

"Scarlett's gonna be pissed," Jameson said with a ghost of a smile.

Gibson looked at the leather-wrapped watch on his wrist. "I don't know about you boys, but I sure could go for a nice, cold drink."

Chapter Thirteen
Scarlett

I knew exactly where to find the rat bastards. "Think they can solve my problems for me," I muttered under my breath as I kicked The Lookout's front door open. There they were, lined up like ducks in a shooting gallery at the bar, laughing.

I wasn't mad enough not to notice Jameson slapping Jonah on the back when he reached the punchline of whatever the hell stupid joke he was telling. Meanwhile Gibs and Devlin had their heads together snickering about something.

"Well, well. If it isn't a whole bunch of jackasses I'm not talkin' to anymore," I announced.

Nicolette, the hard-assed, smart-mouthed bartender, gracefully backed herself into the kitchen.

"Now, Scarlett," Bowie began.

"And why the hell aren't you at school?" I asked, crossing my arms.

"I had a family emergency," he said with a smirk. I glared at him until he ducked behind Devlin who didn't know enough to avoid me when I was like this.

"You don't get that grin off your face right now, I'm going to remove it for you," I warned my brother.

"What's the problem?" Jameson sighed, hefting his beer and knowing full well what the problem was.

"I fight my own battles," I reminded him.

"Yeah, but this way we didn't have to pay bail money," Jameson shot back.

I gritted my teeth together and tried to kill them all with lasers from my eyes.

The bar was mostly empty. It filled up on weeknights starting around five o'clock. But for now, we had the place to ourselves except for a few barflies. I didn't care much about the audience. The whole town was already buzzing about my brothers busting into Wade Zirkel's house and making him piss his pants. I made a mental note to find out later whether that tidbit was true.

"Don't be mad," Gibson ordered, putting his water down on the bar. Gibson was the only one of us who didn't drink. I figured he thought he'd got enough of Daddy's bad genes that he didn't want to tempt alcoholism.

"Who decided I couldn't handle my own problems myself?" I demanded, tapping my foot on the floor. I could damn well handle myself. I didn't need a bunch of overgrown babysitters anymore. I wasn't *actually* going to burn Wade's house down. But I would have sweet-talked his landlady into giving me the spare key for an hour or two so I could get my stuff and pull up the carpet to dump a couple of cans of baby shrimp underneath.

Devlin and Jonah shared a look, and I shook my head. "Oh, no. Not you two. You're both here for four seconds and deciding I can't live my own life?"

"To be fair, Scar, it takes most people less time than that to see you need a babysitter." Gibson was grinning. And while the sisterly part of my heart was happy to see him getting on with Jonah, the independent woman part of me wanted to kick him in the face.

I settled for the shin.

"Ow! Fuck!" he held his abused shin and hopped on his good leg.

"Steel toe, you son of a bitch. Now, for the last time, I'm an adult, and I deal with my own problems."

"What kind of an adult are you if you're still making your high school mistakes over again?" Jameson asked mildly. He was smart enough to keep a barstool in between us. Otherwise he'd be on his knees.

I was too mad to speak.

I wasn't proud of the fact that I'd ended up in bed with Wade Zirkel again. But pickins' were slim in Bootleg, and damn it. The weeks leading up to Dad's death were some of the loneliest of my life. I knew it was coming. I had a feeling I couldn't shake, and rather than dwell on the fact that my dad was drinking himself to death on purpose and my brothers couldn't be roused to care, I'd sought what comfort I could find.

And screw them for judging me for it.

I settled for double middle fingers, flipping them all the bird before I stormed out the way I came in.

"Scarlett, wait."

Devlin was the only one of them dumb enough to come after me when I was in this kind of mood. A sane man would give me the space to get over my mad. Not Devlin. He yanked open the passenger door of my truck.

"Talk to me," he said.

"Either get in or get out of my face," I suggested, breathing fire.

I had a temper. I was aware of that fact. I came by it honestly. My daddy had once thrown a claw hammer through a screen he'd just hung on someone's porch because he couldn't find his tape measure.

Devlin got in, a further testament to his lack of sanity.

"Want to talk?" he asked pleasantly. He clicked his seatbelt into place.

"No, I do *not* want to talk," I insisted. "Why would I want to talk about my brothers and my neighbor running off to do *my* dirty work? Embarrassing me in front of the whole town. I can't believe they still feel like they have to protect me and clean up my messes. And I can't believe you went along with them. What is it about me that screams 'incapable of taking care of myself'? Because I'll have you know I've been taking care of myself for a good, long time. Thank you very much."

He opened his mouth like he was going to say something, but I just plowed right on.

"So what if I slept with the big, dumb loser? So what if he wouldn't give me my stuff back? I would have fixed it. I can handle myself, and I don't appreciate being treated like someone's baby sister all the damn time. I'm twenty-six. I run a damn business. I own property. I haven't starved myself to death or set myself on fire. And yet. *And yet*, you all act like I'm one second from fallin' down a mine shaft."

This time Devlin didn't open his mouth.

He let me rant and rave all the way home. I pulled into my driveway because there was no way I was driving a man home who decided to pay my ex—whatever the hell Wade was—a visit and humiliate me.

I dumped the truck into neutral and yanked on the parking brake.

"So what you're saying is you're angry," Devlin summarized.

I launched at him and nearly gave myself whiplash from the seatbelt that was still securely fastened. I wrestled with it, gnashing my teeth with frustration, until Devlin reached over and calmly released me.

I sat back against the seat and huffed out a breath.

"Maybe you don't like your family getting involved with your mistakes," Devlin began again. "And maybe I know how that feels."

I shot him a glowering look out of the corner of my eye and crossed my arms over my chest. "What would you know about it?"

"I married Johanna, a woman my parents had practically picked out for me. She was 'the right kind of partner,'" he said, adding air quotes. "And when our marriage fell apart—"

"Why are you so polite about it?" I demanded. "This Johanna—what the hell kind of name is that anyway—didn't just let your marriage fall apart. She willfully destroyed it. She's an asshole."

Devlin gave me that ghost of a smile that got that warm feeling lodging in my belly.

"Fine," he conceded. "I married an asshole who publicly destroyed our marriage. My family tried to arrange counseling for us. Too embarrassing, a divorce this early in the relationship."

My jaw dropped. "They tried to force you into counseling?"

Devlin nodded. "My parents and my in-laws decided it was better for everyone if Johanna and I stayed married and worked through our problems. Despite the fact that it's the last thing in the world I'd ever consent to. I may not have been the most attentive husband, but I didn't force her into anyone else's bed. Or our bed as it turns out. But she found a more suitable partner. Someone whose career was progressing a bit faster than mine."

I swore quietly. I hoped that one day I'd get to meet this Johanna and tell her what a steaming piece of shit she was. "I'm willing to admit that you might *possibly* have some small sliver of an idea of the rage that I'm feeling," I said. "So, what happened?"

"I got pissed off and punched her lover in the face at the end of our last day in session—I may have also kicked him while he was on the floor—and refused to go anywhere near a counselor."

"Why do you sound embarrassed by that?" I asked. He'd just described the appropriate reaction to a cheating asshole.

"That's not how McCallisters handle things," he said dryly.

"How do McCallisters handle things? Bend over and take it?" I challenged.

"We handle things privately. Never with violence. Occasionally with attorneys present."

"They really expected you to suck it up and stay with an

unfaithful dickhead?" My family might be a lot of things, but what mattered the most to them—what they were annoyingly vocal about—was what was best for me.

"It's what would adhere to our agenda. A divorce only three years into the marriage suggests instability. In future elections, a divorced candidate would be seen as less secure, less likable, than a married one."

"Bull. Shit. So you're supposed to stay married to a piranha for the sake of your family's agenda? That's horrible."

He rubbed the space between his dark eyebrows. "In this instance, I happen to agree with you."

"So why did you go along with the four stooges today?" I pressed. "You had to know they wouldn't be civilized about it."

"Curiosity. I wanted to see the kind of man you'd choose to spend your time with. Plus, it never hurts to have an attorney with you when you dance across the lines of the law. Also, according to your phone conversation, I was curious about how tiny his balls were."

I dropped my head to the steering wheel.

"You don't have to explain to me. Just because I opened up to you about my painful, humiliating experience. Don't feel obligated to balance the scales. I'd hate for you to talk to me out of guilt."

I flopped back against the seat and groaned.

"Look, it's not like I loved Wade. Hell, I don't think I even like him. It's just I didn't want to go home every night and think about the fact that my father was dying and there wasn't a damn thing I could do about it." My voice broke, and I closed my eyes as the emotions I'd tamped down for so long bubbled to the surface. "My brothers, as you may have guessed, wrote our father off years ago. For me, it was different. We still went to work almost every day together. Went to lunch together. I did his grocery shopping. I took him to the doctor."

I took a steadying breath and stared hard at my sweet little cottage in front of us.

"I was there when the doctor told him he had weeks. And

I was there when he kept right on drinking. And I was there when he didn't wake up."

Devlin leaned over the console and reached for me. He dragged me into his lap and tucked my head against his cheek.

I didn't realize I was crying until my breath hitched. "Dang it. I don't cry. Like ever. This is just stupid."

He just held on to me tighter.

"I just didn't want to have to think. So I stirred things up with Wade again. He was familiar. A familiar asshat, but still he didn't try to make something out of nothing. He let me call the shots and didn't bring any expectations to the table."

Devlin tucked a strand of my hair behind my ear, and I stopped talking so I could listen to the steady thud of his heart under my ear. He stroked my hair slowly, leisurely.

We were quiet for long minutes. I felt the tension slowly seep out of my body, replaced by the heat of his. It felt like a relief to give it all up for a minute.

"You haven't asked me about that kiss," I said finally.

"I haven't had you alone since then," he pointed out.

I picked my head up to look him in the eye. "You've got me alone now."

"All right. Why did you kiss me, Scarlett?"

I loved how my name sounded on his lips. Reaching up, I toyed with the collar of his t-shirt and trailed my fingers over his neck. His breath was hot on my face, the warm sunshine pouring in the windows of the truck. Outside, birds sang, bees buzzed, and the world went on.

"Maybe I was curious," I admitted.

"And what did you find out?" he asked softly, dangerously.

I raised my gaze to his. Those brown eyes warm and interested.

"That I liked it."

He made his move and leaned in, but I pressed my fingers to his lips. "Hang on, Dev. I made myself a promise I wouldn't just hop into someone else's bed after the Zirkel debacle."

He stilled under me.

"But you're not just someone else. And that kiss wasn't just a kiss," I continued. "I haven't decided if I'm sleeping with you or not," I fibbed. "But I'm giving it a whole lot of thought."

"Me too, Scarlett. Me too."

Chapter Fourteen

Devlin

I hadn't heard any gunfire or screaming coming from Scarlett's house since our talk in her driveway yesterday, so I assumed she and her brothers had reached a tentative truce. Or she'd killed them all and quietly buried their bodies in the backyard.

But when Jonah came downstairs the next morning, I figured she had either missed one or they were all alive. She was working on another project today which left me feeling bored and missing her. A McCallister missing a drama queen. I almost didn't recognize myself anymore. And it wasn't just the beard I was growing.

I went for another slow, painful jog and spent the rest of my day catching up on work emails. Feeling so removed from my work was a new experience for me. I'd been groomed for politics since elementary school. My father spent thirty years in and around politics. My mother spent that time dedicated entirely to social events and fundraising. I was the next generation of their efforts.

I loved public service. Sure, the lawmaking was tedious

to the point of impossibility. And party lines were more like trenches divided by minefields. But it was a noble calling.

When I wasn't in session, I was a partner in the family law firm. The law was something I'd long been fascinated with, and I missed practicing. But when there was a legacy to build, the wants of the individual didn't matter.

I stared at the email I'd been ignoring for two days. It was from the family's public relations rep. Blake was responsible for working with our attorneys to clean up the mess I'd left behind. I opened it and noted that both parents were CC-ed.

Devlin,

I hope this message finds you well. We've met with Mr. Ralston, and while he claims he's still mulling assault charges, I'm confident that he doesn't want news of your altercation leaking to the media any more than you do. Things are beginning to quiet down, and in a few weeks, I think it will be safe to have you make a few public appearances. But I do agree with your parents that the divorce should be postponed. Anything that brings attention back to you right now will almost certainly be detrimental to your political career.

Sincerely,

Blake

I closed my laptop and kicked my feet up on the table. I was attempting to enjoy the spring sunshine, the view of the lake. But my thoughts were chaotic. What if I did postpone the divorce? What if I kissed Scarlett again? What if everything I'd worked for my whole life was impossible now?

What if I'd ruined it all by choosing the wrong woman?

"Hey, frowny face," Scarlett said, skipping up the last of the deck stairs. She was smiling at me, and suddenly my questions didn't seem so important anymore. "Please tell me you aren't busy."

Now she had my full attention. I hooked my hands behind

my head and admired the view of her slim legs under short khaki cargos.

"I think I can clear my calendar," I said with a smile.

"Awesome." She threw a t-shirt at me, and it caught me in the face. "Is Jonah free?"

My feet hit the deck, and I unfurled the shirt she'd thrown. It said Bootleg Cock Spurs across the chest around a giant rooster head.

"Oh, no."

"Oh, yes," Scarlett grinned. She pushed the deck door open. "Jonah! Get your ass out here."

"What sport is this?" I asked.

"Fast pitch softball, my handsome neighbor," she winked.

"I just remembered I have plans."

"What's going on?" Jonah asked, poking his head out the door.

"Run," I said dryly.

"Wait till we get to the field."

———

There was a moonshine stand at the ball field. Sure, there was the usual concession stand with hot dogs and mushy French fries. But the moonshine stand had the twenty-person deep line in front of it.

"Come on," Scarlett said, grabbing my hand and pulling me toward the stand.

Jonah trailed along behind us, the spectator stares weighing heavily on the newest Bodine's shoulders.

Scarlett bypassed the line and ordered three apple pie moonshines from a side window that said Players Only. I reached for my wallet.

"Players drink free," Scarlett said, shoving a small mason jar into my hand.

"Are we seriously drinking moonshine before a softball game?"

"League rules. We also drink during the game if that makes you feel any better."

It did not. Jonah shrugged and downed his jar of Bootleg's finest. I followed suit. Maybe a little liquor would loosen me up. It burned in a really good way. My mouth tasted like apples and cinnamon. Like I'd just drunk a slice of apple pie.

"Wow."

Scarlett winked. "That's Great-Granddaddy Jedidiah's recipe."

"What kind of ABV are we talking?" Jonah asked.

Scarlett grinned. "You don't want to know. Come on, boys. Let's get ourselves warmed up."

We followed her to the dugout where the rest of the Bodine family was stretching or frowning at cell phones. There were a few strangers here too.

"Y'all, this is Nash and Buck," Scarlett said, pointing to two guys who were exact physical opposites. Nash was tall and broad like a barn with arms that threatened to explode out of his uniform shirt. Buck was short and lean with a shock of red hair. He looked as though he were a little kid playing dress-up in his father's shirt.

Jonah and I nodded in their direction.

"Nash and Buck, these are our subs Devlin and Jonah. Two of our outfielders caught the pink eye from their kid," she explained. "And this here is Opal Bodine. No relation."

Opal was wiry and tall with short dark hair that she tamed with a ball cap. "Nice to meet y'all," she said, taking a practice swing.

We exchanged pleasantries.

Jonah and I didn't have any cleats to change into, so we let Scarlett lead us through a warm-up. I couldn't help but scan the crowd as I stretched my hamstrings. It appeared as though the entire population of Bootleg had turned out for the game.

Just about everyone of age in the stands had a mason jar of moonshine in hand.

"All right, Base Runners," Gibson grumbled. "We're playing the Eagler Lumberjacks. We're up at bat first. You two okay with outfield?" he asked me and Jonah.

"Sure," I shrugged. I'd played Little League. When I was eight. And I'd been to my fair share of Nationals games. I could handle this.

"Nash, you're up first. Opal you're on deck."

"All rise for the playing of the National Anthem," came the crackly voice over the loudspeaker.

"That's Bernie O'Dell," Scarlett whispered to me as we lined up to face the flag in the outfield.

"He's been announcing since he was in junior high."

Misty Lynn with her bleach blonde hair and very tight t-shirt sashayed up the diamond with a microphone and belted out a reasonably okay and quite dramatic version of the anthem. I noticed Scarlett glaring her down even as she mouthed the words.

The crowd ate it up, cheering and whistling. Misty Lynn curtsied, and Scarlett gave a polite golf clap. "Man, I just hate her guts."

As if she'd heard it, Misty Lynn sauntered up to Gibson and blew him a kiss. Scarlett made vomiting noises behind us.

"Who's your friend, Coach?" Misty Lynn purred to Gibson and looked in my direction.

"Bless your heart, Misty Lynn. Why don't you go call your doctor for your herpes results?" Scarlett suggested sweetly.

"Why don't you go swimmin' in an outhouse, you piece of shit?"

I slipped an arm around Scarlett's shoulders and hauled her to my side hoping further restraint wouldn't be necessary.

"Oh, are you all together?" Misty Lynn asked with interest. She batted her heavily mascaraed eyes at me. "Wonder how long that'll last. Give me a call, tall, dark, and sexy, when you get tired of Miss Scarlett here."

Misty Lynn pranced away on her impractical heeled sandals, and Scarlett growled under my arm.

"I *hate* that dick locker."

"Come on, slugger. Let's get our pregame on," Bowie suggested, towing his sister toward the dugout.

90

The Eagler Lumberjacks looked every bit the part. They played in flannel, and I couldn't be sure without a close up look, but it looked as though even the women had beards.

Between innings, shots of moonshine were handed out to both teams. "It evens the playing field," Scarlett explained knocking back her third shot. "Doesn't matter if you're an all-star athlete if you can't run in a straight line."

Things were getting a little fuzzy in my vision, but I still managed to get my glove on the ball a couple of times. Everyone looked like they were slowing down a bit. Opal was one hell of a catcher, and she hit no less than a double every time she got up to bat. But by the fourth inning, she was listing to the side behind the Lumberjack batter.

Jameson and Jonah got tangled up going for a pop fly and had a hard time getting back on their feet. One of the Eagler players stumbled on his jog to third base and got tagged out while he was laying facedown in the dirt.

The only one who didn't seem to suffer any ill-effects from the moonshine was Scarlett. In the fifth, she hit a bases-loaded triple. And in the sixth, she scored a sweet double play when a bunt made it past Bowie on the pitcher's mound. She moved like the booze made her more graceful, more athletic.

By the seventh inning, I was swilling water and dumping my moonshine on the ground. Jonah was trying to tell the very sober Gibson a story about a horse and a sweater. Opal and Buck broke into a clumsy but energetic two-step in the dugout until Buck smacked his head on the overhang.

Someone in the crowd thought to toss a couple of hot dogs our way. I mainlined two of them hoping they'd soak up some of the alcohol, but in my heart of hearts, I knew it was too late. I watched Scarlett guzzle water and wipe her mouth with the back of her hand.

Why was everything she did so sexy? I loved watching her. The way she moved. The way she laughed. The way her smile reached her eyes. Her dirty mouth.

"Ahem." Jameson elbowed me in the gut. "You're drooling."

I wiped my mouth.

"Metaphorically. Stop staring at my sister."

"He can stare at me all he wants," Scarlett interjected. "I'm starin' right back."

"Ugh," Gibson groaned. "Can you all just not climb on top of each other here in the dugout? That's all I'm asking at this point."

Scarlett grabbed a bat, winked at me, and gave her brother a kiss on his cheek. "Progress," she called cheerfully over her shoulder.

Gibson eyed the other team's dugout. "I think they're about to call the game." I stumbled over to him and closed one eye trying to focus on the Eaglers.

"Are they sleeping?"

"Passed out cold." Gibson gave Scarlett a signal at the plate, and she nodded.

The pitcher threw out his pitch, and Scarlett had to take two big steps to the side to get to it, but damn did she get a piece of it. The bat connected with a clink of aluminum, and the ball soared into the air.

"Go! Go! Go!" Gibson yelled. Scarlett's legs ate up the distance between home plate and first. She was already headed to second by the time the outfielder fumbled the ball.

"Keep goin'!" Bowie slurred next to me.

The crowd was on its feet, listing hard but still cheering. She danced over second by the time the outfielder got the ball under control and threw it.

It was a wild toss. The third basewoman had to leave the base and dive to get her glove on it. Scarlett charged past her without a glance in her direction. She picked up speed and put her head down. The Lumberjacks' catcher was on his knees, unable to stay on his feet, when the third basewoman chucked the ball. I was out of the dugout with the rest of the team cheering as Scarlett threw herself headfirst into the dirt, sliding into the catcher and then June like a heat-seeking bowling ball attacking pins.

I couldn't tell what everyone was cheering about until I saw the ball roll loose from the pile of limbs and drunken laughter.

"Safe!" June shouted.

Chapter Fifteen
Scarlett

Devlin didn't seem to understand the concept of the school bus. "But what about my SUV?" he asked for the third time pointing in the exact opposite direction of where we'd parked.

"Honey, none of us can drive. That's what the school bus is for. They're gonna drive us home."

"But, what about my car?" he asked again.

I grabbed his face in my hands, enjoying the feel of his beard on my palms. "I'll drive you back for it tomorrow."

"Mokah," he said, finally appeased.

I released his cheeks. Bootleg took our fast pitch softball seriously like all our good times. That's why there was a fleet of school buses waiting to drive everyone home. The visiting teams were always required to have their own bus and designated drivers who could enjoy all-you-can-eat hot dogs during the games.

Wednesdays were known as Wasted Wednesday in Bootleg. Everyone was too hungover to do much of anything besides eat greasy foods and tell everyone else to keep it down.

Devlin had held his liquor better than I expected. He was still on his feet. Bowie and Jameson were dragging Jonah onto the bus singing a truly horrible version of "Friends in Low Places." I pulled him into a seat and took the aisle to pin him to the window if need be.

"You're so pretty, Scarlett," he said staring at me with one eye.

"You're pretty far gone, huh, Dev?"

He shook his head. "I am drunk. I'll concede on that point. But there's just something about you. I think I like you a lot," he added in a loud whisper.

"I think I like you a lot too," I said, amused.

"You're like a shot... of..."

"Moonshine?" I suggested.

He shook his head and rapped it off the window. "Ow. No, more like whiskey. You go down with a kick."

That was a compliment I could appreciate. "Well, thanks, Dev. You're not so bad yourself."

"I want to kiss you."

I think he meant to whisper it, but it came out at full volume.

"Oooooooh!" the bus's occupants crooned.

"Hey, Scar, did Devlin pass you a note during third period asking if you liked him?" Cassidy asked, her head popping up over the seat.

"Do you want me to write you a note?" he asked with a frown.

"You should definitely write her a note," Buck agreed.

"I've got a pen and paper," Opal called helpfully from two rows back.

"Y'all are the worst."

Fifteen minutes later, I helped Devlin and Jonah stagger off the bus at my place with a sweetly scrawled note from Devlin in my back pocket.

"Jonah, you go on ahead," Devlin decided. "I'm gonna stay here and kiss your sister."

"'K," Jonah said waving and stumbling over a hydrangea in the flowerbed he was wading through.

I clapped my hands to get his attention. "Through the woods, Jonah. Not through the flowerbeds."

"'K," he said again and walked into a tree.

"He'll be fine," Devlin said optimistically.

"Let's get you some water, big guy." I led him into the house. We made it as far as the foyer before Devlin grabbed me and pinned me against the door. "I'm gonna kiss you now."

"Okay," I breathed.

His mouth seemed to operate just fine under the influence. I certainly had no complaints.

"God," I breathed. Devlin crushed his lips to mine and hoisted me up, wrapping my legs around his hips.

When he touched me, it felt like I had straight whiskey flowing through my veins. He wasn't gentle with me, and I liked that. I liked him rough around the edges, not tip-toeing around being careful.

I just wanted more and more of him. His muscles bunched under the cotton of his t-shirt as he held me there suspended between him and the wood of the door.

"I can't get enough," he whispered.

I was dizzy with it. His words, his touch, his taste. I wanted it all and so much more. I ached for him.

He shoved his hand under my shirt and the feel of his skin against mine made me moan against his mouth.

"Baby, I need you," he confessed. It almost undid me.

"Dev, we can't do this," I whispered.

His hand found my breast through my sports bra, and he made a low rumble in his chest. My head fell back against the door with a thunk. I could feel him harden against me—another body part that didn't need sobriety to function well. I shifted against him desperate to get some of that friction I was so hungry for.

Every touch left me needy for more.

"Dev," I gasped when he sank his teeth into my neck.

96

My arm flailed of its own volition and knocked a painting off the wall.

"Mmm?"

"Honey we can't do this right now," I told him even as I helped him wrestle my shirt over my head.

He pulled back looking dazed, and I felt his cock pulse against me. I shivered with dark, carnal thoughts. "We can't do this because you're drunk."

"Pretty sure all the important parts are working," he said. His cock throbbed in agreement.

I gave a strangled laugh. Never in my life had I been in this position before. "No, I mean, I don't know if you really want to do this because you're drunk or because you want me."

He shifted his hips against me, and I purred like a damn cat when his erection rubbed in exactly the right spot. "I'm sure I want to."

"You are killing me right now, Devlin. I need you to be sober as a judge and then tell me you want me. That's the only way this is going to happen."

He dropped his forehead to mine.

"How long do you think it'll take me to sober up? Five minutes? Ten?"

He let me slide down the door slowly until my feet were on the floor.

I laughed. "Have you ever been drunk before?"

"Pssh. I went to college and law school."

"But since then?" I pressed.

He shook his head. "It doesn't help your career to be seen drunk in public."

"A career in politics sounds really boring."

"Small price to pay to shape our country," he said in a deep voice.

"Are you quoting someone?" I picked up my shirt and pulled him down the short hallway to the kitchen. I gave him a gentle push toward a stool.

"My father. That was his answer to everything. I couldn't

play football because it was too brutish. I couldn't take a summer off and travel Europe because I needed to pad my resume with internships and volunteering."

"What did you do for fun?" I asked, fascinated.

"Made my parents happy, I guess."

I pulled my shirt back on. "Well, guess what, Devlin McCallister? Your parents aren't here. You can do whatever you want for fun."

"I wouldn't even know what to do," he admitted. "I'm still supposed to lay low, so getting into bar fights or tipping cows over wouldn't be a good idea."

"Cow tipping is not a real thing."

"Are you sure?" he asked.

I set a glass of water in front of him. "Drink up, big guy."

I turned to the coffeepot and dumped enough in to make a batch of stand-up-and-dance coffee.

"Have you ever been in a kayak before?" I asked. Not that that would be a good idea today when he couldn't even stand upright.

"A kayak?" he frowned. "I used to row on the weekend in college."

"Like the rich people sport?" I snorted.

"Poor people can row too," he said in exasperation.

"What a man of the people you are," I teased.

"Shut up."

"Did you always want to be in politics?" I asked.

He nodded. "It was understood from birth that I'd go into politics."

"That's not the same as wanting to," I pointed out.

He frowned, considering my words.

My coffee maker beeped and I poured him a mug. "Cream? Sugar?"

He shook his head. "You have any pizza?"

Forty minutes later, the remains of a very large, very greasy pepperoni and mushroom pizza sat on the coffee table, and Devlin McCallister snored on my couch with his socked feet on the table.

He was adorable. And I wanted the hell out of him. If I didn't know it would freak him out, I would have taken a picture of him like this.

I decided I'd make entertaining Devlin my new side project. Maybe it was time he found out what he really wanted out of life. And hopefully Sober Devlin really would want me.

Chapter Sixteen
Scarlett

W hy the hush-hush family meeting?" I asked, barging into Bowie's house in downtown Bootleg on a fine Friday morning.

Bowie lived in a cute little brick duplex with a wide front porch and fancy trim around the windows a whole two blocks from the high school where he worked. Cassidy lived in the other half. And nothing on God's green earth would convince me that was a coincidence.

"I wanted breakfast, and none of you have anything in your kitchens," Bowie called from the back of the house. We Bodines did most of our business over breakfast. We were all early risers by nature and all preferred to pull off the bandage quick when it came to uncomfortable situations.

I followed him back to the kitchen and found the rest of my brothers—minus Jonah—sitting around his kitchen table.

"Well this isn't good," I said, pulling out a chair. Bowie had told me seven, and here I was on the dot, yet all my other brothers managed to beat me here? It meant only one thing. "What do you assholes want me to do?"

"Dad's lawyer called," Bowie began. He dropped a plate of pancakes with whipped cream and sprinkles in front of me. There was a whipped cream smiley face on top.

This was going to be really bad.

"Someone needs to start going through his house," Gibson blurted it.

"Awh, come on, guys. You're going to dump this on me?" I hated them all a little bit at this moment, digging into my stupid smiley face pancakes.

I looked up, and they all had their fingers on their noses. "Yeah, yeah. Not it. I get it."

"Look, Scar," Bowie began. "If one of us went in there, we'd just start pitching things. We don't have the sentimental feelings that you do. We'll handle the hauling. But we need you to go through the house."

"What are we doing with the house?" I asked.

My brothers looked at each other. "What do you want to do with the house?" Gibson asked.

"Wouldn't hurt to keep it for another rental. It's got more bedrooms than most other properties."

"Needs some work," Jameson pointed out.

"Needs a fucking exorcism," Gibson muttered under his breath.

"Can we maybe just choke down our hate for one meal?" I suggested.

Bowie and Jameson shot Gibson stern looks.

"Sorry," he muttered.

"I can't believe y'all are dumping this on me." Just like they'd dumped Dad on me. Just like they'd expected me to handle everything. Maybe I'd just save us all some trouble and burn the damn house to the ground.

Bowie sat down next to me. "Scar, we know it's not fair to ask this of you. But if you want it done right, this is the way to do it."

"I'll clean it out. You all do the hauling, selling, and storage. And then Gibs and I will split the flip work," I decided. "But I want free labor from every one of you. This is gonna take time away from my business, so y'all better show up for me."

"We will," they promised vehemently.

I knew they would, but I was still pissed off and wishing they'd all grow a pair and just get over the grudges they held against our father. He was dead. He couldn't do any more damage.

Business concluded, they all dived into the stack of smile-free hotcakes at the center of the table.

"So. You and Devlin?" Bowie began.

I poked him in the hand with my syrup-covered fork. "Uh-uh. From now on, we're staying out of each other's love lives unless Gibson has a head injury and gets back with Misty Lynn."

"Come on, Scarlett," Jameson said. "We're just looking out for you."

I shook my head. "I mean it, guys. I don't need three—four now—overgrown buffoons overseeing my dating habits."

"Devlin's not horrible," Gibson said, forking up a triple layer of hot cakes into his mouth.

"Seconded," Jameson nodded.

"Well, there's a ringing endorsement," I said dryly.

"But he's also not staying," Bowie said. "He's just passing through. Is that really someone we want Scarlett spending time with?"

"That's a good point." Jameson picked up his coffee.

"You all know I'm not getting married before thirty, right?" I'd made my mother a promise every year on my birthday for as long as I could remember. I would not get married before thirty. Which meant I could have a hell of a lot of fun for now.

"Scarlett, why don't you think about settling down with someone and not marrying them?" Bowie suggested.

"You're ridiculous."

Gibson leaned over his plate. "Look, Scar. We raised you. If you're out screwing around, it's our fault."

"Oh, so you want me to settle down to make you all feel better."

"We just want one of us to turn out to be a well-adjusted adult," Bowie shot back.

"How's that electrician you were seeing?" I asked Bowie, knowing full well he'd dumped her within ten minutes of hearing that Cassidy and Amos Sheridan had called it quits this winter.

"Electrical engineer," he corrected. "And we decided to see other people."

"Like your next-door neighbor?" I asked innocently.

"Burn," Jameson nodded in approval.

Gibson smirked his appreciation.

I pointed my fork at Gibson. "Don't you start. I know you've been taking no one but bar skanks home with you after your shows," I said. My brother was quite the talented singer and guitarist. He played bars within a 50-mile radius for fun... and women.

"My sex life is my business."

"Not if mine isn't mine," I argued. "In fact, I think I'm gonna make a list of your recent conquests. Just so we can all stay up to date on your long, sporadic line of one-night stands."

Jameson was smart enough to stare intently at his plate and not move around too much to catch my eye and wrath. To be honest, I wasn't sure about that particular brother's dating life. I thought he might be seeing someone, but she lived outside of town. He'd never seen fit to introduce her to any of us, so I figured it wasn't serious. But I could find out if I had to. When I was little, spying on my brothers had been one of my favorite past times.

"So, we're agreed," I said. "No one bothers me about my sex life, and I'll leave y'all's alone?"

"Agreed," they mumbled.

I dug back into my pancakes and started thinking about just how long I wanted to wait with Devlin. It was like being on a diet and living next door to an ice cream stand.

I thought about that irresistible hot fudge sundae that was Devlin McCallister all morning in between cursing out my brothers one at a time. I had projects to wrap up before I saddled myself with Daddy's house. And if they had a problem with it, then they could just go and clean out his things themselves. I wasn't avoiding it, I told myself. It was just good business to put paying jobs first.

I'd gone from eking out a living at eighteen to doing real well for myself. The income from my rentals kept me going when work was slow in the winter. And I was building up a nice chunk of savings so I could snatch up another seasonal rental.

With Devlin's job, I'd be pocketing a nice fee. And just like that, I was back to thinking about him. He was quite the fine male specimen. And his time in Bootleg was doing wonders for him. Every time I saw him, he looked stronger, sharper… fitter.

I thought about Dev and his fine form all through the furnace filter swap out at my rental and during my roof patch job at Zadie Rummerfield's parents' house. Hell, I even thought about him when I snaked Cassidy's upstairs toilet because she was too embarrassed to call her plumber cousin.

Devlin kissed me like I was a woman. Not some girl he'd known since kindergarten. Not the youngest of four—five now—Bodines who would throw down if he stepped out of line. And not the poor daughter of a drunk and a loser.

He made me feel mysterious, interesting, sexy. Things I couldn't feel on a daily basis around the people I'd known my whole life.

Try as I might, I couldn't see a downside to a little spring fling with the man.

I pulled my phone out of my bra where I'd stashed it for my little plumbing escapade. Cassidy had paid me for my troubles with a spa gift certificate and a box of condoms. And I was going to put one of them to use tonight.

I dialed Devlin's number, and he answered on the first ring.

"Well, hello there," I purred.

"Hi, Scarlett." I heard a small crash in the background and some quiet swearing. "I mean, hey. What's up?" he said casually.

Devlin had a crush on me. And that warmed my West Virginia heart.

"What are y'all doing tonight?" I asked.

Chapter Seventeen
Devlin

The Lookout was more crowded this time than the last. Generations of Bootleggers cozied up around the bar or held down tables on the main floor space. There were pool tables in the back with the requisite neon beer signs. And peanut shells and dust all over the floor. When I'd asked about it, I was told that no one in Bootleg had peanut allergies. The locals credited the hot springs and their mystical healing powers with the town's lack of life-threatening allergies.

"Hey, Dev," Millie Waggle called out from a table of women in a mix of flannel and spring dresses. "Where's your roommate?"

I waved. They all waved back, smiles curving their lips.

"Jonah's visiting with friends in Virginia," I told them despite the fact that it was none of their business.

I started toward the long L-shaped bar even though I'd already decided I would not be overindulging tonight. My moonshine and softball hangover from earlier in the week was enough to convince me to spend the rest of the week apologizing to my body with a series of grilled meats, salads, and workouts. I now knew I suffered from the week-long, feel-like-I-have-the-flu hangovers that all adults came to experience.

But I needed something to do with my hands. A drink would be the most believable prop to hide my nerves.

Tonight, I was on a mission. Scarlett Bodine was coming home with me, or I was going home with her. One way or another, we were going to end up naked together. And in order to make that happen, I couldn't be the anxiety-ridden hopeful romantic that I currently felt like.

"Devlin," Rhett, Misty Lynn's current burly boy toy, nodded as I passed him.

"Evening, Rhett," I said, slipping past him. It was odd that I was a stranger here, yet I knew more people in Bootleg than I did in Annapolis. That was the small town for you, I supposed. Everyone knew you and your business. I wondered if they all knew my recent history. And if they did, would they advise Scarlett to stay away from me?

She'd invited me here, mentioning that Gibson was playing and I should come. Shit. What if she only invited me to be polite? Or what if it was a group hangout kind of thing, and I'd manscaped for no reason? I mentally prepared myself for that humiliation. At least me and my razor were the only ones who'd know my shame.

I hated the fact that those thoughts crossed my mind. Six months ago, I felt secure in my existence. Thanks to breeding and regular reinforcement, I had the confidence of knowing I was important.

The prenup had protected my accounts, but it hadn't done a damn thing for my ego. I'd taken more than a ding with this divorce. But a night with the beautiful Scarlett? I couldn't think of anything that would make a man feel better than that.

And more than that, I wanted to give her something Wade Zirkel never could. I didn't want to just be a familiar set of arms. I wanted to make this special for her. I wanted to give us both something to remember fondly for the rest of our lives.

The only thing standing between me and that eventuality was the distance between my feet and the bar.

I spotted her. She was talking to two older men at the bar. She was in that short denim skirt, a scooped Bootleg Cock Spurs tank, and a cute little cardigan over it. Her hair was down in thick waves, and she was wearing the cowboy boots from the first time we'd met.

It was official. She was the sexiest woman I'd ever seen in my entire life. Who knew my type would be country cowgirl rather than sleek sophisticate? But there was no fighting it.

I took a deep breath and threaded my way through people laughing around tiny tables.

She spotted me halfway there, and the way her face lit up made the tightness in my chest loosen.

"Hi," I said. *Way to be smooth, jackass.*

"Hi," she said, bringing her straw to her lips.

Was it too early to ask her to go home with me? "Can I buy you a drink?" I asked.

She held up her still full glass and wiggled it. "I'm good. But let me buy one for you." She turned back to the bar, and I skimmed my hand over her hair. "Nicolette! Whatever this tall drink of water wants."

The bartender, Nicolette, was a short brunette who had waited on me and the Bodines last time we were here. Tonight she was wearing an If You Don't Like Tacos, I'm Nacho Type t-shirt. She cocked her head at me. "What'll it be, Devlin?"

"Just a beer," I said. One beer wouldn't get me in trouble with Scarlett's consent concerns.

"What are you drinking?" I asked, leaning into Scarlett's ear so she could hear me. She smelled like sunshine and a field of daisies.

"Pepsi," she said with a wink.

"Any reason why?" I asked, barely daring to breathe.

"I think you and I might have plans later tonight."

Merciful heaven. My heart stopped. I was, for all intents and purposes, dead on my feet with the anticipation of what I thought she was saying. It jump-started with an awkward limp, and then I was breathing again.

"So, want to get out of here?" I was only half joking.

She laughed and ran her hand over my chest, down the buttons of my shirt. I went rock hard when she rose up on her tiptoes and let her lips brush my ear. "I want to spend my evening flirting with you before I spend my night fucking you."

And just like that, any drop of blood I'd had left in my head dropped south so fast I saw black creeping in on the edges of my vision. "Huh," was all I could manage.

"Beer's up," one of the old guys said, handing me a pint glass of whatever the hell I'd ordered. "You sure you don't need smellin' salts, boy?"

Scarlett grinned and grabbed my hand. "Come on, Dev. We've got a table up front," she said, pulling me along.

The group thing was no longer a concern for me. Not when I knew tonight was *the night*. However, I was in no state to make eye contact with Bowie and Jameson, or Cassidy and June for that matter. I nodded to the table and sat, hoping no one would notice the raging erection in my jeans. As if reading my mind, Scarlett dropped her hand in my lap, and I nearly jumped out of my chair.

"You all right there?" Cassidy asked, raising an eyebrow at us.

I grabbed Scarlett's hand and moved it a few inches away from my cock.

"All good," I assured her.

Scarlett smiled smugly.

"Hey, June," I said.

June held up a finger, staring intently at the screen of her phone.

"Don't mind June Bug," Cassidy said. "She's watching some game and absorbing every measurable stat with her big brain."

June intrigued me. Not the way Scarlett did. That was lust and biology and chemistry and a good old-fashioned crush rolled into one potent cocktail. June was different. She was incredibly intelligent and used her powers to store every sports statistic known to man. She also appeared to have no interest in human relationships. Unlike Gibson who just seemed to hate people, June was willing to take or leave human interaction.

Speak of the devil, the crowd broke into scattered applause when Gibson strode onto the tiny stage. He was dressed in jeans and a black t-shirt and had a guitar slung across his chest. He was accompanied by a keyboardist and a drummer of mismatched ages.

"That's Hung on the drums," she said pointing at the gray haired Asian man in a distressed denim jacket. "And the guy on the keyboard is Corbin. He plays a hell of a harmonica, too."

Corbin looked like he was seventeen years old. He had dark, smooth skin and thick hair that stood up on his head. He was wearing a bow tie and Dockers.

There was no preamble, no introductions of the no-named band. Gibson launched them into a song about red Solo cups, and the crowd went wild singing along.

Scarlett sang and swayed next to me, and I put my arm on the back of her chair to keep her close. I didn't want to be disrespectful of her brothers, but I wasn't going to make it through this evening without touching her.

She leaned into me and smiled, and suddenly I wasn't so worried about her brothers anymore.

"I'm glad you're here," she said in my ear.

Hal-le-lu-jah. "Me, too."

"Where would you be if none of the other stuff had happened? What would you be doin' on a Friday night in your old life?" Scarlett asked over the music.

I focused on her lips as she said the words. She had the most beautiful mouth of anyone I'd ever met. A bottom-heavy smile with a plump pout. I knew exactly how it felt to have that mouth on me, and I couldn't wait to experience it again.

She poked me when I didn't answer right away.

"Fridays were usually receptions or some kind of dinner or fundraiser. Networking, making an appearance." I reached over and tucked her hair behind her ear. She nuzzled against my hand.

"Would you get all dressed up? Eat tiny foods and make small talk?" she asked.

I nodded. It was part and parcel of the lifestyle. I wanted to advance my career, and that's how it was done. Sure, it meant a dinner was never just a dinner. And it meant that the work week was never only forty hours long. But public service wasn't an eight-to-five job. It was a calling. Johanna and I, I'd thought, had thrived on the expectations. Rehashing who we'd said what to on the ride home.

And here I was in Bootleg Springs, West Virginia, in jeans with a beer and a beautiful woman looking at me like I was the most interesting man in the bar. There was peanut dust on my loafers, and a country band priming the crowd.

I liked it.

"Is this what you do most Friday nights?" I asked her. At times, I was struck by how little we knew of each other. At other times, I felt like Scarlett Bodine was an old obsession. I was so aware of everything she did, every expression she made, every emotion that passed behind her eyes.

She nodded. "This or sometimes Jameson and me order somethin' bad from every restaurant in town and have a pig-in."

"A pig-in?"

"Yeah, when you eat too much in your own house so no one sees your shame."

I laughed, and she grinned at me like there was nothing I could have done that would please her more. I hoped I had a few moves that would.

Chapter Eighteen
Devlin

Gibson broke into another song, the opening bars of which had The Lookout patrons mobbing up the dance floor. The guy could sing. I'd give him that.

The song was "Save a Horse Ride a Cowboy," a country song even I'd heard in passing. And while Gibson sang, I watched his little sister shake her sweet ass on the dance floor. She and Cassidy danced in the middle of a crowd of women who knew every single word to the song. I tried to imagine the last reception or fundraiser I'd been to. Nothing stood out in high-definition like this.

Bowie sat next to me, staring wistfully at the dance floor.

"Don't you dance?" I asked.

"Huh?" he dragged his eyes away from the dancers.

"Do you dance?" I asked again.

"Oh, sure. We all do." His gaze skated back in Cassidy's direction. "Gym class always included a dance class: line dancing, square dancing, ballroom."

"Then why aren't you out there?"

"The view's better from here."

I had to agree with him. Scarlett had ditched the cardigan and had her toned arms raised to the ceiling. She twirled around, her hair catching the air and floating behind her.

"Jesus, you guys are pathetic," Jameson muttered.

"Huh?" Bowie and I said together.

"It appears they're both sexually frustrated," June said, a scientist observing bacteria under a microscope.

Bowie and I glanced at each other and then looked away quickly.

"You ever date, Juney?" Bowie asked.

She frowned. "Of course. When I find someone who is smart enough not to complicate things with unreasonable expectations and demands."

"Unreasonable?" Jameson guessed.

"Someone who thinks it's okay to schedule dates on the weekends during football season."

"You make a good point," Bowie said.

My eyes found Scarlett again, and I watched her dance until the song changed again and she returned to the table.

"What'd I miss?" she asked.

"June only dates football fans," Jameson announced. "And Bowie and McCallister are sexually frustrated."

"Is that so?" Scarlett regained her seat and snuggled into my side. I threaded my fingers through her hair and thought about how everything in this moment was just about perfect.

"Uh-oh," she breathed.

When I didn't react immediately to whatever country danger she'd spotted, Scarlett poked me in the ribs.

"What's wrong?" I asked.

She pointed at the dance floor where Cassidy was being pulled into the arms of a two-stepping cowboy type.

"That's Amos Sheridan."

"Uh-huh," I said, leaning in to brush my lips against her hair.

"Cassidy's ex."

"They look friendly enough."

"I'm not worried about them," she said, staring pointedly at Bowie.

Amos should have been counting his lucky stars that no one ever died from a stare down. Because the one Bowie was sending in his direction could have incinerated flesh and bone.

Bowie's jaw was set in a tense line. Scarlett leaned across me. "Get out there, Bow," she hissed at him.

He didn't even look in her direction but simply got up and stalked toward the dance floor.

Scarlett clamped her hand on my thigh, and I knew I should be focusing on the action in front of the stage, but her touch was distracting enough that I didn't care whether Bowie punched a guy out or not.

In one smooth move, Bowie cut in and took Cassidy in his arms.

Scarlett breathed a sigh of relief.

"I need water and a game of pool," she announced.

June and Jameson brought their index fingers to their noses. "Not it."

"Well, Devlin. It looks like it's your lucky day," she said with a sly grin.

"Don't bet anything higher than a twenty," Jameson warned me as Scarlett pulled me away from the table.

"Don't listen to them," she said. "I'll go easy on you."

We grabbed waters from Nicolette, who was remarkably relaxed for a woman in charge of the thirty hard-drinking Bootleggers at her bar.

"Come on, handsome. Let's see what you can do with a stick," Scarlett said, leading the way to the pool tables. There was one in the back corner that was empty.

She handed me the pool cue and started racking the balls. I tried not to stare at the rise of her skirt, but it was a futile effort. "You wanna break?" she offered.

I didn't want to do anything that would prevent me from watching her. I shook my head. "Be my guest."

She tucked the rack back in the table and chalked her stick. There wasn't anything overtly sexy about what she was doing, but I was mesmerized. She leaned over, lining up on the ball, and I held my breath. The denim was a millimeter from showing me what I wanted to see. What I needed to see. I willed the skirt higher from my position on the wall, and as if the universe heard my prayer, I caught a peek of simple white cotton.

Instead of relief, my blood started pumping through my veins at adrenaline speeds. I'd seen my share of expensive lingerie. But there was something about that peek of white cotton that had me mesmerized.

I hadn't even realized she'd broke until she moved. She'd already pocketed two balls and was lining up a third. She ran the table, shooting me sexy little looks that made my mouth dry and my dick harder than it had ever been in my life.

Pool as foreplay. I grabbed my water and nearly bobbled it when Scarlett threw her leg over the table to line up a trick shot.

"You like what you see, Devlin?" she asked sweetly.

I nodded, not trusting my voice. She sank the shot and danced a little boogie. "Winner, winner. Chicken dinner. I believe I just kicked your ass, McCallister."

"I never had a chance."

She danced over to me, hips swaying in time to the beat of the music. "How about you break this time?"

Every time she bent over in that skirt, I was on the verge of a heart attack.

She smirked, winked, and I was gone.

I wasn't thinking. I didn't do public displays of affection. It wasn't done. But one second Scarlett was standing in front of me shimmying to the music, and the next, I had her pushed against the table while I plundered her mouth. I loved that moment when she softened into me, when she relaxed into the kiss and I was in control. Control had never mattered to me before, but now when my world had been upended, I craved it.

And Scarlett made me feel like I was both powerful and

powerless. She opened for me, her hands pinned between us. And I pressed my advantage, licking into her mouth, stroking my tongue against hers. I could taste the sugar of her drink, the flavored gloss on her lips. I'd been hard all evening, and now that I was touching her, I thought I might just die.

"Where'd you learn to kiss like that?" she breathed, pulling back. Her hair hung down her back, and I shoved my hands into it and nipped at her bottom lip.

"Like what?" I asked.

"Like I'm the only girl in the world you want to kiss."

I would have dived back in, but she stopped me. "Come on, handsome. I'll let you break this time."

She walked back to the table, and my body missed her as if she'd left the state. I took my yet-to-be-used cue, did my best to adjust my now painful hard-on, and followed her to the table. She was killing me, toying with me. And once again, I was powerless.

She racked the balls for me and leaned against the end of the table, giving me a prime view down the scoop of her tank. There was more white cotton visible, and I felt the sweat break out on my back. Was she testing me?

I lined up behind the ball, gave a few practice thrusts and shot.

The cue ball stopped dead at the top of the triangle, and two other balls slowly limped away from the grouping.

Scarlett raised an eyebrow at me. "That's the worst break I've ever seen."

"I'm a little distracted here," I said dryly.

"Maybe you need some personal coaching." She trailed her fingers along the edge of the green and returned to me. "Excuse me," Scarlett said, giving me a nudge away from the table with her ass.

She re-racked the balls. "Come here, Dev," Scarlett said leaning over the table with her pool stick. I gritted my teeth. I approached her from behind and stopped with a breath of space between us.

She looked over her shoulder at me. "Closer," she ordered.

My cock sang hallelujah when it lined up with the sweet curves of her ass. "Good boy," she praised. "Now come on down here."

I leaned over her like I was taking the shot, holding the stick where her hands were. I glanced around us, but the other pool-playing patrons were busy hustling each other and telling stories. I leaned down and bit her shoulder.

"Mmmm," she purred.

I couldn't help myself. I flexed my hips into her, grinding my cock against her. Even through two layers of denim, I could almost feel her slick opening. She leaned back into me, neither one of us in a hurry to take the shot.

There was a commotion coming from the dance floor and stage, and the rest of the pool players went to investigate. We were all alone in the dark corner of the bar.

"What's going on?" I breathed, nuzzling her hair.

"Probably a fight. There's usually one or two on a Friday night. It's what we do for entertainment in Bootleg."

She wriggled her hips, cuddling against my erection, and I groaned in her ear. "Scarlett."

"Devlin." She said my name like a dare.

And for once in my life, I was up for it. I took my hand off the back of the stick and slid it between her and the table. It took no effort to slip beneath her skirt.

"Yes," she sighed, stepping her feet wider.

I wanted to torture her the way she'd tortured me all night, but one brush of cotton against my fingertip, and I couldn't slow down. There was a damp spot the size of a quarter, and it drove me wild knowing that she'd been wet the whole time I'd been hard for her. I brushed the wet spot over and over again, tracing tight little circles, and Scarlett gasped, rocking back against me. I couldn't help myself. I flipped her skirt up revealing those sexy little briefs covering her sweet, round ass cheeks.

"Touch me, Dev," she breathed. And I obliged.

I slipped my hand down the front of her underwear and

found my personal heaven. She was wet and warm and oh so soft. I ground my cock against her, wishing I could unzip right here and slide home. I wanted her like this, helpless and begging under me while I rode her. I thrust a finger inside her, and she cried out.

Whatever was happening at the stage was getting louder. The music had stopped, and there was shouting. But I didn't care. I was fingering Scarlett Bodine while she rode my dick with her ass. I slid another finger into her, and she sobbed out my name. I held her down by the back of the neck. Her hair falling over her face and fanning out over the green of the table. I'd never seen anything sexier in my life. Submissive Scarlett.

"Dev. I need you to fuck me right now," she hissed. Not completely submissive, I realized with a pained grin.

"Baby, I'd love to take my cock out right now, but I think those flashing lights outside mean the cops are here."

She groaned, and I let her lift her head high enough to look. "Shit!"

"Should we go make sure your brothers—"

"They're fine. They probably started it."

I let her up, and she spun to face me. Her face was flushed, and her gray eyes were glassy and dazed. My fingers were still wet with her arousal, and I wanted to find out what she tasted like. I could see her nipples through her shirt, pebbling against the confines of a thin bra. I wanted to taste those too.

"Come on," Scarlett said, nodding toward the emergency exit.

"Where are we going?"

"To have sex!"

"Isn't that door alarmed?" But she was already bumping the door with her hip. We made it five whole steps outside when we were stopped by a cop.

"Evenin' Sheriff," Scarlett said cheerfully.

"Scarlett," he nodded affectionately at her and then gave me the eye. He was a tall man with a thick graying mustache.

He looked oddly familiar. "Sounds like there's trouble. You start it again?"

Scarlett's eyes widened and crossed her heart. "I swear on a stack of bibles it wasn't me. My guess is Bowie and Amos got into it," Scarlett said, crossing her arms over her chest.

"When's that brother of yours gonna get up the courage to ask my daughter out?" the sheriff sighed.

"Probably about the time they're celebrating their eightieth birthdays in the nursing home," Scarlett predicted.

"Sounds about right. Well, I'd best get in there. See ya next time. Or come by for dinner. You know we love havin' y'all." Again, he gave me the once over. I got the feeling I wasn't included in the "y'all."

"Will do!" Scarlett said. She clamped her hand on my arm, and we hauled ass to her truck while the sheriff went to restore order.

"Buckle up, honey," Scarlett announced as she floored it out of the parking lot. "You might want to take this time to lose some clothes," she suggested.

"You want me to get naked in a truck?"

"I don't care where we are as long as you're naked and doing very bad things to me." Her headlights cut through downtown Bootleg. It was late, and the shops and restaurants were closed. She headed in the opposite direction of our houses.

"Where are we going?"

"With as stirred up as I am right now, there's no way I'm makin' it home. We're gonna have to improvise." She turned down an alley, and within a block the streetlights were gone, and the houses got farther and farther apart. We were on a dirt back road driving too fast, and I wasn't sure if I was going to survive the night.

Chapter Nineteen

Scarlett

The moonlight was bright, and I found what I was looking for, the old For Sale sign on the side of the road. It was pastureland and some lakefront property. Five acres that had been for sale since I was fifteen. I pulled off the road onto the little path that dipped low and then crested again into a slow rolling hill. Anyone driving by could see us. And I liked that.

I pulled the parking brake.

"Here?" Devlin asked, peering into the dark.

"There's no five-star hotel. But it's close and quiet, and all the cops in town are at the bar. Plus, my brothers are hopefully being arrested, so they can't interrupt us. Now take your pants off."

I hopped out of the truck and reached behind my seat. I always kept a spare quilt or two in the back. And tonight I'd be putting them to good use.

Devlin got out of the truck slowly as if he wasn't sure that I was serious. I dropped the tailgate and spread the quilts out in the bed of the truck. He was still fully clothed and looking more confused by the minute.

I didn't want him to start overthinking it.

"We have two perfectly good beds at our houses. More if we use Jonah's or one of the other guest rooms," he said.

I shut him up by taking my tank top off.

"Oh, fuck," he whispered.

"Catch up, Devlin." I didn't wait for him to start. I made a grab for his belt. He resisted for a minute, but when I unzipped his jeans and his cock finally escaped its prison, Devlin came back to life. He gripped the sides of my face and kissed me. He stole my breath when he kissed me. I'd kissed my fair share of men. Hell, I'd been kissing since second grade. That might have been about the time my mama started insisting that I wait until thirty before I settled down.

But I'd never been kissed the way Devlin did it. He kissed me like he had to, like I was air and he needed me to live. I liked it and was terrified by it.

And whenever something scared me, I did it again and again until fear turned to excitement... or boredom. That's what I was going to do to Devlin.

His hands left my face and found my breasts. I wished I'd had something fancier for him. Maybe if he stuck around for a while, I'd invest in some silks and laces. But he didn't seem to mind what I was wearing.

He pulled back for a second, his face serious. "I was with Johanna for five years."

"Uh-huh." My focus was on his belt. The one that I was sliding out of his belt loops.

"I mean, I haven't been with anyone else for five years. So, if there's something new—"

"Honey, I'm gonna take good care of you. Don't you worry about anything," I promised.

Then Devlin's mouth was on mine, bruising my lips with a forceful kiss. I liked him like this, taking what he wanted. Strong and focused. I'd never been one to play the submissive chick in bed, but when he looked at me like he was right now, there wasn't much I wouldn't do.

I reached for the snap on my skirt, but he stopped me. "No. Leave it." His voice was as rough as the stones under the tires.

"Tell me what you want me to do."

He showed me instead. Devlin picked me up and placed me on the tailgate, pushing my legs apart so he could stand between them. I reached for him again. His cock was hard and throbbing in my hand. Moisture pooled at the tip, and I brushed my thumb over it. He groaned his approval. I opened my legs wider and guided his wet crown between my thighs. I stroked him against me, appreciating the sweet torture of not enough.

Devlin yanked my bra straps off my shoulders and made quick work of the front clasp. The bra fell from my breasts, and I saw the breath catch in his chest. He swallowed hard. I gripped his cock harder, and he clenched his teeth.

"Slow it down, Scarlett."

I did as I was told, enjoying the novelty of not being a rebel for once.

"Good girl," he told me. I wanted to hear those words again and again from him.

As my reward, he cupped my breasts, and I moaned at the contact. It felt like I'd been waiting for this forever. My nipples hardened against those big smooth palms, begging for his attention. "Oh, dang," I whispered.

He pulled away from me, his erection sliding out of my grip. And then his mouth was at my breast, soft lips and warm tongue gliding over the sensitive peak. He bit lightly, and I gasped, dropping my head back. I looked up at the sky.

We were surrounded by the night. Crickets and tree frogs, the staggered blink of lightning bugs, and the whispers of wildflowers on the dark breeze. The stars dotted the dark, and the fat moon crouched over the tree line that separated us from the lake. Devlin shifted to my other breast, and I bucked against him.

"You are killing me, Dev."

I wasn't one that needed a lot of foreplay. I knew exactly what I needed to get where I wanted to go. Taking the scenic route always seemed like a bit of a waste of time. I liked to get down and dirty quickly so I could be home wrapped up in my robe eating ice cream.

There might have been a few men who gleefully compared my attitude about sex to theirs.

But Devlin was treating my body like a seven-course meal. Like I was something to be savored. It was freaking killing me.

His mouth was patient, feeding on me and working my nipples into tender points until the stars swam before my eyes. When he finally pulled back, the air felt cold on the wet he'd left behind. "Take off your underwear," he ordered quietly.

I shifted back and shimmied out of them, and as they slid down my legs, Devlin took two of his fingers and sucked them into his mouth.

"Yes." I didn't even realize I'd said the word out loud. But the cocky smirk he sent my way told me I'd moaned it. God, I loved seeing him like this.

"Yes what?" He trailed his wet fingers up the inside of my thigh. I was shaking so hard, I needed him so much, that I couldn't stop the tremors.

"Yes, please," I whispered.

He thrust his fingers inside me, and I lost my damn mind. I grabbed for him, trying to pull him down to me so I could kiss him while I bucked my hips to ride his hand. But he held me down and methodically fingered me until I thought I'd die. I was already so close, and he still had yet to put that magnificent cock inside me. I needed it. I craved it.

Devlin curled his fingers in me brushing some secret spot that I'd never discovered myself. I saw lightning behind my closed eyes. I was on a high wire, and I was destined to fall. "Dev. Dev. You're making me—" I lost my ability to form coherent words when the orgasm slammed into me. I felt my walls clamping down on his fingers as I came. He kissed me then, growling into my mouth, taking possession.

I rode it out as my body spiraled through the pleasure he'd dealt me.

"Good girl," he said again, and I slumped back on my elbows. He grabbed me around the hips and dragged me to the edge of the tailgate.

"Dev!" I was too sensitive. I couldn't possibly take what he wanted to give me.

I felt his fingers parting my sex, and then that clever tongue was dancing over that nub of nerves. He licked it with one long stroke, and my head hit the bed of the truck. He didn't stop to ask if I was okay, and I didn't give one good goddamn if I was okay. I just didn't want him to stop whatever he was doing with his mouth.

That tongue danced from my clit to my opening and thrust inside.

"Gah." It was all I could get out of me. I was still shaking from my orgasm, and he was building me up to wanting another one.

Long, slow strokes of his tongue took me higher and higher. Was this what I'd been missing out on all these years?

I grabbed him by the hair and held on tight. My toes were curling up in the boots I still wore.

"You taste so good, Scarlett."

"Jesus, Dev. What are you doing to me?"

He gave my center another lick and sucked gently on my clit. It was as if every nerve in my body caught fire at once. I sat up like a jack-in-the-box.

"Now, Dev!"

He laughed softly, but started working on the buttons of his shirt. The second it was open, I shoved my hands inside and laid them against his chest. "Do you have a condom, or do you want one of mine?"

"So prepared." He pulled one from his back pocket.

I loved the look of his cock in the moonlight. I'd write a freaking poem about it… after he made me come again.

While he tore the wrapper, I gripped him by the root. Together, we rolled the condom on.

"You're so small," he said. "Don't let me hurt you."

"You're killing me now, so hurry up and get to the hurting." I was desperate to have him inside me.

"Lay back," he said, his voice strained. The tendons on his neck stood out rigidly against his throat.

I leaned back on my elbows. The heels of my boots hooked on to the lip of the tailgate. I was spread bare for him out here under the stars and the sky. Devlin gripped me by my thighs and pulled me even closer, spreading my knees. He stroked his cock in his big fist and watched me. I'd wanted this moment for long enough that I didn't see what the point was in waiting any longer. I moved my hand lower, determined to take care of business myself or at least threaten it to spur him into action.

"Don't," Devlin said darkly.

He slid his hands warmly against my calves around to stroke my knees and then sent them diving down the insides of my thighs as his hard-on hung heavily against where I needed him most. Stroking my flesh, worshipping it. He petted me, electrifying my skin. Shocking my nerve endings to life.

His thumbs slid closer and closer to where I wanted them, where I needed his touch the most. He teased me deliberately, diabolically.

Finally, one thumb brushed over my clit gently, lightly. And then again. He stroked me with tender touches that lured another orgasm into the wings. And just when I thought he'd let me have it, just when my eyes were squeezed shut tight, he stopped.

"Damn it, Dev!"

He gripped my hips and drove into me, sheathing himself in my flesh.

I cried out in surprise, in relieved frustration. So *this* is what I'd been missing. He seated himself in me so that he filled me completely. But rather than pull out and push back in, Devlin held here as deep as he could go in my body. I could feel the pulse of his cock inside me, the throb of his desire. I needed him to move. I could come right now if he'd only just move. But he held fast, buried inside me.

Until I looked at him. Until I met his dark gaze.

He was in control, and I was at his mercy. And I couldn't get enough.

He withdrew slowly, and I bucked my hips against the bed of my truck, begging him to do it all again. Devlin gripped my thighs and pushed into me once more. I was blissfully full, stretched to accommodate him. And then he was moving. He set a leisurely pace as if he had all night to enjoy me spread open for him.

Plunging into me over and over again under his own supreme control. I'd never seen this side of Devlin, and I wondered if he had. I loved watching him shed the anxiety, the self-doubt. And I fucking loved watching him make love to me.

He stared into me as he methodically plundered me. One hand skimmed up my thigh and over my belly so he could palm my breast. I was hanging by a thread, one tenuous thread, and he knew it. I wanted more. Everything that he could give me. But I knew if I asked, he'd hold back.

I had to take what I wanted.

I put my weight in my heels and lifted my hips into his thrusts, daring him to stay under control. Tempting him. I reached down and squeezed my own breast and watched as his hooded eyes tracked the movement. Devlin's hand flexed on my other breast, and I gave a little moan.

I felt him pick up the pace infinitesimally and hid my victor's grin. I closed my eyes and focused on pure sensation. The way his thick crown nudged at my front wall, stirring my pleasure. The broad flat palm plumping my breast, the cold hard metal under me. The bunched material beneath my bare back.

Devlin hinged forward, folding over me and locking me in place between his forearms. He was done torturing me, done drawing out the agony of pleasure. His thrusts went deeper, became more brutal, and I reveled in it.

He was driving me up, higher and higher. Every thrust carried me closer to the building orgasm. "Come on my cock,

Scarlett," he ordered, his breathing ragged. "I want to feel your pussy close around me when you come. I want to see you."

I would have done anything in that moment if it guaranteed the orgasm that I knew would make the last one look like a cute little appetizer to the main course. For someone who, until half an hour ago, thought that multiple orgasms were made up by the same people who told their kids there was a Santa Claus, I was pretty desperate for that second climax.

"Dev? Please?" I could feel it build, brick by brick. I was going to burn down the world with this orgasm.

"I'm here, baby." His voice was strained as he flexed into me grinding his pelvis against me. My clit was so swollen it didn't take much more than that. One second I was begging for it, and the next I was coming apart on him, around him, under him.

He groaned, feeling the pulses and tremors of my walls and those delicate muscles closed around him.

"God, yes," he breathed, pumping into me.

I cried out his name as I shattered into a million pieces, and he never stopped fucking me. Never stopped moving in me. I was spent. The waves gentled and slowly, slowly receded, and still he moved in me. Limp as noodles, I lay there. I tried to build up the energy to offer him a blow job. But I needed another minute before words would form coherently.

Devlin had other ideas. He pulled out of me, a slick slide of flesh, and turned me.

"On your knees," he said, bunching the quilt up under me. "Now, Scarlett."

I scrambled to my hands and knees and turned away from him.

He grabbed my hips and yanked me back. His cock slammed home, impossibly deeper. There was nothing controlled about him now. Nothing civilized or torturous. He was a beast in rut. My hands and knees bit into the truck bed liner, and I knew I'd hurt tomorrow. But I didn't care. And neither did he.

He rode me without letting up, bearing down onto me,

curling over me. His fingers dug into my hips, biting into my flesh. I was nothing but feeling now. My thoughts were gone. My words had abandoned me. All I was was Devlin McCallister's toy.

He was grunting softly now on every thrust. I rocked back into him, and the swat he gave me on my ass startled me. My skin stung from his hand, and miraculously I felt the stirring inside me again. Three? Three orgasms was the stuff of unicorns and genies in bottles and a winning $400 million Powerball lottery ticket.

"I feel you getting tighter on my cock," Devlin gritted out. He gripped my hips harder. "Touch yourself."

I obliged. I didn't want to be rude. When my hand met my swollen, wet clit I trembled.

"That's right, pretty girl."

Using my hips as leverage, he pumped himself into me.

He growled low in his chest. "I've fantasized about doing this to you since the first time I saw you in that skirt."

His confession was the straw that broke my damn back. The edges of my body melted into his as my insides liquefied. I came one last time, a slow glow of molten lava flowing. Every cell in my body bloomed like a field of flowers.

"Yes," he hissed. "Yes." And then he was thrusting into me brokenly, grunting softly. I felt him come with me. I felt his cock release his seed into the condom deep inside me.

"Scarlett!" It was my name that echoed through the night across the meadow.

He was whispering words I couldn't hear and rocking into me while we both rode out our climaxes. Eventually, his grip on me loosened, and then he was leaning over me, stroking me with those warm hands. Pressing soft kisses to my back.

The dark closed in around me like a blanket, and I collapsed onto my stomach. I lay there feeling Devlin above me and hearing the night all around us.

Chapter Twenty

Devlin

Scarlett looked at me like I'd just suggested we shave each other's heads when all I'd done was asked her to spend the night. She looked legitimately confused. "But my bed is two hundred yards that way," she said, pointing through the woods toward her house.

"I know, but my bed is right here, and so are you," I insisted.

I wasn't done with her tonight. Hell, I didn't know if I had the stamina for another round. But I wasn't going to go to bed without her wrapped up in my arms.

I don't know what happened in that field. Something had detonated in my chest, and I'd gone places I'd never been before. I'd never been so possessive, aggressive. It was unsettling. And I wasn't letting Scarlett out of my sight until she told me that everything was okay between us.

She frowned through the windshield at my grandmother's house. "Fine. But you better have food. I'm starving."

"Jonah's got a secret stash of frozen pizzas," I promised.

She brightened considerably, and we went inside.

I gave Scarlett a t-shirt to wear. I was half afraid if she went next door to change, she wouldn't come back. So the t-shirt solved that dilemma. I had no idea that a beautiful woman wearing my shirt that came to her knees would be so sexy, so sweet.

"What?" she asked, giving me a side-long look.

"What what?" I slid the pizza onto the oven rack.

"You keep looking at me and smiling."

"Is that a problem?"

"I don't know. This is weird. Isn't this weird? I feel weird."

I turned to face her and pulled her into my arms. "Very weird. Does that make you feel better?"

She looked up at me, her eyes that soft gray. Her small frame was strong and capable. In her bare feet, Scarlett only came up to mid-chest on me. She'd pulled her hair up in a wild tail. The freckles dusted across the bridge of her nose made her look fragile like a porcelain doll. A deception for sure. She was strong and delicate and wild and tame. So many contradictions wrapped in one small, sexy package.

I liked seeing her like this. I wondered if Johanna had ever looked like this, or had she only traded business suits for cocktail dresses and silk pajamas?

"You're doing it again," Scarlett said softly.

"I can't help it. I think you took a piece of me tonight."

She shot me a coy look. "I think I took three pieces of you tonight. One for each orgasm you gave me."

She did it again. Scarlett had managed to loosen something tight in me, release another worry. How could I not feel like king of the world with this woman in my shirt, in my kitchen, in my arms?

"We should probably talk," I guessed. We hadn't discussed what this would mean in terms of a relationship or my limited time here in Bootleg.

"About the pizza?"

"About us."

"Oh. That."

I felt my newfound confidence begin to deflate like a balloon.

But she smiled brightly. "I think we both know the score. What we did tonight? Definitely happening again. And as often as possible while you're here."

I blinked. "That's it?"

She nodded earnestly. "Yup."

"Soooo…"

"So, we're good," she shrugged.

She rummaged through the fridge and fished out two beers. Making herself at home, she grabbed the bottle opener out of the drawer next to the fridge. An accessory I didn't know I had. Jonah and I had been opening beers using the railing on the deck… like real men.

The terms of our relationship settled, Scarlett and I ate the pizza off of paper towels and drank beers straight from the bottle and listened to music. Her small feet rested in my lap while we sat on opposite ends of the couch.

I realized that this was the first time I'd ever seen her relaxed. Scarlett was always on the move, always in motion.

"I've never seen you like this," I admitted.

She cracked one eye open and gave me a half smile. "Like what?"

"Still."

She laughed. "You seem to have sapped the energy right out of me."

I studied her, stroking my fingers over the soles of her feet. "What do you do to relax?" I asked.

"Relax?" she turned the word over as if she didn't know its meaning.

She didn't watch TV, I noticed. If Scarlett had downtime, it wasn't spent binge-watching a show. She spent it with people. She also wasn't one to spend time on her phone playing games or chatting with friends. I didn't know if it came from growing up in a backwoods town with spotty cell reception or if it was more important to her to be present. I liked to think it was the latter.

"I don't have time to relax. I'm too busy building my Bootleg empire," she yawned. "What about you? What do you do to unwind?"

I thought about it.

"You're frowning," she pointed out.

I shot hoops with friends on the weekends. But they weren't really friends. They were more other lawmakers, other lawyers. And we'd talked shop, made deals, argued cases.

"I guess I spent my time building my empire too." And look where that had gotten me.

She stretched, making her entire body rigid before releasing a mighty yawn.

"Bedtime," I decided for us. I scooped her up, leaving the pizza remains for later.

She squealed and cuddled into my chest. "I don't know what your plans are, but I'm afraid my vagina might turn itself inside out if you try to give it another orgasm so soon."

I laughed the whole way down the hall and dropped her on the mattress. "We'll just sleep then," I promised. I pointed her in the direction of the bathroom and spare toothbrush and whatever else she needed and then sat down on the edge of the mattress. I could hear the water running on the other side of the door.

Absently, I rubbed a hand over my chest. Tonight had been... it felt dramatic to say life-altering. But still. I'd never taken a woman that way, never had a lover so eager to meet my demands. But I'd never had Scarlett before. It felt like a key fitting into a lock, and I knew for sure that moving forward, everything would be different.

She padded back into the room and shucked my t-shirt off. "Hope you don't mind. I sleep naked."

I couldn't think of anything that I'd mind less.

She pulled the quilt back and climbed in. "Just so you know, I'm not a cuddler," she said, punching the pillows under her into submission.

"Duly noted." I felt a spark of disappointment but

dismissed it. Tonight had been otherworldly, and asking for anything more felt greedy.

I brushed my teeth with the door open and watched her in the mirror as she settled under the covers. My wife and I had shared a generously sized king bed. Each sticking to our own sides. Respecting the other's space. Had I given her too much space? Is that why she went outside our relationship? It was something I'd wondered about in passing when I wasn't too blinded by rage and humiliation.

I ran the water in the sink and decided that it didn't matter. I had a tiny, fascinating brunette waiting for me in my bed.

I paused just inside the doorway and watched her. She lay on her side curled up, and when I crawled in next to her, I couldn't resist it. I pulled her into my arms, settling her back against my chest, nestling her ass to my thighs.

"What's this? What's happening?"

"Just go with it," I advised.

"Fine, but I probably won't be able to sleep," she grumbled.

I smiled into the dark and rested my chin on her head.

A minute later, she was snoring softly, and I was still smiling.

And when I woke in the middle of the night, she was sprawled out on top of me, sound asleep, her face pressed into my neck. I smiled into the dark and stroked a hand down her naked back. She cuddled in even closer.

It was going to be a good day.

————

The pounding on the front door started just after seven-thirty. Scarlett frowned in her sleep when I shifted her off of me and onto the mattress. I cursed whoever was trespassing on our first morning together while I pulled on a pair of sweat pants. If Jonah had forgotten his key, I wondered if I could craft a plausible murder defense. I was still shirtless when I yanked the door open.

"What?"

The Bodines ranged themselves on Gran's front porch. I'd

seen this before, but the last time I was on their side of the door. Jonah gave an embarrassed wave from the back of the pack.

"You're not taking my remote batteries," I said, walking back to the kitchen and leaving the front door open.

"Y'all have a good night last night?" Bowie asked casually.

I stabbed the start button on the coffeemaker. Except for Jonah, they were all sporting bruises and minor cuts. "Better than you guys, it looks."

"There was a small skirmish on the dance floor," Gibson said. He had a cut on his lip and some bruising under his left eye.

"Let me guess. Amos?" I said dryly.

"I fucking hate that guy," Bowie said. His right eye was blackened, and his knuckles were scraped and bruised.

"Yeah, because you're too chicken shit to ask out his girl," Gibson said, poking the bear.

"She's *not* his girl," Bowie snapped.

"Ain't yours either," Jameson pointed out mildly. He had a scrape mark on his cheek and a bruise on his chin and a small cut on his forehead.

"Can we please focus?" Bowie demanded.

I lined up the coffee mugs on the counter and glanced toward the bedroom door, which was still closed. "I assume you're all here to kick my ass?"

Gibson crossed his arms. "Why? Do we have a reason to?"

Besides the fact that his sister was naked in my bed?

"I'm guessing you're here because Scarlett came home with me last night."

"Give the man a sucker." Bowie nodded.

"So, what's the Bootleg Justice on this?" I asked, pouring the first cup. "You kick my ass? You drag her out of here and lecture her on premarital sex? Because I'm going to be pissed off if you think either one of those answers is the right one. I mean, I'd hate to sic my gran and Estelle on you when they get back for embarrassing your adult sister and beating me unconscious and stealing half their shit. They'd be very disappointed in you."

"What makes you think we'd beat you unconscious?" Gibson asked innocently. He snagged a mug and poured.

"You're the Bodines. I've seen you in action," I said mildly.

"Why don't we take our coffee on the deck and talk about this like adults," Bowie suggested. His amicable tone wasn't fooling me. But I also didn't think they were going to kick my ass. At least not with their sister twenty feet away. Scarlett would side with me and fight like a wildcat.

Gibson and Bowie led the way, and Jameson and Jonah brought up the rear, neatly boxing me in.

"Look," Bowie drawled. "All we want to do is explain that it's in your best interest not to hurt Scarlett."

Jameson nodded threateningly.

"Why in the hell would you think I'd hurt her?"

"If she falls for you and then you go back to wherever the hell you're from, we're gonna have a problem," Gibson said, stroking his beard. His stance was deceptively relaxed.

They pounced in unison like backwoods ninjas. Even though I fought it, it was three against one. Gibson and Jameson each grabbed one of my arms and Bowie locked on to my left leg. Jonah was suddenly Mr. Switzerland. He sipped his coffee sheepishly a few feet away from the fray.

"Get his leg, Jonah, before he kicks someone in the balls," Gibson said.

Jonah looked surprised to be included in the family fight.

"Hurry up, man," Jameson breathed. "He's a fighter."

Jonah put his coffee down and grabbed my flailing leg.

"I really hate all of you right now," I growled.

They carried me down the deck stairs.

"We're doing this for your own good," Bowie said.

"And for our own entertainment," Gibson added.

"Sorry, man. She's my sister," Jonah said.

Jameson grunted.

"So, are Cassidy and Amos back together?" I asked. I felt the second that Bowie's grip on my leg loosened, and I yanked free, kicking him in the gut.

Gibson hooted. "Serves you right for not keepin' your eye on the prize, Bow."

Bowie recovered and wrestled my leg into submission, but at least I felt like I hadn't gone down without a fight. I heard their footsteps on wood and realized they were carting my ass down my gran's dock. "Oh, come on, guys. Not the lake."

"Would you rather a fist to the face?" Jonah asked cheerfully.

"I'm not going to hurt Scarlett!"

"This is just a little reminder of what'll happen if you do," Bowie said, still a little winded.

"You don't need to do this," I tried again. We were getting closer and closer to the end of the dock.

"Pretty sure we do," Jameson insisted.

"I'll press charges!"

"Good luck with that," Jameson smirked.

"The sheriff is a big fan of our little Scarlett. He's not gonna take a likin' to some guy whose just tryin' to get in her pants," Bowie explained.

"I'm not just trying to get in her pants!"

"Oh, hey, Judge Carwell. Mornin' Carolina Rae," Bowie said, raising his free hand to a couple in a fishing boat.

"Mornin' Bodines," Judge Carwell called. "He courtin' Scarlett?"

"What the hell kind of town is this?" I hissed.

Jonah shrugged and grinned. "Bootleg, man."

"Yes, sir. We're just remindin' him to treat her right," Gibson said.

"Carry on, boys."

The judge motored on, not even staying to watch the four Bodines toss my body into the lake.

Chapter Twenty-One
Scarlett

I stepped back to admire my handiwork and swiped a hand over my forehead. The refinished deck glistened under its new coat of varnish. Just in time for summer, Devlin had a nice new deck for our quiet mornings together.

We could move some of the weekend bonfires here, too, I thought. On a practical level, he had more bathrooms than I did and a bigger fridge for beer. I could string up some lights in the trees, put in a fire pit, and maybe add a paver walkway, something wide and level for Granny Louisa and Estelle to enjoy when they came home.

I had a postcard from them in Madrid. I hoped that when I was that age I'd be doing exactly what they were. Living. Really living.

I'd wrap up my projects here by the weekend. The house gleamed like new inside and out with the improvements I'd talked Devlin into. I gave myself a pat on the back.

I liked working near Devlin. I liked looking up from my sawhorses or disgusting pile of ripped up English rose carpeting and seeing him watching me. I liked our long, naked lunch breaks—when Jonah wasn't around. And I *really* liked how Devlin stood a little taller these days, smiled a little more… and swatted my ass whenever I walked past him.

I skipped down the deck stairs and gathered up my supplies, stashing them in the back of my truck. Whistling, I ducked into the first level. Devlin had finally gotten over his ridiculous, urban-dweller notion of locking every door in the house. I jogged upstairs and into the kitchen.

He'd come here an anxiety-ridden shell of the man he used to be. And now? Now, I liked to think I was seeing the real Devlin McCallister. Not some buttoned-up, white-washed, politically correct version but the real man with his very real desires.

I found him in the living room scowling at his laptop with his feet on the coffee table. Stacks of mail and paperwork were strewn about the floor.

"What's all this?" I asked.

"Playing a little catch up." He pointed to a tall stack of papers by his right foot. "Bills introduced by the legislature this year that didn't pass but that might be reintroduced next session. That stack is ribbon-cutting, fundraiser, and reception invitations. And these are some cases my law firm is working on. Thought I'd do a little digging into some precedents."

"Do you *want* to be doing all this crap?" I asked, eyeing the stacks skeptically.

Devlin dumped his laptop on the couch next to him and pulled me down into his lap. "I'd much rather be distracted by you."

"I was hoping you'd say that," I said, making myself comfortable in his lap. He was already hard. And I loved knowing that I had that effect on him. I threaded my fingers through his hair. It was getting long enough that it curled at the back of his neck. His beard was full but neatly trimmed. He'd kept up with his running and his workouts, and I could see the difference in his body. Lean muscle turned out to be quite the turn on for me.

"Is it weird that I think it's sexy when you smell like

polyurethane?" he asked, pressing his face to my throat and breathing me in.

"Yes," I laughed. "So, listen."

"Oh, god. What? Wait. Don't tell me. You want to tear me away from work so we can go 'wrastle' pigs?"

"Judgey McJudgerson!" I hadn't heard the end of it since I'd dragged him to Chicken Shit Bingo for the Bootleg Fire Company. Devlin had had the time of his life and even won the grand prize when the community chicken, Mona Lisa McNugget, took a respectable crap on his square of grass. Class act that he was, he'd donated the cash prize back to the fire company and bought everyone a round of beer. But since then, he'd assumed everything I wanted to do was some backwoods redneck form of entertainment.

In general, he wasn't far off.

"Just for that attitude, I'm not going to tell you what we're doin'," I said haughtily.

He slipped his hand under my tank top and splayed it across my stomach. "Just tell me it involves me getting you naked."

I tapped my finger to my chin. "Hmm. It does involve fewer clothes than what we've got on now."

He leaned in and nibbled my ear lobe. "Then I'm in."

I bounced in his lap. "Awesome! I'll give y'all an hour to finish up here. I'm gonna run into town and get some supplies."

I scooted out of his lap.

"What kind of supplies, Scarlett? Shit. What did I just agree to?"

"Hey, don't go out on the deck. I just sealed it. See ya in an hour, Dev!"

"Scarlett!"

I laughed the whole way to my truck.

———

June was when tourist season really started to pick up. Families with kids burned out from a school year of overscheduling descend on Bootleg as soon as the last day of school was over with. My rentals were booked solid for four and five weeks out, and I was a happy camper despite the extra service calls that came with occupied rentals.

Part of that could also be due to the regular sex I was now enjoying with my next-door neighbor. Regular only in the timing sense. I had great fears that Devlin McCallister was ruining me for other men. Now that I knew that multiple orgasms were possible, well, why in the hell would I settle for anything less?

I slipped into a parking space in front of Bootleg's version of a mini mart. Sure, the Pop In was a gas station and lotto place, but patrons could also buy bait, hand-dipped ice cream, and most grocery necessities. I pushed through the glass door and waved a hello to Opal Bodine, softball all-star, behind the counter. The shop had been in Opal's family for three generations. They used to sell bathtub gin in baby oil bottles right off the shelf.

Opal was dealing with a family picking up enough fishing supplies for a two-week Alaskan excursion, so I moved on to the deli cooler and grabbed two sandwiches, a couple bags of chips, and a pepperoni roll for later. Dev was addicted.

I juggled my load and headed up to the register.

"Y'all have a great day now," Opal called after the family. "Well, someone sure missed lunch," she said, eyeing my haul.

"It's not all for me."

"I've seen you eat after a game. This ain't nothing but an appetizer when you're hungry."

"Har har. Playin' the hilarious shopkeeper."

"I don't see any dessert there," Opal said ringing me up.

"You got anything I'd be interested in?" I tried to play it cool. But Opal, like everyone else in town, knew I had a sweet tooth that was never sated.

"Oh, I just might have a few Triple Chocolate Death by More Chocolate Tortes fresh from the bakery that I haven't had time to put out—"

"Gimmie!"

Five minutes and one of the three delectable chocolate tortes I bought later, I dumped my supplies in the truck and headed across the street to wash my chocolate and sugar buzz down with some caffeine.

"Well, if it isn't Miss Scarlett Bodine," Cassidy said, coming out of Yee Haw Yarn & Coffee with her shift-starting latte. She blocked the door, her hip cocked, and looked at me over her sunglasses. "You've been avoiding me."

"I have not!" I resented the implication. "I've been busy."

"Busy beddin' down with that sexy next-door neighbor."

"And other things."

"Walk with me," Cassidy said.

I hesitated for a moment.

She wiggled her coffee cup at me. "I'll share my caffeine with you."

"All right. But only for a couple of minutes. I've got some sandwiches in the truck that I don't want to get mushy."

"When are you gonna learn to cook?" Cassidy teased.

"Only when absolutely necessary."

We wandered south on Lake Drive, Bootleg's main street, past the Rusty Tool's window display of deck umbrellas and a yard décor outhouse. I waved at Clarabell through the front window of Moonshine.

"So, what's been goin' on? We haven't hung out. You haven't sent me any blow-by-blows of your sex life—pun intended. You didn't even complain to me when your brothers threw him in the lake."

"Those idiots," I shook my head. Devlin had returned to bed soaking wet from head to toe, and we'd started the fun all over again as kind of a 'fuck you' to my brothers. "Thankfully they seem to like Dev."

"So do you," she pointed out.

"What's with the interrogation? Are you accusing me of something, Deputy Tucker?"

"I'm just trying to get to the bottom of why my friend

141

suddenly drops off the face of the earth in a town as small as Bootleg. You've made yourself so scarce, I'm starting to think of you as Callie Kendall."

"That's not fair, Cass, and you know it."

"Look, I've just never seen you so into a guy before. And you're not showing him off or running around town with him. You've never done that."

It was true. I'd been hoarding Devlin, keeping him all to myself. He made it easy with his natural reluctance to socialize. He was still feeling rough around the edges about his divorce and his violent, yet totally awesome, exit from the legislature. And he was just as eager as I was to get and stay naked. It wasn't really a prime socializing situation.

"I took him to Chicken Shit Bingo," I argued for the sake of arguing.

"Alls I'm sayin' is I miss my friend," Cassidy said, giving the eyeball to Rocky Tobias who had parked his shiny monster truck across two parking spaces in front of the bank.

Rocky gave a guilty wave and jogged to his precious hemi before the good deputy could cite him for assholery.

"Do you like him?" Cassidy asked.

"Who? Rocky? He's a great dancer."

"Devlin, you jackass. Do you like Devlin McCallister?"

"Of course, I do. I wouldn't be sleeping with him otherwise!"

"Not true. Wade Zirkel."

"That was different. I was… bored."

Cassidy gave me the "I don't believe you but keep talking so you get deeper in trouble" look that she'd gotten from her father.

"Ugh. Fine. I like him. Like a lot. And I know he's only here for a few weeks, and I know it's all temporary. But orgasms, Cassidy. Oh, the orgasms!"

People were looking at us. Downtown on a Wednesday during tourism season, Bootleg was packed.

"Tell me more about these orgasms," she said, passing the coffee back to me.

"You know how we read that book where the girl had like thirty orgasms in the span of ten pages?"

Cassidy nodded, a faraway look in her eye. "Yeah, I seem to recall that fictional freak of nature."

"Sex with Devlin is like that."

"You had thirty orgasms?" Cassidy lost her deputy cool and screeched this to the entire block.

I clamped a hand over her mouth. "Will you shut your face? I don't want the entire female population of Bootleg Springs to go knocking on Dev's door asking for handouts!"

"Holy shit, Scar. No wonder I haven't seen you and, when I do, you're walkin' funny."

I dragged her down Bathtub Gin Alley past the natural soaps and lotions store and the Build a Shine—the Bootleg answer to Build-A-Bear for moonshine drinkers.

"Multiple orgasms are a thing, Cass. A beautiful, beautiful thing." I felt exactly like I did the time I'd told my six-year-old best friend that Santa wasn't real. I was unveiling a truth of the universe.

"I think I need to sit down," Cassidy said, sinking onto the stoop in front of The Brunch Club, a popular hideaway for tourists who loved their brunch with strong cocktails. Patrons had to use a secret password to gain entrance.

"Cass, do you know what this means?" I asked, hunkering down next to her and patting her arm.

"That we've been having sex with the wrong men," she moaned.

"Exactly."

"Well, where do I find me a Devlin?"

I wanted to say it. I wanted to shove her into Bowie's waiting arms, but family loyalty came first always and forever with the Bodines. Bowie had to be the one to make the move. And at the rate they were going, one of them would be dead before he did.

"We'll find you one. Heck, I found mine next door."

Chapter Twenty-Two
Devlin

Scarlett's text told me to meet her in the backyard. What she was doing in my backyard without coming into the house was beyond me, but I was beginning to realize most things about Scarlett were beyond me and that it was worth it to just go along for the ride.

Scarlett: Bring your bathing suit.

I texted her back on my way out the door.

Devlin: When you said less clothing I assumed you meant naked.

A shrill whistle brought my attention to the water. Scarlett was lounging in a kayak at the end of Gran's dock. Another kayak was tied on to hers. "Y'all can get naked if you want, but you might startle the tourists," she called.

I walked down the dock to her. She was wearing a red and

white checked bikini, sunglasses, and her cowgirl hat. I stopped and pulled out my phone to snap a picture.

"What are you doing?" she laughed.

I snapped the picture and tucked my phone back in my pocket. I had a feeling I was going to want to remember this day.

"I believe the question should be, what are you doing?"

"I was already interrogated by the police today. Don't you try and put me on the witness stand," she teased. I knelt down on the end of the dock and gave her a kiss.

"Are you ready for our kayak picnic?"

"I have so many questions," I admitted.

"Shoot."

"What's a kayak picnic? How do I get into said kayak? How do we picnic in a kayak? Will we be getting naked at some point? Should I put on sunscreen?"

"A kayak picnic is when we float on the lake and eat. You get into the kayak by taking it into the shallow water and sittin' your ass in it. My kayak has the cooler of food. Yours has the beer and water. The answer to getting naked is always yes. And I brought you some spray on SPF."

"What about my phone?"

She held up a small plastic box. "Dry box, my friend."

"I guess that answers all my questions."

"I guess it does. Get in." She untied the empty kayak and handed me the rope. "Go on now."

I towed it like a puppy to land and, kicking off my sneakers, I walked into the water. The warmth of the lake water always surprised me. "Just kinda straddle it and drop in," Scarlett suggested. She was paddling in circles just off the end of the dock.

I did as she instructed and flopped into the kayak. It rocked side to side for a moment but steadied itself.

"Come on! Let's go!" Scarlett said cheerfully. She dipped her paddle into the water and accelerated away from the dock.

"Wait for me!" I'd spent some time in college in sculls

and shells rowing. But a kayak was a new experience for me. I grabbed the paddle secured to the side with a bungee cord and dipped one end into the water.

"Paddle's upside down," Scarlett called out in a singsong voice.

I had no idea how a paddle could be upside down. Gamely, I pushed off the lake floor and awkwardly propelled myself toward her.

"Told ya you'd like it," Scarlett said smugly.

I couldn't argue. The hidden hot springs she'd directed us to, tucked away on an uninhabited shore of the lake, was like nature's perfect hot tub. We'd pulled the kayaks up on the shore behind some cleverly stacked logs that hid them from view.

Hot water bubbled up from beneath the surface to heat the huge pool. We were hidden from view by rock outcroppings and lush evergreens.

"How are there not thirty people in here right now?" I asked, reclining on a natural rock ledge in the pool worn smooth by the water. Scarlett floated next to me.

"They don't call this the Secret Springs for no reason," she laughed.

"I thought you said Bootleg doesn't keep secrets?"

"From each other. Bootleggers know about this place, but we don't tell tourists. That's why there's a No Trespassing sign on the beach."

"So how are there no Bootleggers drinking gin and country line dancing in here."

"'Cause I signed up for two hours, silly."

"There's a sign-up sheet?"

"Well, yeah. You wouldn't want to come here for some private time and find out that it's occupied by the church ladies would you?"

"No, I would not." But I was getting what she was telling me. We had the place to ourselves. For two whole hours.

Scarlett swam to me and slid a slick leg over mine to settle into my lap. I brought my hands to her tight little ass and pulled her against me. She gave me a silky smile when I started to thicken beneath her. She was so much packed into a petite body. Her breasts were delectably hidden behind the red and white checks of her swimsuit top. It had a little frill of material at the top of both cups. A tease for the eyes.

"I like your suit," I told her gruffly.

"I was hoping you'd approve."

I wanted to kiss her to thank her for today, for everything since I'd shuffled here in misery a few short weeks ago. I came here not able to imagine a way out of the darkness that had descended on my life. And here I was with a beautiful woman who smelled like sunshine sitting in my lap and smiling at me like I was something special. Not Devlin McCallister the state lawmaker. Not the man who had a path to Washington, D.C. mapped out in the next five years. No, she thought I was special. The broken and battered man who lived next door. I felt a sudden rush of gratitude and pulled her against me, hugging her to my chest.

"Mmm," she sighed against my skin, somehow understanding that this wasn't foreplay.

I brushed my lips against her hair. She'd piled it on top of her head and secured it with an elastic band. Even when I looked at her objectively, her appeal was undeniable. It went beyond her sweet smile and those bright, mischievous eyes. Beyond that little, curvy body and that dusting of freckles. It was in her energy, in the happiness that spilled out of her, the ridiculous schemes she plotted up, the way she moved her body on a dance floor as if she were worshipping the music by letting it move through her.

She'd managed to rebuild me, brick by brick, into someone different than I'd been before. She was happiness and fun and sweetness rolled into one tiny package. And right now, she was mine. Somehow, that accomplishment felt bigger and more important than any other success I'd achieved in my old life.

My old life. That's what Scarlett had called it. *When had I started thinking of it that way?*

"Tell me about your wife," she said.

My mellow feelings took a sharp left turn into instant anxiety.

She laughed softly against my chest. "I can feel every muscle in your body tensing."

"It's not my favorite subject," I said dryly.

"Do you mind telling me about her?"

I shrugged. Johanna was a wound that was starting to close, but care still needed to be taken lest it festered again. "What do you want to know?"

"What was she like before all this? How did you meet her?"

I thought back, absently stroking my hands over Scarlett's back pausing to toy with the strings of her top. "I'm not sure how we actually met."

It was ironic considering I knew that I'd never forget the moment I met Scarlett. A little brunette mainlining beer in cowboy boots on the tailgate of a pickup truck. While that image was carved into my mind, Johanna had just always been there in the periphery. "We moved in the same social circles, went to the same events, knew the same people. My parents invited her to dinner one night, and we talked a lot."

I remembered the meal. The knowledge that it was a fix-up. I wasn't overly annoyed. Johanna was a beautiful woman, a requisite for a good partner. She was well-spoken, well-bred, appropriately educated. The boxes checked themselves. Her father was a political consultant. She understood the requirements of a politician's wife.

"Was it love at first sight?" Scarlett asked.

I laughed. "No. Nothing like that. It was more of a mutual respect."

"That's not hot."

I laughed, tracing circles on Scarlett's hips. "No, but in my world, mutual respect and shared goals are more important than heat and love at first sight."

Scarlett leaned back to look at me. "Why do you think she cheated?"

I hadn't said the words aloud to anyone. Hadn't put voice to them because I was afraid doing so would make them true. But keeping them inside was eating away at me.

"I wasn't progressing in my career as quickly as I should have," I confessed.

"What does that mean?"

"It means I found myself frustrated with the whole system. Getting anything done required so many compromises that the end product didn't resemble the original in any way. It wasn't about doing good things for our constituents. It was about careers and grandstanding and choosing sides. My whole life I dreamed of making a difference, of working within the framework that our founders established. And when I got there it was nothing like what I thought it would be."

Scarlett cocked her head but didn't say anything.

"I started to drag my feet, making fewer appearances. It was a two-year term which is very short, so I found myself campaigning to keep a job I didn't really like."

It felt like ripping off a band-aid and letting the wound breathe. No one was here to tell me that was a ridiculous way to feel or that I just needed to be patient and grow my power base to affect change.

"It was supposed to be my calling, and I hated being in session. From January to April, we were on the floor twelve to fourteen hours a day doing nothing productive. Just pushing or fighting agendas. I never said anything to Johanna, but she noticed. When we were first married, our nights and weekends were spent at events. Networking, being seen, showing up for causes. And when I started to pull back…"

"She went looking for someone else," Scarlett filled in.

I nodded. "She had her own goals. She wanted to be a senator's wife. I think she hoped for even more than that, and when she saw me backing away from it, she went looking for someone who could get her there."

"What did your family say?"

"They thought it was just a phase for me. That I just needed to recommit to my path."

"Did that include recommitting to a wife who was a cheating skankface douche?"

I laughed and squeezed her ass with my hands. "Yes, as a matter of fact, it did. They suggested marital counseling. They even went as far to schedule an appointment for us."

Scarlett came back to me, resting her head on my shoulder. "That's bullshit."

"That is an accurate assessment."

"So, not only were you betrayed by your wife, your family jumped aboard the Fuck Devlin Over train. It's not your job to live your life for what they want. They made a human being, not hired an employee."

Hearing her say it, having Scarlett call it out for what it was, felt like a healing of sorts. A validation for the nebulous feelings of discontent I'd felt toward my parents since that day.

"What do you want now, Dev?"

When was the last time anyone had asked me that?

"Right now?"

She nodded earnestly.

"Right now, I want you." I reached up and untied the strings holding her top up.

Chapter Twenty-Three
Scarlett

I bowed backwards into the water until it covered my ears. Here there was no sound, only the sensation of Devlin's mouth at my breasts, licking and sucking. Teasing and tempting. The blue sky above me, warm water all around me. Devlin's hands stroking me.

It felt like a religious experience.

He was gentle with me, not his usual demanding self, and I found myself enjoying this side of him just as much as the dominating one. He lapped at my nipple and bit. Lifting me by my ass, Devlin floated me further away from him. I wanted to complain, wanted to go back to him, but when he untied one side of my bottoms, I realized what he wanted.

I floated there suspended between sky and water while Devlin spread my soft folds with his thumbs. The first stroke of his tongue was rapture. He worshipped me there in the hot springs until I was a tingling ball of sensation. Until every cell, every nerve ending, sparked to life. I felt the sun on my tender nipples, felt the water caress my hair, and surrendered to the nature of it all.

Devlin slid a finger into me and then another, gently massaging from the inside while his mouth played on me. The orgasm flowed over me like a waterfall. I cascaded into pleasure rippling around his fingers.

He was speaking. I could hear the vibrations but couldn't make out the words under the water. But I felt them in my heart. He was praising me, pleasing me. Everything inside me glowed as the pleasure ebbed and flowed and finally faded into bliss.

Then he was pulling me back to him, lifting me out of the water to settle me in his lap. Water flowed down my back, and Devlin fastened his mouth to one pert nipple. "You are perfection," he whispered to me.

Reaching between us, I slipped my hand into his swim trunks. He was achingly hard to the touch.

He raised his head from my breast. "Scarlett, I don't have a condom."

"I have one in the bag," I said breathlessly. I closed my fist around him and stroked him. "I don't think I can walk," he confessed with a half-laugh.

"I got this." I lifted off of him and climbed out of the pool. My untied bikini hung off of me. I discarded it on the way to the dry bag and dumped the contents until I found the foil packet. Victoriously I cannonballed back into the pool.

"You make quite the picture, Scarlett Bodine," Devlin breathed as I ripped the foil with my teeth.

I rolled the latex on him, squeezing his cock at the root. His head fell back against the wet rock, his eyes closed in a tableau of ecstasy. He made me feel powerful and wanton, and I never wanted to lose that feeling.

"I love how it feels when you touch me," he admitted, his long, inky lashes parting to look at me.

"I'm partial to it, too," I teased. I raised up high on my knees and positioned his broad head at my entrance.

"I feel like I should ask about the danger of bacteria in this spring," Devlin said suddenly.

I laughed, dropping my forehead to his. I had half an inch of him inside me, and he was worried about water quality.

"Sometimes you're too sensible for your own good." I moved just a bit, taking just another inch. It wasn't enough, not nearly enough. "And the water is tested weekly with the results posted on the secret online sign-up sheet. So quit worrying and start making me come."

Devlin didn't need any more encouragement than that. He grabbed my hips in a grip that hurt and yanked me down on his erection.

I cried out something unintelligible as he filled me. I'd never get used to this feeling. So full, stretched right up to my limit. And the pain of it was its own special turn on.

Devlin lifted his head and found my breast with his mouth. "I'm going to suck on you while you fuck me," he said, nuzzling my flesh.

Oh, sweet baby Jesus. I was going to die in the hot springs. I was swamped in sensation. The sunshine on my shoulders, the warm touch of the water, Devlin's magical mouth sucking and licking my tight, budded nipple. And his cock sliding into me like hot marble. He was a god, an Adonis, and I was the motherfucking goddess of pleasure.

I slid down his cock and rocked my hips. He growled his approval at my breast. I was riding him faster now.

He released my nipple with a pop. "Take it slow, baby."

But I wasn't listening. I was in charge of setting the pace, and I wanted to call the shots. I shoved his head against my other breast, the nipple needy and desperate for the wet of his mouth. I used my thighs to lift higher, drop harder on him.

Devlin's feet scrambled to find purchase under the water against the rock, and when they did, I rode harder. He didn't fight me. I felt his desperation in the hard pulls of his mouth. His hands aided me, their grip hard enough to bruise, and the thought of his fingerprints on me was dizzying.

"Dev," I gasped out. Every time he pushed that blunt crown into me, my walls convulsed. I was hanging by a thread.

153

"Let go, Scarlett. Give it to me," he ordered, lapping at my nipple. Then he used his teeth. It was like lightning to my core. I shimmered, spiked, and exploded. It wasn't waves that built and crashed. It was a detonation that relayed through my entire body. He groaned as all those greedy muscles closed around him.

He slammed into me, once, twice, and then held me hostage as he came. His mouth stilled at my breast as his body went rigid. I was with him, wild bolts of release shattering me. I wished that I could feel his seed in me. I wished there was nothing between us. Then our releases could mingle inside me in a sacrifice to the gods of euphoria.

Chapter Twenty-Four

Devlin

It was strange to miss someone I'd known only a few weeks and weirder still to do so when she'd left my bed this morning and I'd be in hers tonight. But Scarlett had that kind of effect on me. She'd not only brought me back to life, but she'd started to drag me even further into the world of the living. I couldn't remember ever feeling this light, this unencumbered.

When I tried to explain it to her, she claimed it was the hot springs. The hot springs were Bootleg's answer to everything. Cold cured? Hot springs. Little Freddy finally stopped biting at day care? Hot springs. Won the lottery? Hot springs.

But I knew the truth. It was Scarlett Bodine that had me musing about my life on the new deck with a view of the lake and plans for take-out and a bonfire tonight.

My cellphone rang on the table next to my laptop. The dread I felt now whenever the phone rang dissipated when I saw the caller ID. It was hard to face discussions with my parents and our publicist and attorneys when I wasn't feeling particularly bad about what I'd done to Hayden Ralston.

However, my grandmother wasn't calling to update me on my old life.

"Gran, how are you?"

"Well you certainly sound cheerful," she said shrewdly.

"I'm sitting on your deck catching up on some emails in the sunshine. What's not to be cheerful about?"

"Hmm," she said in her you're-not-fooling-me tone. "If I didn't know better, I'd say you found a nice girl."

I sighed. The Bootleg grapevine obviously had offshoots that extended to Europe.

"I might be enjoying my time with someone," I hedged.

Gran hooted. "He's seeing our Scarlett, Estelle."

"About damn time," Estelle called in the background.

"Don't listen to her," Gran said fondly. "She had her money on y'all getting together a lot earlier. Sometimes you're too stubborn for your own good."

"Tell me there wasn't a pool on me and Scarlett," I sighed.

"If you want me to lie to you, I will," she said cheerfully.

I swiped a hand over my beard, not nearly as annoyed as I should have been.

"If it makes Estelle feel better, I was ready earlier than Scarlett was," I told her.

"That's my boy," she said cheerfully.

"Where are you two globe hoppers today?" I asked, changing the subject.

"We're enjoying the late afternoon sun and some tea at a rooftop restaurant in Malta in our new hats," my grandmother announced.

The corners of my mouth lifted, picturing Gran and Estelle tearing up the island nation with their antics. "How did you end up living this life, Gran?"

She laughed. "You mean, how did I escape?"

I laughed ruefully. "Your life looks nothing like Mom and Dad's." Or mine.

"And thank God for that. Listen, Devlin, and listen good. You only get a set number of days, a limited number of sunrises

156

and sunsets. And it's up to you to make sure you're taking full advantage of them," Gran announced.

"It's not like I've been wasting my life," I began defensively. I was in public service. Politics was an honorable pursuit. I wanted to work for my country, serve my people.

"I didn't say that you were. But I'd look real hard to see if that's your calling or if you're just walking the path your father set out for you. Because I can see how you'd confuse one with the other. He's been grooming you since you were born."

This was the part of Gran that drove my parents nuts. They loved her, of course, but they didn't understand her.

"What else would I do with my life if I wasn't walking that path?"

"If you ask me, I think it's high time that you figure that out. I'll say this because I love you. I didn't see you happy. Not when you were elected, not when you married that shithead Johanna. I saw you following through on a purpose and setting and meeting goals, but I never once saw you happy."

That familiar anxiety settled like a block of ice in my gut. I knew now that I hadn't been happy before, but I'd had a purpose. Sitting here around Bootleg feeling lighter, feeling happy, but not having a purpose wasn't much—if any—better.

"Maybe not everyone is made to be happy. Maybe some of us have to find other things to feel."

"That sounds like some kind of bull that your father would spout about duty and honor and service. If you love being a lawmaker, if it makes you feel good—not important, but *good*—then stick with it. Be that. But I want you to decide, not your parents and sure as hell not that crappy ex-wife of yours."

"Gran, why did you come to Bootleg?" I asked.

She sighed. "It's the realest place I've ever been," she said. "It's not some political epicenter where everyone is constantly scheming. Bootleg lets you know where you stand. People care about you. They're not just calculating what they can get out of being associated with you."

I thought about the casseroles and the cards and the

neighbors popping in on the Bodines. Hell, Millie Waggle had showed up on my doorstep with a pan of sticky buns for Jonah when word spread that he was Bodine blood. Sure, he was the bastard half-brother no one had ever met before, but he was still family and a Bootlegger by association.

The Bodines had a support net in place in their friends and neighbors.

Who had been there for me when Johanna had left me? Who had stood by me during the ensuing scandal? They'd shipped me off like a pariah and left me to grieve my life on my own. Until Bootleg. Until Scarlett.

————

My afternoon passed with a few hours of research on court precedents. I packed it in and went for a run along the lakefront trail. My pace was faster than it had been when I first came. I hoped I'd be able to regain what strength and speed I'd lost in another few weeks. And I vowed never to let something level me like that again.

"How was the run?" Jonah asked when I got back to the house, winded and sweaty.

"Not bad," I said, filling a glass from the tap. "Not bad at all."

"Your phone was blowing up," he said, nodding to where it charged on the counter.

I picked it up and eyed the grilled chicken salad Jonah was assembling. I needed to learn to cook. A quick swipe of the screen and my good mood vanished. I felt a wave of anxiety wash over me just seeing *her* name.

Johanna hadn't reached out since my showdown with Ralston. And at that point, she'd left a chilly voicemail telling me she was disappointed that I didn't seem capable to handle our situation maturely and professionally. The only communication we'd had since had been between our attorneys.

I considered ignoring the text, but that was the chickenshit way out and not the Mona Lisa McNugget kind.

The Bodine brothers wouldn't hide from their past. Hell, Gibson saw his horrible ex on an almost daily basis. I tapped the message.

Johanna: We need to talk.

Hell. No. I didn't have anything left to say to her. Had she sent this text a few weeks ago, when I was sitting in a strange town in a dark house, I would have had a litany of topics to discuss. But now? Everything was different. *I* was different.

I swiped back to the messages and Scarlett's name popped up on the screen. My heart soared, and I marveled at the difference in my reactions to the two women.

Scarlett: Thinking about you and your sexy face. Also, if you're not doing anything, I'm stuck under Judge Carwell's front porch and could use your help. If I call Gibson he'll never let me live it down.

"Oh, shit."

Jonah's head swiveled in my direction. I dialed Scarlett's number and made a grab for my car keys. "Where's Judge Carwell's house?" I asked when she answered.

"Oh, thank God! I thought I was gonna die under this rotted out lumber."

"I'm on my way as soon as you tell me where you are."

"I'm on Rum Runner Avenue. Blue house, black shutters. My truck's out front."

I heard a weird growling noise in the background. "What's that?"

"I'll explain when you get here. Please hurry, and don't you dare say a word to my brothers."

"I'll be there in five." I hung up and headed toward the door.

"Scarlett emergency?" Jonah asked from the kitchen.

"I'm not allowed to tell you. But if I can't fix it, I'll call you," I said, pushing through the screen door.

Chapter Twenty-Five
Scarlett

I was good and stuck. I should have known better than trying to crawl under the damn porch with my damn tool belt on. But the damn cat had gotten out when I planed down the door, and the last thing Carolina Rae Carwell had said before she'd left was "Don't let the cat out." If I didn't find Mr. Fluffers and get him back inside, I'd never get to enjoy Carolina Rae's cornbread again.

It was a fate worse than death.

Though laying flat in the dirt under a sagging front porch with a hissing cat's collar hooked in my fingers wasn't so great either.

"Scarlett?"

I'd never been more relieved in my entire life to hear someone call my name.

"Oh my God, Devlin!"

"Are you hurt?" he asked.

"I'm under the porch, and I have a cat, and my belt's hooked on something, and I hope you're not dressed nice because I'm gonna have to ask you to ruin your clothes and belly crawl on in here."

There was silence. "Dev?" I called.

"I'm here."

"You're recording this, aren't you?"

"Damn right I am."

I kicked my work boots into the ground. "I'm so glad you're amused. Now get your ass in here!"

"Yes, ma'am. Here I come." He was laughing, but I didn't care.

"Jesus, Scarlett. How am I going to fit?" he said from behind me.

"That's what she said," I said miserably.

"Har har. But seriously."

"Just crawl in closer to the house—that's the high point— and then see if you can reach over and unhook whatever has me hooked."

Mr. Fluffers let out a feral snarl.

"Is that a fucking raccoon?" Devlin demanded.

"Yes. I have a rabid raccoon by the dang collar, Devlin," I said dryly.

"It sounds like something you'd do."

I heard him crawling in and turned my head. He made it as far as my feet. "I'm about wedged in," he said.

"You're not claustrophobic are you?" I asked, belatedly.

"I don't seem to be." I felt his hand on my ass.

"Now is not the time for foreplay."

"I'm not feeling you up. Your chisel is wedged in a floor board and stuck in your belt."

"I'm going to die here aren't I?" I wailed. "My skeleton will turn to dust under this porch, and I'll haunt trick or treaters every year unless they give me some of their candy."

I felt a sharp tug and then another one, and my belt jiggled loose.

"Got it," Devlin announced cheerfully.

I yipped. "You're the most amazing man in the world, Devlin McCallister."

He slapped me on the ass. Mr. Fluffers hissed.

"Yeah, yeah. I'm amazing. Now how do we get out of here?"

"You're going to have to back out. And then I think you're going to have to pull me out."

He managed it somehow, first crawling out backwards and then dragging me by my ankles. I pushed with one hand and kept a death grip of Fluffers's collar with the other.

Inch by inch, we scooted and dragged ourselves out of my almost-grave until I was facedown in the grass.

I leaped up, hauling the cat by the scruff of his neck. "In your face, Fluffers!"

Devlin bent at the waist and laughed loud and long. As much as I enjoyed hearing him laugh, I wasn't too thrilled that it was at my expense. I dumped the dirtball cat in the house. I'd pay the Carwell's for a cat bath if I had to. But that son of bitch wasn't getting outside again on my watch.

"Just what's so funny, McCallister?" I demanded, hands on hips and working myself into a heated glare.

He was in gym shorts and a t-shirt that were now smeared with dirt. There wasn't a laundry detergent on earth that could handle that mess. His beard was caked with it too. He looked like a dirty, sexy redneck, and I freakin' loved it.

I could only imagine my own mud monster state.

"Baby, you're something," he said, finally catching his breath.

"I'm gonna pretend that was meant as a compliment." He pulled out his cell phone.

"If you try to take one picture, I'm gonna—"

Click.

"Oh, you're in trouble now." I threw myself at him, heedless of the clods of dirt I flung when I moved. He caught me midflight and spun me around laughing. I didn't know if it was the spinning or his smile. But the bottom dropped out of my stomach, and I forgot all about being mad. All I wanted was his mouth on mine.

I kissed him hard, and he pulled me in tight against him,

162

still holding me aloft. I hoped my tool belt wasn't digging in anywhere important.

"Thanks for calling me, Scarlett."

"Thanks for coming when I called," I told him.

I heard the clearing of a throat, and Dev and I turned around. Carolina Rae was standing on her tidy little walkway staring at us. Her husband Ol' Judge Carwell was behind her peering over her shoulder.

Devlin let me slide down to the ground. "Hi, Carolina Rae, Judge. Door's all fixed, but I've got bad news for you on your porch. The joists are starting to rot out. I think you're gonna need a new porch next year," I was babbling. As progressive as I was, I didn't usually make out on my clients' lawns with my... lover.

"Uh-huh," Carolina Rae said, still staring at us. She was seventy-two but only admitted to sixty-six. "And what were you doing with your tongue down your young man's throat?" she asked sweetly.

"I... uh..." Words, those little traitors, failed me. Even Devlin looked chagrined.

She smiled. "Ah, to be young again. Carry on. But don't trample my coleus."

She headed into the house without another word, leaving Judge Carwell outside with us. He was eyeing up Devlin. The front door closed behind Carolina Rae without the hitch it had before I got here. I braced for it.

"Mr. Fluffers!" Carolina Rae screeched.

"Mr. Fluffers had a little adventure," I explained to Judge Carwell.

He grunted, still eyeing Devlin.

"You the lawyer, son?" he asked gruffly.

Devlin nodded. "Yes sir."

"Y'all ever think of a judgeship?" he asked. Judge Carwell's large white mustache twitched beneath his ruddy nose.

Devlin's eyes widened, and I laughed.

"Still tryin' to retire, sir?" I asked him sweetly. Judge

Carwell ran unopposed every election for the office of county judge. He was so ready to retire he tried to convince June to go to law school.

Mrs. Carwell burst through the front door holding the muddy Mr. Fluffers. "Scarlett Bodine!"

I winced. "Yes ma'am. We'll take him right over to Pet Paradise," I promised.

Chapter Twenty-Six
Scarlett

O h, yeah. Just like that, baby," I purred.

"You sound like you're having intercourse." June's dry tone broke through my hot oil massage bliss. Lula, my masseuse and friend since junior high school, snorted. Lula was tall and willowy with flawless dark skin and a riot of thick hair. She was drop dead gorgeous, an exotic looking beauty who wore denim and plaid. She was also rolling in dough, having capitalized on the tourism boom that began a few years ago. She bought the withering old Victorian and—with a little help from me—had renovated it into a kitschy, cultured day spa.

Now, Bootleg Springs Spa was *the* place to rest, rejuvenate, and drop a crap ton of money.

Cassidy laughed through her hot springs seaweed facial. "I bet that's the sound your neighbors have been hearing since you and Devlin started knockin' boots," she said.

"Devlin *is* my neighbor," I pointed out. "He's usually there making the noise with me."

"I've heard about you two," Lula teased. "Makin' goo-goo

eyes at each other in the diner. Booking two whole hours in the hot springs."

"We used every second of those two hours," I said smugly.

June, bored with our conversation, turned the page in her copy of The Economist that she brought from home. She was having her toes painted a pearly pink. Cassidy picked the color for her when June's apathy on the subject became apparent.

"Tell me more about these magical multiple orgasms," Cassidy sighed.

"Damn, girl," Lula said, digging her strong hands into the knots in my shoulders. "That explains the rug burn back here."

I giggled. I couldn't help it. I felt good. The kind of good that meant everything in my life was going in the right direction. For the first time in a very long time, I didn't have some kind of lingering doubt or anxiety about the future. Growing up, I never knew exactly who I'd be coming home to, the fun, happy Mom and Dad dancing in the kitchen and making mountain pies or the screaming, accusatory parents who fought and then sulked in silence for days.

But now, things felt settled. I had a great job, a sexy neighbor who kept me entertained, friends to have a spa day with, and four brothers who annoyed the shit out of me. Life was about as perfect as it could get.

"He's great. The multiple orgasms are great. And I'm great," I reported with satisfaction.

"I kind of hate you a little bit," Cassidy sighed.

"What happened with you and Amos at The Lookout last time?" I asked her, knowing Bowie's side of the story.

"I gave him one dance for old time's sake, and he was annoying. Thankfully Bowie cut in on him, but he just came right back the next song, talking about missin' me and 'let's give it another chance,'" she mocked in a deep baritone. "Thing is, I haven't missed him not one lick since we broke up, and that says enough to me not to get back on that merry-go-round."

"Then how did the fight start?" I asked. Lula's thumbs found tense muscles in my lower back, and I yelped.

"Girl, you have got to stretch. I tell you this every time. You can't just be on your feet for twelve hours a day and expect your muscles to keep up with you."

"Yeah, yeah. Yoga. Pilates. Stretch. I get it. Back to the fight!"

"I don't even know," Cassidy hedged. She was totally lying. But that's what she did to herself when it came to Bowie Bodine. "One minute Amos and I were dancin', and I was like 'thanks but no thanks.' But he wouldn't let go. He was insistent that I listen to him and give him another chance and blah blah blah. And it must have looked like he was hurting me from the table because Bowie and Jameson showed up and had some words."

I snorted. "As if you couldn't take care of yourself." Cassidy was not only proficient in firearms, but her hands could be considered deadly weapons, too. When I was demanding ballet lessons and cheerleading skirts, Cassidy was earning a rainbow of belts in Tae Kwon Do. She got her black belt at eighteen.

"Right?" Cassidy said with an exasperated sigh. "Thank you!"

"So, Bowie and Jameson had words with Amos," I prompted her.

"Yeah. Words were had, Amos said something stupid, and then Bowie just decks him."

"Mmm-hmm." I lifted my head and made eye contact with Lula. She rolled her dark brown eyes in understanding. The entire town knew that Bowie was gone over Cassidy except dear, sweet, stupid Cassidy.

"Anyway, you know how Bootleg is on a Friday."

"Everyone's ready for a fight."

"Yep."

"You know what I find interesting?" June interjected over her magazine.

"What?" I asked.

"That prisons are noting a significant upswing in the delivery of contraband via recreational drones."

Cassidy laughed. "June Bug, when are you gonna start taking an interest in human relationships?"

June raised an eyebrow. "Not until absolutely necessary."

Lula and I chuckled over that.

"Changing the subject," Cassidy said. "What I find interesting is that I have never seen Scarlett Bodine so giddy."

"I'm *not* giddy," I argued. "I'm drunk on orgasms."

"Giddy. After all the guys I've seen you date, in high school and since, I've never seen you light up like you do when Devlin walks in a room. Who knew your type would be a buttoned-up politician? I mean, it's almost comical."

"I don't discriminate against any kind of penis," I argued. "No matter what the person attached to it does for a living."

"Oh, no, I think it's something more than straight up dick worship," Cassidy decided. "I think you like him."

"Well, of course I like him," I said grumpily. "I wouldn't sleep with him otherwise."

"Wade Zirkel," June said, flipping another page in her magazine.

"Shut up, Juney."

She smirked. "You know, Scarlett. Perhaps the feelings you're experiencing are what someone else would consider romantic love."

My body went rigid.

"Whoa. From the way your ass cheeks just seized up, I'd guess that Juney just hit a nerve," Lula pointed out.

I lifted my head like a sea lion heaving itself onto the ice. "Love? Are you kidding me?" I didn't like that thought one bit. I was a Bodine, after all. Bodines a) weren't capable of love and b) made a huge mess of long-term relationships.

"I know your mama made you promise to wait, but I think she'd be givin' you an exception for Devlin McCallister," Cassidy pointed out innocently.

"We haven't talked relationships. We're not even exclusive," I scoffed. Though if Devlin McCallister thought it was okay to stick that fine dick in someone else, he was sorely mistaken.

I had no intention of ever getting married. Not that it was something I'd ever discussed with anyone. My promise to my mama was just my excuse. After seeing my parents' marriage and all the drama and pain that entailed, I had no interest in ever chaining myself for all of my miserable eternity. So if somehow my heart had gotten confused and stumbled a little bit over Devlin, it was just going to have to unstumble itself right quick.

"We're just having fun," I insisted.

"So, you won't be upset when he packs up and goes home?" Cassidy asked.

I hadn't thought about it. Not really. I'd been too busy getting under his skin, into his head… and into his bed.

"I'm well aware of the fact that he's only here temporarily." My stomach lurched.

"Annapolis isn't that far from here," Cassidy pointed out.

"What? You think we'd sign on for a long-distance relationship?" It wasn't the worst idea, but it sure as hell wasn't as convenient as strolling next door to take my clothes off.

"Or you could move there."

"And do what?" I asked, baffled.

"I believe my sister is suggesting that you could follow Devlin and be in a relationship," June piped up.

"He's a *politician*. Can you really see me being some politician's girlfriend?" The room went silent as everyone present considered the idea. Cassidy started snickering, and then they were all in a full fit of laughter. Even June was smiling.

While I was glad they got my point, I'll admit I was the teensiest sliver hurt by their agreement. I wasn't a politician's anything. I wouldn't keep my mouth shut. I wouldn't prance around in cocktail dresses and bat my lashes while the "menfolk" did the work. I knew it wasn't fair for me to be pissed that they agreed with my own assessment, but sometimes you expect your friends' opinions to be higher than your own. Their easy agreement checked a box that I'd been trying to avoid thinking about.

Why *couldn't* I be a good partner for Devlin?

I'd never backed down from a challenge before, not when it was something I wanted. Maybe I just needed to figure out what it was that I wanted where Devlin was concerned?

Chapter Twenty-Seven
Devlin

I knocked on Scarlett's back door, noting that the tiny table here on the porch was set for two with napkins and utensils. There was a candle on the railing next to the table.

I heard footsteps and watched with pleasure as Scarlett hurried to the door. She wore a long dress with blue watercolor blossoms that swished around her ankles. Her feet were bare.

"Hi," she said. Her cheeks were flushed, and her hair hung loose down her back.

She'd spent the day at the spa with her friends, and I'd expected her to look more relaxed than she did.

I leaned in for a kiss, intending to just brush my mouth against hers. But she shoved her hands into my hair and held on for dear life as she kissed the hell out of me. She pulled back just as abruptly, leaving me stunned and breathless.

"What was that for?" I asked.

She smiled up at me. There was something a little shy and a lot unusual for Scarlett in that smile. "Just an appetizer," she said. "Come on in. Dinner's almost ready."

Uh-oh. Scarlett Bodine was many things. Many wonderful, good, wild things. A cook was not one of those things. Even her sandwiches were borderline terrible. I wasn't much better in the kitchen, but at least I didn't try to kid myself about it.

Something smelled burnt. Something else smelled just plain bad.

"I hope you like chicken. I roasted one," she announced.

"Um. That sounds great." I needed to find a meat thermometer stat. I was sure that chicken was one of those meats that could kill you if it was undercooked. "I didn't know you cooked."

She shrugged, looking slightly ill. I wondered if she'd sampled something she cooked.

"I wanted to try something new," Scarlett said, sticking her chin out. "Just because it's not something I've done before doesn't mean I won't be good at it."

"What can I do to help?" I offered.

"How about you put the potatoes in the microwave while I check the asparagus?"

I glanced in the pot on the stovetop. Dear god, she'd boiled asparagus… from a can.

At least we'd have baked potatoes. I unwrapped them and dumped them onto the microwave tray, hitting the potato button. Idiot proof.

"What's the special occasion?" I asked. She was up to something. That much was clear, but as with everything Scarlett did, I couldn't even begin to predict what it would be.

"Hang on, let me go find the wine opener," she said, hurrying out to the porch. Scarlett's screened-in porch served as a bar of sorts during bonfires. She kept her bottle openers and corkscrew out there.

I yanked open a couple of drawers before finding a rusty meat thermometer. Glancing over my shoulder, I opened the oven and shoved the thermometer in the smoking bird. Two hundred and forty degrees. I hoped that was hot enough to cook off bacteria. I heard her at the door and yanked the thermometer out and tossed it behind a roll of paper towels on the counter.

"Looks great," I said as if I'd been admiring the blackened bird and closed the oven.

She brightened. "Thanks! My mama always used to say there was nothin' easier than roasting a chicken."

Scarlett's mama was a liar.

Casually, I pulled my phone out as if to check my messages. I opened the browser and did a quick search for chicken temperatures. At least we didn't have to worry about salmonella now.

"There's pie for dessert," she said, wiping her hands on a dishtowel.

Oh, hell.

"I didn't have time to bake one so I bought it at the Pop In."

I bit back my sigh of relief.

"Could Johanna cook?" Scarlett asked.

I was unsettled by the quick turn of conversation. Especially since Johanna had recently reared her head in my life with that text message this afternoon. "Uh. I suppose she could. She just generally chose not to. We ate out a lot and had a part-time chef prepare meals for the week for us."

Scarlett looked relieved. I was just about to ask her what this was all about when something exploded. We both ducked behind her tiny kitchen island. When no shrapnel rained down upon us, I realized it was the microwave.

"The potatoes," Scarlett yelped.

I made it to the microwave first and opened the door. One of the idiot-proof baked potatoes had exploded, coating the inside of the microwave with potato particles.

"At least we can split this one," Scarlett said, reaching in to grab the other potato. "Ouch! Hot!" She tossed it back and forth from hand to hand.

She smacked her elbow off of the counter, and the potato landed on the floor with a dull splat. "Well, shit!"

I grabbed it and brushed it off. "Five second rule, right?"

The potato was probably going to be the only edible part of the meal, and I wasn't going to throw it in the trash.

"Should we wash it off?" Scarlett wondered.

I shrugged. "Maybe if we just don't eat the skin it will be fine," I suggested.

She nodded. "I'll get the chicken out, and you can carve it."

"Great." I had no idea how to carve a chicken. *Would she be disappointed in that? Did all Bootleg men know how to carve birds? Hell, they probably went out and shot them first.*

She pulled the roaster out of the oven and put it on the wood top of the island. "It doesn't really look like the picture," Scarlett said, chewing on her lower lip and studying the chicken's coffee-brown skin.

It didn't look like any roast chicken I'd ever seen. "I think it looks really good," I lied.

"Do you need any special utensils?" she asked.

"A knife," I said with authority. I'd never even seen my father carve the turkey at Thanksgiving. We always had it catered.

Scarlett handed me a steak knife, and after burning the hell out of my hand on hot chicken skin, I grabbed a wooden spoon from the pitcher on her counter. Sawing through the skin was like trying to cut my way through shoe leather with a butter knife. The meat under the leathery skin was bone dry. At least we could dump the asparagus soup on top of it. I did my best to saw my way through and scrape meat off of the charcoal skeleton. It hit the plate sounding like jerky.

"How about I just carve one side?" I suggested, wiping the sweat from my brow. "Then the rest of it will stay... fresh."

"That's a great idea. I can use the rest for soup... or something."

Scarlett made up our plates—real ones, not the paper plates like I was used to with her—with half of the non-exploded potato, a soupy dollop of asparagus, and several chunks of chicken leather. "I thought we could eat on the porch," she said nervously.

"I'd like that," I told her, wanting to wipe the worry from her face. I took the plates from her and beckoned toward the door.

We sat at the tiny table, our plates touching. I was just wondering if I should eat the entire potato first to soak up the rest of the "food" on the plate when Scarlett took a deep breath.

"I have something I wanna say."

I looked up from my plate grateful for the distraction.

"I think things are good. Between us, I mean," she added. She looked at me like she was waiting for me to say something.

"I… think they're good too?" I said suspiciously. Was she trying to break up with me? Give me food poisoning and then send me packing? Was this some kind of bizarre Bootleg Justice for not telling her that my almost ex-wife texted me with regrets?

Tentatively, I picked up a chunk of chicken and examined it on my fork.

"Well, I've been thinking that maybe we should… what I mean to say is… Oh, hell. I've never had this conversation before."

"What conversation?" I was getting more anxious by the second.

"You can't leave town without telling me, and you can't get naked with anyone else," she blurted out.

I blinked, at a loss.

"I like you," she said to her plate, sounding like she was choking on the words.

I forgot what I was doing and accidentally put the chicken in my mouth. It tasted like petrified feet.

I cleared my throat, trying to soften the chicken with my saliva. "I like you, too," I said through my mouthful. No amount of chewing was going to make this chicken softer. I was either going to have to swallow it whole and choke on it or spit it out.

"Well, since we like each other. I don't think that you should just up and leave without at least talking to me about it first, and if you think I'd be okay with you having sex with someone else, you are *sorely mistaken*." Her voice rose.

"Are you breaking up with me?" I demanded, moving the chicken to the side of my mouth.

"What? No!" She looked horrified. "I'm doing the opposite."

"You're asking me to be your boyfriend?"

Scarlett looked uncomfortable. She shrugged one shoulder. "I'm not really asking. It's more like telling than asking."

I sucked in a breath to laugh and lodged the chicken between my tonsils. My laugh became a coughing fit.

She jumped up and slapped me on the back. I managed to spit the chicken out into my napkin. "Excuse me," I gasped.

"Are you okay?"

"Just went down the wrong pipe," I said, gulping down my wine.

Scarlett sat back down and forked up a mushy lump of asparagus. I didn't care how much I liked her. I wasn't touching that green slime.

"So, what do you think?" she asked, her pretty gray eyes pulling me in.

I thought the chicken was a biohazard.

"I thought you didn't want to talk about relationships," I said. "The first time we had sex, I tried to bring it up, and you shut me down."

Scarlett took a deep breath. "I just never expected to get so attached to you. And now if you were to just pack up and go home, I'd be… upset." Her eyes narrowed, and she pointed her drippy glob of asparagus at me. "And I'd be real upset if I caught you showing off that cock to anyone else."

"Scarlett, I'm not going anywhere for the time being, and I certainly wouldn't leave without at least talking to you first. And I don't know where you're getting the idea that I'd want to be with anyone else when I have you. There's no one out there like you. I'd be the biggest idiot in the world to keep looking when I have you in my bed."

176

She beamed at me, and I felt the tension in my shoulders relax. "Really?"

"Really."

She grinned and wiggled in her seat. I watched in horror as she shoveled the asparagus into her pretty mouth. Her face froze, and then her eyes widened as the realization hit her. She clamped a hand over her mouth.

I shoved her napkin at her. "Spit it out before you vomit," I ordered.

"Gah!" She grabbed the napkin and pressed it to her mouth. "Ohmygod. Ohmygod. Ohmygod."

I held out her wine glass. "Drink."

She drained the glass like she had the beer the first night I met her.

Scarlett put the glass down with a clunk. "That was the worst thing I've ever put in my mouth."

"You didn't try the chicken yet," I pointed out.

"Man!" she wailed, throwing the napkin of masticated disaster on the table. "I just wanted tonight to be perfect!"

I reached across the table and held her hand. "Baby, it is."

"No. It's not! The food is horrible, and I got all nervous and basically forced you to be my boyfriend, and I'm really hungry and all we've got is half a potato each!"

I used my grip on her hand to pull her out of her chair and over into my lap.

She sat stiffly against me, and I hid my smile. Her stubborn streak was a mile-wide like my gran would say.

"I'd like to point out that I haven't turned you down, and we have pie."

"You didn't say yes," she said, pouting at her hands in her lap.

"Scarlett, when's the last time anyone said no to you?"

"It happens on occasion."

"Not this occasion," I told her.

She raised her gaze to mine, and I felt my heart glow a little brighter.

"I'll be your boyfriend on one condition."

"What's that?"

"You promise to never cook again."

Chapter Twenty-Eight
Scarlett

I gave the front door a good kick. Warmer weather always made the front door of my father's house stick. I hadn't been back here since that morning I'd found him. Even in death, Jonah Bodine Sr. hadn't looked peaceful.

I took a deep breath and stepped inside. My childhood home was a bungalow. The yellow siding had always struck me as too cheerful for the family that lived within its walls. Especially after Mama died.

I dropped the keys on the skinny table Gibson had made in his high school shop class. Dad's keys were there too. Dropped there the afternoon before he died. I'd muscled him into the house. He'd snuck a flask along to a job site, and I'd had to bring him home early before the clients saw him shit-faced on the job. I remembered tossing his keys on the table one last time.

It was stuffy and dark inside, reminding me that this was now an empty house. There was no more life in the Bodine bungalow. The blinds had been drawn the night Daddy died and remained closed since then. I'd been avoiding this place and the memories just like my brothers. But I was the only one of us who had the memory of him dead in his bed.

I turned into the long skinny living room on the left. Everything here was exactly the same as it always had been. A saggy plaid couch. The recliner that didn't recline quite right. The flat screen TV I'd bought Dad two years ago when his rabbit-eared dinosaur had finally called it quits. I'd mounted it above the fireplace for him with the sad hope that having something nice would make him want to make an effort in other areas of his life.

My father had taught me a lot of things. He'd shown me how to use every tool known to man to fix just about every problem created by man. But he'd also taught me that no matter how much I hoped or prayed or tried, I couldn't control other people. I couldn't make them make the choices I wanted them to. I couldn't drag them into health and happiness.

It was a painful, essential lesson.

With a sigh, I set about opening the blinds and windows in the long room. Maybe some fresh June air would sweep out some of those memories that haunted us all.

One by one, I worked my way around the room, opening them before moving on to the eat-in kitchen on the opposite side of the house and doing the same. The first floor was divided in half by the stairs to the second floor. I tried to look at the house objectively, like a new project for which history didn't matter.

I'd always wanted to expand the kitchen into the useless breakfast nook. Now I could.

I skipped Daddy's bedroom in the back of the house. I wasn't ready to revisit that room. Not with its most recent memories.

Growing up, it had been mine. The only one on the first floor. There were three small rooms upstairs. When I'd moved out at nineteen, I'd moved Daddy to the first floor since his drinking made him unsteady on his feet.

I looked around trying to decide where to begin.

Overwhelmed, I sat down on the first step of the staircase. It still squeaked as it had for fifteen years. We'd all learned to skip that step when it would have been faster and smarter to just fix the damn thing.

I sighed out a long breath. Jonah, bless his big heart, had offered to come help me today. But it wasn't exactly fair to him, asking him to clean out the home of the father who'd abandoned him.

So, it fell to me. I put my face in my hands and allowed myself a moment of pathetic self-pity. What did I really have to be upset about? I, Scarlett Bodine, age 26, had my very first official boyfriend. We'd sealed the deal last night with baked potato and pie and some vigorous, acrobatic sex on my porch swing. At least until the chain had snapped and we'd fallen in a heap to the floor.

Totally worth the bruises.

In the grand scheme of things, having to tackle my father's house alone was an emotional inconvenience, but my good stuff outweighed the bad. Now, if I could just get up the gumption to start...

The crunch of tires on gravel out front had me lifting my head.

Had one of my brothers felt guilty enough about dumping this on me that they—

It wasn't a Bodine climbing up the porch steps. It was Devlin. And I wanted to cry.

"Hey, I thought I'd see if you needed a hand—"

The velocity of my body colliding with his cut him off. He was here to help me clean up a mess that wasn't his because he cared. I clung to him like Virginia creeper. Gratitude made my eyes sting.

"Thank you," I whispered against his t-shirt. He held me close and stroked a hand down my ponytail. I breathed him in, stealing a bit of his strength, and then unwound myself from him.

He was watching me with a soft look on his face. "Do you think you could greet me like that every time you see me for a while?" he asked.

"Yeah. I think I could do that," I said softly. I stepped back and let him inside. "Welcome to Bodine Bungalow."

Devlin glanced around, and I couldn't help but wonder what kind of home he'd grown up in. I'd be willing to bet it was a bit grander than my own childhood home.

"It's nice," he said. "Cozy. I bet there are a lot of memories here."

There were. Enough bad memories to be haunted by and enough good ones to make the loss still hurt.

"Yeah. Lots of memories," I agreed, my throat tight.

"Where do you want me to start?" he asked. "You have me for the day. I've got cleaning supplies in the car, garbage bags, a couple of plastic totes. I have a scanner back at Gran's if there's any paperwork you want to save."

My eyes started to water. It was the dust, I told myself. Not the freely offered help.

"Let's start with the fridge. That'll be the worst of it. Then, we can look for any paperwork and photo albums. Things I want to keep," I decided.

He nodded. "I'll grab the supplies."

I watched him walk back down the porch steps—the same steps that I'd bounded down in a bid to run away from home twice in my teens—and fell just a little, tiny bit in love with Devlin McCallister.

———

Devlin hadn't said a word when we'd cleared the dozen empty bottles of cheap Kentucky bourbon from the kitchen cabinets. He hadn't mentioned the fact that the refrigerator was empty except for beer and moonshine and a really old jar of mayonnaise. And he hadn't raised an eyebrow when I'd opened each and every bottle and dumped it all straight down the drain.

He was too polite to ask any questions. He knew the basics. But I was tired of not saying anything, tired of accepting.

"My father was an alcoholic," I announced as we carted two waste baskets of recyclables out onto the front porch.

"Okay," Devlin said.

"He always drank, but it got worse after my mom died," I continued.

"How old were you when she died?" Devlin asked.

"I was fifteen. Car accident."

His hand settled on my shoulder, and I stopped my fidgeting. "I'm sorry," he said simply.

"She was a good mom, mostly." It was important to me that he believed me. "She and my dad got pregnant in high school and married. In some ways, they never grew up. They fought a lot. There was a lot of jealousy. And obviously at least one of them wasn't faithful. Daddy drank too much. Mama didn't handle it well. And they raised four basket cases."

Devlin leaned in close and cupped my cheek in his hand. "Baby. Nothing about you says basket case."

I closed my eyes, relaxing into his soothing touch.

"I started going to work with my daddy in the summers at twelve because Mama thought he was drinking on the job. He was. By thirteen, I was driving his ass home. By fifteen, I was doing most of the work."

Devlin towed me into him, wrapping his arms around me, creating a safe, warm space. "Gibson hates him. Daddy never kept it quiet that Gibs was the reason he and Mama got married. Bowie is the good guy trying to undo all the bad that Daddy did. Jameson just kept his head down and tried to live his own life outside of the drama."

"And your mother?" Devlin asked.

"She hung in there for us. She didn't know what happiness was. But she knew what was right and wrong. Made me make that promise not to get married before thirty and made my brothers promise not to get married for any reason other than stupid in love."

183

"Did he ever hurt you?" Devlin asked.

I leaned back and looked up into those stormy eyes. "Daddy? No! Of course not. At least not physically."

He relaxed his hold on me.

"If not physically, then how?"

I shrugged and pressed my cheek against his chest. It was my new favorite place to be. "I just wanted to be important enough to him that he didn't need to drink," I confessed.

"Baby."

Devlin said it so softly, so sweetly.

"I know. I know that he was an alcoholic, and I know you can't just matter enough to someone to make them quit. But I really, really wanted to," I told him.

Again, he ran his hand through the tail of my hair.

"I can't remember a time growing up that I wasn't worried about Mama and Daddy gettin' a divorce. Looking back, I don't know why they didn't. I mean, it wasn't like they were happy."

"Maybe they felt like it was the right thing to do," Devlin offered gruffly.

"But the right thing shouldn't be so unhappy. Should it?" I asked.

"Easy doesn't mean right," Devlin pointed out.

I sighed. "There was a time—right after Callie disappeared—that things were good. Everyone was trying. Even Gibson," I recalled. "I think it scared everyone and made them want to hold on to what we're all lucky enough to have."

"But it didn't last?" Devlin asked.

I shook my head. "Never does, I guess." I looked into the front yard at the trees I used to climb as a kid, pretending I was in the jungle far, far away. "Anyway, thanks for listening."

Devlin leaned in and stroked his thumb across my cheek. "Scarlett, anything that's important to you is important to me."

God help me, I believed him.

My sigh this time was one of relief. "Thanks, Dev. How do you feel about snooping for important papers?"

He grinned. "I feel pretty damn good about that."

Chapter Twenty-Nine

Scarlett

Even with Devlin present for moral support, I wasn't prepared to tackle Daddy's bedroom so we headed upstairs. "Mama and Daddy used to use this bedroom," I told him, shoving open the white painted door. It creaked like a dang haunted house.

The walls still boasted that English rose wallpaper that Daddy had sworn he'd take down. The mattress still sagged on its old iron frame. There was a bookcase built into the wall, the one change my father had managed to make in his years here. It was a jumble of paperwork and books and old magazines. Judging from the layer of dust, no one had been up here in a few years.

"Gross. Let's start with this allergy factory," I suggested. "We're makin' sure there's no outstanding bills, looking for anything on property taxes, any titles to the house or his truck or whatever. At least we don't have to worry about any life insurance or retirement paperwork," I said dryly.

"Paperwork is my specialty," Devlin said. "Why don't you

look for photos and mementos? I'm sure Jonah would be interested in seeing what your childhood looked like."

It was a thoughtful gesture that I don't know if I would have thought of making on my own. I knew just where to start. Mama's trunk was shoved in the corner by the closet and buried under an entire family history stashed into shoe boxes and manila folders. Photos, report cards, drawings. We'd never made it through the mess when she died. And we'd ended up just adding to it in the years after. After pawing through some of it for pictures for Mama's funeral, we'd left it for Daddy to take care of and—as expected—everything sat exactly as he'd left it.

I cleared the top of the trunk, making neat stacks on the bare mattress. Keep. Recycle. Burn to the Motherfucking Ground.

When I tried to lift the lid, I found the trunk locked. I frowned at the lock. I'd played with this trunk a million times as a kid. Hell, my brothers used to take turns hiding in it when we'd played hide and seek. It had never been locked.

I glanced over at Devlin. He was sitting on the whitewashed floor sorting stacks of paperwork. I studied the lock. It wasn't as if it was a particularly challenging lock. One or two whacks with a hammer would break the clasp easy enough. And I was curious enough to know what my parents had thought was worth locking away. But I didn't like the idea of busting up something Mama valued.

I glanced over at Devlin who was happily sorting papers like the hot closet nerd he was.

Obviously, there was a key of some sort that locked the damn thing. I closed my eyes and let my mind wander. The trunk was old. It wouldn't be an ordinary key that fit the lock. I opened my eyes. It couldn't be that easy, could it? I rose and jogged downstairs to the front door. Dad's key ring was right there. I picked it up and thumbed through them. Front door, back door, garage. My house. Truck keys. And one stubby, brass, unlabeled key.

I held my breath and headed back upstairs, the weight of the keys heavy in my hand. What secrets could my parents possibly have kept? They were an open book of misery and dedication to commitment. It was probably a stack of *Sports Illustrated* issues or doll clothes. Or, ugh, a fat pile of unpaid bills that my father hadn't told me about. That would be a nice slap in the face.

I returned to the bedroom and stepped over Devlin's incomprehensible organizational system. Kneeling in front of the trunk, I slid the key into the lock. It turned with no resistance.

I felt a nostalgic tug when I saw the green flowered fabric lining. The smell was the same, old and musty, but now instead of being an empty hiding place for kids, the interior of the trunk was packed full. I brushed a hand over my mother's favorite dress. I'd boxed up her clothing the week after the funeral and given it to the Bootleg Community Church to distribute to the needy. I hadn't even noticed that her soft, spring green dress was missing.

My father must have tucked it away, I realized. Along with her bed pillow and it's carefully cross-stitched pillow case. I unpacked them slowly, running my fingers over long familiar mementos. Their wedding album came next. They'd married in a hurry and without their families' joyful acceptance. So, their album consisted of a dozen sepia-toned shots of my mother in a high-necked lace dress that her cousin lent her. Daddy was oh-so-young in his baby blue suit. His shirt had ruffles on it, something that never ceased to entertain me. As a little girl, I'd insisted on perusing the album hundreds of times and never once had I realized it was like admiring the chain that tied my parents to their unhappy life.

I flipped through the thick pages, studying each picture. There were no glowing smiles during the ceremony, but the last shot was a candid of my father looking down at Mama with a tenderness that rarely showed in the ensuing years. Mama was looking up at him and laughing. In that picture, she sparkled.

It wasn't all bad, their life together. And this picture was living proof of that. There were pockets of happiness in that lifetime. But I wanted more than pockets.

I shot a look at Devlin and found him watching me. "You had about a million emotions go across your pretty face in the last minute," he told me.

"Oh, yeah?" I asked. He gave me that half smile that I liked so much.

"What did you find?" he asked, standing up and stepping over his neat piles to get to me.

I stroked a hand over the dress, remembering endless hugs and Easter mornings. Everything always ended. The good and the bad. And while I hated it, it was also a comfort. Daddy was no longer suffering. And maybe now my brothers could start to move on.

Devlin's hand squeezed my shoulder. He sank down next to me on the floor.

"This is some of my mama's stuff," I told him, handing over the photo album.

"May I?" he asked. I nodded.

He turned the pages. "I like your dad's suit," he grinned.

"He wore it to their prom and then their wedding. And one more time to Gibson's christening. I don't think he wore so much as a necktie after that."

"Do you think Jonah would like to see this?" Devlin asked.

I looked at the album in his big hands. "I'd like to show him," I decided.

"We'll start another pile then." He placed the ivory book on the bare mattress.

I gave him the dress. "This too."

We dug back into the next layer of goodies in the trunk. I was delighted to find Jameson's baby album and a stack of disciplinary reports from the high school regarding Gibson. These I could use for blackmail.

Devlin laughed his way through the reports, making sure there wasn't anything important stuck between the pages of

Gibson's juvenile delinquent-ism. I found more loose family photos and the veil Mama had worn on her wedding day. There was a grimy folder of Sunday school lessons Mama had taught and my father's neat collection of every single program of the Bootleg Annual Jedidiah Bodine Still Explosion Re-Enactment. We found odds and ends of family life. Mama had kept every sketch and drawing Jameson had done growing up. Even at seven, he'd shown artistic promise. Bowie's good citizenship trophies and soccer team pictures were stacked neatly in an acrylic box.

"Oh, Dev. Look at this," I said, lifting a photo triumphantly from the bowels of the trunk. "Me at prom."

Devlin studied it, smiling sweetly at the 17-year-old me. I'd worn an electric blue two-piece dress because everyone else was wearing black. My hair, it had been even longer then, was piled on top of my head in Medusa-like coils. I was the punky Tinkerbell to Freddie Sleeth's smirking seventeen.

"What was your prom night like?" Devlin asked.

"Well, a lady never kisses and tells," I told him. "But I can tell you that Freddie's pickup got a flat on the way to the dance, and we had to change it in a mud puddle. He got flustered and dropped the lug nuts right into the mud, and I ended up having to fish 'em up. Changed the tire too since *someone's* daddy never showed him how. Still made prom queen even covered in mud," I said smugly. "How about yours?"

Devlin looked embarrassed. "I borrowed my parents' driver and Town Car in the tux I already owned and took Lilibeth Paxton to a candlelit seafood dinner on the water followed by an evening of elegant entertainment and dancing."

"Could we possibly be more different?" I asked him.

He tucked a strand of hair behind my ears. "I don't know, Scarlett. I think we've got enough in common to outweigh those very different differences."

I liked that answer, and I told him so with a kiss. I kept it sweet and light. I wasn't about to jump Devlin's sexy ass here in my parents' house surrounded by their ghosts. "Thank you for your help," I whispered, pulling back to admire his just kissed mouth and that neat beard.

"Anything you need Scarlett, ever. Just ask."

"I wouldn't say no to some lunch after we finish this trunk," I said hopefully.

He kissed the tip of my nose. "Anything you want."

Happy again, I dug into the depths of the trunk. It looked like we'd already found all the good stuff. What was left were lace curtains—probably my gram's—that needed a good washing and a balled up plastic bag at the bottom. I pulled the curtains out and sneezed. If I could clean them up, they sure would look pretty in my front windows. I plucked the plastic bag out of the back corner of the trunk and was surprised that it had some weight to it.

"Not empty," I said, peering inside. Something cherry red that rang a distant bell in my head. "Huh." I pulled it out. It was a cardigan. I spread it out on the floor and ran my finger over the buttons. Four big, red buttons, and the top one was a white button with yellow daisies on it. "Oh, my God." The memories flooded back. "This is Callie Kendall's sweater."

"The girl who disappeared?" Devlin asked, peering over my shoulder.

I nodded. "She always had the coolest clothes. She lost a button off of her favorite sweater climbing trees or something, and the next day she came back with this button sewn on. By the next week, all the girls were swapping out their top buttons."

"How did it end up here?" Devlin asked.

I shrugged. "I don't know. All of us Bootleggers played together. She was practically one of us since she spent every single summer here. I probably had her over to play or something. She was the coolest girl I knew," I sighed. "Smart, pretty, nice. She was real quiet, but sometimes she just broke out of her shell, and you felt lucky just to be around her. I was jealous of her, and I looked up to her. If that makes sense. I was devastated when she went missing."

Something was tugging at my memory and then pulled hard. I was missing something important.

"How about we collect our spoils for today and..."

The missing poster flashed into my mind. The piece of paper I'd studied thousands of times in the years since Callie vanished, willing it to give me a clue, to give us all answers.

Last seen wearing denim shorts and a red cardigan sweater.

I dropped the sweater as if it were a rattlesnake.

Chapter Thirty

Devlin

I need you to text the Bodines—just the brothers," I said to Jonah without preamble when I stormed through Gran's door.

"Okaaaay." He drew out the word and put down his sandwich.

"Text them and tell them to get their cowardly asses over here now."

I stomped into the living room and dumped the stack of papers I'd promised Scarlett I'd scan for her and then headed for my bedroom. I needed to shower off the dust and mustiness of Jonah Bodine's house. And I needed to calm myself down before I told three grown men who weren't afraid of a little violence that they needed to grow a collective pair and stop dumping shit on their sister.

She'd been exhausted when we left her father's house. Had even begged off on lunch saying she just wanted to take a nap. She was shaky and overwrought, and I placed the blame squarely on each pair of broad Bodine shoulders. They shouldn't have made her see to their father's house on her own. It had obviously taken a toll. We'd no sooner finished going through the trunk than she'd collapsed in on herself. I'd driven her home—with no argument from her—leaving her truck there.

I stepped under the stream of hot water from the shower head that Scarlett had replaced herself. Just because the woman could do it all didn't mean that she should be expected to do it all. I let the anger simmer. Anger was a welcome change to what I'd felt when I'd first come here. There was strength in anger.

Ten minutes later, I was dressed and pacing the living room when the first car pulled up outside. Bowie didn't even bother knocking. He rushed in through the kitchen door. "Is Scarlett okay? She's not answering her texts."

"No thanks to you," I snapped. "Sit down." If he was surprised by my tone, he didn't show it. I caught Jonah trying to sneak down the hallway toward the stairs. "You too, Bodine."

Jonah slunk into the living room and, shooting me a curious look, took Gran's favorite wingback.

"This better be fucking good," Gibson drawled when he came through the front door. Jameson was behind him. Both were dressed as if I'd interrupted them at work.

Bowie sniffed the air. "Is that burnt arm hair?"

Jameson shrugged. "Phone scared me."

"Sit," I said, jerking my thumb toward the living room.

"What the hell is this, McCallister?" Gibson demanded.

"This is about the three of you acting like chicken shits and dumping everything on your sister."

"Now just a minute here—" Bowie began.

"No. I talk. You fix it. I just came from your father's house with your sister. As you may recall, you dumped the settling of your father's estate on her. Just like you saddled her with the responsibility of his care. She took him to doctor's appointments, filled his refrigerator, drove him to work. What did you three cowards do?"

Gibson rose from the couch, his hands clenched into fists.

"This is none of your fucking business. You don't know what it was like to grow up with him."

I stood in front of him, daring him to take a swing. "No. I don't. But your little sister does. And you're too busy holding onto grudges with a dead man to act like a fucking family."

Gibson narrowed his eyes at me.

"Go ahead," I shrugged. "Take a shot at me, but you know it's true. You know that you three washed your hands and saddled your sister with a responsibility that never should have been hers alone."

I think Gibson was growling at me. But I was going to say it all.

"I just drove her home from your father's house where she was so overwhelmed by memories that she was too upset to drive herself. And which one of you was there for her? Not a single one of you."

"I feel like this is a family thing—" Jonah said, starting to rise from the chair.

"You are family," I told him. "You came here to see what your brothers and sister were like, and here it is. Your brothers are selfish, negligent assholes who expect someone else to clean up their family's mess."

"Scarlett never said she didn't want to do all that," Bowie argued.

"That's not true." Jameson scratched the back of his neck. The room went silent. "She told us all the time. Asked us to run him to appointments toward the end. Wanted us to check in on him when she was working long days and he wasn't with her. She sure as hell didn't want to clean out his house by herself."

Bowie swore quietly and looked at his hands.

"You all think she escaped your collective childhood unscathed? She didn't. She's just the only one of you with the balls to face it and to forgive. And if you keep using her to do the dirty work, you're all cowards."

"She should have come to us rather than sending you—"

I laughed a dry, humorless laugh. "You think she knows I

194

called you all here? You think she wants to ask you to help her? She's tired of being disappointed by you. You'll stick your noses in her love life, but you won't lift a finger to help her take care of your own father. You should be ashamed of yourselves."

They sat, stewing in silence.

"You want to hear the ironic part? The only one of you who volunteered to help her was Jonah. He's also the one with the best reason for not lifting a damn finger. So why don't y'all think about that and get the hell out of my house and fix this for Scarlett."

It was my first official "y'all," and I embraced it.

They left, jaws tight, eyes dark, anger snapping off of their bodies. But not a single one of them bothered trying to defend themselves.

"Man, you must have been one hell of an attorney," Jonah said from his chair.

"Still am. Want a drink?"

"Hell yeah."

I grabbed a couple of beers and headed out to the deck. Summer was slowly sliding into Bootleg, one toe at a time. It was in the midseventies today, and the lake was busy. Fishing boats, pontoon boats, floating decks lazily motored past Gran's deck. People were out enjoying their Saturday without a care to what was going on within the houses that dotted the lake.

I wondered what other secrets, what other skeletons existed in this little lake town.

Jonah joined me on the deck. "That was quite the verbal ass-kicking you gave them."

I opened my beer. "They deserved it. They expect her to take care of everything because they think she wasn't hurt by any of it. But she was the only one of them strong enough to deal with it."

"Think they'll apologize?" Jonah asked.

My lips quirked. "In their own stupid, ineffective way. And maybe Scarlett will finally lay into them like they deserve. And then maybe things will change at least a little bit." My thoughts shifted to my own family. Had I ever really stood up for myself, or had I let myself be pushed down a path I didn't want? Did I even know what I wanted?

"What's all this?" Jonah asked, looking in the tote I'd carried in from the car.

"Scarlett wanted you to see some family history. I think she wanted to look through them with you. But she was pretty worn out and told me to show you."

I saw his hesitation. But Jonah didn't seem like the kind of guy who backed away from discomfort. He pulled the first album out of the bag and settled back in the deck chair. "Is this Scarlett?" he asked, a smile tugging at his lips.

I pulled up the chair next to him and looked. The little girl in pigtails and a pink dress sat astride her father's shoulders, grinning for all she was worth.

For the next half hour, we sat in silence and paged through another family's history.

Chapter Thirty-One

Scarlett

I'd talked myself down from hysteria twice so far and was working my way back up once more as I paced my living room rug. I tried coming at it from every conceivable angle and could not come up with a single reason why my father would have had the sweater Callie Kendall disappeared wearing. Unless he had something to do with that disappearance.

I'd begged off of lunch with Devlin and made up an excuse about being tired. I was so wired with adrenaline I thought I might actually launch into orbit on the ride home. But Devlin didn't ask any questions. Instead, he held my hand the whole way home and then deposited me on my doorstep, promising to take me back to my dad's to get my truck whenever I was ready.

I might never be ready.

I couldn't wrap my head around it. Daddy was many things, lots of them bad. But he wasn't a kidnapper, a killer. I couldn't believe it. I wouldn't believe it.

I shot an apprehensive glance at the sweater, folded neatly

on my kitchen counter. By itself, it was harmless. It was just cotton and buttons. But the bigger picture was much darker. This could be the first clue in a twelve-year-old cold case, and it pointed squarely at my father.

Maybe he'd found it somewhere? Alongside the road or in a ditch. There was no crime in that. But then why would it have been tucked away, hidden like a family memento... or a trophy?

I shook the thought out of my head. I couldn't go there.

My father was no murderer.

And how many others would believe like I did, I thought. I couldn't even count on my own brothers to know that Daddy wouldn't have done this. Gibson wouldn't even be surprised. He'd take it as a vindication that our father was as bad as he'd claimed him to be for all these years.

"Fuck," I muttered to myself. "And things were going so good, too."

The knock at my door shoved my heart into my throat. I raced the four steps into the kitchen and grabbed the sweater that I'd shoved in a sealable freezer bag. It was evidence.

"Scar? Open up." It was Bowie.

"Shit, shit, shit." I ran around in a circle like a teenage boy about to get busted in his girlfriend's bedroom. Finally, I stuffed the sweater under the couch cushion and tried to look natural when I opened the door.

"What's wrong?" Bowie asked.

Damn him and his stupid sensitive nature.

"Nothing. What do you want?" I asked woodenly.

Jameson stared at me. "We're sorry," he announced.

"Great. I accept. Now, if you'll excuse me, I'm busy." I tried to shut the door on them, but they muscled their way inside.

"Now, Scarlett," Bowie drawled. It's how he always talked me down with his annoying logic and his shiny good nature.

"Don't 'now Scarlett' me. I just don't feel like talking right now."

"And we're here to talk about why you don't feel like talking."

There was no fucking way in the entire world that they could know what I'd found. *Unless, they were in on it? Oh my God. What if my brothers caught Daddy—*

"Sit," Jameson ordered, shoving me into Gram's rocking chair.

"Jesus, Scar. You look like you're gonna pass out. Do you need a doctor?" Bowie asked, crouching down in front of me.

I sprang out of the chair like a jack-in-the-box and side-stepped him. "Can y'all just tell me why you're here so we can all get on with our lives?" I demanded.

Bowie and Jameson exchanged a look. I'd seen that look every time I had my period in my teens and they bore the brunt of my hormones.

"Do you want like a hot pad or some chocolate?" Bowie ventured.

"What I want is for you to get to the point and then get out."

"We're sorry for being assholes," Jameson said. He made himself comfortable on my couch. On the cushion under which I'd just shoved evidence in a case that had fascinated the east coast for over a decade.

I swallowed hard. "Be more specific."

Bowie took a deep breath. "We're sorry for expecting you to take care of everything related to Dad, including his house."

"Apology accepted. Go away."

"Now, don't be like that, Scarlett. We were wrong. And it was unfair of us to expect you to handle everything just because we had grudges and hard feelings."

"Speaking of grudges and hard feelings, where's Gibson?" I asked.

They shared another look. Gibson's MO was to run off when things got tricky or sticky or annoying. "Y'all have been doing this for years. Why the sudden apology?" I caught the winces.

"It's been brought to our attention that—"

"Devlin called us chickenshits," Jameson said, cutting to the chase.

"He saw how hard all of this is on you. Something that none of us ever noticed before, and we're sorry," Bowie added.

I did not have time for this. "I get it. You're sorry. Can we just skip ahead to the 'everybody's fine' part and call it a day?" That sweater was going to develop a telltale heartbeat any second now.

"I don't think we should skip ahead in this situation," Bowie argued. "See, I feel like we've spent several years screwing up, and a couple of apologies aren't really enough."

"And Gibson feels like he doesn't have anything to apologize for, right?" I added.

"You know, Gibs," Jameson said cryptically. I did. And there were certain things we all knew without talking about. One of those things was that Gibson saw my loyalty to our father as a disloyalty to him.

I avoided looking at the couch, just in case they'd notice my attention.

"Scar, we're family," Bowie said, taking my chin in his hand. "We should be in things together, and I'm sorry for expecting you to handle all of this shit on your own. It's not gonna be that way anymore. I'm goin' to Dad's tomorrow."

"Me, too," Jameson sighed.

"We'll get this settled together, and then we'll move on together," Bowie promised. "That's how it should have been from the beginning. You've been toughing it out for a long time on your own, and I don't want you to ever feel like that again."

"Damn it, Bowie." I stomped my foot on the wood floor. "You couldn't just leave, could you?"

"What?" He looked startled.

Sonsabitches wanted to be family? Then they deserved to suffer with me. "Get up, Jameson." My brother did as he was told while looking at me like I was having a breakdown. Who knows? Maybe I was.

I pulled the sweater out from under the cushion and threw

the baggy on the coffee table. "Now, how are we going to deal with this as a family?" I demanded.

They stared down on it.

"Um. Is it too small?" Bowie asked. "Maybe we could order a new one?"

"It's a nice color for you," Jameson offered.

"Christ!" I stormed over to my kitchen and dug through drawers until I found what I was looking for. "Here."

I threw the old Missing poster on top of the sweater. Jameson picked it up and frowned. I saw the instant he got the connection. The tightening of his jaw, the narrowing of his eyes. He handed the poster to Bowie and stared at me.

"Where did it come from?" he asked me flatly.

"Holy fucking shit, Scar. You didn't kill her, did you?" Bowie asked, dumbfounded.

I don't know why I found it funny. Or maybe I didn't find it funny at all and was just flat out hysterical. But I collapsed to the floor laughing so hard I cried.

"You automatically assume I had something to do with it?" Hadn't I done the same toward my father?

"It was a knee-jerk reaction," Bowie said defensively, staring at Callie's sweater like it was an angry boar.

"I found it in Mama's trunk upstairs," I told them. "I recognized it right away because of the button. Remember how every girl in Bootleg swapped out their top button for a year afterwards? He'd packed a bunch of stuff in there. Family photos, some of Mama's clothes, and this was in the very bottom."

Jameson picked up the bag and examined the sweater. He dropped it, his face pale. "It's stained."

"What?" I asked, snatching it back from him. I held it up to the light, and there was a little pattern of stains. "It looks like drops or splatter."

"Blood," Jameson said quietly.

"He didn't do it," I said, shaking my head. Someone needed to say the words out loud. I braced for their argument, held my breath.

Bowie, still staring at the offending sweater, remained silent. "Devlin know about this?" he finally asked.

I shook my head. "He knows I found the sweater, and he knows it was hers, but he doesn't know she disappeared wearing it."

"He's a smart guy, Scar. How long does he have to be in Bootleg before he knows every detail of the Kendall girl's disappearance?"

I scrubbed my hands over my face. "What do we do? I mean, I know we have to turn it over to the cops, but…"

The "but" hung in the air.

"But what?" Bowie asked. "We have to take this to Sheriff Tucker."

Jameson swiped a hand over his forehead. "I don't know man. What if it was an accident?"

"What kind of accident?" Bowie demanded.

"What if he was driving drunk that night. She left the lake, and it was dark, right?"

My stomach dropped out. My brothers believed there was a possibility that our father had done this.

"And then what?" I demanded, my voice a near shriek. "He dumped her body in the lake? He buried her in our backyard? He wouldn't have done that. You can't believe that."

"What's the other option, Scar?" Jameson demanded. "Why else would he have her blood-stained sweater hidden away?"

"We have to take this to the sheriff," Bowie said again.

"And say what? Our dad might be a murderer? You know what that will do," Jameson argued.

"We'll all be guilty by gossip," I said to myself.

"We can't not take this to the cops. There's blood on it. This might be the answer that that poor girl's parents have been looking for," Bowie said.

"But it might not be the right answer, Bowie," I argued. "Before we throw ourselves on the mercy of this town and beg them to believe us, don't you think we owe it to Daddy to at least dig a little deeper ourselves?"

"We're not crime scene investigators," Bowie snapped. "We have evidence in the highest profile missing person case in the state, and you want to sit on it and hope that our father had nothing to do with it?"

"We vote then," I said. Jameson was with me. Together we could overrule Bowie.

"We're not all here," Bowie said.

Gibson would love to crucify Daddy in the court of public opinion. To have the rest of the town believe like he did, that Daddy was a low down, dirty loser? Gibson would gladly sell us all out for that tasty slice of revenge.

"Look," I began. "I agree that we need the police at some point. But can we just sleep on it? Bow, I'm not ready for everyone to start looking at us as the reason she's gone. Think about it. Your job could be on the line. What will your friends say? Your neighbors?" I was shamelessly pushing him to think of Cassidy. And it was all selfish.

The second the sweater went to the cops was the moment I'd have to say goodbye to Devlin.

"This is a fucking nightmare," he said.

"No one can know about this for now, Bowie," I told him. Not Dev, not Cass. And I wasn't even sure about Gibson at this point.

"So, what do we do?" Bowie asked.

"We think back. Where were we when Callie went missing? Do we remember anything specific about Dad at the time?"

"How the hell are we supposed to remember?" Bowie growled in irritation. "It was over a decade ago."

"It's one of those things where you always remember where you were when it happened," I told him.

"Gibson's," Jameson said suddenly.

I looked at him, the memory dawning. "Yeah. That's right. We were all at Gibson's. Cassidy called over to tell us."

"Why were we all at Gibson's apartment?" Bowie asked, frown lines carving into his forehead.

Chapter Thirty-Two
Scarlett

The subterfuge was killing me. I'd been avoiding Devlin for twenty-four hours. Good guy that he was, he was giving me space with the occasional sweet reminder by text or voicemail that he was around if I wanted to talk or not talk.

I didn't go back to Daddy's house. I'd promised I wouldn't go there without Bowie or Jameson, and to be honest, it hadn't been a hard promise to make. One little sweater, tucked in the corner of memories, and the whole house felt foreign to me. Everything felt strange and new as if my childhood hadn't been what I thought it had. My family hadn't been who I was sure they were.

There was one person who might have some answers, and I wasn't looking forward to asking him the questions. After he ignored my texts and calls for a full day, I decided enough was enough. Gibson Bodine would talk to me if I had to string him upside down over a camp fire.

I hopped in my pickup that Devlin and Jonah had thoughtfully returned to me and headed up the mountain. Gibson took his outsider role seriously, building himself a cabin on three acres of woods on a dead-end lane half a mile back from the road. The land had belonged to our grandfather. The shack that still stood at the backside of the property was where Great-Granddaddy Jedidiah hid his still during Prohibition.

Gibson's only neighbors were deer and bear and birds. Just the way he liked it.

His house was dark, but the lights were on in his shop. He'd built a metal pole building to house his cabinetry business and spent more time out there than inside the house. He was a restless soul, preferring to work long into the night than make small talk with acquaintances over beer. Everyone in town believed him to be the asshole our father had told him he was his whole life, and they accepted it about him. Gibson had never seemed inclined to prove them wrong, even though I knew there was more to him than a bad temper and broody looks.

I pushed open the heavy door next to the garage bay. He was sanding down a set of base cabinets. The space smelled of sawdust and stain. Gibson, asshole that he was, was a master craftsman and made beautiful cabinetry. He charged a hell of a premium, too. But he poured his heart and soul into every piece, making them perfect in ways he could never be.

"I'm busy," he said without turning around.

In a way, Gibson and I were the closest out of the siblings. Jameson was off in his own world, creating art, avoiding people. Helpful, friendly Bowie, on the other hand, immersed himself in the outside world. But Gibs and I understood each other. Even though we didn't always agree.

"I need to talk to you about something," I told him, sliding onto a padded stool against his lacquer red metal cabinets. "It's bad."

I saw the hitch in his shoulders, and then he turned to face me. "What?"

No matter what went on in our normal daily life, no matter how much my love of our daddy upset him, I could always count on him. "I found something when I was cleaning out his house."

Gibson wiped his hands with a cloth and tossed his safety glasses onto a work table. He strolled over to a mini fridge and pulled out two bottles of water. He tossed one to me, and I caught it in midair.

"Go on."

I wasn't going to sugar coat it for him. "I found the sweater that Callie Kendall disappeared in. It's stained with what might be blood."

He stared at me as if I weren't speaking English. "You're fucking with me."

I shook my head. "I wish I were. It's hers, Gibs. The top button—"

"Daisies," he said, interrupting me. And I wondered how in the hell he remembered that. But then again, everyone in Bootleg knew everything about Callie except where she disappeared to.

I pressed on. "We were all at your apartment when she went missing. We spent the night."

He took another drink and looked away. Remembering.

"Why were we there, Gibs? I was fourteen, Jameson sixteen, and Bowie eighteen. Why did we spend the night at your apartment?"

I closed my eyes and prayed for an answer that wouldn't gut me.

"It was a long time ago," he hedged.

"Gibs."

He sighed and pulled out a stool that matched mine from under a sawdust-encrusted table. "Mom called. She asked."

"She just asked you to keep the three of us at your place that night?"

He shrugged tired shoulders. "I don't know. It was late. Like after ten. She sounded upset. Said it would help her out. I assumed they were fighting."

What did Mama know? What was there for her to know?

206

I rubbed my forehead, a new worry blooming bright. "It wouldn't have been the first time," I said. They'd fought before. Usually Gibs or Bowie would keep me entertained in their rooms until the shouting stopped. Sometimes we went to Cassidy and June's house and stayed there until the fight was over and all was normal again.

"Bowie drove y'all over," Gibson said with a small smile.

"Did you think it was odd that she asked you to keep us for the night and then Callie up and went missing?" I asked.

"The connection never occurred to me," he said. "You think he didn't have anything to do with it."

"He" meaning our father. And it definitely wasn't a question.

I shook my head and jumped on the defensive. "I know what you're gonna say, Gibs. Daddy was many things. But he didn't take Callie. He didn't hurt her."

"Then how the fuck did her sweater end up in his house?"

"He could have found it—"

His rage, poker hot, surprised me. He threw his half-empty water bottle across the room. "When are you going to finally realize what a low-life he was, Scar?"

"He never hit us," I said, rallying. It was an old argument.

"Since when in the fuck should that ever be the line?" Gibson demanded. "Why would everything else up to physical abuse be okay? He told me over and over again that I ruined his life. That I was the reason he wasn't off playin' in a band or makin' something of himself. He told me I was *nothing*."

Gibson came by his musical talent honestly. But as a "fuck you" to our father, he purposely never pursued it.

I wasn't hurt by the anger I heard behind the words. That was Gibson, a walking fit of rage. It was the pain that got me.

"I'm so sorry," I whispered.

"He told me I was nothing. And you know what? He was right. Because I'm just like him. He made sure Bowie knew he'd never be good enough for him no matter how hard he tried. And Jameson? He shut that boy down every time he came in for a hug, every time he asked to go fishing, every time he made that fucker a special drawing. Jonah Bodine crushed his spirit, Scarlett, and the sooner you realize what a monster he was, the better."

I had tears spilling down my cheeks now. We'd danced around this topic for years, neither one of us ever daring to say all of the words.

"He was sick, Gibs. Sick. Alcoholism is a fucking disease like cancer or Alzheimer's."

"He had a damn choice in the way he treated us."

"Did you deserve better?" I asked, my voice breaking and echoing around the metal walls. "Of course, you did. We *all* did. We deserved a dad who would be there for us. One who'd coach the soccer team or cook dinner or even just listen when we spoke. One who didn't look at each one of us as the ball and chain to a life he never wanted. But we didn't have that. We had him."

"And he's gone now. Finally," Gibson spat out.

"Jesus, Gibs. He was our father."

"He was *nothing* to me. And now? Now, you expect me to give him the benefit of the doubt and say maybe this drunken asshole didn't have something to do with that girl's disappearance? Then how the fuck did that sweater end up in his house?"

"I don't know, but I believe—"

"Goddamn it, Scarlett!" Gibson snarled. "Stop it. Just stop defending him!"

"Jameson doesn't think he did it—"

Gibson rounded on me. "They know?"

I nodded. "I told them when they came to apologize to me for being fucking lousy brothers and dumping all of the responsibility on me!" It wasn't fair, but I was tired of being fair. I was tired of brushing things under the rug and hoping they'd get better. "You saddled me with him for all these years because you couldn't handle dealing with him."

"Fuck you, Scarlett."

"Fuck you back, Gibson."

I hopped off my stool and flipped him the bird for good

measure. "You have fun up here in your lair avoiding life while I clean all of this up for you. As usual!"

I didn't hear his response because I slammed the door so hard the garage doors rattled. I'd expected it to go this way. But that didn't mean I was happy about being right just this once.

Chapter Thirty-Three

Devlin

"You can't just will her to appear, man," Jonah said as I peered through the deck doors at the bright midmorning. It was Day Three of no Scarlett.

"Don't you have something to do?" I asked mildly, knowing full well he didn't.

Between the two of us spending just about all day, every day, together, we were entering territory where someone's face was going to get beat.

One of us needed a job. Or my fucking girlfriend needed to come back. She was still responding to texts. But she wouldn't pick up the damn phone, and she wouldn't talk to me about what was wrong. That wasn't like her. Scarlett Bodine didn't *not* talk about what was on her mind.

I'd given her about as much space as I was willing.

"I've got nothing but time on my hands," Jonah said airily, but I could hear the irritation in his tone.

We needed to get out of the house.

"You want to get out of here? Maybe get a pepperoni roll?" I suggested.

"Yes and yes."

We took Jonah's car, a late model Mustang, and dropped the top to cruise into Bootleg. In the sunshine, we drove down crowded Main Street and turned onto Bathtub Gin Alley to complete the circuit. There wasn't much to Bootleg. Most of the retail spaces occupied those two streets. And it was a busy day in town with tourists enjoying the charm.

We ordered pepperoni rolls to go from the Moonshine Diner. It seemed a crime to avoid the fine early summer weather, so we took the food down to the lakefront. There were people here. Families on the sandy beach. Kids splashing in the bath water warm lake. Teenage girls sunning themselves and giggling over the antics of sunburnt teenage boys.

I pointed to an empty picnic table under a copse of trees, and we snagged it and sat.

We ate in silence, staring off at the blue of the lake, the reflections of the sun on its choppy surface.

"What would you be doing on a morning like this a couple of weeks ago?" I asked Jonah.

He chewed his mouthful of pepperoni goodness and thought. "I'd be telling Mike that he didn't need that donut, and if he thought about it again, he'd have to give me twenty."

"Why can't Mike have the donut?"

"Because he paid me a lot of money to be his personal trainer. And part of that job was slapping food out of his hands. Same with his wife Betsy who *did* listen to me and dropped thirty pounds over the course of a year."

"Do you like what you do?" I asked. I'd been giving a lot of thought to actually loving something versus doing what was expected. The difference had never been more striking.

"Yeah. I do. The human body is an amazing thing. It's capable of miracles, even with all the abuse and donuts we heap upon ourselves," Jonah said.

I stared out at the lake and thought about the toll I'd allowed stress to take on me. How much better I felt now that I was—sporadically—putting forth a physical effort.

"How about you?" Jonah asked.

I sighed. "If we were in session, I'd be sitting surrounded by my party delegates while we tried to stop the other side from accomplishing anything. Then, around lunch time, we'd switch. There were some days that felt like our entire focus was stopping the state from accomplishing anything."

"How about when you weren't in session?"

"I'm a partner in the family law firm. There are always cases to consult on, court dates, clients."

"Sounds busy," Jonah ventured.

I shrugged. "Most of my time was spent focusing on how to get to the next step. How to get re-elected. How to go from state legislator to federal. Who to meet. Who to side with. Who to befriend."

We sat in silence for a few minutes watching everyone else around us.

"Do you ever feel like your whole life is in limbo?" Jonah asked finally.

"Only from the second I wake up until I close my eyes at night."

He gave a half-laugh. "What are we doing here?" he asked. Jonah didn't mean here at the lake on a weekday morning.

"I'm not sure. Recuperating? Restarting? Reviving?"

"Until I got here, I didn't even know I had anything to recuperate from," Jonah admitted.

"I guess sometimes it can just sneak up on you."

"Did you like your life? I mean, before here."

"I thought I did. Until it all fell apart, and then I realized I couldn't remember the last time I felt happy. You?"

Jonah shrugged. "I don't know. I was happy. I liked my job, my apartment, my life. But maybe something always felt like it was missing?"

I nodded. "And if you just kept busy, just kept moving forward, maybe that feeling would go away."

"Yeah. I didn't want my mom to ever think that she wasn't enough. That I was wishing for a father she couldn't give me."

"Have you told her you're here?" I asked.

He blew out a breath and wadded up the wax paper from his pepperoni roll. "Yeah. After Scarlett gave you the albums to give to me. It wasn't a great conversation. But I wasn't going to lie to her about where I am and what I'm doing."

"Do you think the Bodines are the missing piece?"

He arched an eyebrow at me. "Do you think Scarlett Bodine is *your* missing piece?" he shot back.

"I'd like to request a recess," I joked.

"Motion denied."

I tilted my head back, enjoying the feel of the sun warm on my face. "I don't know what I think. But I sure like her, and I sure like this pepperoni roll."

"I guess that's good enough for today. You know, sooner or later, we're both going to have to decide if it's time to move on, stay put, or go back."

Sooner or later was not today.

———

We headed home happy to have at least left the house.

I unlocked the front door—a habit I just couldn't quite give up—and let us in. I was delighted to spy a lithe brunette lounging on the back deck.

"What do you know?" Jonah said. "You did will her to appear."

"Must have been the hot springs," I joked. I headed down the hallway and crossed the living room, trying not to appear too eager. When I opened the deck door, Scarlett tilted her head backwards and raised her sunglasses.

"Hi," I said quietly.

"Howdy, neighbor."

"Long time, no see."

She grimaced. "Yeah, about that…"

I shook my head. "Yeah, about that…" I parroted. I wished I could see her eyes because something flickered across her face, an emotion I couldn't quite define.

"I had a rougher time than I thought at Daddy's house. Thank you for verbally kicking my brothers' asses."

"It had to be done."

She nodded. "It did, and maybe my own needed a little kick too to finally tell them I didn't want to do all this on my own."

"I just hope it wasn't too little too late."

She stood and padded to me barefoot. Her toenails were sparkly red. She slipped her lean arms around my waist and squeezed. "I have a favor to ask you, but first I was wondering if Jonah would like to see some more albums. I brought mine."

She wasn't telling me everything, and I already knew what that felt like, already knew what that did to a relationship. I wasn't signing up for that again.

"I think Jonah would appreciate that," I said stiffly. I pulled out of her embrace to leave.

"It doesn't have anything to do with you, Dev," she said. "It's a family thing."

That was one thing I did understand: family secrets. Everything my family did was cloaked from the outside world so as to remain above reproach in public. A shiny veneer cloaking the humanity beneath.

I nodded, still not appeased. "I'll get Jonah."

I found him inside flipping through a fishing magazine. *God, we both needed to get a life. And soon.* "Hey, Scarlett has something for you," I said, jerking my head toward the deck.

He straightened out of his slump on the couch.

"Cool. Hey, listen. I noticed you've been working out a bit. If you need any guidance, I can help."

"It beats sitting around waiting on the Bodines," I said.

He gave a crooked grin. "Ain't that the truth."

I left them alone and powered up my laptop in the little room Estelle had converted into an office on the first floor. For the first time since I'd laid eyes on Scarlett, I wondered if I was making a mistake staying here.

There were more emails from my attorney. One from

Blake, the PR rep, and two from Johanna herself. They'd been sent two days apart. Just seeing her name in my inbox sent my blood pressure skyrocketing. I was a bandage ripper. I always had been, at least until my life imploded leaving me abundantly cautious... or cowardly. I opened them both and held my breath.

To: Devlin
From: Johanna
Subject: Us

I think we need to talk. Please call me.
J

To: Devlin
From: Johanna
Subject: Need to talk

I think I made a mistake.
J

I didn't ask to be her ex. She'd given me no choice. But there was nothing gratifying about seeing that email. She had made a mistake, but I had no interest in fixing it. It had been a mistake to marry on the premise as tenuous as shared goals. People changed. Goals changed. I'd married a teammate, not a soulmate. And that teammate had let me down. I wasn't going to hang around waiting for her to do it again.

I decided not to respond. I didn't owe her anything. Not with the generous pre-nup that our marriage had been built upon. Not with the divorce settlement that our attorneys had hashed out. I was done.

I opened the attorney's email next. Antonia was a partner in my family's law firm. Smart, sharp, and mean as a snake when it came to negotiations.

To: Devlin
From: Antonia
Subject: Divorce update

The papers will be signed and filed within two weeks.
You're almost a free man. Try not to fuck it up.
Antonia

I skimmed Blake's email. It was more of the same. With an interesting tidbit at the end. Stephan Channing, a fellow legislator, was under investigation by an ethics committee for improper conduct. Word on the street was sexual harassment that escalated into the state senator being reported for trespassing at the homes of two female aides.

This could be your ticket back. Keeping my ear to the ground for more news.

A new scandal meant mine could be quietly swept under the rug. By the time my next session began, my divorce would be settled, and someone else would be under the microscope. I'd be free to start back on my path.

Why didn't that make me feel vindicated? Bootleg was messing with my motivation.

I answered a few more emails, scrolled through my texts, and gave my two cents on a few cases at the firm. I touched base with my assistant who'd become rather free range since my abrupt departure, and we discussed the latest rounds of invites and events. The only one that sounded remotely interesting to me was an outdoor barbeque reception for Maryland Legal Aid, a cause I was particularly passionate about. The event was in Annapolis tonight.

I could make it. But did I want to test the waters?

I put it on the back burner along with the handful of requests for comment from a few of the more tenacious media members who bypassed the family mouthpiece. It appeared that interest in my divorce was indeed fading.

"Devlin!" Two voices called in singsong.

I sighed and closed my laptop. "What?" I called back.

"Come out here," Scarlett pleaded.

I took my time, stopping for a glass of water in the kitchen before joining them on the deck.

"Devlin, look what Jonah's mama sent him," Scarlett said, tapping a photo album with her unpainted fingernail.

"I told her we were exchanging childhood memories, and she reluctantly agreed to send this," Jonah explained. "It's my early years."

The picnic table was scattered with other albums, Scarlett's I guessed. The resemblance between Jonah and the rest of the Bodines in childhood was unmistakable.

"Is your mama okay with you bein' here?" Scarlett asked, flipping the page and cooing over a little Jonah on a spotted pony.

Jonah kicked back in his chair. "She's not thrilled, but she did overnight the album."

Scarlett raised her gaze to mine. "I can understand how family bonds get tricky."

She was sending me a message, begging me to understand. I looked away.

"What's your mama like?" Scarlett asked Jonah.

"She's the best. Tough lady. Takes no crap but has a real soft center."

"She sounds wonderful. I hope I can meet her sometime. Is there anything you want to know about our daddy?" she asked softly.

Jonah looked pensive for a moment. "I don't know. I guess, was it all bad? Did I miss out on not having him around?"

Scarlett sat thoughtfully with the questions. "It wasn't all bad, no. But it was all inconsistent. Never knowing if you were coming home to happy Mom and Dad or miserable Mom and Dad. That takes a toll. Daddy got worse after Mama died. There wasn't much good after that. You had to look for it pretty hard. But I still would have liked for you to get to know him. At least then you'd have some answers."

They flipped through photos and shared stories. And from the outside, I could see the bond they were forging strengthen. Scarlett was claiming Jonah as family. I wondered what she'd do when he decided to go back or move on. I wondered what she'd do when I decided.

After a while, Jonah excused himself to make some calls, and I took his seat at the table next to Scarlett.

"Gibson and I are fightin'," she admitted as she packed up her albums into the tote.

"I'm sorry to hear that."

"It was a long time coming," she sighed. "Can I ask you that favor now?" Her sweet gray eyes pleaded with me.

"Sure," I said. Just because she was asking didn't mean I had to say yes. She shut me out, and thanks to my family's reaction to my failed marriage and the near implosion of my career, I had a sore spot in that area.

"I was wondering if you wanted to get away for a night? You know. Get out of Bootleg and go someplace."

"Don't you have work?" I asked.

She shook her head. "I have a handyman I can pawn the maintenance calls off on for twenty-four hours or so."

"Where do you want to go?" I asked.

"Anywhere."

Chapter Thirty-Four

Scarlett

Are you sure I'm dressed all right?" I asked, brushing my palms over the hem of my strapless sun dress. It was blue and white with giant flowers all over it. The waist nipped in and the skirt flared out. I'd bought it on a whim and found no occasions to wear it in Bootleg.

"You look amazing," Devlin assured me. He was wearing stone gray trousers and a simple white button-down that looked way too good on him.

"I feel pretty fancy for a barbeque," I confessed.

He grinned at me from behind his sunglasses as he drove. And my heart gave that awkward flip-flop. He seemed less mad at me now, and I was grateful for it. I didn't like keeping secrets, but this was one mess I wasn't eager to drag anyone into.

"It's a pretty fancy barbeque," he said.

"What if I don't fit in?" I asked.

"Is that fear I hear? Who are you, and what have you done with Scarlett?" he teased.

"I'm not scared," I said, horrified at the accusation. "I've just never gone to a political function with my politician boyfriend before."

"I think you'll be just fine. Keep in mind that they're all people too."

"Yeah," I scoffed. "People with trust funds and ivy league degrees. I'm Scarlett Bodine from Bootleg, West Virginia. My roots include an alcoholic daddy and a bootleggin' great-granddad."

I laughed. "Everyone's got their dirty little secrets. They're just not as up front about them as you are."

"Will Johanna be there?" I asked.

The smile evaporated from his face, and I wished I hadn't asked the question.

"She won't be, but people who know her—knew us—will be."

"Do you want me to pretend we're not having sex?" I offered. If he said yes, I was going to forget that I was trying to make it up to him for avoiding him.

"Scarlett, I don't want you to pretend anything ever with me. Least of all that everything's okay when it clearly isn't."

Ah, shit. A direct hit.

"I know I owe you an explanation."

"Yeah, you do."

"And I know I owe you an apology."

"Yep."

"But I can't give you an explanation because I don't want to drag you into family business. And I'm no damn good at apologies."

"So I'm just supposed to leave it at that?" Devlin didn't look happy.

"No! You're supposed to let me make it up to you."

He muttered something under his breath about the "fucking Bodines," and we rode the rest of the way to Annapolis in silence.

I'd been here years ago in junior high for a field trip. But back then, I'd been more interested in flirting with boys and giggling with Cassidy to pay much attention.

"This is the cutest town I've ever seen," I said, peering through the window at the red brick buildings and narrow streets. "It's so neat and tidy."

"There's the marina," Devlin said, pointing through the windshield. Sailboats and fishing boats bobbed tied up to docks and mooring balls. A huge wooden schooner cruised out into open water. "And down this street is where I used to live. The house went up for sale as part of the divorce settlement."

"Where do you live now?" I asked, craning my neck to get a better look at his past.

"My family has a condo no one was using. It's mine to use until I figure out what I'm doing next."

I didn't say anything, but I linked my fingers through his. I wondered if he noticed how he tensed up when he talked about the unknown of the future.

"So where is this shindig tonight?" I asked, changing the subject.

Fifteen minutes later, we'd left the city limits behind us and turned onto a paved private drive that snaked its way toward the bay. I whistled when the house came into view. It was a sprawling New England Colonial with dark, faded cedar shingles and trim. The dizzying rooflines made the home look even grander. There was a fountain in the center of the circular driveway. And between the house and the glint of the bay stood a huge white tent billowing in the breeze. Devlin pulled his SUV up to the front porch, and I eyed the long line of brand new cars that looked like they were on a luxury car lot.

"This is Dr. and Mrs. Contee's house. They're hefty campaign donors with a laundry list of pet causes. Tonight we're raising awareness for Maryland Legal Aid."

My hands had gone icy in my lap. I didn't usually intimidate easily. But I felt like I'd turned into Cinderella for a night when all I really wanted to be was a pumpkin… or a bumpkin.

I stuck my chin out. *I was going to be the best damn bumpkin these folks had ever had the misfortune of meeting.*

Devlin squeezed my hand as if he was reading my mind.

"If you're not having a good time, we can leave at any time," he promised.

I nodded.

"And they're probably going to pump you for information about the divorce, my work, bad blood between me and Johanna's whatever-he-is. They're going to assume that you're a gold digger or that we were also having an affair. Also, they won't say anything bad to your face. So, take comfort in that."

I laughed. "Basically, I'm the new kid walking into my first day of high school."

"Essentially. Just with more gray hair and money in this cafeteria."

I nodded, happy to at least know the score. "Let's do this."

We turned the SUV over to the smartly uniformed valet and entered through the front door where we were greeted by one of the party organizers. "Devlin McCallister, so lovely to see you again," a woman in a smart red blazer said with a wan smile. "Please join the others in the backyard. Have a lovely time."

Devlin's grip tightened on my hand, and I realized I wasn't the only nervous one.

"Everything is going to be just fine," I assured him. "If you're not having fun, we can leave after half an hour."

He laughed at me turning his words back on him and slung his arm around my shoulder, drawing me into his side. "I'm glad you're here for my first foray back into real life," he whispered in my ear.

I got goosebumps from his lips brushing my ear lobe. I realized this was more of a test for him than me. If Devlin could be welcomed back, he could resume his career and carry on with his life. A life that was two hours away from Bootleg Springs.

"Devlin McCallister! I haven't seen you since…"

Devlin kept his arm anchored firmly around my waist and made a dozen introductions that I promptly forgot. We met the hosts, a lovely couple in their midsixties who were half in the bag from the signature punch the caterer had whipped up.

Someone handed me a glass of champagne. An actual glass, outside on the stamped concrete patio. Either rich people didn't drop things, or they didn't care if something broke since they weren't the ones cleaning it up.

Every time someone tried to squirrel me away for some gossip, Devlin reclaimed me and expertly ended the interaction.

"You are good at this," I whispered to him as we walked away from a curvy lady with a Liza Minnelli-worthy wig who'd done her damnedest to get Devlin to admit he was devastated over his divorce.

"You're not half bad yourself," he said, leaning in to press a kiss to my cheek.

Liza had shut the hell up when I'd giggled and batted my eye lashes. "Are people still talking about that? That was months ago! I swear, sometimes I feel like some of us never got out of junior high," I'd said.

"McCallister."

I felt Devlin tense against me, and I turned to face the enemy. He was tall and lean with sandy hair and a toothpaste commercial smile. He was wearing dark blue slacks a striped button-down and glossy loafers. Everything about him said subtle and successful.

"Anderson, good to see you," Devlin said offering his hand. The man shook it with energy. Definitely a politician in the making. "This is Scarlett Bodine. Scarlett this is Les Anderson."

"A pleasure," Les said smoothly.

"How y'all doin'?"

He seemed delighted by my accent. His professional smile disappeared and was replaced with a real one. "Well, well. We've all been wondering where McCallister was, and judging by your voice, I can hedge a guess."

I slid my arm through Devlin's. "Dev and I have been enjoying our time together in West Virginia."

Les's eyes widened just the slightest bit. "And here I thought you were off licking your wounds," he said.

"He's been too busy licking other things," I announced.

Devlin coughed, and I realized I may have gone a bit too far. I was used to throwing down insults with Misty Lynn. We didn't have to worry about holding back for polite society being that there was no polite society in Bootleg.

Les smiled approvingly. I couldn't tell if he actually liked me or liked the gossip I was providing. "You two up for some horseshoes?"

I perked up. If I was good at pool—and I sure as shootin' was—I was even better at horseshoes. "That's up to Scarlett," Devlin said, deferring to me.

"Maybe you can show me, just like you taught me how to play pool." I winked.

Devlin laughed, catching my drift.

Les signaled to another man, short and stout, wearing a red tie and a sheen of sweat, and pointed toward the horseshoe court.

Introductions were made. The sweaty newcomer was Lewis, a junior assistant district attorney. He seemed relieved that his small talk duties were officially over.

"Teams?" Les drawled, flagging down a server and distributing beers amongst our foursome.

"Dibs on Scarlett," Devlin said.

———

"Well, my, my. I believe I just won again," I said feigning surprise as my last horseshoe encircled the stake.

"You, Scarlett, are a sneaky, scheming, scam artist. Have you thought about getting into politics?" Les asked with a quick grin.

"Only so far as it involves getting into Devlin's pants," I teased.

Les threw his head back and laughed. "Your Scarlett is a breath of fresh air," he told Devlin when he approached.

Devlin slid his hands around my waist in easy affection.

"That she is," he agreed. I leaned into him. Maybe this whole politician party thing wasn't so bad after all?

"If y'all will excuse me, I'm going to find the restroom and another round of beers," I said excusing myself.

"Don't get lost," Devlin said gruffly. I winked at him and followed the brass walkway lights back to the patio. A mustached man wearing a bow tie held the door for me and gave me a mock bow.

I was killing this politician's girlfriend thing. Everyone was so happy to see Devlin being so happy. I stepped into the powder room. When I was done, I checked my makeup and was carefully reapplying my lipstick when I heard voices in the hallway.

"Can you believe he had the nerve to show up here with her?" a woman asked in gratuitous glee.

"Johanna is not going to be happy that her soon-to-be ex is slumming it with some redneck. I mean, she said *y'all!*"

They laughed, a tinkling cultured laugh that they probably practiced, and I saw red. Bloody murder, bleeding nose red.

"Devlin acts like this was just a little ding to his career, but he's hanging by a thread. One false step, one wrong move, and he's done. Everything his parents have worked for will have been a complete waste."

"I know," the other woman crowed. "Him showing up with some twenty-year-old hillbilly is just too much. He's going to need a permanent mental health leave, not just a temporary one."

I stared at my reflection long and hard. I was Scarlett Motherfucking Bodine. And I was a liability. I had no idea what a politician's girlfriend would do. What Johanna would do. So I did what I'd do.

I yanked the door open. "Hey, y'all. Funny thing. These walls are so thin!"

They gawked at me, looking as though they'd been cut from the same perfect postured, no-assed cloth.

"I feel real bad about eavesdroppin' on y'all because now I'm just gonna make it my personal mission to find out everything there is to know about you. I'm gonna know which one of you is sleepin' with your golf pro and which one of you binge eats cartons of ice cream until you vomit." I took a step closer, and they both took one back, crowding closer to each other for support.

"I'm going to find out where you volunteer and get you kicked off of every board of every organization. And I'll make it my j-o-b to ruin your boring little lives. Just for fun."

I wiggled my fingers at them and started to walk away. When I felt them relax, I turned around and smiled. "Oh, and just so you don't think no one talks behind your back, a woman in a pink dress called y'all bony bitches, and two gentlemen in sport coats were talking about which one of you gives worse head."

I had heard no such things, but judging from their expressions, both were completely plausible. I patted myself on my back and walked back out to the party with a skip in my step.

Bootleg Justice for the win.

Chapter Thirty-Five
Devlin

Scarlett lasted longer at the party than I thought she would. She hung in there patiently while I worked my way through the crowd. Using every weapon in my arsenal, I reassured each person that I was happy and healthy and ready to work. If the questions went beyond probing, Scarlett stepped in with a redirect that usually dizzied the interrogator into submission.

"My great-granddaddy was one of the founders of our town," she was saying proudly. I loved watching stuffy society try to cover their shock at learning the Bodine family's bootlegging history told with the same pride as their Mayflower ancestral lineage stories.

An hour after I'd intended to leave, I finally got Scarlett in the car.

We both collapsed against our head rests with twin sighs of relief.

"Well that was somethin'," Scarlett said.

"You can say that again."

"I would, but I'm too tired."

"Are you too tired for—"

"Sex? No, I think I can rouse the energy for a couple of orgasms," she said, smiling without opening her eyes.

"I was going to suggest pizza."

"I could definitely eat and then have some of those orgasms."

I brought her hand to my lips and brushed a kiss over her knuckles. "Pizza and sex sound like exactly the perfect thing."

"Did you have a good time?" she asked, turning her head to look at me.

"As good of a time as you can have at a work function."

"Do you miss it?" she asked.

Did I?

"There's a certain satisfaction in successfully navigating the social minefield of politics," I said. "But it's no night at The Lookout."

She laughed. "I know you're making fun. But you promised me pizza, and I'm still making up to you, so I'll choose not to fire back."

"I appreciate your restraint," I laughed. I turned the key in the ignition. "Did you have a good time?"

"It was… interesting," she said slowly.

"Hmm. That certainly sounds definitive."

"I learned a lot," she said.

"For instance?"

"For instance, there are catty Misty-Lynn-like assholes in every town."

I was curious who she'd labeled as a Misty Lynn. There were quite a few likely choices.

"And I learned that it's never appropriate to use plastic dishes and utensils. And that everyone will like you more if you let them talk about themselves."

"All accurate assessments. Although I personally believe that Solo cups and paper plates have their place."

She looked out the window, a ghost of a smile playing on

228

her lips. "I liked seeing you in action, but I felt like I was watching an actor playing a part."

"That's pretty much exactly what it is," I admitted.

"Why can't people just be real?" she asked. "Why can't they say, 'You know what, Stuart? I don't want to support your initiative to jail the homeless.' Why does everyone have to pretend to be polite?"

"It's how things get done," I explained. "Everyone pretends to play nicely together until we can't pretend anymore."

"I heard you were on leave. Mental health leave," Scarlett said.

I swore quietly. "Let me guess. Misty Lynn the Second?"

"And third."

"When I hit Ralston, my ex-wife's lover, my family went into damage control mode. Everyone knew what I'd done. Most would have done the same in my position. But, in the eyes of the constituents…"

"You come off as unstable. Can't keep a wife. Now you're violent," Scarlett filled in the blanks.

"I basically handed everyone a weapon to use against me. I took a leave from my job. My parents and our publicist told everyone that it was an unfortunate reaction to too much stress."

"And now you're left proving that you're not mentally unstable. You're just a normal guy who decked an asshole."

"But I have to prove it by playing the game, following the rules."

She shot me a look. "And not decking anyone else?"

"I've got a second chance to make the next session a good one. Improve my chances for re-election. Then I can start thinking bigger."

"Do you want to?"

I turned down a side street and drove past the pizza parlor in a hunt for a parking space. "My goal is Congress."

She was still watching me. "That, Mr. McCallister, doesn't answer my question."

"Politicians don't know how to answer direct questions."

"Maybe you don't know what you really want," she ventured.

I squeezed into a space a block down.

"That's the hunger talking. Come on. I'll let you pick the toppings… on your half."

Chapter Thirty-Six
Scarlett

Devlin unlocked the door to his condo and motioned for me to enter. We were on the water five stories up. The Chesapeake Bay stretched out in front of the building, dark water meeting a dark horizon.

He flipped light switches, and the exterior view disappeared. The condo was spacious and well-furnished if lacking personality and devoid of color. The living room furniture was arranged around a gas fireplace and marble mantel. The floors were a light hardwood scattered with black-and-white throw rugs. The art on the walls, mostly maritime scenes, was black-and-white as well. The kitchen, small but still twice the size of my own, was black again with white counters. There was a round glass dining table and four clear acrylic chairs.

"I know. It's a little stark," Devlin said, bringing my overnight bag in.

"You're living *here*?" I asked. No wonder he'd been depressed. This place looked like a fancy furnished hospital room. Everything was glass and leather and chrome.

"I'm living in Bootleg Springs," he corrected me. "I stayed here temporarily."

"You're staying in Bootleg temporarily," I reminded him. There was no point in us pretending otherwise. Devlin's life was here. Well, not here in this soulless condo but in the general vicinity.

Devlin put my bag down and drew me into his arms. "We should probably talk about what we'll do when I come back here."

We.

"I don't want to think about you leaving right now. Is that okay? Can we just pretend that we don't have to worry about that yet?" I begged.

"There are a lot of things you don't seem to want to talk about," he pointed out. He was frustrated with me, and I understood why. But I needed Devlin to cut me a break. Everything I was doing was for his own good. He didn't need to be rolling around down in the mud with me.

I sat down on an unyielding white leather and metal chair in front of the wall of windows. "There are just some situations that are best handled privately."

"Fine, then why don't you want to talk about our future?"

I was not about to nail down Devlin to a commitment that would ruin his career.

"Because I just want to have a nice time with you tonight without worrying about where we're going and what we're doing," I lied.

"We're going to need to talk about those things at some point," Devlin said, his frustration palpable.

But whatever he wanted to say, whether it was reasons why we should try a long-distance relationship or break up now, I didn't want to deal with anything else in this moment.

"Now can you point me in the direction of your restroom?" I asked.

He showed me to the powder room, and I shut myself in and stared at my reflection and let the mask drop.

I didn't fit. I would never fit here with him. My chest hurt as if something was breaking open or collapsing in on itself.

Devlin's calling was politics. His family had invested everything in him and his career. He was just coming back from one scandal. They had exiled him over a little ol' divorce, treating it like he'd murdered an entire litter of puppies on live TV. He'd never survive the fallout of dating the daughter of a potential kidnapper... or murderer. I believed my father to be innocent. But that didn't mean anyone else would.

If Devlin and his parents thought a divorce was a nail in the coffin, what would they say over his girlfriend being at the center of a cold case murder investigation?

Thanks to the Misty Lynn twins tonight, I had a better grasp of what this life was like. It wasn't the truth that mattered. It was the appearance. And me in my cute little Target frock and my self-styled hair with my thick-as-honey accent would be a liability to Devlin. And that's even without being the daughter of an accused murderer. Talk about a real scandal. His career and quite possibly his relationship with his family would be over.

Sins of the father carried weight here, even if they were only perceived.

My breath hitched. Somewhere along the way, I'd started to think that we could survive long distance and different worlds. Now, I knew better. Our days were numbered. Devlin and I had an expiration date.

Chapter Thirty-Seven
Devlin

I opened the bottle of wine and set two glasses on the counter. A good wine and a great pizza. Our meal reflected our balance. A combination of refinement and casual charm. I'd do my best to pretend there weren't things we needed to discuss. For tonight. But if Scarlett thought I'd be willing to stay in another relationship where I was kept in the dark, she had another thing coming.

She'd done so well tonight, I thought, pouring the wine.

Scarlett never pretended to be someone she wasn't. That was her power. Her unapologetic authenticity. There was a danger in being yourself in this space. Everyone was always looking for a weakness, a vulnerability, to exploit. But with Scarlett, was that possible? Did the weakness lie in me? Was I vulnerable because I worked so hard to hide my flaws rather than embracing them? Would Scarlett end up being my greatest strength or my most bitter weakness?

My phone buzzed in my pocket. It was late for a non-emergency call. When I saw my mother's number on the screen, I answered.

"Is everything all right?"

"No, everything is decidedly *not* all right, Devlin," she said, her tone clipped.

"What's wrong?"

"You were supposed to stay out of sight. Not parade your bumpkin girlfriend around the city, rubbing her in Johanna's face. Just imagine how it looks. Like you're trying to get revenge by traipsing around some trophy—"

"Scarlett isn't a trophy," I interrupted, annoyed at the comparison. "And I don't give a good goddamn what Johanna thinks about me moving on with my life. She moved on with hers while we were still married!"

"She at least did it discreetly," my mother shot back.

"I can't believe you're defending her."

"And I can't believe my son who has been groomed for this life is so willing to throw it all away. People were just starting to forget, and then you have to surprise everyone with Redneck Ruby."

"Scarlett," I corrected.

"Devlin, forgive me for saying so, but does it sound like I care what her name is? I'm not having some barefoot country hillbilly ruining your career. We've worked so hard for this, given you every opportunity, and to see you just throwing it away on a girl…" she trailed off as if she couldn't bear to finish the thought.

"I'm not throwing anything away. I'm finally enjoying myself for the first time in thirty-some years, Mother."

"Enjoying yourself?" her tone was reaching into the upper octaves of horror. "Do you think you have the liberty to enjoy yourself? McCallisters serve. It's a responsibility and an honor."

"You're overreacting," I told her. My blood pressure was rising. It wasn't the first time one of my parents had laid a guilt trip to keep me on the straight and narrow. I always caved.

"You're not grasping the damage you've done tonight.

Everyone is talking about you and her. Blake is going to have to work overtime just to sweep this under the rug."

"I didn't do anything wrong. I took my girlfriend to an event where we both had a nice time," I said evenly.

"The fact that you refuse to even consider the ramifications just proves that you're not ready to come back. Your father is going to be devastated. You're acting like you don't even want this anymore."

I scraped my hand through my hair, pacing the kitchen. "I have to go, Mother."

She huffed out a few more insults and guilt trips and I disconnected.

Once they met her, they'd understand the draw. But I wasn't about to force Scarlett into a visit with them. Certainly not now. She'd done nothing wrong. Hell, I wasn't convinced that I had either. Why would being with someone who made me happy, made me feel stronger, be wrong? Scarlett had been there for me when my own family closed ranks against me, shunning me. It had been Scarlett who'd picked up the pieces and put them back together again. It was Scarlett who—

"You look like you're contemplating a word problem on the SATs," she said lightly from behind me. I turned to admire the view.

She wore a cami and short set in soft heather gray with pink trim. Pajamas had never looked so sexy. My anger over my mother's phone call was already dulling.

I handed her a glass of wine.

"I heard you talking," she confessed, perching on the arm of the leather armchair.

"My mother called," I told her, pushing her hair over her shoulder and trailing my fingertips down her neck.

"Is everything okay?" she asked, her gray eyes wide and worried.

I nodded. "Everything is good," I murmured.

She perked up. "So we can eat that pizza that smells like heaven?"

I smiled down at her. "I'll get the plates."

"Can we eat on the balcony?" she asked, nodding toward the glass wall.

"Of course." We divided up slices and plates and spices—garlic salt for her, oregano for me—and juggled everything to the sliding door. Annapolis on the water was always quiet at night. I could hear the faraway echoes of late night diners on a restaurant patio overlooking the bay.

Boat mooring lights glowed and bobbed gently in the night.

Scarlett flopped down in one of the cushioned patio chairs and propped her bare feet up on the railing. She was so different from Johanna. I didn't know why I felt the need to make the comparison other than the fact that my ex-wife and I had attended so many events like the one tonight. Johanna had never picked up a horseshoe or caused a scene over malicious gossip. And when we'd come home, she'd change into silk pajamas and sip hot tea while we discussed who said what to whom. She wasn't a woman to prop her feet up on anything or to ever consider pizza a meal.

"I can practically hear you thinking," Scarlett said dryly, with her mouth full.

I gave her a half smile. "Just thinking about tonight."

"You're thinking about a lot more than just tonight. Did it feel good to be back?" she asked, mopping at the sauce on the corner of her mouth.

"It felt…" I paused and thought. "Familiar. Comfortable."

"Hmm," she said without further comment.

"My mother was unhappy that I came back. She felt it was too early."

Scarlett rolled her eyes. "A mother who doesn't want to see her son. Nice."

"There are *appearances* to be maintained," I said in a falsetto.

Scarlett laughed in appreciation. "Let me guess, she wasn't happy with you parading your redneck girlfriend all over the place."

"She may have mentioned something along those lines," I hedged.

Scarlett laid her hand on my wrist. "It's okay. Because I probably won't like her either."

I choked on my wine laughing. It made my nose burn.

We ate in silence for a few minutes. "What are you and Gibson fighting about?" I asked.

"Devlin McCallister! You are tenacious!"

"It's the attorney side of me."

She sighed heavily, and I felt a sliver of guilt for pushing her. "Cleaning out our father's house brought up a lot of... history," she explained. "Gibson has always hated Daddy. And the one thing he hates more than that is my loyalty to him."

"He saw you caring for your dad as a slap in the face?"

She nodded, sipping her wine slowly. "It's an issue we've kept buried for a long time. He never understood why I kept forgiving our dad and kept trying. Gibson didn't have a healthy relationship with my father. He got the worst of it, and he's hurt that I chose to forgive rather than hold grudges alongside him."

"And this all just came to a head?" I asked.

"We finally said all the words we'd been holdin' in. It wasn't pretty, and now we have to wait for the dust to settle."

"So why shut me out?" I asked.

She gave a little one-shouldered shrug and stared straight ahead into the night. "I don't know. I guess I'm just used to handling things on my own."

"When your mother was upset with your father or one of you, what would she do?"

"Ugh. It was the worst. She'd give us the silent treatment for days. Just freeze everyone out."

I lifted an eyebrow and waited.

"Wait... you're not saying—"

"Maybe you're seeing the other side of that?" I suggested mildly. "You were angry and overwhelmed and froze me out."

She opened her mouth and shut it again. "I don't like this conversation. Not one bit."

"We all carry pieces of our parents," I reminded her.

"Your mama just called to yell at you for showing your face in town. What part of her are you carrying around like a cross to bear?" Scarlett demanded.

She was angry at the implication, but at least she was still talking to me.

"From my mother?" I mused. Suddenly I wasn't liking this conversation either.

"Yeah, not so much fun now, is it buddy?" Scarlett said smugly.

"Let's just boil it down to this. It hurt me when you froze me out, Scarlett. I've already had one relationship end because someone was keeping secrets and holding things back from me. I'm not interested in a repeat."

She swallowed hard, keeping her gaze straight ahead into the darkness. I couldn't read her thoughts and felt unsettled.

"The thing about secrets is some of them need to be kept," she said quietly.

"Bullshit."

She put her wine down on the concrete, placed her plate beside it, and rose. She moved to me in the dark and pulled her hair out of the confines of the band she'd secured it with. She was a goddess of the night. I knew I should press. I should insist on continuing the conversation, but she was taking my glass, my plate, and setting them aside.

And then she was settling herself astride my lap.

I opened my mouth, but no words came forth. She scooted higher so that my hardening cock was buried at the apex of her thighs, begging to be released from my pants.

The need was instantaneous. She purred and circled her hips against me. And then she brushed her full lips against mine. An aphrodisiac. That's what the taste of Scarlett Bodine was. I kissed her like a deprived man, shoving my hands into her hair, thrusting my hips up against her. I wanted in, regardless of the thin layers of clothing that separated us.

She poured herself into the kiss, and as our tongues slid and danced around each other, I ghosted my palms over her breasts. Her nipples budded under the fabric of her shirt instantly at my touch. She made me feel powerful and weak in the same breath. Invincible and desperate.

"We should go inside," I whispered, pressing fevered kisses to her lips, her jaw, her neck.

"Why?"

"I don't have a condom on me." My dick twitched between us, trying to convince me that we didn't need one.

Scarlett grinned, slow and feline. "Check my pocket."

"What pocket?"

She tapped the tiny square of pink fabric just above her breast.

I dipped a finger into the pocket and felt the brush of foil. "Ingenious little devil, aren't you?" I asked.

"Less talking. More nudity," she insisted.

I glanced around us. There was no one in front of us, but the balconies were separated by brick walls. No one could see us without leaning out over their balcony to peer around the wall, but anyone could hear us. "We have to be quiet," I warned her.

"I'll make sure you don't scream my name too loud," she promised.

I groaned as she shifted against me, grinding against my insistent erection.

"I want you fast," she said. Without preamble, she shoved her hand in the waistband of my pants and gripped my shaft.

I let out a hiss of breath. This woman would be the death of me eventually. But hopefully not in the next half an hour.

I spread my legs wider for her, and Scarlett rose on her knees, freeing my cock from the confines of the pants. She ripped the foil with her teeth, and I helped her shaking hands roll the condom down my aching dick.

Her little shorts sported a small wet spot, and I pressed my thumb against it. I could feel her heat through the thin cotton. She shivered and let out a quiet little moan. I stroked her with the pad of my thumb, pressing through her shorts, and then she was gripping my cock and guiding it between her legs. Understanding her intent, I tugged the crotch of her shorts to the side and lined myself up with her opening. She settled onto my tip, enveloping the first inch in that slick, wet heat. I was desperate for more. I didn't care if she wasn't ready to accept me. I didn't care if anyone heard us. I only wanted to be inside her.

I grabbed her hips and, with one quick thrust, drove into her, sheathing myself to the hilt. Scarlett's head fell back as she held me there, deep inside her, gripped by those delicate walls. I could feel her quivering around me, feel her need buzzing in her blood.

I yanked the neck of her tank top down, baring one breast. And when I latched on with my mouth to that straining peak, she cried out and began to ride me.

I plumped her breast with one hand while I sucked hard, walking that fine line between pleasure and pain.

She rode me with desperation, chasing down an orgasm that was just within her reach. I loved her like this. Reckless, out of her mind with desire for me. I wanted to take her over the edge into the abyss of pleasure. Her little whimpers were making my cock even harder.

"Dev," she whispered, pleaded. The sound of her ass meeting my thighs, damp slaps of flesh, nearly broke my mind. Everything about this woman was a fantasy of perfection. Except she was real. So real. I squeezed her breast, forcing her nipple further into my mouth, and lapped with my tongue.

"I'm coming," she hissed. I felt her explode around me. Hot, wet squeezes gripped my aching dick like strong fingers. Scarlett stopped breathing and rode me. Hard. I didn't want to come yet. I didn't want this to be over as quickly as it started, but her pussy gripped me, and it took every ounce of my focus not to come right then and there.

"Damn it, Scarlett," I groaned. She rode me relentlessly, and her orgasm flowed through her until finally she was spent, collapsing against my chest. I held her to me, locked in my arms as the climax that had threatened to kill me slowly receded to the wings.

I thought that I could just hold her like this forever. Wrapped around each other, sated and still hungry. But then she was pushing away from me and climbing off my lap.

My cock slid out of her regretfully.

"Where are you going?" I demanded.

"Right here." She sank between my open knees and dragged the condom off of my shaft. "I want to see you come."

And just like that, my orgasm was back, demanding me to find it. She used both hands on me, her breast still bare. And when she leaned forward to flick her tongue over my crown, I'd never seen anything like it. I was there, on the edge already.

She watched my crown in glee as clear liquid beaded at the tip. "You like this, don't you Dev?" she whispered, pumping my cock harder.

I wanted to close my eyes, to give myself over to the climax she was milking out of me, but I didn't want to miss a second of those hungry gray eyes, the way her rosy lips parted when she felt me pulse against her.

"You're going to come for me, and I'm going to watch," she said, licking her lips. She brushed her thumbs over my balls, and that was it. I was coming. We both watched, hypnotized as the first thick rope of my release wrenched itself free, landing across my stomach. I gritted my teeth together but couldn't quite cover the grunt of satisfaction, of relief. The next one reached my chest and glistened in the dim light from inside.

Scarlett worked my dick with her small, strong hands, pumping me until every drop I'd been holding back lay patterned across my abs and chest. Only then did I drop my head back against the chair. Only then did I start to breathe again.

"That was fucking awesome," Scarlett said with satisfaction, her head resting on my thigh. With the last of my energy, I stroked her hair and started planning the best way to convince her to give us a real shot.

Chapter Thirty-Eight
Devlin

I dumped my contribution to dinner—one of those large bagged salad kits—into a mixing bowl on the island. I could smell the sizzle of steaks on the grill out on the deck, hear the murmur of conversation. We'd invited the Bodines over for a cookout. Even Gibson had reluctantly come. Scarlett wasn't here yet. She'd been called in to help a plumber friend handle a drainage emergency at a rental property.

Gibson and Scarlett had yet to patch things up, and I hoped that a cookout on neutral ground would pave the way.

I heard a car in the driveway and felt my heart lift. Just the anticipation of seeing Scarlett made me happy. Ever since our trip to Annapolis, I'd been thinking seriously about the future, and I knew one thing. I wanted Scarlett in mine.

I heard the knock at the front door and frowned. Scarlett wasn't a knocker. None of the Bodines were. They either pushed right through your unlocked doors or made themselves at home in your yard and on your deck. It was the Bootleg way.

Maybe it was Millie Waggle with another delectable baked

good. The woman could perform miracles with flour and cocoa. I think she had a secret crush on Jonah, and I was happy to encourage it if it meant I got to enjoy homemade pies and sticky buns and cookies.

I wiped my hands on the dishtowel, shoved the salad into the fridge, and headed toward the front of the house.

It was not Millie Waggle standing on my doorstep. It was Johanna.

I blinked, not believing my eyes. It had been long enough since I'd seen her last. I'd already forgotten little details about her. The beauty mark at the side of her mouth. The pearly pink lipstick she was never without, even though I'd preferred to kiss her without it.

She was tall and slim, bordering on too thin, I realized. She exercised ruthlessly and managed her diet with the focus of a general at war. Her blonde hair was swept back into a low roll at the base of her neck. She wore a sleeveless sheath dress in dove gray and a string of pearls around her neck that matched the studs in her ears. It was her "casual" wardrobe.

"What are you doing here?" I demanded, not quite trusting my voice. The woman before me had once shared my life, my bed, my goals. Now, she was a stranger.

"Devlin," she said with a soft smile. "So good to see you. I'd like to come in."

"I have company," I told her. My brain was still shocked at seeing her on my doorstep and didn't form the "get the hell out" that I felt she deserved.

She cocked her head to the side, still smiling wanly. "It's important," she insisted.

I should have slammed the damn door in her damn face and joined the party on the deck, but decades of etiquette training and social graces wouldn't let me. I held the door open, and she walked inside.

"Such a quaint home," she said brightly. I followed her back the hallway to the living room. The deck doors were open, and music and laughter spilled inside.

Johanna turned away from the view and the fun outside

and faced me, lacing her fingers together in front of her. "You've been avoiding me," she stated.

"I have." I didn't see a reason to lie or make her feel more comfortable with the situation. "Most men do that when it comes to their ex-wives."

"The divorce isn't final yet," Johanna pointed out. "And that's what I'd like to talk to you about."

"Believe me, if there were anything I could do to speed the process along, I would have," I snapped.

"I want to call it off. I want you to give us another try."

Baffled, I stared at her. "What about Ralston?" I demanded.

"He was a… poor choice. A mistake which I deeply regret."

"And so you thought you'd just come back, and we could pick back up where we left off."

Her cheeks flushed slightly, but it was the only show of emotion. "Quite frankly, yes. I've known for some time that I hadn't made the right choice. I hurt you deeply, embarrassed you. And, for that, I'm sorry."

She was speaking Klingon or Portuguese because I wasn't comprehending a word she was saying. Nothing made sense.

"I don't think I'm understanding. Why would I ever take you back?"

"We make sense, Devlin. Together, we make a very good team. If we get back together, this whole scandal goes away. I understand it will take some time before you can trust me, but I promise to be a good partner. The *right* partner."

It was becoming clear through the fog in my brain. "You're here because of Scarlett."

"I wanted to give you some time to clear your head and possibly even forgive me. But I didn't expect you to move on so quickly or with someone so… unsuited."

"You sound like my mother."

"Your mother is justifiably concerned. If you get re-elected, you have a very real shot at Congress in a handful of years, and from there, who knows where we could go. It's your dream, and I can help you make that happen," she insisted calmly.

245

"All I have to do is take you back?" I asked bitterly.

She nodded, looking hopeful. "We can find a new house together. It might even be fun."

"Why is Ralston suddenly a mistake? Did he move on to someone else already?"

I saw the shadow in her eyes and knew my accusation had hit its mark.

"I see," I said quietly.

"I made a mistake," she pleaded.

I shook my head. "No. You didn't."

"And just *what the hell is this*?" a sweet voice drawled with Southern charm. Scarlett stood with her hands on her hips just above her tool belt. She wore jeans and a Bootleg Cockspurs tank top.

"*This* is Scarlett?" Johanna asked, aghast.

"Oh, you must be the lying, cheating, piece of garbage ex-wife. Bless your heart," Scarlett said, batting her lashes.

Oh, shit.

The music stopped on the deck, and the door darkened with frames of four men all watching in rapt attention.

"Who's that?" Gibson hissed.

"How the hell should I know?" Bowie whispered back. "I know all the same people you know."

"Guessing she's the ex," Jonah added.

Jameson grunted.

If Scarlett noticed the audience, she didn't care.

"Now what would a disgraced ex-wife be doing at her ex-husband's lookin' all pretty in her pearls?" she mused, tapping a finger to her chin. "Did you come to renegotiate the divorce? Are you here to lay claim to the Crock-pot and the fine china?"

Johanna had gotten both of those in the divorce.

"I'm saving my marriage," Johanna said icily.

"Like hell you are," Scarlett announced. She was pure fire to Johanna's ice. She was magnificent.

"You're obviously not feeling like yourself," Johanna said,

246

addressing her comment to me and dismissing Scarlett. "And I take ownership of my part in that. I was the one that sent you into a tailspin, but Devlin, you can't accomplish all you're meant to do with her by your side."

"At least he doesn't have to worry about me soliciting dick all the time," Scarlett shot back.

I heard snickers from the deck. Johanna's mouth dropped open. I doubted that she'd ever heard anything so crass before in her entire life.

"I beg your pardon. You're a child and an ignorant one at that. You couldn't possibly understand the kind of partner that Devlin needs."

"He doesn't need a fucking partner," Scarlett enunciated. "He needs a best friend. Someone who will have his back, not end up on hers under someone else."

Her brothers were howling with laughter behind me, and I inched my way toward them. I needed to put myself between Scarlett and Johanna, but I wasn't sure if I could count on any of them for backup.

"You need to leave," Johanna announced. "You need to leave so I can talk to my husband."

"Oh, hell no," Scarlett said, crossing her arms in front of her chest. Johanna had six inches in height on her, but Scarlett had a good fifteen pounds of muscle in her favor. She also had a hammer and a few screwdrivers in her tool belt. "In fact, I think it's time you left. You have to the count of three to get your non-existent ass out of this house."

Johanna sputtered. "I'm not leaving. This is Devlin's house, and I am welcome in it as long as he says I am!"

"Oh, are you?" Scarlett drawled. "Devlin?"

"Devlin?" Johanna glared at me, willing me to choose her.

I wanted to calm things down. "Let's just take a step back—"

The Bodines groaned behind me, and I knew immediately I'd made a huge mistake.

Scarlett's eyes narrowed at me. "Not good enough, McCallister."

"Johanna, I think you should leave," I said calmly.

Scarlett bared her teeth, and I knew it was too little too late.

"Devlin, I feel like we should continue this discussion—"

"Get out of this house now!" Scarlett shrieked. She took a threatening step toward Johanna who hopped behind the wingback armchair. "Take your skinny, cheating ass all the way back to Annapolis and find someone else to fuck over! And if I ever see your face around Bootleg again—"

She was reaching for her hammer, trying to wrestle it free. The sliding screen door imploded behind me as four bodies shoved their way through it. Gibson dived for Scarlett while Jameson and Bowie ushered Johanna down the hall toward the front door. Jonah blocked Scarlett's attempt to chase her down, and I stood there wondering what in the hell had just happened.

"Get her out of here!" Scarlett yelled at the top of her lungs. "If she comes near Devlin again, I am shoving her in Rocky Tobias's septic tank!" Gibson wrestled her to the ground and sat on her. Jonah jogged down the hallway to the front door. I could hear raised voices outside before he closed it.

I couldn't quite comprehend what had just happened. All I knew is that the squirming ball of fury on my grandmother's living room rug cared more about me than any appearance or any plan. She wanted to protect me when no one else in my family or circle of friends had been willing to.

I loved Scarlett Bodine. She might not know it yet, but she sure as hell loved me back.

Jameson and Bowie returned to the living room where Scarlett was swearing a blue streak.

"When I let her up, she's gonna try to kill you," Gibson predicted.

"Me?"

"You invited your ex-wife into your house. The woman who treated you like dog shit. You don't play nice with that," Bowie explained.

"Unless of course you're hoping to get back together with her," Jameson added.

Scarlett stilled and glared at me. "Devlin McCallister, if you even think for one second of getting back together with that frosty, pearl-wearing beanpole, I will hold you down, shave your head, and... and..."

She was so mad she couldn't even string together an insult.

"I'm not getting back together with her, Scarlett. I'm with you." I probably should have chosen a less exasperated tone because she was now snarling into the carpet.

"Where's your self-respect, man?" Gibson demanded.

"Fuck self-respect. Where's his survival instinct?" Bowie wondered.

I shoved my hands into my hair. "I don't even know what's happening. Why is everyone mad at me?"

"Because you're an idiot," the Bodine men said together.

"I'm letting her up," Gibson decided. "He needs some sense knocked into him."

He slid off of Scarlett, and she jumped to her feet. "What the hell is wrong with you?" she demanded, shoving her finger in my face.

"I'm not really sure. Maybe you could help me figure it out?" I suggested.

She let out a groan of frustration and took the throw pillow off the couch and hurled it into the kitchen.

"On that note..." Jameson headed for the door.

"Why don't we take the steaks and eat them anywhere but here," Jonah suggested.

"Good luck," Bowie said, clapping a hand on my back.

They disappeared through the trampled screen door, leaving me and the seething Scarlett alone.

Chapter Thirty-Nine
Scarlett

"Why are you so mad?"

Devlin's stupid question pissed me off even more.

"I walk in and find you and your ex-wife talking about giving it another try. And you ask me why I'm mad?" I shrieked. The pitch hurt my own ears.

"*She* was talking about reconciling. *I* was not!"

"I didn't hear a resounding 'oh, hell no' from your mouth," I shot back.

He sank weakly into the plaid wingback chair and rubbed his hands over his face. "Scarlett, I'm a little overwhelmed right now."

"Do you want to get back together with Johanna?" I asked calmly, quietly.

"No! I don't. That's not an option or a possibility or something I'd ever want to revisit no matter what."

I thrust my arms into the air. "Then why in the everlasting hell didn't you *say so*?"

He frowned, confused. "I was trying to explain to her—"

I cut him off with a wave of my hand. "Devlin, I understand that seeing her was a shock, and I get that you're required to be professionally courteous in most situations, but that woman lied, cheated, and deceived you and then decided you should take her back."

"Wait," he said, holding up his hands. "You're not mad because she showed up here—uninvited, I might add?"

I looked up at the ceiling and prayed for patience. The etiquette was bred bone deep in this man. "No! Who could blame her? You're a fucking catch, and she's only just now realizing what a stupid disaster she's made of her life because she got greedy! I'm mad because you felt like you needed to break the news to her so gently she still thought she had a chance!"

"Scarlett, not everyone is like you, and not every place is like Bootleg. There are rules to social interactions."

"She hurt you, humiliated you, and put your career at risk. And you can't even get a good 'fuck you' past your lips. I can't send you back into the world being so vulnerable, Dev. I can't do it!"

"What are you ranting about?"

He looked shell-shocked, like the survivor of a traumatic accident. That's probably the way the abrupt end to his marriage had felt. Traumatic. And she'd come waltzing back in like the entitled asshole she was.

I crossed to him and knelt down in front of him. "You came here cracked, if not broken. And you need to take care not to put yourself in that position again. You opened the door to JoSkanka, and she walked right in, figuratively and literally. You can't let her think she has a chance. You have to forget about being polite all the time and focus on being powerful."

"I thought you were mad because I was talking to my ex-wife," he said.

"Crap on a cracker! Catch up, McCallister. You've spent your whole life playing by the rules, and look where it got you. I want you to take charge just like you do in the bedroom."

He looked around us as if worrying about an audience.

"See? That right there!" I pointed an accusing finger at him and rose to pace off my mad. "You're concerned about how it looks, how it sounds. Why not just speak the truth and move on?"

"It's not the way things are—"

"Done. I know. I know. Okay. But did it ever occur to you that things are done wrong?" I returned to him and put my hands on his knees. He looked dazed. "I'm not trying to be mean here, Dev. I don't want you to ever be in the position that Johanna put you in again. And I sure as shit don't want someone feeling like they deserve a second chance with you."

"You're acting like I'm some helpless child," Devlin said, fully irritated.

Had he seen what she had when he came here? A man bent to breaking. A man alone and adrift. She wasn't sending him back to the family that abandoned him and the woman who took advantage of him without improving his arsenal.

"I don't think you're a helpless child. I think you're only willing to take what you want when you're naked."

"Now you're being ridiculous," Devlin announced, surging to his feet.

"I'm being ridiculous? I'm being ridiculous?" I jumped up, pushing away from him.

He stalked toward me. "Let's get a few things straight," he said quietly. I felt my pulse kick. He wasn't the shell-shocked ex-husband now. He was a predator, a hunter. I loved him like this, all graceful power and single-minded desire.

The air charged between us with the change. It wasn't just anger now. It was anger warring with want. And I could tell he liked it. This is what I wanted for him. But I needed to set him free. He needed to be able to stand on his own two feet without me.

"Why are you acting like I'm going to go back and never see you again?" Devlin demanded.

I didn't want to say it. It felt wrong to say it.

"What are you keeping from me?"

Too many damn things. Until I knew I could prove that my father had nothing to do with Callie's disappearance, there could be no Devlin and me.

"We aren't going to work together," I said quietly. My own words cut at me. He didn't pull back, and I thanked God for tiny miracles.

"Scarlett, you and I work better together than anyone."

I shook my head. I didn't know how to tell him without telling him. "I'm a liability to you. I don't operate the way you'd need me to."

"Where is this coming from?"

"Dev, when we were at that party, people were nice to my face. But behind my back? They were gleefully discussing your midlife crisis spent slumming it with a bumpkin. I won't help your career. The one you've been working toward your entire life. That's one thing that gazelle you were married to got right."

"Fuck them," he snapped. "And fuck her. This is our life we're talking about here, Scarlett."

"But we haven't been talking about it. Really talking about it. We have sex. We hang out. But we both know you're not staying here. And I don't fit there. I'm not what you need."

"You're what I *want*." The vehemence in his voice made me feel twin pangs of hurt and a desire so fierce I didn't think I could stand it.

I wanted to be right for him. I wanted to have his back and have him on his back. But until I knew how that sweater ended up in my father's house, I couldn't ask him to be mine. I couldn't demand that kind of commitment. Not when it would mean giving up everything he'd worked his whole life for.

"I think deep down you know it," I said, pretending his last remark didn't mean anything to me. "Your parents know it. Your stupid, bitchy acquaintances know it. Hell, even Johanna knows it. Why do you think she was so confident you'd let her come back? They told her about me. I'll hurt your career, and you'll resent me. Or I'll resent you for taking me away from my home and trying to turn me into someone I'm not."

He'd stopped arguing, and my heart broke just a little bit.

"We don't need to talk about this now," he said finally. I couldn't tell if he was resigned to the truth or regrouping.

I was relieved. "Look, the only thing we need to be discussing right this second is that when you go back to your old life, you aren't the same polite doormat. You fought for me. You confronted my brothers for me. I expect you to do the same for yourself."

"You want me to take what I want?" he said, low and rough.

I nodded, my eyes going wide at the change in him.

He kicked the ottoman out of his way, a show of temper I hadn't seen from him before. Devlin exercised control in all things. And sometimes that control got in the way of real life. The only time he ever let himself off the leash was in bed with me.

"Bottling things up isn't gonna help, Dev," I reminded him. "You gotta let it out. You went mean on my brothers, which they deserved. Why can't you do the same for yourself?"

"I have responsibilities," he insisted.

"Fuck your responsibilities! Are they really your responsibilities if someone else dumps them on you?" And didn't I know that first hand?

"You know what I want, Scarlett?" His voice was a rasp of gravel.

I nodded. I knew exactly what he needed. *Release*.

I reached for the waistband of his shorts.

"Get on your knees," he hissed.

Chapter Forty
Scarlett

M y legs went out from under me, and I sank to the floor and unzipped him. When I shoved my hand into the opening, I found him already halfway hard. "You like seeing me on my knees?" I whispered.

His cock swelled in my hand. Oh, yeah. He liked seeing me like this in front of him. Willing and waiting.

I stroked his shaft with my hand, keeping my grip loose. He watched my every move, and I was happy to give him a show. I licked my lips and leaned in to sweep my tongue over the crown. His breath came out in a hiss. Using the flat of my tongue, I licked my way up the underside of his shaft, and when I got to the slit where moisture was starting to pool, Devlin's knees shook.

"Again," he rasped. I obliged, using my tongue like a weapon on him.

This time when I got to his purple, swollen head, I opened my lips and took his cock into my mouth.

His groan was music to my soul. I felt that insistent throb

between my legs warm. Pleasing him made me wet and needy. I'd never felt this with anyone before. The mechanics were the same—tabs and slots—but somehow every touch meant more with Devlin.

I took him to the back of my throat and held there. He let me, a low rumble rising from his chest. "I've never seen anything more beautiful than you on your knees like this," he growled.

My thighs clamped together of their own volition. I wanted the invasion of him. I wanted him driving into me until I screamed. But I wanted to give him this more.

I fisted the last inches of him that I couldn't get to and began to work him with hand and mouth.

Devlin's head fell back for a moment, but when I flicked my tongue over the underside of his crown, everything changed.

"Fuck, Scarlett," he hissed. He shoved his hands into my hair, roughly assuming control. His fingers closed in my hair, gripping it until my scalp hurt. Devlin used it to control my rhythm on his cock.

He started slowly, leisurely fucking my mouth. His head burying itself in my mouth to the back of my throat. I swallowed convulsively around his girth. "Yes, baby. Just like that." He wasn't so slow now. I reached up with my free hand to cup his balls. I loved the velvet feel of them in my palm.

I looked up at him and found him watching me from hooded eyes. His breath was ragged, and I could tell he was close. I tugged his balls, and he winced in a mix of pleasure and pain.

He wrapped my hair around one hand and placed the other hand on the wall behind us. "I'm gonna come in your mouth, sweet Scarlett."

I moaned and swallowed hard.

"Fuck, baby." He gritted the words out.

My jaw ached. But I needed to taste him, needed to give him this moment. To pour himself into me and lose himself. Release the anger, the frustration, the anxiety. I felt him harden painfully, felt his balls drawing up. I felt everything. The ache between my own legs, the pounding of my heart as adrenaline coursed through me pushing me past discomfort. And then he was coming.

On a long, guttural noise, Devlin orgasmed down my throat. Thick and salty and oh so satisfying. He flexed his fingers in my hair, bringing his forehead to the wall behind me, and loosed his seed in me. He grunted, both pained and satisfied, as I swallowed every wave of his release.

We collapsed to the floor, gasping for breath. He was still shamelessly hard. "Goddamn it, Scarlett," he breathed.

"You're welcome," I said on a breathy half-laugh.

He spun me around on the rug, stretching out on top of me. "You have two seconds to get these jeans off."

I didn't move fast enough for his liking, and Devlin released my belt and yanked my pants down. I got one leg free, and then he was pushing into me. I made a noise between a sigh and a scream as he filled me without any preparation. I was wet, but so tight, and he had to force his way into the hilt. I was so wound up that I was already teetering on the edge.

"How are you still fucking hard?" I gasped, my breasts crushed against his chest. He wasn't being careful with me, and I liked it.

He pulled out and sank back into me, rocking against that needy bundle of nerves. The power of his thrust moved us backward on the floor.

"You make me this way," he said accusingly. I pulled my knees up, giving him the deepest possible access.

On his fourth thrust, I was coming. My walls closing around him in a death grip that had him groaning in my ear as he fucked me against the rug. The hardwood and wool biting into my back. But I was coming in explosions of color and light and heat.

"Scarlett!" It was a question, a cry, and then he was filling me with a second release. I felt him come raw inside me, felt the tremor of it and the hot wave of his seed as it spilled into me.

We came together, orgasms milking each other and mixing in one beautiful, dark moment of holiness. Devlin thrust his hips against me and held there until our climaxes slowed and faded.

"I probably should have asked if you were on birth control," he said, his face buried in my neck.

"I think we just made a baby," I whispered.

He lifted his head, panic giving him swift energy.

I laughed at the startled look on his face. "I'm kidding!" I poked him on the shoulder. "Of course I'm on birth control."

He lowered back down and bit my shoulder. "You're evil."

"You love it."

"Yeah. I do."

Chapter Forty-One

Devlin

We'd settled nothing in the two days since Johanna had showed up on my doorstep. And in remaining unsettled, we both tried our best to pretend that everything was fine. But now I knew Scarlett had been seeing a countdown clock in her head when it came to us.

And now I was seeing it, too.

I held the diner door for Scarlett and followed her back to the booth that Clarabell pointed us to. It was early, and she was booked with jobs for the day, so we decided to grab breakfast together instead of dinner.

She slid into the booth and picked up the menu. I noticed that she ordered something different every time. Variety was the spice of Scarlett's life, which gave us one unforgettable summer together and nothing more. I was hurt that she wasn't willing to at least try, that she was so ready to write us off.

But she'd made up her mind. And I didn't know how to convince her otherwise. What would she do in Annapolis? Hang a shingle up and offer her handyman services? I couldn't expect her to give up everything just to support me and my dreams. If they were still my dreams… It wasn't a mistake I'd make again, asking a woman to give herself over to my goals.

Scarlett smiled across the table at me, but it didn't quite reach her eyes. We'd both taken to avoiding the "what's wrong question." She was dressed in jeans and a tank top. Her work uniform for summer in Bootleg. There was nothing Scarlett could put on that I wouldn't find sexy. From plaid pajama bottoms to cutoff shorts to paint-splattered tank tops. If it was on her body, I wanted to take it off. Even though we'd labeled ourselves as temporary and both seemed to be carrying baggage from that decision, I still found myself plunging into her every damn night and coming like I was losing part of my soul.

"I think I'm going for an omelet today," she decided cheerfully.

"Egg whites and turkey bacon for me," I said with less enthusiasm. Jonah had become my trainer and was guiding me out of weakling phase. I'd already gained a few pounds of muscle back.

Clarabell arrived with the usual beverages we didn't even need to order. "What'll it be today, lovebirds?"

I watched Scarlett closely for a wince but didn't see one. We ordered and then sat back in the awkward silence that was our new norm.

"So—" we both began.

"You first," she said, deferring to me.

"I was just going to ask how things at your father's house are going." I'd offered to go back to help, but she'd insisted that she and her brothers had a handle on it.

Scarlett stirred her ice water with her straw. "Slow going."

"Are you and Gibson on speaking terms?" I asked her.

She nodded and gave me an honest grin. "Yeah. And thank you for that. We're all on the same page now."

"Where you need to be."

She nodded, but the smile faded, and I saw the shadows in her eyes. "What are you doing today?" she asked.

"I'm wading my way through constituent communications and a couple of drafts for next session," I said. "We should be able to pass some significant legislation finally."

"You must love what you do," she ventured, looking at me with those big sterling eyes.

"I love the idea of it more than the reality of it," I confessed.

"Really?" she asked.

"There's a lot that gets in the way of actually doing the job I was elected to do."

"Do you ever wish you did something else?"

I felt the weight of the question and wondered if that was hope in her eyes. But I'd never once lied to Scarlett. We didn't do that.

"I've never considered doing anything else," I said.

Her face fell.

Clarabell returned with our breakfast, and we ate in silence until Scarlett threw down her fork. "This is the stupidest thing in the world, Dev. I like you. I want good things for you. Can we please make the most of our time together?"

"I'm still hung up on the fact that you insist we don't fit together."

She stood up and rounded the table, sliding into my side of the booth so that we were hip-to-hip.

"Do you think I'm happy about this? If I thought for one second that I would be good for you, I'd be packing my shit, getting my nails done, learning to lose the accent, and heading to Annapolis. But we both know I'd be a complete disaster as a politician's... girlfriend. I don't fit. And I don't think you'd like the changing I'd have to do to fit."

She was right. And I hated that. Scarlett leaned into me, her bare arm brushing my forearm.

"This sucks," I said succinctly.

"But it doesn't have to," she insisted. She wrapped a slim hand around my arm and squeezed.

"Just because we don't make a permanent fit doesn't mean that we should throw away the rest of our time together. I love being with you, Devlin. And I'm going to treasure these memories for the rest of my life. Also probably become a lesbian because no man is going to live up to you in the sack."

I laughed even though I didn't want to. Scarlett had that effect on me, and I wondered how in a few short weeks I'd gone from wondering how I'd ever sweep up the pieces of my life to wishing I could spend the rest of it with a sexy little brunette that could outdrink me.

"I just want to make the most of our time together. Okay?"

How could any man in the world look into the gray depths of those eyes and say no?

"Okay, Scarlett."

She smiled at me, and some of the ice in my chest melted.

We ate our breakfasts on the same side of the booth, shutting out the rest of the restaurant, and made plans for the rest of the week. I felt lighter than I had when we came in, but the thought of a Scarlett-less life still left me feeling empty.

I walked behind her to the door and waited for her casual ritual with the Missing poster. True to Scarlett's word, as an adopted Bootlegger, I'd been indoctrinated into the theories, conspiracy and otherwise, every time I stepped foot into town.

I saw the hitch in her stride, the slight pause, before Scarlett bypassed the poster and pushed the front door open looking straight ahead.

Odd.

I'd never seen her walk right out the door before. I stopped and stared at the poster.

"Come on, Dev," Scarlett said, her voice tight. "I'll give you a ride back before I go to work."

Chapter Forty-Two
Devlin

I browsed the grocery shelves and consulted my list, frowning at Jonah's handwriting. I was cooking for Scarlett tonight. Jonah had given me a protein-heavy menu that "even an idiot could make." I glared at the selection of chicken breasts. I was too distracted to pick the proper poultry.

"You keep staring at the chicken like that, and they're all gonna get up and fly away," Opal Bodine said. She was wearing overalls over her tall, lean frame. Her short dark hair was tucked under a ball cap.

I relaxed my face and offered her a smile. "Cooking stresses me out," I said lamely.

"That's what they make take-out for," Opal said with a wink. She reached across me for a pack of chicken thighs and dumped them in her basket. "See ya at the game!"

I hadn't played another inning for the Bootleg Cock Spurs. The hangover wasn't worth it. But I had attended a few games since—and kept well hydrated.

I pushed the cart down the aisle, moving on to the

spices portion of Jonah's list, and my mind wandered back to Scarlett.

As an attorney, I'd developed a certain sense for when people were holding out on me. As a politician, that sense sharpened to a razor's edge. Scarlett was keeping something from me. Something that had made her edgy and nervous. Something that kept her so tied up in her own mind that she'd checked out on me.

Was it even any of my business? I wondered, grabbing a jar of thyme and throwing it into the cart. Scarlett had, for all intents and purposes, broken up with me as soon as I headed back to Annapolis. She was convinced she'd be a hindrance to me, to my ambitions. And I didn't understand how she'd come to that conclusion. Or why she hadn't at least demanded a compromise. Yes, people had talked during and after the barbecue. However, very little of it had been negative. She was refreshing, honest, and interesting. That made her stand out.

Why couldn't we try the long-distance thing at first? Or why hadn't she demanded that I give up everything and move here. I had to admit, I'd at least consider it. Scarlett made me happy in a way I had never experienced before. But she was hell-bent on the idea that she was bad for me.

Her behavior had changed even before the barbecue. I thought back to the day at her father's house. I wondered if I'd missed something.

I picked up a bottle of dried rosemary and held it up against the fresh sprigs Jonah had put on the list.

"What's the damn difference?" I muttered.

"The one in the plastic packaging is fresh. The other is dried, giving it a strong flavor in smaller quantity."

"Hi, June," I said, shoving the herb back on the shelf.

"Hello." She picked up a bottle of dill weed and tossed it in her basket.

"Know much about cooking?" I asked, making small talk.

"I know a lot about a lot of subjects."

"Well, hi there handsome," someone else purred from behind me.

I turned and found Misty Lynn in cutoffs that would be considered indecent in a strip club and a belly-baring t-shirt. She had a pack of Nicorette gum and a box of platinum blonde hair dye in her cart.

"Hello, Misty Lynn," I said flatly. No matter what was going on between me and Scarlett, I wasn't about to get tangled up in whatever web Misty Lynn was spinning.

"And look! It's Bootleg's favorite robot, JuneBot." Misty Lynn's smile turned to a sneer.

June sighed beside me. She ignored Misty Lynn and plucked a bottle of lemon pepper off the shelf.

"I hope she's not bothering you," Misty Lynn said to me in a stage whisper. "She's just not good with people. I think she's on the S-P-E-K-T-R-O-M."

I blinked, trying to process.

"She means spectrum," June filled in for me. "She's claiming that I've been diagnosed with a form of autism when really she's just threatened by my superior intellect. While I was weighing college scholarship offers as a junior in high school, Misty Lynn was offering oral sex in exchange for Cs."

June didn't seem like the type to lie. And, judging from Misty Lynn's scowl, she'd just delivered the truth.

"Now that's a low down, dirty lie, June Tucker! You take it back!"

June looked perplexed. "Mr. Hower the trigonometry teacher was terminated because of your relationship. Don't you remember? Mrs. Hower filed for a divorce—"

"You shut the hell up right now! You hear me?" Misty Lynn poked a purple finger nail into June's chest.

I stepped between them. "Why don't we all just take a breath?" I suggested before Misty Lynn went for June's eyes with those talons.

Misty Lynn's face transformed to flirtation. A social chameleon. "Don't listen to Juney. She's not right in the head, if you know what I mean," she drawled, twirling a finger around her ear. "You know, Devlin. I sure would like to get to know you better." She lowered her lashes in a screen siren-worthy wink.

I cleared my throat. What was it with women this week? "I'm with Scarlett," I reminded her. Temporary though it may be, I was committed to our relationship.

And Misty Lynn terrified me.

She pouted. "I'm just bein' friendly," she assured me, running her fingernails down my forearm.

Fuck. There was no Scarlett here to bail me out this time.

I grabbed Misty Lynn's hand off my arm and dropped it. "Look, Misty Lynn, I'm just not interested."

"Not interested?" Her mouth was open so wide I could see her gum. Apparently, she wasn't on the receiving end of "not interested" often.

I stomped down the need to soften the blow.

"That's right. Not interested. Now, how about we all get on with our shopping?"

Misty Lynn glared at June who was staring blankly at her.

"What the hell are you looking at?" she hissed, knocking into June's shoulder as she stormed past.

"A woman who seems incapable of taking a hint," June said flatly.

I pinched the bridge of my nose and hoped the jibe wouldn't bring her back. But Misty Lynn just flipped us the bird over her shoulder and stomped away, her flip-flops flapping against the tile floor.

Between Scarlett, Johanna, and Misty Lynn, I'd had my fill of estrogen-fueled theatrics for the week.

"Goodbye," June said abruptly and wandered off, leaving me alone with my herbs and spices.

I finished off the rest of the shopping and successfully avoided any other unnecessary human contact until the cashier.

Marge, as her name tag read, cheerfully scanned and bagged while carrying on a gossip session with every customer. Myself included.

My gaze drifted to the Missing poster that hung under her register lane light. I nodded, half listening to the latest news about a falling out between the dueling banjo trio made up of the mayor, the police chief, and Mrs. Morganson the third-grade teacher.

Marge followed my gaze. "Such a shame, isn't it?" she said. That's how all conversations about Callie's disappearance started. "The anniversary of her kidnappin' slash murder is comin' up in a couple of weeks. Her daddy's back in town for a little bit at least. He's a judge, but he usually takes a month or so here in the summers. What do *you* think happened to her?" Marge asked cheerfully.

I opened my mouth to answer when the text caught my eye.

Last seen wearing denim shorts and a red cardigan sweater.

Chapter Forty-Three
Devlin

I drove home in a daze while my mind turned it all over.

Last seen wearing denim shorts and a red cardigan sweater.

Scarlett had found a red cardigan sweater tucked away in her father's things. A sweater she identified as Callie's. Shortly after the discovery, Scarlett had pleaded exhaustion, and I'd driven her home. And then I hadn't seen her again for two days. When she finally did come back around, it was with the idea that we were too incompatible to make this relationship work beyond a summer in Bootleg.

I slapped the steering wheel in frustration.

She'd cut me out. She'd kept something huge from me when I was the one person who could help her. If that sweater was indeed the one that Callie Kendall had last been seen wearing, the Bodines could use an attorney. There'd be an investigation. The press would swarm all over a new development in a cold case like this. That kind of attention would bleed over into everything, turning their private lives into a public circus…

And that's why she was ending things with me.

I pulled into the driveway and dropped my head against the seat.

There'd been no sign of the sheriff or any other law enforcement next door, and if Scarlett had reported the sweater, I was certain word would have spread like fire. I could only assume that she'd decided to keep the discovery to herself… perhaps her brothers as well.

I was having a lot of feelings about this. Conflicting ones. Scarlett didn't trust me to let me in on this. And I wasn't going to let that stop me from helping.

I carted the groceries inside and stashed them away. I grabbed a water, my laptop, and a legal pad and set up shop in Estelle's tiny office. Research was one of my nerd-like obsessions. I excelled at finding answers.

Starting with the original articles of the disappearance, I dug in. The articles were mostly local at first and then spreading nationwide as hours turned to days and days turned to weeks. They shared the same information over and over again. The last people who saw her were teenage friends who had gathered at the lake on a rocky beach often frequented by locals on the warm July night.

Witnesses—some of whom I've met including Nash, Misty Lynn, and Cassidy Tucker—recalled seeing her walk back toward town on Hooch Road. According to her parents, Judge and Mrs. Kendall, Callie never made it back to their house on the lakefront Speakeasy Drive.

I printed out a map and highlighted her potential path. The beach that she'd left was less than an eighth of a mile from the Bodine house, but she'd have walked in the opposite direction toward town, keeping the lake on her left as she traveled west.

She'd been wearing a long sleeve cardigan on a hot summer

night. Which I found odd. Wasn't it usually warm enough to forgo a sweater? Curiosity had me calling up an image search. The pictures all showed a pretty young girl with a shy smile who always wore long sleeves. I scratched another note and moved on to the next thread to tug on.

I gave myself two hours to binge on everything related to Callie's disappearance. I stumbled on a forum of conspiracy theories about the disappearance. The rabbit hole danger was real, but I did make a list of every suspect forum members named. It was a short list, and it didn't include Jonah Bodine Sr. or any of the Bodine boys. I needed to know who had been investigated, interviewed. I needed access to those notes.

I tapped out a beat with my pen on the tablet now scrawled with notes.

There was one person that Scarlett trusted implicitly. And she was the same person who could get me information. I debated for a solid ten minutes, weighing just how pissed off Scarlett would be at me for making the call against what I could learn from it.

She didn't want my help, but she was damn well going to get it.

———

Thirty minutes later I pulled up a chair next to Cassidy Tucker at The Lookout. She wasn't wearing her deputy uniform, and it made me feel like I was just having a casual conversation.

"If this is about Scarlett's favorite kind of diamond, you might as well save your money, Dev. She promised her mama she wouldn't get married before thirty," Cassidy said hefting her beer.

I caught Nicolette's eye and pointed at Cassidy's beer.

"This isn't about diamonds," I said. "This is about something... delicate."

Cassidy's eyes narrowed. Nicolette dropped my beer off with a nod and left again. "Define delicate."

"Say I was representing the family of someone accused of

a crime." I waited a beat and looked at her hard. I wanted to know if Scarlett had already spilled to Cassidy.

"Jesus, what did Scarlett do now?"

"Scarlett didn't do anything this time. No one did anything. Let's say this is all hypothetical."

"I'm not liking how this conversation is going," she said, sitting back in her chair and crossing her arms. She had the cool, flat eyes of a cop.

"Did a good friend of yours come to you recently with something he or she found?" I asked.

"Like what? A missing dog?"

"Like something connected to a crime."

"What are you getting at, Devlin?"

I waited a beat and repeated the question.

Cassidy sighed, grudgingly. "No. No one brought me any evidence recently."

Scarlett trusted Cassidy with her life but not with this. Either I'd have to trust her, or I needed to get up and walk out of here right now.

"Spill, McCallister."

I leaned in and lowered my voice. "What if someone found something in a deceased relative's house? Something that was connected to the biggest crime ever committed in Bootleg?" I asked.

Cassidy stiffened. She glanced around us and leaned in. "What did Scarlett find?" she asked in a voice barely above a whisper.

"Let's say my client," I said.

"Fine. What did your client find?" Cassidy asked.

"First, what wouldn't you do for Scarlett Bodine?" I pressed.

Cassidy's eyebrows winged up toward her hairline. "What *wouldn't* I do? There's not a damn thing in this world that I wouldn't do for her. If she needs help burying a body, I'm there with a shovel and duct tape."

I nodded. It was the answer I wanted. And I believed her.

"What was Callie Kendall wearing when she disappeared?"

"Cut off shorts, a blue tank top, red sweater, and blue flip-flops." She rattled off the list, and I remembered that Cassidy had been one of the last people to see Callie alive.

"My client," I said, placing emphasis on the words, "found a red cardigan sweater that matches the description tucked away in her deceased parents' possessions."

Cassidy leaned in until we were almost nose to nose. "Are you fucking kidding me?" she hissed.

I shook my head and glanced around to make sure none of the bar flies were listening.

"And she told you and not me?" Cassidy hissed. "And she didn't go to the cops? What is wrong with her? I'm going to kill her."

I put a hand on her arm. "She didn't tell me. I was there when she found it. But she didn't tell me that it's what Callie was wearing when she disappeared."

"Then why are you here? How did you find out?"

I shrugged. "I connected the dots. I'm guessing Scarlett's trying to handle this on her own. Whatever that means."

"If word gets out that the first clue in a decade has turned up in that case, we'll have the state police and FBI and media crawling all over this place. Jesus, Judge Kendall just got back in town."

I nodded. "And the Bodines will be under the microscope."

She flopped back in her chair. "Dang it, Devlin. I thought you asked me here to talk about engagement rings."

I looked into the depths of my beer. "I wish. Scarlett decided this is just a summer fling and that, when I go back to Annapolis, we're over."

"What?" Cassidy slapped a hand on the table. My beer sloshed over the rim. "That girl is ass over head in love with you."

"She said we wouldn't work. Said she'd be a liability to my career."

"Because of the sweater," Cassidy sighed, connecting the dots. "She doesn't want you to get dragged into the circus."

"I think that's why she didn't tell you either," I pointed out.

"Well fuck her," Cassidy announced, picking up her beer. "I'm going to help the shit out of her."

"We both will. Whether she wants us to or not," I agreed.

Chapter Forty-Four
Scarlett

Devlin's house smelled like charcoal. All the first-floor windows and doors were wide open. Dressed in gym shorts and a t-shirt, he ushered smoke out onto the deck with a dish towel.

"Something sure smells good," I drawled, eyeing him with amusement.

"Hilarious," Devlin said dryly. But I noticed the way his gaze lingered just for a second on the scoop neck of my tank top. "Grab a towel and help me."

I pulled a rooster towel out of the drawer and fanned from the front door until the smoke dissipated.

"What's for dinner?" I asked, strolling back into the kitchen where blackened pieces of some kind of meat smoldered like coals.

"It's Jonah's fault," Devlin said. "His handwriting is illegible."

"Awh. Jonah's teaching you to cook?"

He swung an arm around the wrecked, smoky kitchen. "Obviously it's not working."

I laid my hand on his arm, pleased at the muscles that bunched under my touch. "Maybe we should just face facts that neither one of us belongs in a kitchen."

"I refuse to accept that," he announced, giving me a perfunctory kiss on the forehead.

I poked my nose into the covered bowl on the island and found a yellow-ish potato salad. I plucked a potato cube out and popped it into my mouth. It was inexplicably crunchy. I swallowed hard.

Devlin seemed tense, a little moody. I could relate.

Nothing between us had been normal since that day at my father's house. I'd stashed the sweater in a kitchen cabinet and tried to pretend it didn't exist. In the middle of the night, I'd had a moment of pure insanity and wondered what would happen if I just threw it out. But I couldn't do it. I knew I had to take it to the police. I had to pull the plug on my own life as I knew it, and it sucked.

Everything in my life had frozen at that moment. I couldn't move forward in my father's house knowing that there could be other evidence tying him to Callie. I couldn't just enjoy my time with Devlin while he was here because the closer we got, the deeper he'd get dragged for this. But I wasn't going to break. I wasn't going to be selfish and spill my guts to him dragging him and his newly repaired reputation into this mess.

I needed to do what needed to be done. And I just wanted a few more days with him.

Devlin shoved the take-out menus at me. "Take your pick," he said.

Our fingers brushed, and I felt that electric zing swim through my blood. It had been selfish of me to continue seeing him while he was here.

"You know, Scarlett, if you need help all you have to do is ask."

I frowned. "I think I can pick take-out just fine on my own."

He eyed me and rubbed a hand over his beard. God, I

hoped he'd keep the beard even after he moved back. "You have friends who'd be willing to help you."

I felt a tingle crawl up the back of my neck. He was talking like he knew something.

The take-out menus fell through my limp fingers, and I bent to pick them up. The front door opened and shut.

"It smells like someone set the house on fire," Jonah announced, strolling into the kitchen.

"I blame you," Devlin said.

"I wasn't even here," he argued.

"He's blaming your handwriting, and let's just skip ahead to the part where we all decide what kind of take-out we're orderin'," I suggested.

Jonah pulled out a stool and plopped down to study the menus. It's not like he hadn't memorized them already. There were three places in town that did decent take-out, and we'd eaten them all in a rotation for the past few weeks.

"While you're both here," Jonah said, studying the pizza menu like it was the most fascinating novel in the world. "I'm thinking it might be time for me to head home."

"What do you mean *home*?" I demanded. I knew I hadn't been making much time for Jonah the past week since the "discovery." But I wasn't ready to let my new brother go because, odds were, he wouldn't come back.

"I've been here long enough. I'm getting antsy. I'd like to get back to work and let everyone else get back to their routines."

"But you can't go!" I noticed Devlin take a step back, his face a mask of hurt, and then it was gone. I plowed on. "Jonah, we just met. You can't just pack up and go home. Don't you want to stay and… and…"

"Be part of the family, the community," Devlin said flatly.

"Yeah! That!" I agreed, pointing at him.

Jonah looked at Devlin, and they telegraphed something between them. "Listen, I think I'm going to go for a drive," Devlin announced. "Why don't you two stay and talk?"

He picked up his keys and was gone before I could say another word.

"Well, what in the hell was that all about?" I asked when the front door shut soundly behind him.

"Scarlett. Seriously?" Jonah looked at me with disapproval.

"What? What's wrong with everybody all of the sudden?"

"You begged me to stay because you're not done getting to know me in front of the guy you told to go home without you."

"But that's different! You're my brother," I argued.

Jonah shook his head. "Did you ask Devlin to stay?"

"Why in the heck would Devlin stay here? He's got his career path all planned out. He's worked for it his whole life. He's not gonna give all that up for some redneck girl in some backwoods town."

Jonah opened the fridge and pulled out a beer. "I guess you'll never know the answer if you can't ask the question."

I sputtered after him as he strolled out of the room, beer in hand.

"I guess I'll just make myself dinner then," I said to the empty room. With Devlin gone to sulk and Jonah judging me, I figured it was safer and kinder back at my house. I'd make a sandwich and then figure out if I should go to Cass or straight to her daddy. Maybe I could beg them not to tell anyone until after Devlin went home?

My stomach flip-flopped on itself as I ducked out the back door and scurried down the stairs.

Maybe I should call my brothers first? Then we could provide a united front. I hurried through the woods. I'd fucked up, keeping the sweater this long. Callie's family deserved answers, even if we were the ones to pay the price for them.

I broke through the woods into my yard, and I saw the police cruiser in my driveway. Cassidy was leaning against the hood in her uniform. I'd seen her in uniform about ten thousand times. Hell, I'd even seen her arrest people. Once it was even me. But I'd never felt nervous being around Cop Cass before now.

"Evenin', Scarlett," she said.

She fucking knew. "Bowie's got a damn big mouth where you're concerned," I said flatly. I couldn't believe my own brother had gone behind my back.

"I don't know what you're talking about," she said mildly, pushing away from the car. "But I do know you have something that you want to tell me."

Cassidy wasn't usually such a good liar. I'd deal with Bowie and his head-up-his-ass crush later.

I sighed. There was no turning back now. "Come on in then."

Cassidy followed me inside. She'd been in my home hundreds of times. We'd giggled drunkenly over men and eaten way too many pizzas and dozens of wings under this roof. We'd guzzled beers and sunned ourselves on the dock. And now I was about to confess to withholding evidence. A crime. I'd looked it up online.

"Are you mad?" I asked.

"Hell yes, I'm mad! I'm mad that you didn't tell me, Scar. What the hell were you thinking?"

I scrubbed my hands over my face. "Are you asking as a cop or my best friend?"

In answer, she smacked me on the back of the head. "What do you think, jackass?"

I gave a weak laugh. "I found it, and it took me a few minutes to put it together. I knew it was hers, but I didn't realize she'd gone missing in it, and when I did…" I took a breath and shook my head. "I just wanted to get Dev as far away from that sweater as I could."

"He wouldn't have turned you in, idiot."

"I know that. But he'd want to get involved, and he's running for re-election next year. That wouldn't be an option if he were tangled up with the daughter of a potential… whatever you're going to say Daddy is. It's one thing to date me. I think we could have made it work. But there's no way Dev's career would survive a murder investigation."

"Even if your daddy had something to do with it—which

I'm not saying he did—you had nothing to do with it. None of you did."

"Yeah, but we're the ones left. We're the ones who'd be gossiped about half to death. We're the ones who'd have the media on our front steps. I can't ask Devlin to stand by me through all that."

"He would," Cassidy pointed out bluntly.

"I *know* he would. And I'm not asking him to do that."

"Because you love him."

I didn't want to talk about me loving or not loving Devlin when what we really needed to talk about was in a freezer bag in the cabinet.

"Let's get this part over with," I said. I opened the cabinet door and pulled out the bag.

Cassidy handled it with care. "Jesus. I didn't quite believe it until right this second," she confessed.

"It's not that we didn't trust you, Cass. I just didn't want to drag you into this mess… yet. If it makes you feel better, Bowie wanted to drag you in right away." And apparently he'd gone scampering next door with a guilty conscience and hearts in his eyes.

Cassidy grunted, not appeased, and I didn't blame her. If she would have kept something like this from me, I'd be good and pissed. But now wasn't the time for apologies. It was the time for truth.

"There's stains splattered on it," I said, jerking my chin toward the sweater. "I didn't notice them, but Jameson did."

"Hmm," Cassidy said.

I could see her cop wheels turning.

"Who all's handled this?" she asked.

I winced. "Just me without the bag. Bowie and Jameson with the bag."

"Why not invite the Bootleg High School football team to play keep away with it?" Cassidy was snarky when she was pissed. "I'm gonna need you to take me to where you found it," she said.

I nodded. "FYI, we didn't touch anything else in the house after I found this."

"At least you did one thing sorta right," Cassidy sighed. "That's why we bring these things to law enforcement immediately. We find things the average person doesn't. Forensics and all that." She flopped down in a chair. "Jesus, I remember the night she disappeared. I remember my daddy getting the call the next morning that she never came home. I remember watching her walk away from the lake wearing this exact sweater."

"Brings it all back," I agreed.

"Did you know this is why I went into law enforcement?" Cassidy asked.

"I had no idea. I thought you wanted to be like your daddy," I told her.

"That was part of it. But I remember the need for answers, you know? Someone out there knows exactly what happened to Callie. And I want to know too. Her family deserves answers. Hell, I think we all deserve answers."

"Was my daddy ever a suspect in the case?" I asked.

Cassidy shrugged. "Just about every adult in Bootleg was interviewed within forty-eight hours of Callie's disappearance," she said. "I pulled the files. Jonah showed up at the police station the next morning and offered to help organize a search party. My daddy did an informal interview on the spot. Jonah was alibied by your mama. None of you kids were home that night."

"We were all at Gibson's," I said.

"I remember calling your house as soon as Daddy got the news. Your daddy answered and said y'all were at Gibson's."

At least my father had been home that morning. That was one answer. I'd been wracking my brain trying to recall the specifics of a day twelve years ago. Parts of it were burned into my brain like a brand. The rest was like trying to remember what I ate for breakfast on a Tuesday a decade ago.

"Now look, Scarlett. You're gonna need an attorney. Someone who can stand between you and us *and* you and the media."

"I'm not asking Devlin," I railed.

"I'm not asking you to ask Devlin," she snapped back. "I'm telling you to get a lawyer."

"Dang it, Cass! That's gonna eat into my savings," I groaned. I'd planned to start scouting for another rental property this fall and have it ready for renters by next spring.

"Price you pay for being an asshole who doesn't trust her friends and boyfriend, if you ask me."

Chapter Forty-Five

Devlin

Cassidy: That thing we talked about happened. All is good.

I read the text again through bleary eyes. It was two in the morning, and I still hadn't fallen asleep. When I came home from my drive, I saw Scarlett's house was dark, and I knew Cassidy had made her move. If I couldn't convince her over dinner to go to the police, Cassidy was Plan B.

I'd walked away tonight, wanting to give up on her the way she'd given up on me. But I couldn't. She'd begged Jonah to stay. Hell, she'd been horrified by the idea of him leaving. But me? She'd written me off.

What wouldn't I have done for her if she'd only asked?

I was mad and hurt. But that didn't stop me from calling in a favor from my friend from law school. Jayme was a sharp lawyer who ran her own firm in Charleston. She was a shark in a pretty package and used it to her advantage. She was exactly the kind of attorney I'd want in my corner, and that's who Scarlett was getting whether she wanted her or not. I could at least do that for her.

I'd come home and holed up in the office, intending to work. But I found myself digging back into my Callie research. Cassidy had told me confidentially that Jonah Bodine Sr. had never been considered a suspect. And beside the fact that he was alibi'd the night of her disappearance, there was no record of his movements before or after.

> **Devlin:** Thanks. I talked to Jayme. She'll be here in the morning.
> **Cassidy:** We'll hold off on the formal interview until she's here. Dad's on board with keeping their names out of the papers. But there's no way Bootleg won't know whose house we're searching.

I blew out a breath and hoped that Bootleg's loyalty would remain intact when it came to the Bodines.

> **Devlin:** Good work, deputy
> **Cassidy:** She loves you, you know. She's just thick-headed about it.

I put my phone down and laid back to stare at my ceiling and think about the fact that Scarlett Bodine was too stubborn to trust me...or love me.

———

The insistent knocking woke me. I squinted at the clock on my nightstand. It was seven-thirty in the morning, and I'd fallen asleep only an hour or two before. I shuffled into some shorts and cut through the kitchen to get to the front door. It was probably Jayme. She'd always been an annoying early bird.

I pulled the door open on a yawn.

"Oh, my lord! You grew a beard. He grew a beard, Thomas," my mother gasped.

"Mom? Dad?"

My parents were standing on my doorstep. I wasn't mentally prepared for this. From now on, I was never answering my door again. Bad things always happened.

"Hello, son," my father said gruffly.

"Well. Aren't you going to invite us in?" my mother demanded, and she stepped past me into the house. "I swear a few weeks in this place, and he's forgotten his manners. A beard, answering the door half naked. I don't know what they put in the water here." Her litany of complaints faded when she rounded the corner into the kitchen.

"You look good," my dad said, pulling me in for a one-armed hug and clapping me on the back. I realized the last time he'd seen me was the day after I'd decked Hayden Ralston on the legislative floor. I'd been drunk and hollow. And Thomas McCallister had sent me packing. I'd been a liability, something to sweep under the rug.

"Is she here?" my mother shouted from the kitchen. "Your little friend?"

"You mean, Scarlett?" I called back dryly.

"Scar—aaaaah!" My mother's shrill shout of panic had my father and me jogging down the hallway to see what threat she was facing down.

Jonah—poor, disheveled, sleep-deprived Jonah—was staring stupefied at the blonde woman who was flapping her arms like a bird. "Who are you?" she demanded.

"Mom, this is Jonah," I said, rubbing my eyes. "Jonah, these are my parents, Thomas and Geneva McCallister."

"Nice to meet you," Jonah said with a yawn. He was wearing only pajama bottoms.

My mother's wild eyes flashed back and forth between the two of us. "Are you two…" she glanced around the kitchen as if she were about to impart a secret. "*Seeing* each other?" she asked.

I looked at Jonah's bare chest. He cracked a crooked smile.

"What is with this house and turning people gay?" my dad wondered. "Not that there's anything wrong with that," he added quickly. The McCallisters were liberal to the bone but always had one eye on what constituents would think.

"I think we can spin this in the appropriate way, and it might even be a bonus come election time," my mother mused still staring at Jonah's chest.

"Jonah is Scarlett's brother. He's staying here."

My parents looked vaguely disappointed.

"I'm going to go back to bed," Jonah announced and disappeared in the direction of the stairs.

He left, and I was again alone with my parents. I started up the coffeemaker. Caffeine was required for most conversations with them. "What are you two doing here so early?" I asked.

"We wanted to give you the good news in person," my mother chirped.

"What's that?"

"Hayden Ralston was arrested last night for soliciting a prostitute. An *underage* prostitute." She was breathless with glee and clapped her hands together.

"While we don't want to celebrate the misfortune of another, we are happy that the attention has shifted from you and your situation," my father interjected diplomatically.

My mother grabbed my hands. "You realize what this means, don't you? You can come back. There's no reason for you to stay here another minute."

Everything in my brain came to a screeching halt.

"I don't know about you two, but I certainly wouldn't mind some breakfast," my father said, patting his flat stomach.

I rubbed a hand over my beard. "Let me get dressed, and we'll go to Moonshine."

My mother's nose wrinkled. "Honestly, I don't know what my mother sees in this place."

The problem was, I did.

———

Clarabell fussed over my parents at the diner and talked them into a couple of specials. She didn't even laugh when my mother tried to order a cappuccino. While Mom chatted about a day sail they'd taken on the bay, I tried to listen to the conversations around us. As far as I could tell, no one was talking about the Bodines or Callie.

That wouldn't last long. It would be good if I could get my parents out of Bootleg before the news broke.

I was on edge. I wanted to be with Scarlett right now, making sure the Bodines were as removed from the situation as legally possible. Hell, I just wanted to be with Scarlett. She was probably terrified… or pissed off. And I hated the fact that she hadn't called.

Clarabell delivered our orders with a flourish. "Are y'all spendin' the weekend?" she asked.

"Oh, lord no," my mother laughed. "We're all leaving for home today."

Clarabell's eyebrows shot up her forehead. "Is that so?" she asked, topping off my father's coffee. She telegraphed a look to me that asked if Scarlett was aware of this news.

"I'm not sure when I'm leaving," I amended, not wanting the grapevine to get to Scarlett before I did. I wasn't leaving if I could help her. If she needed me.

"Don't be silly. Devlin is very busy as a state legislator," Mom bragged to Clarabell.

"He's certainly kept busy this summer," she said. I caught the veiled criticism loud and clear. "Do y'all know Judge Kendall?" she asked, swinging her coffee pot in the direction of an older gentleman in the corner who looked like he was dressed for a tennis match. "He's a district court judge."

My father looked interested. He lived for networking, collecting connections like some did stamps or shot glasses. "I believe we've crossed paths in Annapolis." I gave it thirty seconds before he decided to wander over to introduce himself.

If Judge Kendall was enjoying a diner breakfast, he hadn't been notified of a break in his daughter's case. It was only a matter of time.

"Well, give us a holler if you need anythin'," Clarabell said and bustled away. I winced when I saw her fish her cell phone out of her apron pocket.

"It's like they're speaking a different language here," Mom whispered.

"Come on, son," Dad wiped his mouth on his napkin. "Let's go introduce ourselves to the judge."

"Dad, let him eat," I said. "His daughter went missing here—"

"That's why he sounds so familiar," my mom gasped. "His daughter was kidnapped or murdered or something. That happened *here*?" She looked around the diner as if expecting to see the guilty party plopped down at the table next to us.

Allowing the man to enjoy a peaceful last breakfast before discovering new evidence had been uncovered in his daughter's disappearance was reason enough to leave him alone.

"Come on, Devlin. He won't mind," my father insisted.

I suppose it was morbid curiosity that had me following my father to the man's table. I saw his immediate future, and it would be a painful one after what I could only assume was a painful past.

He had thinning gray hair that he combed neatly over his head. He wore wire rimmed spectacles and a white polo shirt. His watch was expensive. His breakfast was sensible.

"Excuse me, Judge Kendall?" my father said, interjecting himself into the man's breakfast.

"Yes?" He looked up with a hint of resignation as if he was used to being interrupted. The honorable judge, tired of his people. I wanted to leave him alone, leave him to the last peaceful breakfast he'd have for a long time.

"I wanted to stop by and say hello. I'm Thomas McCallister, and this is my son, Devlin. We met a few years ago at a gala for the Maryland State Historical Society." My father's mind was a meticulously organized filing cabinet of people, events, and connections.

"Ah, of course." The judge warmed slightly, slipping smoothly into political mode. Only other insiders would notice the lack of sincerity in the man's polite smile. He offered his hand to my father, and they shook. "It's good to see you again."

"Devlin is in the state legislature," my father explained. They were making small talk, discussing mutual friends, when the bells on the diner door chimed and Scarlett strolled in. She was wearing ripped up cutoffs and one of those damned tank tops that hugged her curves. Her hair was tied up in a ponytail. She looked every inch the beautiful girl-next-door.

Our gazes met, and I saw a dozen emotions flit across her face. When her eyes scanned to my father and then Judge Kendall, she froze.

Chapter Forty-Six

Scarlett

Of all the shit things to happen on a shit day, I had to get a text from Clarabell saying she was sorry to hear Devlin was leaving town. And then I had to walk on into Moonshine and see Devlin making small talk with Callie's daddy. The man who was about to find out that my father was a person of interest in his daughter's missing person case.

I swallowed hard, and Devlin crossed the black-and-white tile floor to me.

"Hey," he said softly.

I wanted to fall into his arms and press my face into his chest. I'd spent the better part of the night showing Cassidy and then Sheriff Tucker where I found the sweater. In an hour, my brothers and I were going to present a united front at the police station and have our statements taken.

Jonah Bodine Sr. was officially a "person of interest." And while our names were being kept out of the paperwork, it was a matter of time before forensic investigators tore my daddy's house apart and the news spread far and wide.

And Devlin McCallister needed to get as far away from me as possible.

"Got a minute?" I asked, shoving my hands in my back pockets.

"Of course," he said. "My parents are here. Do you want to meet them?"

I shook my head and felt the tail of my hair brush my back. "Now's not a good time." I wasn't lying.

We stepped outside onto the sidewalk into the warm morning sun.

"Clarabell texted and said you're leaving today," I said.

Devlin opened his mouth, but I cut him off with a wave of my hand.

"I think it's good for you to go. You should go." I said. My stomach flip-flopped, and I felt tears tickle the back of my eyes.

"You want me to leave?" he asked slowly.

I nodded. "We both knew this was temporary, and you're in such a better place now. It would be silly for you to hang around here." The words tumbled out in a rush. I had to make him leave before he found out, before he knew. I couldn't stand the idea of him looking at me like I was the daughter of a murderer. I'd die if my family's hot mess damaged his reputation.

"Scarlett, there's no reason I have to leave today," he began. "If you need me for something, I want to be here for you."

Always the good guy. Dang it. Here I was kicking him to the curb, and he was offering to stick around for me. He probably thought I was a mental case after the past few days. Everything had spiraled out of control. If Devlin didn't leave Bootleg now, he'd end up in the middle of this mess with me.

"I don't need anything, Dev. You gave me the most fun I've had in a long time." I reached out and cupped his jaw, feeling the bristle of his beard against my palm. "I hope you'll keep the beard," I whispered.

"This is what you want?" he asked, his hand snaking up to hold my wrist.

"It's what we agreed on," I said, skirting the truth. I wanted

Dev here with me. I wanted to lean on him. But that was selfish. Someone had to look out for Dev. And if a career in politics, a life in the spotlight, was what he wanted? That's what I'd make sure he got.

He released my wrist, his expression unreadable. I couldn't stop myself from reaching out and running my palms over his broad chest.

"I can't just pack up and leave," he said. "What about Jonah? My grandmother's house—"

"Granny Louisa will be fine with Jonah staying on. She trusts my judgment."

I saw Devlin's jaw clench once and then relax.

"This is what we'd planned all along," I reminded him. "A great time and a friendly parting."

"I thought we'd be saying goodbye in a different way," Devlin admitted.

I gave him a saucy wink. "Naked, you mean?"

"Well. Yeah. A romantic dinner on the deck watching the sun set," he said, tracing the back of his knuckles over my cheek. "A good bottle of wine. Candles."

I was melting into him when I needed to be walking away. I let my fingers dig in to his chest.

"Thanks for all the orgasms," I said, desperate to keep it light.

I saw a flash of amusement and sadness in his brown eyes, and then he slid his hands around my waist. "Thanks for an unforgettable summer," he whispered.

I closed the distance between our mouths and kissed him hungrily. This was no sweet goodbye. This was desperation, a need unmet. I felt him thicken and harden against my belly. God, I wanted him. Not one last time though. I wanted him every night forever. I knew for sure that no one else would make me feel the way Devlin Brooks McCallister did. And in that moment, I almost hated my daddy just a little bit.

"There's an alley six feet from here," Devlin said, pulling back, his breathing ragged.

I laughed breathlessly. "That's not a good idea."

"Right. My parents might catch us," he said casting a glance in the diner window. Half of the customers had their noses pressed up against the plate glass window.

"Oh, for Pete's sake! Sit down and eat your breakfasts," I hollered.

Mona Lisa McNugget, Bootleg's official mascot chicken, strutted past pecking her little beak at the piece of toast Moonshine staff left for her every morning.

"I'm going to miss this place," Devlin said, waving to Mrs. Morganson through the window.

"Look at us bein' all civilized about this," I said. "You must have rubbed off on me."

Devlin threaded his fingers through my ponytail. "I think the rubbing was mutual."

"I sure hope so," I breathed. He was put back together. That was for sure. Gone was the shadowed, anxious man who'd arrived in Bootleg. In his place was a strong, smart, capable man who had better not take shit from anyone or else I'd have to track him down and give him another lesson.

"Dev, promise me you won't get back with Johanna," I said. "I know it's not fair to try to dictate who you date and don't date. But she's no good for you. You can do better."

"I've already done better, Scarlett."

Chapter Forty-Seven
Scarlett

I f you have no further questions for my clients, we'll leave you to do your jobs." Jayme, our surprise lawyer, was a shark in a sleek pantsuit and sky-high heels. She'd nearly tackled me and my brothers on our way into the police station, claiming to be our representation. Jayme had already been briefed on our situation and claimed that a friend had called in a favor. I assumed it was Sheriff Tucker worried about us Bodines. Old habits were hard to break.

Sheriff Tucker exchanged a long look with the homicide detective who'd driven in to stick his nose into the case. Detective Connelly wore his years of experience in the deep lines of his face. "We'll do our best to keep your clients' names out of this mess," Sheriff Tucker promised. "But with forensics going over their daddy's house, it's only a matter of time before every busybody in the tri-county area knows."

Gibson shifted in his chair, no happier about a team of investigators ripping through our childhood home than I was.

"We appreciate every effort you make to ensure my clients'

privacy." Jayme said, cool as the cucumber eye masks at Bootleg Springs Spa.

I took my cue from her and stood up while she packed her briefcase. "Gentlemen," I said, nodding at the sheriff I'd known my entire life. His mustache twitched. And I knew this was as hard on him as it was on us.

Cassidy was pacing outside the door and grabbed me by the tank top straps. "You were in there for fucking ever!"

"Excuse me, deputy. My clients and I were just leaving." Jayme hauled me out of Cassidy's grip and through the back door of the station where our lawyer had ordered Gibson to park in the alley. "We're having a meeting," she announced. "Where can we go?"

"We can go to my house," I sighed.

"I'll follow you." Jayme slid behind the wheel of a sexy little crossover vehicle.

I climbed in the backseat behind Bowie.

"Well, that was fun," Jameson drawled.

"We did the right thing," Bowie said. "Callie's father has a right to know, and who knows? Maybe they'll turn up evidence that leads them to the real killer."

Gibson's eyes found mine in the rearview mirror. Neither one of us said anything. It was a tentative truce.

"I can't believe you went to Cassidy behind my back," I said, slapping Bowie's head from behind.

"Ow! What are you talking about? She said *you* went to *her*."

I leaned around the seat and grabbed my brother in a choke hold. "Are you sayin' you didn't tell her?" I demanded, applying just enough pressure to make him uncomfortable.

"Gibs, I'm gonna kill you for teachin' her this one," Bowie gasped.

"Swear it, Bow! Swear you didn't tell Cassidy," I growled.

He slapped at my arm. "I didn't say a damn word to anyone."

"Wrote an unsigned letter? Made an anonymous call? Hired a sketchy skywriter?" I pressed.

His neck was turning a deep shade of raspberry.

"Jesus, Scar. I swear I didn't tell anyone."

I released him and sat back to glare at Jameson. He held up a hand before I could attack from the side. "It wasn't me either."

All eyes slid to Gibson.

"Don't look at me. I've been holed up in the workshop for three days. I didn't even see the sweater."

"None of y'all talked?"

Gibson made the turn into my driveway. "How do we know *you* didn't tell her?"

"I *did* tell her but only because she already knew!"

Jayme pulled in next to us, and I couldn't help but look next door. Jonah's car was in the driveway, but there was no sign of Devlin's. Was he already gone? Had he really vanished from my life just like that? It was what he needed to do, what he should do. But why did that half-empty driveway hit me like a fist to the gut?

"Cute place," Jayme said, pulling off her designer sunglasses and studying my cottage. I couldn't tell if she was being sincere or sarcastic.

"Come on in, y'all," I said, leading the way.

I put the coffee on and poured glasses of ice water while Jayme arranged her files just so on my dining table.

"Okay, here's the deal," she said, launching into business. "The sweater is being sent off for forensic testing. It'll take weeks for any results to come back, so that's a little bit of a reprieve. However, the crime scene investigation team already started on your father's house. The sheriff and Detective Connelly have agreed to refer to you all only as 'witnesses' in any official statements and paperwork. But I grew up in a small town, and I know how fast news travels. You're not to comment to anyone about anything," she said. "Got it?"

I nodded, and Jayme zeroed in on me. "That includes your deputy friend."

"Cassidy is trustworthy," I argued. "She's on our side."

"Say nothing to anyone," Jayme enunciated crisply. "This

is now a police matter, and I don't want you to get tangled up in this any further. None of you are suspects. None of you are to blame for any potential actions by your parent or parents. That being said, they will name Jonah Bodine as a person of interest. That plus the sweater when it leaks—and it will—will have the media swarming you like fleas."

My brothers and I looked at each other. "Okay," I said. "What else?"

Jayme consulted the notes she'd scrawled during our formal interview. "Stay the hell away from Judge Kendall. I know you share a town the size of a city block, but don't talk to him, don't try to defend your family, and for God's sake don't apologize."

Avoiding someone in Bootleg was about as easy as finishing a marathon with only one leg.

"If you feel threatened by anyone, go to the police," Jayme continued.

I snorted. "Who exactly would we feel threatened by?"

"Judge Kendall. Overzealous media. Drunk townsfolk."

Gibson rolled his eyes. "We can hold our own."

"Not saying you can't," Jayme said. "I'm saying your family doesn't need any additional legal trouble for the foreseeable future."

I laughed weakly. "Guess y'all can't start any more bar fights."

Jayme rolled her shoulders. "God, I hate favors," she muttered.

———

It was better and worse than we thought it would be.

All it took for word to spread like spilled gin was Rocky Tobias to drive past Daddy's house when the state police were roping off the driveway.

Approximately ten minutes later, everyone in Bootleg was informed that somethin' was goin' down at the Bodine homestead. Less than an hour later, the sheriff's office was so inundated with calls and drop-ins that they issued a vague statement.

Bootleg Springs Police Department Memo

Evidence relating to a crime was recently discovered by anonymous witnesses at a home outside of town. There is no reason to believe there is any threat to the community at this time. Please go about your business.

By lunchtime, the rumor mill had more grist than it knew what to do with. I didn't know who was the first to whisper Callie's name, but it ignited like gasoline fumes. And when Sheriff Tucker's cruiser was spotted in Judge Kendall's driveway, everyone's suspicions were confirmed.

Bootleg Springs Police Department Memo

In response to the flood of calls and questions, the Bootleg Springs Police Department would like to remind our citizens that there is no call for concern. There is no threat to our community. We are simply investigating a police matter relating to an old crime.

Bootleg Springs Police Department Memo

Y'all really need to stop gossiping. That's an official order from your sheriff. Also, please stop standing outside Judge Kendall's house. And we'd like to take this opportunity to remind you that harassing private citizens—which includes inundating someone with phone calls demanding answers even if it is just for a betting pool—is still against the law in Bootleg Springs.

Lines were drawn. And my hometown chose sides faster than the Yankees and Confederates.

Chapter Forty-Eight
Scarlett

I had the flu. Or the plague. Or a case of food poisoning that had lasted six straight days. My body hurt like I'd decided to swim the length of the lake and then gotten run over by Jimmy Bob Prosser's monster pickup truck.

I heard my back door open and pulled the quilt over my head. The male Bodines had decided that we needed to host a bonfire and pretend that everything was peachy keen. I didn't know if they were doing it to pull me out of my funk or test the waters to see who in Bootleg we could still call friends.

Whatever their motivation, I wasn't moving from my bed cave. If the pile of maintenance calls coming in didn't rouse me from my deathbed, then some dumb party wouldn't either. I didn't have the energy to fix a damn thing let alone make small talk and swill beer.

I wanted to lay here and think about Devlin. Wonder what he was doing. Was he missing me? Had he stepped right back into his old life? Why hadn't he texted or called? Had he heard the news that Jonah Bodine Sr. was a person of interest in Callie Kendall's disappearance?

I'd started to text him a thousand times and deleted every single one of them without hitting Send. Only once had I seen the dots in our last text conversation that meant he was typing. I'd clutched my phone so tight my fingers hurt. But the dots disappeared without a text.

"Scarlett Rose Bodine." Cassidy's voice snuck through the cotton of the quilt.

"Go away. I'm contagious."

She unceremoniously ripped the quilt off of me. "Get your ass out of bed!"

"She looks terrible," June announced from the doorway, pulling her tank top over her nose as if to ward off germs. "Maybe she is ill."

"Oh, she's ill all right," Cassidy confirmed. "Ill in the head."

"Just go away and leave me to die," I moaned dramatically. "I think it's the flu." I coughed as if to prove my point.

"You don't have the flu any more than I have a dick," Cassidy announced.

"Oh, so you're a doctor now?"

"Do you have fever, chills, and body aches?" June asked.

"Yes!" Well probably not the fever or the chills part. And the body aches were really more of a lethargy that hooked its talons into me… but it was clearly the flu.

"No, she doesn't," Cassidy said without pity. "She's got a broken heart, and she did it to her own damn self."

I sat straight up in bed indignantly. "What in the hell are you talking about, Cassidy Tucker?"

"You pushed Devlin away because you loved him, and we all know it was a huge mistake."

I ignored the ridiculous part of her statement and zeroed in on the other. "We all?"

"The fifty people in your backyard. We voted. You need to get your ass up and go after Devlin."

"We parted ways. It was very civilized," I argued.

June snorted.

"Since when do you do anything civilized, Scarlett?" Cassidy demanded. "You love Devlin."

"We had a fling—"

Cassidy shook her head. "You fell sloppy stupid head-over-boots for the man. Admit it."

"I'd like to share my theory," June interjected. "I believe Scarlett's romantic feelings for Devlin scared her, and she rejected him to protect herself."

"June, are y'all calling me a chicken shit?" I gasped.

"Essentially? Yes."

"I am no such thing!" I put my feet on the floor and stood up.

"Good job, Juney. You got her out of bed, now insult her again so she gets in the shower. She smells like a junior high boys basketball team."

"I don't smell—" I gave my armpit a sniff and reconsidered my words.

"Call him," Cassidy said, thrusting my phone at me. "Call him and tell him you're a sorry idiot and you miss him and you want to make it work." She had no idea how many times in the past week I'd wanted to do just that. I missed him. I physically ached for a man I'd chased away.

"Cass, I appreciate your concern. But I am not dragging Devlin into this Dumpster fire of a mess. He's got a career to worry about."

"Did you ever bother asking him what he wanted, or did you just make the decision for him?"

"God, you sound like Jonah."

"Speaking of Jonah, how do you think your half-brother feels finding out about his father from Bootleg and not you."

"Hell."

"Let me guess. You didn't want to burden him with it either?" Cassidy crossed her arms over her chest.

I could only face one mistake at a time.

"What if Devlin didn't want to stick? What if I told him

300

everything, and he still left?" I demanded. "Do you know what that would have done to me?"

"Newsflash, dumbass. He does know. He figured it out on his own. Who do you think told me so I could protect your ass? Who do you think called in Jayme the Terrifying? You think me or my dad have those kind of connections?"

I gaped at her. "That's not true. Is it?"

"Damn straight it's true. He was ready to stay, to help. And you sent him away. You didn't trust him to love you back."

"He loves me?" I whispered.

"Either that or perhaps he just has masochistic tendencies," June piped up.

I shook my head. "It doesn't even matter if he loves me or is a masochist. We'd just end up like my parents."

Cassidy threw her hands up in the air and screeched. "Did someone drop you on your head recently? What makes you think you're destined to repeat your parents' mistakes? Did you get knocked up in high school? Uh. No! Did you marry your high school sweetheart and then proceed to never mature past the eleventh grade? Also no! You and Devlin had something special, and you got scared and shit all over it!"

"I didn't shit all over anything!" I hollered.

"You know what?" Cassidy said, looking at me with disdain. "The longer I talk to you, the more I just wanna punch you right in the face."

"Bring it on, Deputy Assface."

Cassidy sucker punched me right in the dang face. I was so surprised I fell back on the bed. But the second my ass hit mattress I launched myself at her. The force of our bodies hitting the wall dented the drywall.

Growing up in Bootleg, Cassidy and I learned how to fight dirty. I grabbed a hold of her hair and gave her a shot to the gut with my knee.

She grunted and threw an elbow that connected with my right boob.

I got off a short shot to her jaw that snapped her head

301

back. But Cassidy wasn't weak from a week of moping. She gripped me by my t-shirt—Devlin's Cock Spurs t-shirt that I hadn't given back—and threw me on the mattress. She climbed on and we traded shots, shouting insults.

"You're the thick-headedest mule in three counties!" Cassidy yelled.

"You're a redneck douchecanoe!"

"I can't believe we're friends!"

I tasted blood and wasn't sure if it was my own or if it was dripping from Cassidy's nose.

"Okay. That's enough of that." Bowie's voice was amused when he picked Cassidy up off me. That pissed us both off. Cassidy kicked him in the shin with her bare foot, and I grabbed his hair.

"Ow! Fuck! Jameson!" Bowie screeched. "Get in here!"

Jameson hauled me over his shoulder and carted me into the living room, which was filled with gawkers.

"What in the hell are you two doing?" Gibson demanded, hands on hips. "Y'all have been best friends since birth."

"She started it," I snapped.

"I did! Because she's a dumbass," Cassidy growled, still fighting Bowie's hold on her. "Bootleg Justice!"

"Don't make me call my lawyer," I yelled.

There was dead silence for five whole seconds in my house, and then Cassidy and I started to laugh. And we couldn't stop. Calling a lawyer over Bootleg Justice? It just wasn't done. Everyone was howling now, and the human restraints were no longer necessary. I met Cassidy in the middle of the room.

"Friends again?" I offered.

"Yeah. Just maybe stop being such a dumbass."

We hugged it out and the crowd applauded.

"Now, what are you going to do about Devlin?" Bowie asked me.

"Yeah," the crowd demanded.

"Bring him back!" someone started chanting.

"Pepperoni roll!" someone else chanted.

I climbed up on my coffee table, surrounded by people I'd loved since kindergarten. Friends and neighbors who had been there through the deaths of my parents and were willing to stand with me now even in this mess.

"I'll tell you what I'm gonna do! I'm gonna get a shower!"

The crowd cheered.

"And then I'm gonna drive to Annapolis!"

They cheered louder.

"And I'm gonna bring me back my man!"

They were rioting in my living room. I was picked up and carried to my bathroom on the shoulders of Freddy Sleeth and Corbin the keyboardist.

They dumped me inside and slammed the door behind me.

"Find me something conservative to wear," I yelled to Cassidy. "I'll show him what a politician's girlfriend looks like!"

My reflection in the mirror over my tiny vanity caught my eye. "I can do this," I told myself. "At least I think I can."

I showered quickly and brushed my teeth. Cassidy shoved a dress and shoes into my hands. Once I was dressed, Opal Bodine squeezed into the bathroom and, standing on the lip of my tub, styled my hair into a chic twist. I slapped on some makeup over the fresh bruises going for a look that said board-room, not brothel, and called it done.

I strolled out of the bathroom and struck a pose for the twenty-some people still crammed inside my house.

"What do y'all think?"

"Are your boobs tryin' to escape?" Millie Waggle asked.

I looked down and grabbed my girls. The dress Cassidy had picked was a remnant from my short stint in 10th grade band. It turned out that I hated the clarinet, and the trumpet player I was trying to impress was more interested in one of the trombonists, if you know what I mean. I lasted for one concert, in this high-necked dress, before quitting.

"I don't think your breasts like their incarceration," EmmaLeigh, a homemaker and mama of four wild boys, said

303

eyeing the flesh spilling out the sides of the dress. EmmaLeigh was nice as pie and sweet as tea. "Maybe if you wore a little wrap?"

"Here!" Buck whipped the gauzy pink cloth off of the lamp shade closest to him, and Opal wrapped it around me like a little jacket.

Cassidy stepped forward with a to-go box in her hands. "Here's a pepperoni roll in case he tries to say no. Clarabell says good luck and bring your boy home."

My eyes stung as I accepted the box.

"He won't say no," Gibson said, stepping up to take his turn. He nudged my chin up. "But if he does. You call us. And we'll kick his ass."

I nodded, the little gold earrings danced in my earlobes. "Are we good, Gibs?" I asked.

"We're good." He lifted a hand to ruffle my hair, but Opal slapped his hand away.

"We gotta fix things with Jonah," I told him.

He scrubbed a hand over the back of his neck. "Yeah, I know. You let us worry about that."

I nodded, trusting him to do what needed to be done. Bowie held up my truck keys. "Gassed up and ready to go."

"Thanks, Bow."

"Go get your guy."

I looked around at the people crowded in my kitchen and living room. "What if I can't stay in Bootleg anymore? What if I have to move?"

"Then we'll come visit you," Bowie promised. "We'll bring the moonshine and pepperoni rolls."

"I'm scared about things changing," I whispered.

"Sometimes change is better than keepin' things the same," he said sagely.

Jameson was next. He gave me a nod and patted me on the head. In Jameson's world, that was the equivalent of a five-minute hug and a conversation. He handed me a brown paper bag. I peered in it and found a sandwich and a box of condoms.

"Just in case," he said stoically.

I laughed and squared my shoulders. "See y'all. I'm gonna go get me a boyfriend!"

Chapter Forty-Nine
Scarlett

I was ten miles down the road hurtling toward Annapolis as fast as my pickup would go when Cassidy called.

"Little snafu," she said.

"What?" I asked, putting down the sandwich I'd been inhaling as I drove.

"Devlin isn't in Annapolis."

"Well where in the hell is he?" I demanded.

"He's at Granny Louisa's house."

"The hell you say! He came back, and he didn't even *call* me?"

I threw the phone on the passenger seat and executed a U-turn that put the ass end of my truck in the ditch. Gravel and mud flew, and then I was flooring it back to Bootleg.

"That son of a bitch came back without a word!" I fumed. I was gonna kill him and then tell him that I loved him so much it hurt to take a breath without him in my life. But definitely kill him first.

Devlin McCallister was going to feel the Bodine Wrath.

I fired myself up for my second fight of the night and

vowed that no one would break this one up until I was declared the winner.

Judging from the cars in my driveway, the bonfire was still in full swing. I bypassed my house and pulled into Granny Louisa's driveway behind Devlin's SUV. There would be no escape for him.

I yanked the emergency brake and turned off the truck, leaving the keys in the ignition. Devlin had come back and hadn't called or texted or showed up naked and begging on my front porch? He was a dead man.

I went around back because that's how sneak attacks worked. I was no Johanna ringing the doorbell proper as can be. Oh, hell no. I fought dirty and played mean. I kicked off my heels and jogged up the deck stairs that I'd refinished just a few weeks earlier. At least I didn't have to worry about splinters before extracting my justice all over his ball sack.

The lights were on, and I deducted even more points from Devlin after noticing he wasn't on the deck pining over me. He deserved a kick in the balls. Dang it. I should have left my shoes on. They were pointy.

I had a full head of steam behind me that nearly carried me through the screen door before I realized it wasn't Devlin sitting in the wingback chair with his feet up. It was Granny Louisa.

"Thank you again for riding to my rescue, Devlin honey," she said.

I glared imaginary lasers at the man who adjusted her footstool. He didn't look emaciated and depressed. He just looked stupidly handsome.

Maybe if I messed his face up a little, he wouldn't be so beautiful?

"I'm glad you called, Gran. But I can't stay. Mom's driving in tomorrow morning to help you and Estelle."

Estelle, a svelte black woman with silver hair and a hallelujah voice, poked her head into the living room. She held a cast iron fry pan in her hand. "I don't know why y'all are treating us like we're two old ladies," she announced.

"Well, one of you fell out of a gondola in Venice and broke her foot," Devlin said dryly.

"Hush up, Estelle," Granny Louisa said, waving at her girlfriend. Devlin appeared to miss the wink she sent her partner, but I caught it just fine. Granny Louisa was up to no good.

"Now, boy of mine, why are you in such a rush to go back to something that makes you so miserable?"

My ass perked up at that. Miserable was good. Very good.

"I'm not miserable," that asshole said. "I have a responsibility—"

Granny Louisa interrupted him by making a prolonged fart noise with her mouth. "Do you love the girl or not?"

My feet were frozen to the spot. I couldn't have moved if I tried.

Devlin, the potential asshole, flopped down into the chair across from Granny Louisa. His broody expression didn't give me the words I longed to hear.

"You've spent fifty minutes of every hour since you got here moping on the deck and staring through the woods in her direction. Do. You. Love. Her?"

"She didn't trust me. She didn't ask me to stay. And now she's throwing a party."

"That doesn't mean you don't love her and she doesn't love you. It means y'all are young and dumb."

I saw it then. The pain of my heart was plastered across Devlin's sexy AF face. He hurt for me. He missed me. He loved me.

Like *hell* was I going to let him say it first. I wanted that honor… and the ability to throw it in his face for the rest of our lives.

In my haste to shout the words first, I forgot about the screen door that I'd replaced after my brothers wrecked it. I half dived, half tripped through it, yanking it from its tracks and sending it crashing to the living room floor. It rattled against the hardwood, crumpled and mangled just like my heart.

Devlin came out of his chair looking shocked and maybe the slightest bit scared.

"I love you," I shouted.

Granny Louisa looked a little surprised. Estelle reappeared and gaped at the evidence of my spectacular entrance.

"Speak up, honey. I don't think he heard you," Estelle insisted.

I opened my mouth to make my proclamation again, but Devlin held up a hand. "I think we all heard Scarlett," he said dryly. His gaze scanned my face, and I saw his Adam's apple work in his throat.

Granny Louisa bent down and ripped open the Velcro on her boot. She kicked it off and hopped to her feet, spry as a forty-year-old. "Our work here is done, Estelle. Why don't we meander on over to The Lookout for a round of mystic moonshines?"

Estelle tossed her dish towel on the floor. "Sounds good to me. I'll get my drinkin' pants on."

They hustled out of the room, leaving me and Devlin to stare at each other.

"You broke Gran's door," he said quietly.

"I also announced that I'm in love with you," I pointed out just in case he'd missed the announcement.

"See y'all later," Granny Louisa said as she and Estelle giggled their way out the front door.

Silence reigned. I could hear my heart thumping away in my chest. Devlin stalked toward me and didn't stop until he had his hands on my hips. He leaned in, and I thought I just might embarrass myself by passing out on the man. My body had missed him like sun… or beer. I'd been kidding myself to think I could just walk away from him and be fine.

I was anything but fine.

"One more time," he whispered, his thumb brushing my lower lip, and I felt the touch in every nerve ending in my body.

"I, Scarlett Rose Bodine, love you, Devlin Brooks McCallister. And you're a fucking idiot if you think I'm letting you leave again without me."

"You dumped me, remember?"

"I didn't say you were the only idiot," I argued.

"You were an idiot," he agreed. "And I left without telling you how I feel," he said, tugging me close enough that every inch of me was touching him.

"And how exactly do you feel?" I asked him.

"Like without you I'd spend my whole life knowing I was missing out on something special. Like I walked away from the only woman I ever loved because I'm an idiot."

"Keep talkin'," I prodded.

"I went home to that sterile condo. I attended half a dozen luncheons and ribbon cuttings and fundraisers. It sucked. You're the color and music and flavor in my day. And life without you isn't worth crawling out of bed for. I want you, Scarlett. I love you, and you better get that through your thick Bodine head."

My breath was shaky on the inhale and got stuck in my throat. "What do we do about it?"

"I have some ideas," he said, a slow smile curving the corners of his mouth.

"I think that sounds right nice," I breathed. "But do we need to talk about your grandmother faking an injury to lure you back to town?"

"Do we need to talk about why you didn't tell me about Callie's sweater?"

"Do we need to talk about the cluster your life's about to become if you start datin' a girl in the middle of a murder investigation?"

"Do we need to talk about why you didn't even give me the choice to stay or go?"

I bit my lip. Yeah, we had a lot to talk about. And maybe even some apologizing to do, which I wasn't excited about at all.

"Why don't we leave that all for later? It'll keep, won't it?"

"It'll keep," he agreed.

The thump of music next door echoed, and Devlin shook his head. "Just like the first night I met you."

"Not quite," I said, reaching into my hair and yanking the pins free. I let my hair tumble down my back and grabbed him by the hand. "C'mon."

We ran through the night, navigating the skinny trail through the woods. When we came out on the other side, the crowd cheered.

"I found myself a man, y'all!" I shouted.

Devlin tossed me over his shoulder and jogged to Buck's pickup by the fire. He put me down feet first on the tailgate. "Someone get the lady a beer," he called.

Someone shoved a beer into my hand. I leaned forward and pulled Devlin up next to me in the bed of the truck.

"Ladies and gentlemen," I said. "I dedicate this to all of y'all."

Devlin raised a beer as well. I saw my brothers in the crowd raising their drinks. Jonah stood between Bowie and Jameson. He tipped his beer in my direction.

Devlin and I clinked cans, and on the count of three, we started to chug.

Chapter Fifty

Scarlett

Hours later, Devlin and I were slow dancing in my backyard, the party still going strong around us. "Sorry about Granny Louisa's sliding door," I said.

"Excuse me. Did you just apologize?" Devlin asked feigning shock.

"I figured I'd start with one of the smaller things and work my way up."

"Easing into it," he teased.

"There's a lot we're gonna have to talk about, Dev. Half the town thinks my daddy did it. When news breaks about that sweater, nothing's gonna be the same. The media will be breathing down our necks." I needed him to know the risks. To understand them. And then still pick me.

"You know, it's a good thing your boyfriend is an attorney. It's even better that he's been thinking about opening up his own practice in West Virginia."

I gasped. "Are you serious? Won't your parents hate your guts?"

"They are currently bitterly disappointed."

"You already told them?"

"Scarlett, I went back, but part of me never left here. You're what I want. God help me, but Bootleg is what I want."

"I need to show you something," I announced.

"Is it under that dress?"

He wasn't exactly excited when I pulled him away from my house and bed and headed for my truck instead. But I had one hell of an idea, and I didn't want to lose it in a cloud of lust.

"It's worth the wait. I promise."

Devlin held my free hand as I floored it toward our destination. There was only one thing I wanted more than to get him naked and under me. And it was important.

I turned onto the bumping lane and stopped by the peeling For Sale sign. The fields stretched out, bright under the nearly full moon. The tree line whispered quietly in the light breeze that stirred up. I could just make out the sparkle of lake water beyond.

I patted the For Sale sign. "What do you say, Dev? Build a life with me here? You can open your practice or do something else. Teach yoga, sell nuts and bolts, keep my books. I've got some money saved, and I can do some of the work myself. I'm thinking four bedrooms and one of those big soaker tubs in a window facing the lake."

I could feel him practically vibrating next to me, and I wasn't sure if it was the physical need to strip me down and make me come or if it was the plan I was laying out.

"We can build a house, a life, a family. And someday, when the kids are being obnoxious, we'll tell them how it all started right here on the tailgate of my truck."

His mouth lifted. "Why Scarlett Bodine, are you proposing marriage?" he teased.

I wrinkled my nose at him. "Not yet. I promised Mama not 'til thirty, and a Bodine doesn't—"

"Break promises," Devlin filled in, reeling me into him.

"I want this with you, Dev. I want a big house and wild kids and bonfires."

"I want to give you anything and everything you want," he reminded me.

"Is that a yes?"

"Honey, that's a hell yes." He kissed me hard under the moon on the land we'd buy together. "Why are you wearing this, by the way?"

He'd pulled back and was studying my dress. "I was planning to impress you with my chameleon-like ability to blend in when I crashed your place in Annapolis. Because I came to my senses first."

Devlin threw his head back and laughed. "Scarlett, honey, you couldn't blend in if you were invisible. Please don't ever try. I'd miss my beer-drinking, boot-wearing Bootleg girl."

I grabbed him by the tie and yanked him down to me. "Yeah, just remember who said 'I love you' first."

Epilogue
Devlin

I was already awake when Scarlett's alarm went off. Today was a big day, not that Scarlett Bodine let anyone forget that it was finally her thirtieth birthday. Four years together, I thought, rolling to my side, and I was finally going to ask her to marry me.

Her brothers had given me their perfunctory approval ages ago. It was totally ceremonial—they'd dunked my ass in the lake again—but I was a part of them now. And it was time to make it official.

Scarlett stirred when I dragged her up against me, kissing her bare shoulder.

The morning light poured through the windows facing the lake. We'd built this home together, Scarlett doing a good portion of the work herself and teaching me a few things along the way. And every damn day, I counted my blessings when I pulled up the long drive. Everything I cared about most in this life was here.

The ring was in the drawer of my nightstand. I'd thought

of a million ways to do this over the past four years. As with everything involving Scarlett, I had a Plan A, B, C, and D on top. It was a necessity when your girlfriend was as unpredictable and wild as Scarlett.

My soon-to-be fiancée let out an inelegant snort and sat straight up. "Christ on a cracker! What time is it?"

"It's early," I said, propping myself on my elbow and watching her spring naked from the bed. "What's the hurry, birthday girl?"

She paused midhop as she dragged on a pair of cutoffs and grinned at me.

"I've got birthday things to attend to. Hair, massage, and facials with the girls," she said. She hopped in my direction and laid a kiss on me that turned my morning wood into a raging hard-on.

"What about me? Don't I get to spend your day with you?" I asked.

Her grin was as honeyed as her accent. "Don't you worry, Dev. You'll be the highlight of my big day."

"We have dinner plans," I reminded her.

"Oh, those mysterious dinner plans you've been reminding me about?" She winked. "I'll make sure I'm showered, sexy, and ready for action."

I was ready for action now. I climbed out of bed, my cock demanding her full attention.

"Uh-uh. You keep that sex stick away from me. I gotta go." Scarlett grabbed a bra and tank top and half-ran to the bathroom, slamming the door in my face. "Nice try, honey," she called through the door.

Plan A—a sweet, romantic, quiet, naked gesture—was officially defunct.

Undeterred, I grabbed a pair of gym shorts and ambled down the hall toward the kitchen. The house was the perfect mingling of McCallister and Bodine.

There were windows everywhere they could be squeezed into the design. The entire back of the house was one panoramic lake view. There was a study off the front door for me, and Scarlett used the formal room on the opposite side as her disaster of an office.

We had five bedrooms perfect for overnight visits with my parents and our future "pack of kids." The living space and kitchen were one big room, which made entertaining easy. The huge mountain stone fireplace in the living room gave Scarlett the excuse she was looking for to host monthly "indoor bonfires" in the middle of winter.

I opened the fridge and collected the ingredients for my protein shake. My phone buzzed on the counter.

Cassidy Bodine: Are y'all engaged yet???

I shook my head. It was going to be a long-ass day if I couldn't pin down my fireball girlfriend and put a ring on her little finger. All of Bootleg Springs was waiting for the signal and then the town would descend upon our backyard for the biggest, craziest bonfire Scarlett had ever seen.

I heard her jogging down the hallway, bare feet slapping on the hardwood.

"I'm late, honey. Otherwise I'd be demanding my presents," she said, rising on tip toe to kiss my cheek.

I grabbed a handful of her shirt and pulled her in and up for a birthday-worthy kiss.

Scarlett melted into me, but before I could revive Plan A, she was wriggling out of my grasp. "Nice try, hot stuff! To be continued!"

She disappeared in the direction of the garage and left me with my protein shake and another unsatisfied hard-on.

I hefted the canoe over my head, droplets of water raining down on me, and headed for the lake. Scarlett and I had been through it all in the last four years. Her brothers' weddings, endless nights of making love, fiery arguments, soft conversations under the stars, lazy Sundays on the lake, not to mention the investigation that we'd all finally moved on from.

Scarlett Bodine had saved me from a life I'd thought I wanted.

She'd picked me back up at my lowest point, and then two years ago, she'd stood next to me, trembling with pride in her cowboy boots when I was sworn in as Olamette County judge. She'd campaigned so hard for me I think most folks were afraid not to vote for me. And so Ol' Judge Carwell was able to retire, and I stepped into my own courtroom.

It wasn't Washington, D.C.—my courtroom had six deer heads mounted on the wall above the bench—but I was happier than I'd ever been. Happier than I would have been. And my parents were vaguely less disappointed now that they had a judge in the family. They just tended to leave out the "county" part of my title. And they'd warmed up to Scarlett, which I'd had no doubt would happen. The woman could thaw the coldest of hearts with her sweet smiles and honeyed drawl. And if that didn't work, she bull-headedly wore down every rough edge she encountered until the other party couldn't remember a time when they didn't love Scarlett.

I eased the canoe down onto the sandy beach and shoved it into the shallow lake water. Lashing the lead ropes to the dock, I tossed the quilts and the picnic basket into the belly of the canoe.

The beer cooler came next. I patted my front pocket, reassuring myself that the ring was still in its place.

"Mornin'." Jonah, Scarlett's half-brother sauntered across the lawn, his hands in the pockets of his athletic shorts. "Thought I'd drop by and see if you needed any help setting up for the bonfire tonight," he said.

My phone rang, and I picked it up off the dock.

"Hey, Scarlett."

"I'm grabbing lunch with the girls," she chirped.

"Oh. Uh." I eyed the engagement canoe. "Okay. When will you be back?"

"I'm not real sure. Just called to tell you I miss you, and I'll see you tonight for dinner."

Well, hell. Plan B had just taken a steaming crap. "Try to be back by five," I said, hoping I sounded casual and not disappointed and panicked.

"I think I can manage that," she said, cheerfully unaware that she was ruining the biggest day of our life.

"You *are* coming back, right?" *Hell, what if after all these years she'd gotten cold feet?* I felt my stomach do a slow roll.

Her laugh was husky. "Why, your honor, you know you're the one I want to spend my birthday night with. In fact, if I were you, I'd spend the afternoon hydrating and stretching."

"Promise?" I said softly.

"I promise, Dev. I can't wait to celebrate with you, and I'll be thinking about you all afternoon. I love you."

"I love you, too," I said, mostly appeased.

"Just remember who said it first," she sang before hanging up.

I swore quietly and stared down at the canoe of romance. "Well, shit."

"Problem?" Jonah asked.

"Scarlett's spending the afternoon with her friends."

Jonah ran a hand through his dark hair. "Yeah, she rounded up the girls for a spa day and lunch and whatever."

The girls were the women the Bodine men and I had fallen for. I wasn't the only man to show up in Bootleg only to get blindsided by love. The last few years had been a whirlwind of lust, love, and a shit ton of weddings, some of which I'd presided over. I'd been hoping to add my own to the list. And it was looking like the universe—or worse, Scarlett Bodine herself—was conspiring against me.

"You were going to propose in a canoe?" Jonah asked.

I shrugged. "I thought a picnic lunch and some time at the hot springs would be… you know… romantic and nostalgic."

Jonah nodded. "Yeah, totally." His gaze landed on the picnic basket. "Shame for it to go to waste."

I had half a pound of Scarlett's favorite chicken salad, a

six-pack of cold beer, and three or four hours to kill before my parents showed up to celebrate the engagement that wasn't.

"You wanna go?" I asked Jonah.

He shrugged. "Got an extra pair of trunks?"

———

Scarlett was definitely avoiding me. Jonah and I worked up a sweat paddling over to the secret hot springs where we ate my engagement lunch and talked sports, women, and work. Jonah's personal training business was the perfect complement to Bootleg's day spas. Tourists could spend their morning sweating through a lakefront boot camp and then stuff their faces at any of the town's dining establishments before having the kinks worked out at one of the half-dozen spas in town.

I had a few kinks of my own now. My shoulders were tight with worry that Scarlett was avoiding me or skipping town or getting arrested again. I was beyond ready to make our love "official." And I thought she'd felt the same way. I couldn't have misread the last four years. *Could I?*

The catering crew showed up as we were unloading the canoe. Jonah volunteered to direct them so I could shower. By the time I came out with wet hair and clean clothes—the ring safely tucked in my front pocket again—my parents were pulling up the drive, and the Bodines had descended upon our house.

Gibson and Jameson were stocking the fire pit with wood. Bowie was carrying my mother's full-sized suitcase. The woman was staying for thirty-six hours and had packed as if she were going to Paris for a week. My father was poking his nose in all the covered dishes the caterers set up in the kitchen.

My gran and her girlfriend Estelle were pouring everyone who walked through the door little cups of strawberry moonshine.

I greeted them all and tried to hide my distraction.

There was still no Scarlett. Her responses to my texts had been vague. At least that's the way my starting-to-panic mind read them.

"Your home is lovely," my mother said, admiring the grand fireplace. "Maybe I could bring my DAR group here for a retreat in the fall?" she mused.

She wasn't actually asking. She was planning.

"Dev, you got a minute to help go over the setup of the tables?" Gibson asked, sticking his head in the backdoor.

"Sure," I nodded dumbly and followed him outside.

"You look like you're gonna be sick," he observed.

"I haven't proposed yet," I told him. "How can we have an engagement party with no engagement?"

"I wouldn't worry about it if I were you," Gibson drawled. Easy for him to say. He had a shiny gold band on his ring finger and a fucking permanent smile on his face these days.

"The girls here, yet?" Jameson asked from the yard.

"Not yet," Gibson called back. "Be here soon."

"Wait a second." I stopped on the deck. "She's up to something. Isn't she?" I dared them to lie to my face.

Gibson put his hands on my shoulders and helpfully shoved me in the direction of the stairs. "Scarlett? Up to something?" he asked innocently.

Jameson stuffed his hands in his pockets and whistled tunelessly while avoiding my gaze.

"If you don't start spilling your guts, I'm canceling poker this week," I threatened.

"Look. You want to get engaged, don't you?" Gibson said, pointing me in the direction of the box truck from which a two dozen round tables were being unloaded.

I slapped my thigh. "That little sneak thinks she's going to propose, doesn't she?"

Gibson and Jameson shared a long look.

"Damn it. She's held the fact that she said 'I love you' first over my head for four years. Can you imagine what she'll do if she's the one who pops the question?"

They nodded stoically, not willing to officially break the Bodine family code of blabbing on each other.

Bowie and Jonah wandered up.

"Why don't you two take McCallister here for a little walk before he blows his top," Gibson suggested.

"Did you know about this?" I asked, poking Jonah in the chest.

"Of *course* I knew. My wife can't keep a secret to save her life."

"None of them can," Jameson grinned.

Four phones dinged, chirped, and tinkled simultaneously. The brothers glanced at their screens, four matching grins splitting their faces. God, they were annoying.

"Girls are here," Jonah said.

I spun back toward the house. There was no way in hell that I was letting Scarlett Bodine propose to me. I was getting this one first.

"Where y'all goin'?" Bowie called after me.

"To ruin Scarlett's plan!"

"What about the tables?" Gibson yelled.

"Fuck the tables!"

I stormed into the house under a full head of steam and followed the sounds of giggling and squealing in the direction of the upstairs bathroom.

"Wait until Devlin gets a load of you," I heard Cassidy sing when I tackled the last of the stairs.

"You look attractive," Cassidy's sister agreed. "Not at all like your usual mess."

"Thanks, y'all," my future wife drawled.

I gave the door a boot and scared the hell out of the six women crammed inside.

"Devlin! What's gotten into you?" Scarlett demanded, hands on hips, elbows jabbing the others in the confined space. Her hair, a sexy sable color, hung long and loose down her back, just the way I liked it best. She wore a white lace dress that hit just above her knees and fluffed out at the skirt.

It was the perfect look to propose.

I was irrationally furious, which is the only excuse for what I did next.

I, Devlin McCallister, Olamette County judge, hauled my girlfriend over my shoulder and carried her kicking and screaming out of the bathroom. Her friends stared after us, mouths agape. Cassidy was recording it on her phone, and I didn't give a damn. We passed my parents and Jonah's mother on the stairs. Scarlett quit her hollering long enough to give them a little "hey there, fresh towels are in the linen closet," before I slammed our bedroom door behind us.

I dumped her on the bed so hard she bounced.

"If you mess up my hair, I will never forgive you, Devlin Brooks McCallister," she howled.

Before she could jump to her feet and kick me in the balls or put me in a headlock, I stretched out on top of her and clamped a hand over her mouth. Her eyes went from furious to ready-to-get-naked in less than two seconds. I was already hard. Something about seeing her in all that white lace made my blood thicken.

"Marry me," I demanded. My carefully drafted, ruthlessly memorized speech was out the window. Hell, I was on Plan Quadruple Z by this point. And I wasn't going to spend another second of my life without putting a ring on this woman's finger. Whether I'd have to wrestle it on remained to be seen. "Marry me, Scarlett. Be my wife."

She made a muffled sound, and I removed my hand before she could bite me. Scarlett never hesitated to fight dirty. It was one of my favorite things about her.

"About damn time," she said with a cocky grin.

"About time?" I shouted. "You've been avoiding me all fucking day."

"I had to get ready for tonight," she said, rolling her hips against me.

I gritted my teeth, trying to focus. She hadn't said yes yet.

"Say yes, Scarlett." I nibbled at her lower lip and felt her pulse kick up under my fingers on her throat.

"Yes, of course I'll marry you," she sighed, begging me to deepen the kiss.

"And I get the credit for proposing?" I asked, a little worried that she'd said yes so easily. "I asked first."

She dropped her head to the mattress and laughed. "I think I can give you that one."

"I can't believe you thought you were going to propose," I said gruffly, tracing my fingers over the soft skin of her neck.

"Oh, I never planned to propose," Scarlett countered.

I lifted up, resting my weight in my elbows. "What?"

"I knew you'd do right by me and propose today," she said smugly. "I just figured if we were gettin' engaged and I was turning thirty and all, why not get married tonight?"

My mouth opened, and no words came out. Scarlett giggled beneath me. "Y'all sure are sexy when you're speechless."

"I'm going to need you to run that by me again," I finally managed.

"As soon as you put a ring on me—I'm *assumin'* there's a ring—" she said pointedly. "We're gonna go say some vows in front of most of Bootleg, eat some barbecue, drink some beer, shove cake in each other's faces, and then you and I are gonna get real naked and biblical."

I dropped my forehead to Scarlett's. "I love you more than anything in this world. Do you know that?"

"I sure do. And the feelin' is mutual. You're my one, Dev. I want more of all of this with you. I want babies upstairs and grandkids on the lake. I want you every night for the rest of my life." She cupped her hand to my cheek, rubbing her palm over my beard. "Now, about that ring…"

———

At dusk, Scarlett marched down the grassy backyard aisle lined with Citronella candles with her four brothers as an escort. That didn't surprise me. What did was the Bodines handing Scarlett over and then lining up next to me, a perfect bookend to the bridesmaids on Scarlett's side. Family. Blood and otherwise.

As Old Judge Carwell launched into his southern-accented recitation of the vows, I couldn't stop rubbing my thumbs over Scarlett's palms, reassuring myself that this was indeed happening. My mother was politely sniffling into my father's handkerchief in the front row. Gran and Estelle sat next to them snapping about a thousand pictures with their phones. Jonah's mom and Cassidy's parents took up Scarlett's side. Beyond them was the better part of all of Bootleg. And above us, someone had thought to turn on the strings of lights we used for parties.

I could smell bonfire and brisket. Everyone in the audience had a drink in hand.

And when Scarlett looked up at me, eyes sparkling with a joy that mirrored my own, I knew that I was more than ready for another fifty or sixty years with her. She was my adventure and my safe place. My best friend. And I was going to spend the rest of my life loving the hell out of her.

We all had a good laugh when Old Judge Carwell got to the honor and obey part.

And, when I got the go-ahead to give my wife our first kiss, I leaned in so only Scarlett could hear me. "Just remember who proposed first."

Author's Note

Dear Reader,

Welcome to Bootleg Springs where the liquor flows and the neighbors know your every move! I hope you enjoyed your first visit. I'm not going to lie, I knew exactly who Scarlett Bodine was before I even started writing this book. It all started with that scene of Devlin seeing her for the first time chugging a beer from the tailgate of a pickup.

I just fell in love with the idea of this blue-collar country girl who thought about sex like a man, did the dirty work in her family, and still had time to chase down every ounce of fun she could find. And I love a town that breaks all those stereotypes. Sure there's y'alling and the mayor plays a mean banjo, but Bootleg is a prosperous tourist town with a big heart, smart neighbors, and canny entrepreneurs.

I'm really excited about this series, and not just for my usual reasons (small town, crazy family, hilarity). The suspense aspect has been so much fun to plan out with Claire. There will be six books, each with a couple and an HEA, but the mystery won't be wrapped up until Book 6 and YOU GUYS, you *really* want to know what happened!

So, once again, welcome to the moonshiniest town in the whole dang country. I hope you'll stick around! If you loved Whiskey Chaser, please feel free to tell seven hundred of your closest friends or leave a review on Amazon.

Are you getting the BFF vibe from me? Follow me on Facebook and join me in my reader's group: Lucy Score's Binge Readers Anonymous. And if you want first dibs on preorders and sales and awesome bonus content, definitely sign up for my newsletter! I hope to see you around!

Xoxo,
Lucy

Acknowledgments

Claire Kingsley for being like "Hey, we should co-write a series together!" and then holding my hand through Whiskey Chaser.

Dinosaur chicken nuggets.

Author Kathryn Nolan for insisting that the book blurb was so good, my readers would throw up with excitement!

Mr. Lucy for doing literally all the things while I buried myself in this book! And for rubbing my head for an hour when I had that gross headache. And for always restocking the toilet paper in the powder room. And for bookmarking Porsche 356 convertibles because he plans to surprise me with one someday!

Dawn and those sharp eyes for typos and enduring love of all romance. For Amanda Edens for her professional proofreading.

My Binge Readers for their endless support, their diabolical sense of humor, and their acceptance of my taco obsession. Also, for those of you who provided much needed background about West Virginia.

Ready for more from Bootleg Springs?

BOOK #2 BY CLAIRE KINGSLEY
WITH LUCY SCORE!

Continue for an excerpt from *Sidecar Crush*.

Chapter One
Jameson

I didn't care what my sister said, being here tonight wasn't *good for me*.

She'd called no less than half a dozen times today, insisting I needed to get out of the house. Why? Who knew with Scarlett. Once that girl got an idea in her head, it was damn hard to get it out. And apparently Miss Scarlett Rose had decided her brother needed a drink at The Lookout.

Now that I'd been sitting here awhile, I'd decided she was wrong. I didn't need to be here. I'd have been much happier if I'd stayed in my shop. I made my living as a metal artist, and I was working on a big commission—had plenty to keep me busy. Granted, I liked a cold beer as much as the next guy, and Nicolette served 'em up good. But what I did *not* like was the fact that half the people in here were looking at me.

They thought they were being so damn sneaky. Little glances over their shoulders. Heads together to whisper.

Moving my gaze back to the table, I shifted on my stool. The noise of a dozen conversations drifted around me. I knew what people were whispering about. All us Bodines knew. They were wondering if our dad—a man who was no longer among the living—had been responsible for the disappearance, and possible murder, of Callie Kendall a dozen years ago.

Did I think he'd done it? I didn't rightly know. There'd never been a lot of love between me and my father, but that didn't mean I believed he'd been a murderer.

Hadn't been a lot of love between our father and any of his children, save Scarlett. She'd always tried the hardest with him. Maybe because she was the baby, or the only girl. Hell if I knew.

There had been good times with him, and with our mama. A lot of 'em, in fact. But Dad had made it hard. Drank too much. Blamed us kids for every problem in his life. My brother, Gibson, had taken the worst of it. Turned him into a mean son of a bitch if you weren't related to him. Sometimes even if you were. Bowie seemed to have decided he'd be Dad's opposite. Nice guy, Bowie. Upstanding sort. Our half-brother, named Jonah after our father, hadn't the pleasure—or misfortune—of growing up with Dad. That seemed to have been a blessing, far as I could tell.

Me? I'd always tried to stay out of his way. Keep my head down. Be invisible. Kinda what I did in general, and it usually worked out fine.

Wasn't working no more. Not with the whole town whispering about Jonah Bodine Sr. and Callie Kendall's damn sweater. Now eyes were on me, and I did not like it. Not one bit.

Moisture beaded on my beer bottle and the scent of garlic fries and whiskey wafted by. I took a sip and ran my thumb down the cool glass.

Bowie sat across from me, staring into his beer. He was usually a bit more talkative, but tonight he'd been quiet. I hadn't asked why. June Tucker sat next to him, reading a book. I liked Juney. I found her bewildering sometimes, but she also didn't talk too much, or expect me to. Although she did tend to ask awkward questions.

Jonah sat on her other side. We'd only found out about

Jonah's existence a couple of months ago when he showed up in town looking for us. He'd heard about dad's death, and saw he had siblings he'd never known. Of course Scarlett had claimed him as a Bodine after about ninety seconds of knowing him. I reckoned she'd been right to do so. Jonah was a decent sort. He hadn't been sure about staying in Bootleg, and I wasn't sure if he'd wind up settling here long-term. Somehow—I wasn't quite sure how, seeing as the agreement had been made in the sixth inning of a Bootleg Cock Spurs softball game, and I'd been pretty far gone on moonshine—Jonah had recently become my roommate.

I took another sip of my beer and Scarlett flashed me a sweet smile. She was standing by another table with her beau, Devlin. My brothers and I had reluctantly agreed that Dev was all right for Scarlett. She'd made us promise we wouldn't toss him in the lake again. We got around it by promising we wouldn't *unless he deserved it.* She'd thank us later. Devlin was obviously crazy about Scar, but every man deserves to get his ass thrown in the lake once in a while. Even the good ones.

Normally I wasn't one to start a conversation where one wasn't already happening, but I glanced up at June. "Where's Cass tonight, Juney?"

She blinked at me once. "On a date."

My eyes flicked to Bowie. His jaw tightened, and his eyelid twitched. Now I knew why Bowie was playing the part of the broody Bodine tonight. He had eyes for June's sister, Cassidy Tucker, but for reasons none of us could fathom, he'd never done a thing about it.

"A date, huh?" I said. "Who's she seeing?"

"Someone she met online," June said. "I told her the probability of finding a suitable match using an appropriate online resource was high."

"*You* gave her this idea?" Bowie asked.

"It's perfectly logical," June said. "Cassidy would like to meet, and date, a man with potential for long-term commitment. Utilizing a dating application will widen her range of potential mates."

"Potential mates?" Jonah asked. "You make it sound like she's an animal."

"Technically speaking, we're all animals," June said. "*Homo sapiens* are classified within kingdom Animalia."

"Thanks for the science lesson, June Bug," Bowie said.

"Bowie, are you experiencing feelings of jealousy because Cassidy is having a potentially romantic encounter with another man?" June asked, her voice flat. There was no sarcasm or humor in her question. She was really just asking.

I tried to cover my smirk by taking a drink of my beer.

"No," Bowie said. "I'm good."

June shrugged and went back to her book.

Scarlett swept up next to me and elbowed me in the ribs. "See, Jame. I told you this would be good for you. Aren't you glad you came out of hiding?"

"Not especially."

"Oh, stop," she said. "Y'all are a bunch of negative Nancys over here. Bowie, quit your scowling. You look like Gibs."

"Who looks like me?" Gibson asked.

He'd come up behind Scarlett, a bottle of water in his hand. The oldest and youngest Bodines were opposites, and not just in gender. Scarlett was tiny, while Gibs was the tallest of all of us. Looked the most like Dad, too, which I was pretty sure he hated.

"Bowie," Scarlett said. "He's over there trying to turn his beer sour."

Gibson just grunted.

"Y'all are a sad-lookin' lot," Scarlett said. "And I know exactly why."

"Why is that?" Bowie asked.

I wanted to kick him under the table for encouraging her.

"Because you're single," Scarlett said. "Here I am, the youngest Bodine, and I've got this great man. And you poor things are still waiting to find someone."

"Who says we want to?" Gibson asked.

She smacked his arm. "I wasn't talking about your grumpy

336

ass. You find a woman who can put up with you, and I swear I'll learn to cook just so I can bake her the best pecan pie in Olamette County. She'll deserve it."

Gibson snorted and took a drink of his water.

"But y'all," she said, pointing to the rest of us sitting at the table. "You need to think about it. Finding somebody. Settling down. It'd be good for you."

"Like coming out for a beer'd be good for me?" I asked.

"Yes," she said, poking me in the shoulder. "Just like that, only better. Come on, Jame, that girl you've been seeing doesn't count if you can't even bring her around to introduce to your family."

"I ain't seein' her anymore," I said.

"What?" Scarlett asked, her voice going up several octaves. Devlin paused behind her, like he wasn't sure if he should come near or wait to see if it was safe. "Since when?"

I rolled my eyes and hunched down over my beer. Half the place was looking at us openly now. And the other half was straining to listen.

"Jesus, don't make a scene," I said. "It ended quite a while ago. It's fine."

I'd been seeing Willa Sawyer, a girl who lived over in Maryland, for a couple of years. It was an on-again, off-again type thing. Long distance. Sometimes she'd come out here and see me; other times I went to her. Wasn't ever real serious, but we had a nice time when we were together. She'd decided she wanted more commitment than I could give her. Met someone else—planned to get married soon. Kinda left me without as much to look forward to, but I was glad for her. She was a nice girl—deserved that sort of thing.

"Well, you could have told us," Scarlett said. "Here I thought you were keeping her a secret for a reason. Like maybe you were ashamed of us."

Devlin seemed to have decided it was safe to come near. He stepped up next to Scarlett and slipped his arm around her waist.

"Don't be dumb, Scar," I said. "I wasn't keeping secrets, and you know I'm not ashamed of y'all. It just wasn't a big deal."

"Too bad it's over," Gibson said. "Seemed like you had a good thing going. Got a little action when you wanted it, and none of the bullshit."

"Isn't that exactly what you have?" Scarlett asked, her disdain for Gibson's dating habits—or lack thereof—evident in her tone. "Action when you want it. No bullshit… That is, no commitment or connection to anyone."

"Scarlett, just because y'all are acting like lovesick puppies doesn't mean the rest of us need to go out and get ourselves attached," Gibson said.

Scarlett rolled her eyes and turned her back to him. "What about you, June? Got your eye on anyone special?"

June looked over the top of her book. "No."

"Jonah?" she asked.

"Sorry, Scarlett," Jonah said. "Not really."

Scarlett huffed and grabbed Devlin's arm. "Y'all are no fun. Come on, let's go play pool."

Our table quieted down considerably in the absence of Scarlett. She pranced around the pool table, shaking her backside at Devlin. The way he watched her still got my hackles up, and I had to remind myself that Scarlett was his girl now. He could look at her like that. Truth was, he *should* look at her like that.

I reckoned any guy in Scarlett's life couldn't win, not with us as her brothers. If he looked at her with those hungry eyes, we wanted to bust his face. But if he hadn't been looking at her like that, we'd have hated him for not appreciating her enough.

The TV behind me caught my attention and the noise level in the bar went down a notch. Nicolette had just changed the channel to a reality TV show, *Roughing It*.

The premise wasn't all that exciting. A bunch of minor celebrities stuck in a cabin out in the woods somewhere, expected to get by without a lot of modern conveniences. Mostly it was just a bunch of drama between the cast members while they fumbled around in the woods. Definitely not something I'd watch under normal circumstances.

But my interest—and the interest of everyone else in Bootleg—stemmed from the fact that Leah Mae Larkin was on the show.

Leah Mae was one of us. A Bootlegger. She'd lived here until she was twelve. Then her mama had divorced her daddy and moved her away. After that, she'd spent summers here for a while—at least until the rest of the world discovered how pretty she was and she became a model. She'd dropped the Mae—went by Leah Larkin now.

Back when she'd still been Leah Mae, she'd been one of my only friends. Maybe my best friend.

I hadn't seen her in a long time. And it wasn't like I was harboring any foolish unrequited feelings for her. She was basically a celebrity now. I was only interested in what she was up to because it wasn't every day that a Bootlegger was on TV.

Shifting in my seat, I looked at the screen. There was Leah Mae, standing in front of a mirror, pulling all that long blond hair up into a ponytail. She'd always wanted to be on TV. When we were kids, we'd spent more hours than I could count with her making up plays and starring in them. Playing dress-up and twirling around. Telling me how she was going to be a famous actress.

The scene cut to the cast going out to the nearby lake to fish. Maybe it was one of those challenges they were always putting them through. People got voted off the show each week, and so far, Leah Mae had made it every time.

I tried not to pay attention, but they kept showing Leah Mae struggling with her fishing pole. Kinda looked like she didn't know which end was which, but that couldn't be the case. Leah Mae could out-fish anyone, and we all knew it. Sure, with her glamorous lifestyle now, posing for pictures and walking in fashion shows, she probably didn't get out fishing much. But fishing was like riding a bike. You didn't just up and forget.

The guy in the boat with her asked if she needed help. Brock Winston. That guitar-toting pansy-ass. His music wasn't terrible, but I'd hated him from the first minute I saw him on that show with Leah Mae. He was married to some actress, but he sure seemed to be cozying up to Leah Mae in a way a man shouldn't if he already had a girl.

Damn celebrities. One famous girl wasn't enough for that guy? He had to go flirting with another?

Brock got her pole fixed and the camera zoomed in. Her eyes caught me, held me fast. Back when we were kids, she'd always had this sparkle in her eyes when she was acting. But there was no sparkle now. They were flat. Still damn pretty, but this wasn't Leah Mae. It didn't look like her, the girl I'd once known. She looked like a girl in a cage, being made to do tricks.

Leah Mae turned her gaze to Brock and the camera panned in on him. He was giving her a look I knew all too well. A distinct *I want to fuck you tonight* look. All men had one, and we could spot them in each other if we were paying attention. And that was exactly how Brock Winston was looking at Leah Mae Larkin on Nicolette's stupid big-screen TV.

I turned back to my beer. Didn't much want to see the rest.

"I bet those two are gettin' busy in the back when the cameras are off," Rhett Ginsler said behind me.

"You think?" Trent McCulty asked.

"Sure as shit," Rhett said. "She's actin' all coy, but I'd bet ten bucks and a jar of moonshine she's spending her nights getting plowed by that Brock guy."

The muscles in my back clenched and I tightened my grip on my beer.

"Maybe she's just playing it up for the camera," Trent said.

"Could be," Rhett said. "Leah Mae's an attention whore anyway."

I rose so fast my stool fell backward behind me, crashing to the floor with a loud bang. Without much awareness of how I got there, I stood behind Rhett and Trent, my hands balled into fists.

"I reckon you need to stop talking shit about her," I said, my voice a low growl.

Before I finished speaking, Bowie and Gibs were already flanking me, ready to throw down. They probably didn't know what had me so riled, but they wouldn't care. This was how we did things. Backed each other. They might kick my ass later if I got them into something stupid—although it was usually Gibson getting the rest of us into something stupid, not me. I was prepared to deal with the consequences. No one used the word *whore* in a sentence with Leah Mae's name. Not in my hearing.

Rhett shifted on his stool, turning to face me. "What's it to you?"

"She's one of ours."

He snorted and took a swig of his beer. "I guess. How long since she's even set foot in Bootleg, though?"

"Doesn't matter," Bowie said, and Gibson growled in agreement. "Jameson's right."

"And I suppose you think you're gonna do something about it?" Rhett asked.

Eyes were on us. Lines being drawn. A couple more guys stood nearby, clearly on Rhett's side. Like I gave a shit. Jonah stood on Gibson's right. He hadn't grown up here, but he understood.

"You're damn right I'm gonna do something about it," I said.

Rhett got off the stool. He was about my height—could look me in the eyes. I stared back, my face hard, my jaw set.

"Y'all better back away from my bar if you're gettin' rough," Nicolette said.

"Well, shit." Scarlett's voice.

I saw Devlin come up next to Bowie. He was rolling up his sleeves, but he leaned closer and spoke under his breath. "Watch it, guys. You're supposed to stay out of trouble."

"Bootleg justice, Dev," Bowie said, his eyes never leaving Rhett and Trent.

"I know, I know," Devlin said.

I wasn't an idiot. Hitting first was a bad idea, if you could avoid it. But if I didn't hit first…

"What are you hanging out in here for, anyway, Rhett?" I asked. "Shouldn't you be keeping tabs on your girlfriend?"

"What's that supposed to mean?" Rhett asked.

I shrugged. "Word around town is Misty Lynn's been messin' around with Wade Zirkel. I reckon you ain't man enough, so she had to go look elsewhere."

"You son of a bitch." Rhett drew his fist back, and I let it come. Took it across the jaw.

Rhett's punch was the invitation I was looking for. I clocked him square in the nose while all hell broke loose around me. Rhett grabbed his face and hollered, blood running down his chin. Gibson and Bowie dived in, pushing and punching at anyone who dared face them. Even Dev and Jonah got in on it.

The scuffle was broken up quick, and I let someone pull me back. I'd bloodied Rhett's nose, and I was satisfied with that. Didn't seem like too many punches had landed on anyone. The only blood was Rhett's, although Trent looked like he might wind up with a shiner. Gibson flexed his fingers a few times. Everyone else gave each other a good mean glower and went back to their places.

"Jameson, what in the hell were you doing?" Scarlett asked. She touched my jaw and tipped my face to see if I was hurt.

"Rhett needs to remember himself, is all," I said, jerking my chin out of her reach. "I'm going home. See y'all later."

"If you wanted to go home so bad, you could have just left. You didn't have to punch someone in the dang face," Scarlett called after me.

I walked out, ignoring the eyes that followed me. Yeah, starting a bar fight meant people would look—and talk. Although a scuffle in The Lookout was pretty typical for a Friday night. But I could not abide that good-for-nothing pond scum Rhett Ginsler talking about Leah Mae like that. She'd been my friend once, and that still meant something to me. That jackass needed to remember his manners.

After I got home, I might have scrolled through her Instagram a little bit. And that might have been a habit I'd gotten into recently. A habit that was right stupid, and I knew it. Nothing had ever happened between Leah Mae and me when she'd been a normal girl, visiting her daddy for the summer. Sure as shit wasn't any chance of something happening between us now.

About the Author

Lucy Score is a #1 *New York Times, USA Today,* and *Wall Street Journal* bestselling author. She grew up in a literary family who insisted that the dinner table was for reading and earned a degree in journalism. She writes full-time from the Pennsylvania home she and Mr. Lucy share with their obnoxious cat, Cleo. When not spending hours crafting heartbreaker heroes and kick-ass heroines, Lucy can be found on the couch, in the kitchen, or at the gym. She hopes to someday write from a sailboat, ocean-front condo, or tropical island with reliable Wi-Fi.

Sign up for her newsletter by scanning the QR code below and stay up on all the latest Lucy book news. You can also follow her here:

Website: Lucyscore.net
Facebook: lucyscorewrites
Instagram: scorelucy
TikTok: @lucyferscore
Binge Books: bingebooks.com/author/lucy_score
Readers Group: facebook.com/groups/
BingeReadersAnonymous Newsletter sign up:

Printed in the USA
CPSIA information can be obtained
at www.ICGtesting.com
LVHW051223290924
792438LV00030B/403